F.C N.

The Life and Work of the Ven. J.B. de La Salle

The Founder of the Institute of the Brothers of the Christian Schools

F.C N.

The Life and Work of the Ven. J.B. de La Salle
The Founder of the Institute of the Brothers of the Christian Schools

ISBN/EAN: 9783337141585

Printed in Europe, USA, Canada, Australia, Japan

Cover: Foto ©Raphael Reischuk / pixelio.de

More available books at **www.hansebooks.com**

Hon. J. George Hodgins, LL.D.
Deputy Minister of Education
Ontario Canada.

with

Compliments of

Brother Maurelian
of
Memphis, Tenn

JEAN BAPTISTE DE LA SALLE.

THE
LIFE AND WORK

OF THE

VEN. J. B. DE LA SALLE,

THE FOUNDER OF THE INSTITUTE OF THE BROTHERS OF THE CHRISTIAN SCHOOLS.

BY

F. C. N.

D. & J. SADLIER & Co.

NEW YORK: MONTREAL:
31 BARCLAY STREET.   275 NOTRE DAME STREET.

1883.

PROTESTATION.

IF, in the course of this narrative, we give the title SAINT to the Venerable de La Salle, or to other persons mentioned therein, it is merely to use the expression ordinarily received among the faithful, who at times apply this term to persons whose piety is universally acknowledged. We have no intention to forestall the judgment of the Sovereign Pontiff, to whom we humbly submit our sentiments, our writings and our person.

PREFACE.

THE present Life does not pretend to be exhaustive. It is merely a sketch. It is only in the English language that there is any lack of biographies of the Venerable de La Salle. But many of those written take partial views of their subject. Some consider only the saint enduring suffering and persecution for the greater honor and glory of God, and for the good of souls. Others look but to the mere human side of his character, and dwell solely upon the achievements of the great educational reformer.

The writer's is a different view. To his mind the great educator was so successful, because he was also a great saint. The one trait is inseparable from the other. Had he been less holy, the work would have produced less fruit. In the following pages, while it is sought to do justice to the educator, the saint is not lost sight of. With what success, it is left to the reader to determine.

In preparing the work, the following Lives have been consulted :

Vie de M. Jean-Baptiste de La Salle, 2 vols. 4to. (1733), *par P. Blain.*

La Vie de M. de La Salle, Instituteur des Frères des Écoles Chrétiennes, par M. l'Abbé de Montis. Paris, 1785. 321 pp.

Vie de M. de La Salle, par P. Garreau, S. J. 1750.

Vie du Vénérable J. B. de La Salle, Fondateur des Écoles Chrétiennes, par L. Ayma, pp. 432. *Deuxième édition.* Aix, 1858.

L'Abbé de La Salle et l'Institut des Frères des Écoles Chrétiennes. Depuis, 1651. Jusqu'en, 1842.

Par un Professeur de l'Université. 198 pp. Paris, 1842.

Vie du Vénérable J. B. de La Salle, Fondateur des Frères des Écoles Chrétiennes. Suivre de l'Histoire de cet Institut. Jusqu'a 1734. Par un Frère des Écoles Chrétiennes. 500 pp. Rouen, 1874.

Histoire du Vénérable Jean-Baptiste de La Salle, Fondateur de l'Institut des Frères des Écoles Chrétiennes, par Armand Ravelet. 496 pp. Paris, 1874.

La Vie de Monsieur Jean-Baptiste de La Salle, par le R. P. D. François E. Maillefer, Prê. R. Bn. de la Congrégation de St. Maur, a Rheims. 1766. (This life is in manuscript; there are but six or eight copies extant.)

Leben J. B. de La Sallen, von Jos. Aloys Krebs, C. SS. R.

Le Monument du Vénérable Jean-Baptiste de La Salle, Rouen. Fête du 2 Juin, 1875. Deuxième édition, 256 pp. *Par J. Chantrel.*

Œuvre des Écoles, par L. Ayma. Aix, 1859. 312 pp.

Vie du Frère Philippe, par M. Poujoulat, 1875. 376 pp.

Also many documents in the archives of the mother-house in Paris, and several papers we had previously published on kindred subjects.

INTRODUCTION.

THE Venerable John Baptist de La Salle has many claims upon the attention of the reading world. He was a holy man, who practised virtue in a heroic degree. The study of such a soul must be elevating and invigorating. It is a soul that has soared upon the wings of heavenward aspirations above the level of humanity ; it is an example worthy of admiration : and who knows but that, from admiring, God may inspire the reader to imitate its noble career? This were certainly a grace worth praying for. When one becomes so saturated with the Spirit of God that he snaps all the ties that bind him to the things of earth, and lives only for heaven, his is necessarily a glorious and successful career. The world may pronounce it a failure, and to all seeming it may be so ; but it is the reverse. The good has been done, the seed has been sown, and in due time Providence will draw out plant and fruit. The work cannot remain barren, for it has been blessed. Such is one of the numerous lessons written upon the face of the life sketched in the present volume. We see therein a man who runs counter to the ways and maxims of the world ; who abandons his wealth to the poor, and becomes one of themselves, that he may the better do good among them ; who leaves the high road to preferment and renown, that he may be ignored ; and withal, a man whose existence has been a benediction to millions, and whose career has been made resplendent by the accumulating gratitude of two centuries. The principle of action animating such a life is worthy of our most diligent research. The high moral qualities that supported it ought not to be left unstudied. We find before us a man of iron will, overcoming obstacles numerous and difficult ; a man of faith, receiving successes and disappointments, patronage and persecution, as so many blessings coming from the hand of God ; a devoted child of the Church, refusing a mitre when to accept it were to renounce his allegiance to Rome, and preferring, in the stead, a crown set with the thorns of persecution. The story of such a life shows how much good may be done when a man is really in earnest. It is an eloquent protest against the petty selfishness of so many with ready hands and willing hearts, who defeat the designs of God upon them, because of their want of the spirit of sacrifice.

It is not only the spiritual life of this great man that is worthy of our study and imitation ; it is also his works. His mission was not merely to sanctify his own soul ; it was, furthermore, that of inaugurating a new era in education. He began where he found the need the most pressing : he placed primary education upon a new basis. Living in the golden age of Louis XIV, he saw beneath the glitter of his day, and found that in many cases what men called gold was only gilding. He found the splendors of the court built upon the impoverishment of the people, and his heart bled for them. Others might bask in the sunshine of royal and episcopal power ; he would none of it. He had a work to do. The poor were in suffering and neglect ; their children were without a proper education. He saw a people growing up in ignorance of their religion and their duties, a prey to all the accompanying vices, and he shuddered at the consequences. Perhaps he foresaw, perhaps there flitted across his vision, the horrors of the French Revolution. Be that as it may, had there been more La Salles, the people would not have become so estranged from the clergy ; and though the Revolution might not have been avoided, its horrors would have remained unwritten in the blood of the best in the land. There were universities and colleges enough for the wealthy and middle classes, but the poor were sadly neglected Primary education was at a low ebb. Anybody was considered good enough to be a teacher. At Paris, Claude Joly is accused of employing the very scum of society to teach his schools.* In Lyons, M. Demia finds "that the greater number of teachers not only did not know how to read and write well, but were also ignorant of the principles of their religion."† The Bishop of Toul, in 1686, draws a disgusting picture of the masters of his day : "They are gamblers, drunkards, libertines, ignorant and brutal. They pass their

* *Factum,* attributed to E. Purchot, of the Paris University.
† " *Vie de M. Demia,*" p. 81.

days in taverns, playing cards, and are engaged to fiddle in haunts of pleasure, and at the village festivals. In church they are not modestly dressed, and instead of applying themselves to the ecclesiastical chant, they sing, during the Divine Offices, whatever comes into their heads." * But little good was to be expected from such men ; on the contrary, the evil they did was incalculable. "Since you force me," said a prelate, "to say what I would wish to have hidden in eternal forgetfulness, I have been obliged to interdict a dozen of *magisters*, because these unfortunate individuals had become the corrupters of those confided to their instruction." † "We ought not to be astonished," says M. Bourdoise, "if we see so few of the children educated at the free schools live like good Christians. For a school to become useful to Christianity, it must have masters who labor as apostles, and not as mercenaries. To remedy so loud-crying an evil, and raise up masters worthy of their sublime mission, became the life-work of La Salle. And he succeeded. He gave a new method of teaching : the mutual-simultaneous, which time has sanctioned. "It is by the simultaneous method that the Brothers have raised the level of education ; that they have regulated its progress, and caused it to be useful to the masses, and not to the chosen few."‡ He based the acquisition of knowledge rather upon reason and judgment than upon memory. He laid a hitherto unheard-of stress upon the study of the vernacular. Prior to his day, the study of Latin was made the basis of all other studies; children should know it before undertaking to learn their mother-tongue. He reversed the process, though not without much opposition. Nor did he neglect higher education. He found that many of the colleges of his day were calculated to give young men a knowledge of the ancient classics, and unfit them for the industrial and commercial pursuits of life ; he accordingly established colleges, in which were inaugurated special courses in mathematics, the fine arts and the natural sciences.

But it was not enough to begin all these and other innovations and reforms ; the good work should be perpetuated. For this purpose La Salle gathered around him men with a kindred spirit, and drew up for them a rule of life which he

---

* Synodal Statutes of 1686.   † Père Blain, vol. i, p. 52
‡ "*Rapport sur l' Instruction Primaire,*" by M. Buisson, p. 252. 1873.

himself was the first to follow ; and he and they pledged themselves to devote their lives and energies to the noble work of educating youth. He displayed rare tact as an organizer. The rules and constitutions he prepared for the Brothers have been regarded as a masterpiece of wisdom. They embody his genius, and the more closely they are followed, the more successful is the result. He showed the way for the numerous religious orders of laymen devoted to teaching, since established in the Church. Be their names what they may, to him must they all look as their spiritual father. He was the pioneer. "He is," says Ravelet, "the Columbus of a new world." * He showed how such institutions might be made to flourish and do good. And we may add that in every instance La Salle was ahead of his age, and worked more for the future than for his own day. There is scarce a modern educational improvement that he did not anticipate. "That method must be excellent," says M. 'Ayma, "which has remained the same for two centuries, and yet ceases not to suit our time, the character of youth, our present needs, and the requirements of families." † But his greatest title to the gratitude of men is that he is the modern apostle of Christian education. At no time was it more necessary to lay stress upon the religious training of youth than in these days of scepticism and godless education. At no time is the Brother of the Christian Schools more called for. The school-room has become the battle-ground between Christianity and atheism. Therein the enemies of religion are putting forth all their strength.

---

* "*Histoire du Ven. J. B. de La Salle*," p. 5.
† "*Œuvre des Écoles*," pp. 37, 38.

CONTENTS.

BOOK I.

THE PREPARATION.

CHAPTER I.

CHAPTER II.

CHAPTER III.

CHAPTER IV.

BOOK II.

THE VOCATION.

CHAPTER I.

CHAPTER II.

CHAPTER III.

CHAPTER IV.

CHAPTER V.

CHAPTER VI.

CHAPTER VII.

CHAPTER VIII.

CHAPTER IX.

BOOK III.

THE WORK AND ITS FRUITS.

CHAPTER I.

BOOK I.

THE PREPARATION.

CHAP. I.

The Church as an Educator.—Some Leaves from her past Record.—
The early Monks Civilizers.—Decrees of Councils in Favor of
Education.—The Work of Religious Orders.—The work of the
Reformation.—How the Church counteracted it.

THE author who undertakes to write a faithful
history of one of those distinguished characters
that the Catholic Church can alone produce, finds
a preparatory task before him. Prior to building
up, he has to clear away the historical rubbish. De
Maistre has truly said that history, for the past three
centuries, has been a conspiracy against truth, and
he who would determine what any Catholic undertaking or Catholic character has been, must first find
out what each has not been. Thus, when we peruse
the pages of history, as written by the greater number of authors, we find them almost unanimously
proclaiming that the Church is the enemy of popular
instruction, and that she dreads lest her children
become intellectually vigorous. Were we to believe these writers, we would conclude that she has
hold only upon ignorance ; that, in these days of
enlightenment, she is a fossilized institution, whose
life and energy have all passed from her ; that she

only cumbers the ground, and shuts out the light.
But the fact that learning still exists, that it flourishes as a vigorous tree, whose branches outspread
themselves more and more, and that all the nations
of the earth now take shelter under its protecting
shade, is the living refutation of the monstrous pre-
tension that the Church allowed instruction to perish, or that she was the enemy of learned men, and
of the sciences they developed.

Justice requires us to judge men, not only by the
results of their actions, but also by the principles
which have directed them. This rule is of general
acceptance, when applied to the individual; it is
equally applicable to society at large. Now, it is
the Church that has moulded the better phases of
modern society, and inspired the humane elements in
the laws by which she is governed. She may not
have given it all the finish that modern reformers
think it might have attained; but we must not forget that, in this case, the Church is much like the
skilful master, who gives his scholar, not all the instruction that he would desire to impart, but all that
the latter has aptitude to receive. Moreover, society when properly constituted, depends for the
legality of its existence upon the principles of which
the Church is the guardian and best exponent. But
though a Divine institution, we must not forget
that this Church accomplishes her mission to men,
in part, by human agencies. She forms and associates, she fosters and encourages; but it is not
given, even to her, to create. This is why the
work of the Church is not an absolutely perfect

work, in all its details. But let us be just; let us judge her as we would judge any representative body; let us consult her official declarations, and examine the efforts she has made to render these declarations effective; above all, let us not forget the feeble instruments with which she has worked, and the great obstacles she has had to surmount.

We shall not attempt to speak of those famous universities, the names of which are known to every educated person, and which owed their vigor and intellectual prowess to learned priests and monks; we prefer to see whether the masses of the people were provided for; whether they were left in ignorance and servility, or if the Church raised her voice, and employed her power and influence to ameliorate their condition.

Primary Christian education begins with the organization of the Church. Christ was Himself a primary teacher; His apostles were the earliest Christian educators. "Suffer little children to come unto me," said the Divine Master; thereby He made of His Church a grand school, in which there is room for all. None are exempt from the invitation; for the sublimest genius, as well as the most limited intelligence, is that of a child when there is question of the mysteries of our holy religion. A sublime origin is this of Christian education. The foundation was laid; the erection of the superstructure was only a question of time. During the first three centuries the work of instructing had to be done by stealth. The Church was recognized only to be hunted down. Under the ban of persecuting

emperors and blood-thirsty governors, her home
was the catacombs, her pulpit the executioner's
block. The only privilege granted her was an
occasional apology; her rights were limited to
that of sealing her faith, and watering the seed of
her belief, with the blood of her children. But, the
first ages of persecution ended, she walked abroad
among the peoples, scattering her benefits to all;
she renewed her educational efforts, and proved her
love of learning by the schools she established in
all principal cities. " The Church and the school
have been always inseparable for the people."*   As
time rolled on, and revolution followed revolution,
she still clung to her divine mission. Driven from
their cells and their monasteries, her sons seek new
retreats. Even when success crowns their efforts,
and princes encourage their labors, these pioneers
forget not their vocation. When more than sufficiently numerous, they form colonies, and are not
afraid to exchange the comforts of an established
home for the miasma of the marsh, and the terrors
of the forest. Everywhere the children of Benedict
and Bruno, of Columba and Clement, spread the
good odor of Jesus Christ, and saved the world from
falling into barbarism. But, as our object is to
draw attention to the efforts that prepared the way
for the work of the Venerable de la Salle, we limit
ourselves chiefly to the consideration of what had
been accomplished in France previous to his time.

The decrees of the early councils in France
furnish us with positive evidence concerning the

---

* Gregory VII, p. 216.

universality of schools in that country during the fifth and sixth centuries. But this did not last. Under the degenerate sons of Clovis, learning and sanctity became buried in the disorders that prevailed throughout the kingdom. The genius of Charlemagne remedied the evil.

He collected a body of learned men about him; he required the bishops and the abbots, in his dominions, to establish schools for the education of the people. His orders were faithfully obeyed. France became a nursery of learning; throughout the empire, from the court to the remotest village, schools were established, in which reading, writing, the psalter, singing, computation, and orthography, were taught.

The schools then founded were of various grades: there were those of country curates, in which the parish children were to be gratuitously taught, and especially instructed in the elements of Christian Doctrine; those attached to bishoprics or abbeys, where the instruction was of a higher grade, chiefly intended for youths who were preparing for ecclesiastical duties; finally, the school established in the emperor's palace, where the most distinguished men of the empire assembled, and where the emperor personally took part in their literary labors.

Despite the ruin caused by the invasion of the Normans, these schools were continued under the patronage of the bishops, the clergy, and the monasteries—even by laymen, under ecclesiastical supervision. In his Capitulary of 797, Theodolphus, Bishop of Orleans, one of the first restorers of let-

ters in France, enjoins upon pastors to give gratuitous instruction to the children of the people, and
nothing was to be exacted, nothing accepted, save
what might voluntarily be given by the parents.*
Gautier, successor of Theodolphus, renewed the
decree by which this pious bishop had ordained
" that each priest shall have a cleric, whom he will
religiously train; and, if it be possible, he shall not
neglect to have a school in his church, and he shall
watch attentively to nourish, in a chaste and modest manner, those whom his cleric undertakes to
instruct." Hincmar, Archbishop of Rheims (845),
the spiritual adviser of kings, four of whom he had
consecrated, and whom Guizot not inappropriately
compared to Bossuet, believed it a duty to
introduce, among other regulations for the direction of his archdiocese, that the proper authorities
should examine " *if each parish priest had a cleric
able to direct a school.*" In an ancient council, held
at Macon, we find the same idea in almost the same
words: " Each priest in charge of souls shall have
a competent cleric to teach school, and he shall
notify his parishioners to send their children to the
church, to be instructed in the faith." The Council
held at Mayence, in 813, imposes it as an obligation
upon all priests to employ every means in their
power "to oblige the faithful to send their children
to the schools, to be instructed in the truths of faith."
In 855, the Council of Valence earnestly recommended the *reëstablishment* of Christian schools, and
chiefly attributes the ignorance of the things of God

---

* Labbe, t. vii, p. 1140.

so manifest in those days, to the fact that these schools had been allowed to perish.

Later, we find the Church working in the same spirit. In 1179, the third Council of Lateran, held under Alexander III, decreed : " The Church of God being obliged, as a good and tender mother, to provide for the spiritual and corporal wants of her children; desirous of procuring for the poor, who are deprived of the necessary pecuniary resources, the facility to learn to read, and to advance in the study of letters, ordains that each cathedral church shall have a master, whose duty it will be to gratuitously instruct the clerics of this church and the poor scholars, and this master shall be given a salary that will suffice to support him, thus opening the way to learning. A school will also be established in the monasteries, where there formerly were foundations for this purpose. No one shall exact remuneration for a license to teach, nor, under pretext of any customs whatever, shall he extort aught from these already engaged in teaching ; neither shall he refuse any competent and worthy person permission to teach. Those who will presume to contravene this order, shall be deprived of their ecclesiastical revenues; for it is but just that, in the Church of God, he who, through cupidity, would sell the right to teach, and thus prevent the progress of the Church, should himself be deprived of the fruits of his labor."* The fourth Council of Lateran, held under Innocent III, in 1215, renewed these instructions. They were followed as far

---

* Labbe, t. x, p. 1518.

as the troublesome character of the times would permit.

In 1235, Pierre de Colmien, Archbishop of Rouen, published an ordinance, in which he made it obligatory upon the clergy "frequently to impress upon their parishioners the obligation under which they were to instruct their children, and to make them attend school assiduously." The recommendations were not lost upon those to whom they were addressed. At the beginning of the twelfth century we find schools opened, not only in the cities, but also in the villages. In the thirteenth and fourteenth centuries they spread in many directions. Thus, in little villages like Saint Seine and Lucenay-en-Morvan, there were flourishing establishments. In the diocese of Langres, there were schools in no less than thirty-one districts, some of which, even at the present day, are insignificant places. In 1465–6, the diocese of Rouen, alone, had given the tonsure to three thousand nine hundred and fifty-four youths, all of whom, to receive this distinction, must have obtained, at least, a partial education. We can conceive some idea of the extent to which these schools were disseminated, when we read that Gerson, in his treatise upon the " Visitation of Dioceses," written about the year 1400, counselled the bishops to inquire diligently "if each parish has a school, how the children are taught therein, and to establish schools where none have been opened." With the multiplication of schools came an increasing demand for teachers. The profession was one so highly honored in those days, that it became a convenient cloak with which to veil rascality, and then the Church began to be more choice in her appointments. She laid stress upon the faith and morals of those to whom she intrusted the education of her youth. To this effect we read several canons and decrees of Councils. Thus, the thirteenth canon of the Council of Rouen, in 1445, declared that none save those whose age, morals, and talents fitted them for the profession, should be employed as teachers of youth. In 1551, the Council of Narbonne prescribed that teachers, before being engaged, should be presented to the bishop, to submit to an examination as to morals, faith, and learning. The General Assembly of France, held at Melun in 1579, remarks that the lives of teachers should, in themselves, be a subject of instruction.

The first canon of the Council of Rouen, in 1631, ordained that the bishops shall reëstablish the ancient schools, open others in localities where they do not exist, and see that youth be educated in the ways of the Lord.

Similar regulations may be found in the decrees of the Council of Bordeaux, in 1533, of Aix, in 1585, of Toulouse, in 1590, and Chalons, in 1662. Thus, the last-mentioned assembly says: "*Prefer the payment of a teacher to any other pious work, which may be neither so necessary nor so pressing.*"

As time advanced, it became still more necessary to attend to the faith and morals of teachers, inasmuch as the Protestant Reformation had sent abroad a number of illiterate but bold adventurers, who had left the anvil or the bench to become preachers of doctrine and teachers of youth,—veritable blind leaders of the blind. The Reformation breathed a spirit of disintegration. Naturally, it tended to the total forgetfulness of all that tradition held dear. It was a spirit that taught each man to believe himself inspired, and the framer of his own faith. It was the negation of all authority. How did the Church meet the difficulty? It was a serious one; the remedy must be powerful.

To oppose this spirit of independence, this pride of intellect, the Church continued to offer, as she had hitherto done, the doctrine of submission of will and intellect, as embodied in her religious orders. St. Ignatius, after having been the hero in earthly warfare, founds a Society, which, since, has been foremost in every religious battle—first to enter the field, last to leave it. The learning of his sons is one of the lights of the Council of Trent, and their zeal brings hitherto unknown, forgotten peoples into the fold of the Church. Later, St. Alphonsus hastens to do his share in the work of staying the progress of infidelity, and of rebuilding that which irreligion has torn down. His children devote themselves to the wants of the villages, and preserve the traditions and expound the doctrines of the Church so well, that their father has been rewarded by being placed, with the Gregorys and the Basils, in the list of the doctors of the Church. Not only had heresy made sad havoc in the souls of the people, but war, instigated by the passions which the hour created, had filled Europe with desolation, and all hearts with dread, when St. Vincent appears, to stem the tide of misery and suffering. He, too, founds an order that will not only have for its object to instruct the people, but that will attack evil most successfully, by preparing the athletes who are to enter the field against irreligion and infidelity. His fathers of the mission open seminaries and retreats : in the former, young men are trained for the service of the altar ; in the latter, such as have already entered the field, and who need repose for a short while, to recuperate, physically and morally, may retire, always certain of a welcome reception. St. Vincent does more. He establishes the Sisters of Charity, whose veil is their modesty, whose cloister is the sick-chamber or the battle-field ; who are to be found everywhere, since there is no place in which they are not needed. But the age in which the Reformation sought to establish itself, was not only an era of incredulity and negation ; necessarily it became one of sensuality. The founders of the new doctrines had given the example ; the disciples followed. Then did the Church prove that she possessed vitality. St. Philip Neri, in his holy simplicity, and St. Paul of the Cross, in a spirit of mortification, which rivals that of the seraphic St. Francis,—each founds a Society, whose work is its best recommendation,—a work that to-day admires, and to-morrow will not cease to need.

Is the list complete? Not yet; there is one character whose genius is to turn the tide of thought upon this rapid-moving globe. He needs only to be mentioned, to be known: the Venerable

de La Salle. " He," says Ravelet, " is the most
distinguished person in the history of the eighteenth
century." He appears at the beginning of the
reign of Louis XIV. While this prince is at the
zenith of his glory, an humble priest prepares, in
silence and in seclusion, a work, the future development of which he does not foresee. He lays the
foundation of this enterprise in all humility, the very
year in which Louis, through pride, contests the
rights of the Holy See. This modest priest founds
an association of Christian teachers at a time when
those who govern the people forget the most important principles of Christianity. But long after
the great monarch has tottered into his grave, and
his power has fallen, the work of this unknown priest
grows apace, and his name becomes revered by all
who love religion and youth.

CHAPTER II.

Birth of Jean Baptiste de La Salle.—His family.—Early Years.—He enters the University of Rheims.—First Communion.—He receives the Tonsure.—Duty of Christian Parents.—M. Dozet resigns his Canonry in Favor of M. de La Salle.—St. Sulpice.—Père Baüyn.—Death of Father and Mother.—He returns to Rheims.—Père Roland.—M. de La Salle receives Minor Orders.—Ordained Priest in 1678.—First Mass.—He is sought as Spiritual Director.—His Humility.

THE traveller, who visits the city of Rheims, and enters Rue l'Arbalète, will there find a hotel, known as the Hotel de la Cloche-Perse, and also as Hotel de la Croix-d'Or. Recent researches have established that it was in this house, on the thirtieth day of April, 1651, Jean Baptiste de La Salle was born; the same day he was baptized in the church of Saint-Hilaire, his grandfather and grandmother being sponsors. A marble slab, placed in a conspicuous part of the front of the house, marks its historical importance.

It may be remarked that, from the foundation of the Apostolic College, certain families have been specially favored by heaven, in regard to religious vocations. In the family of which Jean Baptiste de La Salle was the first-born, history presents another illustration. Four of the seven children consecrated themselves to God: a daughter became a religious among the Ladies of St. Stephen; one of the sons, a canon-regular of St. Genevieve, at Senlis; two others were successively canons in the Metropolitan Church of Rheims. The family of La Salle has other glories, partially of a religious, partially of a national, character. The name and family are found connected with some of the most eminent explorers or missionaries in the New World. Marquette, the Jesuit, was connected with La Salle, Rose de La Salle, a relative of Jean Baptiste, being Père Marquette's mother; and in the French army which aided in securing American independence, there were three Marquettes, who gave their lives for the cause.

There is but one verdict as to the early years of Jean Baptiste de La Salle. "Gifted with the most happy disposition of mind and heart," says one of his latest biographers,* "this child of benediction produced early fruits of virtue. Simple in his tastes, charitable to the poor, affectionate toward his brothers, submissive, respectful, and considerate toward those whom he looked upon as superiors, he was the ornament and the joy of this noble family. He never manifested any affection for those amusements or brilliant feasts at which he was at times constrained to assist; yet, in his external conduct, nothing could be detected that bespoke either a gloomy disposition, or a superficial character; he was gay, without giddiness; devout, without affectation." Moreover, it was easy to foresee that Providence had special designs upon this remarkable child. All that related to religion charmed him; his greatest delight was to read the

---

* F. Lucard.

Lives of the Saints. When his parents wished to reward him for his application to study, they could give him no greater gratification than to relate some pious legend, or to read a portion of the Acts of the Martyrs. The ceremonies of the Church produced a marked effect upon him; he loved to repeat them, as best he could, before a miniature altar, which he had erected in his room. Possessing a rich, sympathetic voice, his greatest satisfaction was to sing pious hymns and canticles, though his father offered him the opportunity of training his musical taste in another direction. He learned to serve Mass, and afterward asked, as a signal favor, to be given a place among the sanctuary boys of his parish. So determined was his opposition to worldly amusements, that, on one occasion, while the entire family was engaged in the enjoyment of a *soirée* given at his parents' residence, he could only be consoled when one of the pious ladies present consented to relate to him some traits in the lives of the saints.

His virtuous mother, Nicolle Moët, had a large share in the development of these pious sentiments, but she did not limit herself to this part of his education. At an early age she inured him to the love of labor, and this strengthened the foundation of his future persevering character. When about eight years of age, he was placed in the university which had been founded at Rheims in 1554. It was then under the rectorship of the distinguished Thomas Mercier. The precocious talents of the young scholar, his keenness of judgment, and his close attention to study, gave his parents reason to expect a most brilliant future for their son. The new scholar realized the hopes of his family; ere long he attracted the attention of his professors, and soon gained their esteem. Under their intelligent direction he made rapid progress, to such an extent, indeed, that they more than once involuntarily asked themselves: "For what work has Providence predestined this remarkable child? What shall be his future?" *

The attentions of a religious mother, joined to the instructions of intelligent pastors, prepared Jean Baptiste for the important act toward the accomplishment of which his heart yearned with childlike faith and love. His first communion was an act that not only united him with his Divine Lord, but also made known his future vocation. Rich in the innocence and fervor of his youth, he approached Jesus with candor, love, confidence, and simplicity. Fully impressed with the greatness of the favor he had received, he desired to make, as nearly as possible, an adequate return. What could he give but his own heart? The sacrifice was intuitively called for at the moment when, for the first time, he found himself united with the sacred heart of his Lord. Instinctively the sacrifice was asked, spontaneously it was given. From that moment his choice was made, and young La Salle cried out, in the fulness of his gratitude: "Henceforth the Lord is my portion; no creature shall deprive me of this Divine treasure; in Him, alone, shall my soul seek light, peace, rest, and happiness."

---

* F. Lucard, t. i, p. 11, 2ᵐᵉ ed.

Hitherto, Louis de La Salle had fondly hoped that his son would, in course of time, attain the highest positions within the gift of the profession of law. He had looked upon Jean Baptiste as one who would fittingly continue to preserve the noble traditions of the family, while perpetuating its existence. What was his surprise, his momentary sorrow even, when informed that he must renounce all such fond parental aspirations? His son had but one desire: that of abandoning the world, with all its allurements; one ambition: that of " entering the house of the Lord," of offering each day the sacrifice that is unceasingly immolated from the rising of the sun till the going down thereof. But, if the child was highly favored in the call, he was not less blessed in the courage of his father. After a brief struggle, which only increased the value of the offering, this new Abraham resigned himself to the will of God, as expressed in the determination taken by his son.

Christian parents, do you understand the nobleness of such conduct? Do you see your own duty traced in the action of this Christian father? If urged, even at the risk of your lives, to break open the door of the tabernacle, to seize the sacred vessels, and to use them for profane purposes, the blood-stained altar-steps would attest the courage with which you had resisted so sacrilegious an outrage! Yet what less criminal act do you commit, when you thwart the religious vocations of your children; when you take these vessels of election, and constrain them to serve a purpose for which Providence had never intended them? Had such unchristian principles directed the conduct of Louis de La Salle, we should not have one of the brightest pages furnished for our information and encouragement in the extensive volume of Catholic history, while the Church, and, through her, society, might have had fewer laborers in the great cause of popular education.

In the conduct of Jean Baptiste de La Salle, at this early age, we see that his retiring disposition did not indicate want of force of character. It was his first great sacrifice, and his Christian fortitude proved equal to the exigency. True courage is never demonstrative. Like still waters, which run deep, it is only the occasion which manifests its power.

The angels rejoiced, and happy parents and friends applauded, when, on the eleventh of March, 1662, Jean Baptiste received the tonsure from Jean de Maltreau, Bishop of Olonne. The ceremony took place in the archiepiscopal chapel of Rheims. "Young de La Salle, like another Samuel, seemed formed for the service of the tabernacle. The tonsure," continues his earliest biographer,* " was not for him an idle ceremony, nor simply a semblance of renunciation of worldly manners and customs, as it is for so many others. His mouth spoke only what his heart dictated, when he declared that he took God for his portion, and that he desired no other inheritance. Once a cleric, Jean Baptiste de La Salle seems a new man. His piety, his modesty,

---

* Père Blain, 1733.

the innocence of his morals, all shone with greater lustre than before he had vested himself with the surplice, and had approached the steps of the altar. Among the clerics, as in the midst of his school-mates, he was a shining example. It was a candle which the bishop had lighted, and had placed upon a candlestick, that it might spread its rays upon the church of Rheims. Soon this luminary was to shine over all France. His love for chanting the praises of the Lord increased each day. Providence was pleased soon to give this young disciple the opportunity to follow Him more closely."

At this time the University of Rheims had, for chancellor, Pierre Dozet, Archdeacon of Champagne, who had been, for fifty-three years, canon in the cathedral of that city. He was a man of great information, and of profound piety.* He wished, before dying, to resign his canonry in favor of some scholar who united on his brow the double halo of science and virtue.† For this reason, he believed that he would be rendering an important service to the chapter of the metropolitan church of Rheims, by resigning his canonry in favor of the Abbé de La Salle. The church of Rheims, so noted for the multitude of saints and of learned persons that it has furnished, could felicitate itself upon the acquisition it had just made in the person of this holy young man. It was not the ambition of his family that procured him the honor. He owed the preferment to the great idea that had been formed of his worth.‡

---

* Ravelet, Vie du Ven., p. 83.   † Ibid., p. 7.
‡ P. Garreau, S. J., Vie de M. de La Salle, p. 11.

Not satisfied with the general testimony in the Abbé de La Salle's favor, M. Dozet desired to examine the young cleric. In him the experienced chancellor discovered one of those souls selected by the Almighty for a great work. He was happy in considering himself an effective, though distant, instrument in its furtherance. Abbé Dozet's resignation occurred on the ninth of July, 1666; his successor took possession of his appointment on the seventeenth of January following. He had not quite completed his sixteenth year. Once installed in this new dignity, "his assiduity at choir was remarkable; but the devotion with which he sang the Divine Office attracted even greater attention. The old considered themselves happy in having the new canon in their midst; the young respected his virtues: even had the latter been inclined to less regularity, they would have found their conduct condemned by his example."*

Here we find the subject of our narrative installed in the chapter of one of the most remarkable churches in France,—a body of men which, in 1798, counted thirty-one of its former members bishops; twenty had occupied the archiepiscopal see of Rheims; twenty-one had worn the Roman purple; four had occupied the chair of Peter, under the names of Sylvester II, Urban II, Adrian IV, and Adrian V.

That the retiring incumbent understood the character and disposition of him he had chosen to be his successor, will be seen by the counsel he

---

* P. Garreau, S. J., Vie de M. de La Salle, p. 12.

gave, when informing him of his generous intentions. " Remember," said M. Dozet, "that a canon should be like a Carthusian monk: he must pass his life in solitude and in retreat." The Venerable de La Salle never forgot this advice. Though naturally given to study, the position in which he now found himself rendered it a double duty for him to devote his whole intellectual energy to the acquisition of those sciences in which canons were required to distinguish themselves. The Council of Trent demands that the cathedral chapter be composed, at least two-thirds, of doctors. St. Charles Borromeo selected none but doctors as canons. A laudable pride, not to say a Christian sentiment, therefore, induced M. de La Salle to devote himself with renewed ardor to study. Having finished his course of philosophy at Rheims, he took the degree of Master of Arts; and attracted by the superior advantages to be secured in the schools of Paris, he determined to pursue his theological studies in that city. "I am convinced," said he to his parents, "that there I shall find fewer distractions, and a more complete course."

Once more Providence directed the steps of His servant. In Paris there were three seminaries, each presenting special claims to the attention of industrious and piously inclined students: that designated as Saint Nicholas du Chardonnet; that known as the Bons Enfants, in which M. Olier had made a retreat—St. Vincent de Paul had also been connected with it, and had extended its usefulness; and, finally, that of St. Sulpice, founded by M.

Olier. This last was the one selected by the Abbé
de La Salle. Besides the ordinary advantages,
this seminary required its students to devote a
certain time each week to the catechising of the
young and the ignorant. At least four thousand
children received religious instruction in this way,
through the instrumentality of M. Olier, who had
rented several places in which to assemble the youth
of his parish. St. Vincent de Paul regretted that
he could not offer this advantage to the students
of the seminary of the Bons Enfants. " Experience
has taught us," said he, " that, where there is a
seminary, it is well to have a parish in which to
exercise the seminarians." Thus, in preferring St.
Sulpice, the Abbé de La Salle entered a step further into the designs of Providence, and prepared
himself to be the future founder of an institute, one
of whose chief duties would be to instruct children
in the doctrine and the fear of the Lord.

He entered St. Sulpice on the eighteenth of
October, 1670, and came under the enlightened
direction of the celebrated M. Louis Tronson,
known till our day as the author of " Subjects of
Particular Examen," still used in many religious
communities. M. Tronson was rector, and M. le
Ragois de Bretonvilliers, superior. Both kindly
received the young abbé; they admired his candor, his genial disposition, his amiable manner, and
treated him accordingly, yet he chose neither for
his spiritual director. At this time a distinguished
Calvinist convert, Père Baüyn, was particularly
remarked by the Abbé de La Salle. He was

in charge of the catechism classes, to which he devoted himself with untiring zeal. To him the new student opened his heart, and begged for direction. M. Tronson had already selected Père Baüyn as confessor: it is not surprising that this should have influenced the choice of M. de La Salle. A single incident will show that he had not overrated the virtues of his spiritual guide :—

One day Bossuet visited M. Tronson, and expressed his regret that there could no longer be found in the Church such heroic examples of obedience as were narrated of the ancient religious. " It is true," replied M. Tronson, " that such examples are rare, and that they were numerous in times past; yet, through the mercy of God, there are still striking illustrations furnished us: perhaps I might give you one at this moment." M. Tronson left his room, and requested a seminarian to send him M. Baüyn. The latter soon arrived, and, according to custom, tapped lightly at the door, before entering. Hearing no response, and supposing M. Tronson occupied, he took his New Testament from his pocket, and continued to read it, till the superior would tell him to enter. When the Bishop of Meaux desired to leave, M. Tronson accompanied him to the door, where he found Père Baüyn. " What does this mean, sir?" he said, in a severe tone. " Is it possible that you have had the audacity to come to the door of my room, and to listen to the conversation I have held with Monseigneur? . . . Leave this place immediately. . . . such conduct is unworthy a priest." M. Baüyn, without uttering a word, bowed most respectfully, and retired, to the great astonishment and edification of the Bishop of Meaux.

It may easily be supposed that, under the direction of so experienced a guide, the Abbé de La Salle made rapid progress in virtue. One of his professors, afterward Superior-General of the Congregation of St. Sulpice, has left this enviable testimony in his favor: "M. de La Salle was constantly a faithful observer of the rules; his conversation was always pleasing and becoming; he seems *never to have given offence to any one, nor to have incurred any one's censure.*"

None can live with the disciples of M. Olier without partaking of their zeal for souls; their influence insensibly, but surely, makes itself felt. With the Abbé de La Salle, the union thus cemented has been continued through his children. Says M. Poujoulat: " To assist the Christian Brothers is a tradition with the priests of St. Sulpice. It was they who, in Paris" (as we shall see hereafter), "first assisted the Abbé de La Salle. Two centuries after, they were the first to welcome the children of the Venerable to the shores of the New World. The sons in each case were true to the early friendship." * While at St. Sulpice, the Abbé de La Salle distinguished himself, not only by his piety, but likewise by his vigor of intellect, and the aptness with which he treated theological subjects. One of his biographers bears this flattering testimony, which, moreover, is substantiated by all

---

* " Vie du Frère Philippe," p. 200,

authorities on the subject: " He courageously wrestled with theological difficulties, and familiarized himself with all the subtleties that error opposes to the unshaken principles of truth. To arm himself entirely against dangerous sophisms, he joined practice to the advantage of serious and continued reading. He might be heard discussing, not in that tone which pride and self-sufficiency would suggest, but with that assurance which is the fruit of zeal for the defence of truth. When stopped by any difficulty, he consulted his masters, committed their answers to writing, thought over their meaning at his leisure, and applied them when occasions presented. By observing this method, even with ordinary talents he would have distinguished himself; we may thence form an idea of the rank he attained as a scholar, since Providence had so largely favored him with remarkable talents." * However, those who would thoroughly understand the life of the Abbé de La Salle, must remember that the future Founder was destined, during all his days, to live, labor, and succeed, without any large share of human sympathy. At the time we now speak of, the young abbé was to begin his painful experience of the uncertainty of worldly prosperity.

When he left Rheims, in 1670, to enter the Seminary of St. Sulpice, his beloved mother was in the enjoyment of perfect health. She had smiled upon her son, had blessed him, and had promised herself to see him return, when his studies were

---

* P. Garreau, S. J., " Vie de M. L. S.," vol. i, p. 16.

completed, to be the future guide and consoler of the household. But all her anticipations were not to be fulfilled; little more than a year had elapsed when the mournful intelligence reached the young levite that his mother, from whom he had never received aught save kindness and affection, and whose pleasure had been his delight, was no more. Even the sad satisfaction of kissing the brow of this departed parent was refused him. The only legacy that he prized, was her blessing. He had not seen her dying; he was to meet her only in heaven. "Lord," said this affectionate son, "Thou knowest how dear to me was the mother I have lost. If I have the happiness to find favor in Thy sight, I beg of Thee to take pity upon her soul: place her in the haven of Thy eternal rest."

The shock he had just received was one that required all his manhood to bear up against. It demanded more: grace was needed; and this he obtained by the outpouring of his soul into the bosom of the God of all consolation. Deep as was his draught of sorrow, the measure of his sufferings was to be filled within a few months, by the death of his beloved father, thus leaving him an orphan, the protector of a household, and the administrator of a considerable patrimony. Before expiring, the father had earnestly recommended the care of his other children to their eldest brother; the abbé, therefore, left the Seminary of St. Sulpice, and returned to Rheims, the better to oversee the education of his brothers and sisters, and to administer the revenues of his family.

" When," says Père Blain, " one possesses the ecclesiastical spirit, and loves the source from which it is drawn, he may easily conceive the pain that our young abbé must have experienced, when obliged to interrupt his course of study ; to leave a house in which he delighted to dwell, and in departing from which he lost at once the greatest assistance in his studies, and the grandest models of priestly virtue. Filled with joy, he had entered the Seminary of St. Sulpice on the eighteenth of October, 1670 ; his heart crushed with affliction, he left it on the nineteenth of April, 1672 ; but in retiring, he bore with him the spirit of a cleric, and was already a man, as far as his age had allowed him to become so."

It was a difficult task for the Abbé de La Salle, at the age of twenty-one, to replace father and mother toward his family ; but he devoted his whole attention to his domestic affairs, provided for every circumstance by his discreet administration, and foresaw each emergency by his prudence. At an age when so many are flattered with the thought of being free, La Salle was not only his own master, but the temptation inseparable from the care of many was before him. Others would have fallen, under such circumstances. Among the mental struggles that he must have experienced was, " whether he should pursue the vocation that he had thus far selected." Many plausible arguments, which the world and nature would have pronounced unanswerable, might have been advanced ; but the future Founder, distrusting his own lights, had recourse to his usual method: prayer, and the direction of discreet advisers; and therein lay his safeguard. The friend he needed, and whom Providence had provided for the occasion, was found in the person of M. Roland, canon and theologian of Rheims. He was born the second of December, 1642. "M. Roland," says Père Garreau, "seemed born only to do good to the public; he had received great talents from God, and did not render them sterile, by living apart from those he was to benefit. His whole time was occupied in good works." The Abbé de La Salle, at the age of twenty-one, places himself under the direction of a guide who was but twenty-nine. But his choice was a wise one.

His biographers give this testimony of M. Roland: "He was pious and enlightened, detached from the world, and recommended the practice of poverty, humiliation, and penance. He wore a hair-shirt, and an iron waist-band; slept in a modest and poorly-furnished room, and refused himself all that might savor of luxury or effeminacy. In his home he had a certain number of young men, whom he prepared for the ecclesiastical state; he had established in this way a sort of preparatory seminary, wherein he directed their studies, and formed their interior. M. de La Salle was not one of his students, but he was one of his most docile penitents, and most faithful disciples." "There were other ecclesiastics in the city of Rheims, quite as distinguished for their learning and their piety; none equalled him in his zeal for the Christian education of the poor." In 1670, M. Roland preached the Lenten sermons in the city of Rouen. During this time he held frequent conversations with the pastor of Saint Amand, under whose direction he had spent the first six months after ordination. He also frequently saw Père Barré, with whom he contracted a holy and lasting friendship. These two founders of the Sisters of Providence gave M. Roland a full idea of the object and the end of the pious association which they had organized.

" No one," says F. Lucard, " could at that time undertake any good in Rouen, without becoming acquainted with Madame de Maillefer. Born at Rheims, of the Dubois family, which was allied with that of M. de La Salle, she had at first been very vain and selfish. Harsh toward the poor, she was extremely careful to procure for herself all that could gratify her sensuality, or pamper her love of luxury. Like Dives, she one day gave a cruel refusal to a poor person, whom she might, by an alms, have saved from misery, but who, unfortunately, died the following night in one of her stables, where the servants had sheltered him. Stung with remorse, she at once entered seriously into herself. The sight of her spiritual condition affrighted her, and she was converted to the Lord. From that hour she endeavored to obliterate her past record, by the most heroic acts of penance and humility ; she assisted Père Barré in all his charitable undertakings, and M. Roland, who had known her at Rheims, met her occasionally. She promised to found a school for boys in her native city. About this time the 'Remonstrances' of M. Demia appeared. They produced such effect upon M. Roland, that he determined to establish schools for the poor, under his immediate direction. He realized his design, by establishing the Sisters of the Infant Jesus. Madame de Maillefer obtained a worthy daughter of Père Barré's congregation, Sister Françoise, to be the superior of this new community." The Abbé de La Salle occasionally saw the members of the new Society, when he visited his spiritual director. His heart was in their work, as soon as he had learned its charitable object. M. Roland found it an easy task to interest him in the rising undertaking; and thus, without his knowing it, was La Salle gradually preparing for his own great labor.

In the midst of these circumstances, the Abbé de La Salle did not forget the duties of his position. He remembered that a stewardship was confided to him, and he did not wish to be an unjust servant. Six talents had been given him, and our history shows that he caused them to bear interest for his Master. He established a rule for his brothers and sisters, to which they were obliged to submit. The hours of rising, those for meals, the time for study and recreation,—all was determined with remarkable foresight. He felt that order was heaven's first law, and that, where happiness was possible, it was probable only where order reigned. His brothers and sisters, seeing that he was the first to fulfil the injunctions given, cheerfully submitted; and the spirit of union with which heaven blessed these orphans, took from the rule the monotony it would otherwise have inspired.

The Abbé de La Salle's general object in selecting M. Roland as his spiritual director, was to secure a guide who would replace Père Baüyn; his immediate desire was to learn the will of God as to his future course. Père Roland's virtue had merited the entire confidence of M. de La Salle; the latter, in return, gave him complete obedience, and, in submission to his wise counsels, determined, without further delay, to enter the ecclesiastical state, by taking upon himself its irrevocable obligations. In the absence of Cardinal Barberini, Archbishop of Rheims, he received minor orders from the hands of Charles de Bourbon, Bishop of Soissons, on the seventeenth of March, 1668. The Church, on that day, was celebrating the feast of St. Patrick, whose children, at that very hour, were sealing with their blood their attachment to the faith which their patron had given them. Thousands of their descendants were afterward to become children and disciples of this young levite. On Pentecost Sunday, 1672, M. de La Salle advanced another step toward his sublime vocation, by receiving subdeaconship at Cambrai, from Ladislas Jounart, archbishop and duke of that city. As he progressed toward the object of his desires, Providence permitted that many churches should divide the honor of having initiated the future Founder of the Brothers of the Christian Schools. He wished to return to Paris to receive university honors, but his domestic duties preventing, he obtained this distinction in his native city.

By the advice of M. Roland, M. de La Salle
went to Paris, in 1675, and was there ordained
deacon by the Bishop of Bethlehem. "Let me
be permitted," writes Père Blain, "without wishing
to compare our young deacon to the first who
received this honor in the Church, let me be
permitted to apply to him those words which the
Holy Ghost uses in canonizing Saint Stephen: '*He
was full of peace, and of the Holy Spirit.*' His
modest demeanor, the tranquil and even tenor of
his countenance, inspired every one with this favorable impression toward him; more than once, when
at the altar, in prayer or elsewhere, people thought
that they perceived in him another Stephen, whose
face shone as that of an angel."

Thus we see that six years were spent in preparing for the solemn act which was to be the
culmination of the Abbé de La Salle's desires. He
had taken no step without counsel; he had not
advanced without having first assured himself, by
the wisest means, that he was going in the direction in which Providence desired him to proceed.
What, then, must have been his joy, his soul-filling
happiness, when, on the ninth of April, 1678,
Easter-Eve, he knelt before Mgr. Le Tellier, his
archbishop, and received at his hands the sacerdotal
unction, in the Cathedral of Rheims!

Ordained priest, the Abbé de La Salle thought
only of approaching the altar. He redoubled his
fervor in preparing to offer his first Mass. His
whole life had been a preparation for the bright
day he had just passed; and the following morning,

while the Church celebrated the feast of the resurrection, La Salle offered up the divine sacrifice, the unbloody repetition of Calvary's drama, through which are taken away the sins of the world. No pomp attached to the abbé's first offering. No father and mother were there to receive from the consecrated hands of their first-born the Bread of Angels. No numerous retinue of friends assembled to do honor to this joyful occasion. In silence and retirement, alone, in converse with God, the young priest offered the Lamb without stain. He was not long to enjoy the quiet which was his on this occasion.

All his biographers agree with Père Blain, in saying that "persons afterward went to his Mass to be edified, to be impressed by, and to share, his piety. The assistants were recollected and touched; they felt themselves renewed, when witnessing the piety, the profound respect, the majestic air, with which he performed the divine ceremonies. As he retired from the altar, the worshippers still remained in their places, that they might partake, as he passed by, of the graces with which his soul had been filled. His thanksgiving completed, he found himself surrounded by numbers who insisted upon receiving his advice. He was another Moses, who returned from conversing with God, and who brought with him a heavenly light, which he shed upon all those who approached him. His youth was no obstacle to the confidence which his piety inspired; for, if he was a young priest, he already appeared a great saint." *

---

* "Vie de J. B. de La Salle," vol. i, p. 131.

Such manifestations of confidence were a source
of suffering and humiliation for him in whom
they were centred. "Many recommended themselves to his prayers, but he answered that he
was the one most in need of being prayed for. The
hour in which he would devote himself entirely to
the salvation of others, had not yet arrived. He
left the church without heeding those who so
earnestly asked his advice. In the quietude of
his home, he devoted himself to the duties imposed
by his guardianship. When he had given the required time to this obligation, he retired to his room,
where study and prayer occupied the hours in
which he was not engaged in chanting the praises
of God among the canons, in the cathedral church
of Rheims." *

* "Vie de M. de La Salle," vol. i, p. 28.

CHAPTER III.

Abbé de La Salle's Trials.—He desires to exchange his Canonry for a Curateship.—Mgr. Le Tellier refuses.—Death of M. Roland.—Sisters of the Holy Child Jesus.—M. de La Salle procures them Letters-patent.—Renewed Trials.—M. Nyel and Companion.—Efforts to establish Communities for the Instruction of the Children of the Poor. —Gerard Groot, St. Joseph Calasanzio, Venerable Cesar de Bus, M. Demia, Blessed Peter Fourier, Peter Tranchot, Père Barré, M. Nyel.—M. de La Salle providentially rescued.—He lodges M. Nyel and Companion.—M. Dorigny.—School at St. Jacques.

So far La Salle has appeared as the student, anxious to realize the designs of God, and as the faithful administrator of an important stewardship. Apart from the trials and the agony of heart to which the bereavement of his parents had subjected him, we have found few difficulties in his way. We now come to a period of his life in which the immediate preparations for his great mission are manifested ; and wherein we perceive that, like all the chosen soldiers of Christ, he had to tread the painful way of the cross. Much as La Salle was worthy of admiration as a cleric, he appears in all the dignity of his character as a priest. To offer the holy sacrifice of the Mass was his greatest delight. In the early days of his ministry sickness was frequently his portion. Yet, even in such cases, " he often found sufficient strength in his courage to satisfy his devotion ; and he was seen many times painfully walking alone, or assisted by others, to the altar." Indeed, he had been but a few days priest when the Abbé Roland desired to give his zeal a wider field of labor. He proposed that M. de La Salle should exchange his canonry for a parish. The director and the disciple agreed that, since this would afford an opportunity to save many souls, it was a desirable step to take. The Abbé de La Salle's only wish was to procure the glory of God, as far as possible : such an offer appeared to him a call from above. Yet he was willing in this, as in all else, to submit to the guidance of his superiors.

To appreciate the heroism of this determination, it is well to remember that parishes were at that time anything but desirable, in a worldly sense. " The position of parish-priest," says M. Faillon, " had fallen into such discredit, that, from time immemorial, previous to M. Olier, no person of distinguished family connections had been known to fill a curacy." Père Rapin also admits that " the care of parishes was so little esteemed that, in Paris, even the most considerable parishes were given to strangers, as positions unworthy of persons of distinction."

However, great difficulties presented themselves in the way of making the exchange. The curateship of the parish proposed to La Salle demanded a person of mature age and experience. He had neither. The burden seemed too great for his youth. Besides, he had his family still in charge. Was he to abandon these natural, legitimate, and essential duties? Could he combine the responsibilities of pastor with those of a tutorship? Either M. Roland had not thought of these things, or else he was impelled by an extraordinary grace. However, God inspires many pious designs, whose execution He often defers, or permits to be accomplished by others, who did not at first think of such undertakings. Inspired by God, David proposes to build a temple, yet he is informed by the prophet Nathan that the execution of this project is reserved for his son. St. Louis makes a vow to go in person to deliver the holy places from the hands of the Mahometans, and yet he sees himself discomfited in a work that religion had inspired. "After all," continues Père Blain, "perhaps God was thus preparing the Abbé de La Salle to relinquish, not immediately, but in a short while, not only his canonry, but all his earthly goods. Perhaps, even in the eternal designs, he was thus to draw upon himself the grace, which was afterward given him, to leave all, as did the apostles, to follow Jesus Christ, poor, naked, and abject.

The intelligence soon spread throughout Rheims that the Abbé de La Salle intended to exchange his canonry for a poor curateship. His relatives became alarmed. They had certain intentions upon his position, and expected that it would remain in the family. They made known their feelings to the canons of the chapter; word was sent to Mgr. Le Tellier, inducing him to refuse his consent. The prelate needed no pressing to take this step. He understood and appreciated the greatness of soul of the incumbent, and did not wish to deprive his chapter of one so edifying. When the latter presented himself before the archbishop to make known his intentions, he was told that he was to retain the position to which he had already given such honor. This word was an oracle for the Abbé de La Salle ; he did not make the slightest objection. False virtue is headstrong and persistent ; it desires only to follow its own ideas, and looks upon everything that contradicts it as so much opposition to the voice of heaven ; true virtue, on the contrary, mistrusts its own light, submits at once, and knows not what it is to oppose lawful authority.

Soon after, Providence offered M. de La Salle a rich field in which to labor for the good of souls. His friend, M. Roland, lay dangerously ill at his country-seat. Perceiving that his last hour was at hand, he sent for M. de La Salle, and named him his executor. " I confide to you, also," said the dying clergyman, " my newly established congregation of the Sisters of the Child Jesus: this is the noblest inheritance you will receive from my profound friendship. Your zeal will cause it to prosper. Through love for the souls of poor children, purchased with the blood of Jesus Christ, you will complete the work I have begun. Rev. Père Barré will, in all this, be your sure model and guide." M. Roland gave his soul to God on the twenty-seventh of April, 1678. He was but thirty-six years old.

M. de La Salle was gradually brought into the paths in which he was afterward to walk with such rapid strides. He was already acquainted with the details of the management of a numerous family. Providence now had imposed upon him the direction of a partially-established religious community. He considered the dying words of his former spiritual director as those of a departed father. He foresaw that, in promising to fulfil them, he would be placing himself in many new difficulties; but it sufficed that the spiritual good of his neighbor was in question, to induce his consent. No sooner had the worthy priest breathed his last, than M. de La Salle took charge of the infant community. What he had foreseen, occurred immediately after M. Roland's death: the dissolution of the Daughters of the Child Jesus was spoken of. The mayor, and other authorities, declared that a new religious community was an additional burden upon the city, and that there was already a large number of such associations. The Sisters believed themselves destined to speedy destruction. Their struggling society, which M. Roland had so dearly loved, which he had sustained with all his influence,—this society, which he had endowed with his wealth at death, would have fallen shortly after him, had not the faithful depositary of his last will and testament come to its assistance. He addressed the city magistrates in its favor; the archbishop, at his request, bestowed the greatest marks of interest upon it, and promised, through his brother, Louis XIV's minister, to obtain letters-patent for the new society. These were granted as soon as asked, and were afterward registered at the prelate's expense. They were placed in the hands of M. de La Salle, and from that moment the good Sisters looked upon their new father as one to whom they owed at least a great part of the esteem and affection they had previously bestowed upon M. Roland. Free from all disquietude as to their future, they labored with confidence, under the conduct of the canon who had procured their legal existence. Jean-Baptiste de La Salle began to be considered at Rheims as a public benefactor. The Daughters of the Child Jesus were not, perhaps, aware of an earlier obligation under which this new protector of theirs had placed them. In 1677 M. Roland had gone to Paris to obtain the legal existence of his society, through the influence of the archbishop; but the latter paid no attention to his request. He allowed M. Roland to remain in the antechamber, without even giving him an audience. Sadly disappointed, the holy priest returned to Rheims, and poured the anguish of his soul into the bosom of his nearest friend, M. de La Salle, who not only consoled, but encouraged him to persevere in his work, assuring him that Providence would bring all to a proper issue in His own good time.

In the lives of those whom God selects as examples by which we are to direct ourselves, it will be noticed that continued prosperity was never their portion. "No cross, no crown," is a motto applicable to the career of every person whose name is held in veneration by the Church. This the Abbé de La Salle experienced shortly after his successful efforts in formally establishing the Sisters of the Holy Child Jesus. One would suppose that a conduct remarkable as his for its zeal and self-sacrifice would have received naught but praise; yet at this moment the anger, the jealousy, and the ill-will of the world, were let loose upon him. His public trials were to begin.

His household affairs were administered with such rare prudence, he spoke so little to others of what he was doing for his brothers and sisters, that public curiosity was brought to bear upon his actions: solely occupied with his domestic affairs, responsible only to God and to his selected superiors, he acquainted none others with the course of life he pursued with those under his care. What the world did not know, it imagined; what it could not understand, it misinterpreted. Gossip undertook to explain matters; exaggerated reports were circulated. The more than fatherly care with which he kept his tender charges aloof from everything savoring of worldliness and vanity, was set down as unbearable harshness. It was bringing disgrace upon a highly respectable family. It was transferring the cloister into the world. He had made of his household a model of virtue and piety, which was a living protest against the frivolity of the fault-finders. This is what could not be endured, and it was seriously discussed whether young persons, subject to such regulations as their brother had imposed upon them, should not be withdrawn from so impracticable and unworldly a guardianship. But the persecution only raised him in the estimation of all well-meaning and intelligent persons.

These are terrible trials for one who still clings to creatures, and who has not made an entire sacrifice of himself to God ; but M. de La Salle humbly submitted to all the attacks of which he was the victim.   He preserved his equanimity; he changed nothing in his conduct; rather he endeavored to render it more in keeping with what he believed he owed to the Almighty. Previously he thought that he had reduced his manner of living to what was solely necessary ; after renewed examination, he found that there were still superfluities; he reformed his dress, and rendered it still more despicable in the eyes of a world which seeks but vanity ; he became more generous to the poor, and more frequently visited the sick. On several occasions he must have called upon the " Man of Sorrows," while under these trials, and in the lan-guage of one whose heart felt the keenness of affliction, imposed upon him in the home of his friends, he must have repeated to himself :

" Lead, kindly Light, amid the encircling gloom, lead Thou me on!
*　　*　　*　　*　　*　　*　　*
So long Thy power has kept me sure, it still will lead me on,
O'er moor and fen, o'er crag and torrent, till the night is gone." *

The day for the life-work to which Providence called him, was at hand. It had an insignificant beginning ; one which made the worldly-wise to smile ; still it was a work which, in its continuation and successful establishment, has given the Abbé de La Salle the enviable title, BENEFACTOR OF MANKIND.

---

* John Henry Newman.

While thus exposed to the gibes and sneers of a world which could not understand, and therefore did not respect, his intentions, the Abbé de La Salle was adding personal trials to those which Providence allowed to befall him. One of the chief difficulties he experienced at this time was to resist a persistent inclination to sleep. He resolved to overcome this enemy of meditation and spiritual communing with God. He ordered his servant to wake him every morning at four o'clock, and not to leave the room till he saw him dressed. The valet obeyed these instructions implicitly. As soon as the Abbé de La Salle had made his toilet, he began his prayer, but sleep soon overcame him; a continued and lengthy struggle ensued. He entered into a holy anger against himself, and, in the fervor of his determination, went so far as to kneel upon broken shells; no sooner did he fall asleep than the sharp pain awoke him. God was pleased with his goodwill, and gave him a complete victory over the enemy he so vigorously fought against.

During this time M. de La Salle did not forget to watch over and to protect the interests of the Daughters of the Child Jesus. One day, in the month of June, as he approached the door of the convent, he was met by two travellers, careworn and fatigued: one was of mature years, the other was young, and apparently the former's domestic. In them, without knowing it, La Salle was meeting the first two laborers who were to join him in tilling a field, some of the former workers in which we shall forthwith introduce to our readers.

Congregations of ladies had been established in large numbers. Their usefulness was generally admitted, and their relative missions of labor were easily determined. Many attempts had been made to establish similar orders among men, whose office was chiefly to be the education of sons of the laboring and middle classes. So far none had succeeded in France.

In the fourteenth century, a canon named Gerard Groot, born, in 1340, at Deventer, in Holland, traced the first outlines of an institute, which, in many respects, resembled that to be established by the Venerable de La Salle. At first a canon at Utrecht, and afterward at Aix-la-Chapelle, he abandoned his canonry, and established a body of clerics known as Brothers of the Common Life, to teach elementary schools, where children might learn reading, writing, and catechism. The Brothers supplied their wants, by copying books. The institute was approved, in 1376, by Gregory XI. The holy founder of this meritorious work died in 1384.

In November, 1597, St. Joseph Calasanzio opened a public free school, for the reception of indigent scholars, in Rome: the pastor of St. Dorotheus, in Trastevere, had given him a large room for this purpose. St. Joseph Calasanzio was at this time a member of the Confraternity of the Holy Apostles, whose mission was to distribute alms to the poor. Seeing the sad state of ignorance in which youths, unable to pay for their schooling, were found, he sought a religious order, whose object was to take charge of such. Finding none, he established a teaching body. Two priests joined him in the good work. This school soon numbered several hundred children. They were taught the catechism, reading, writing, and arithmetic. Rome had thus early the honor, which very modern institutions claim for themselves: that of gratuitously furnishing the children who attended their schools with all articles of stationery, and such books as they needed. The congregation instituted by St. Joseph Calasanzio was recognized, in 1607, by Paul V, and four years afterward was established as a regular congregation; and the members were permitted to take the three ordinary vows of religion, to which a fourth was added, by which they devoted themselves to teaching. These religious were known as the Fathers of the Pious Schools. St. Joseph Calasanzio died in 1648, at the advanced age of ninety two years. His schools prove their usefulness by the fact of their continuance till the present time. Still their diffusion has been quite limited.

In 1592, Venerable Cesar de Bus founded the Congregation of the Christian Doctrine at Cavaillon, in the diocese of Avignon. It was approved by Clement VIII, and was composed of priests and laymen, who were united by the vow of perseverance. They devoted themselves chiefly to the instruction of the poor in the doctrines of the Church. On certain days their pupils held public discussions among themselves, upon some point of Christian Doctrine. Venerable de Bus died in 1607. The better to succeed in their mission, his disciples opened public free schools, some of which continued in the south of France till the Revolution.

In this connection, there is another name worthy of honorable mention: M. Demia, a priest of Bourg, was named archpriest of Bresse, by His Grace, the Archbishop of Lyons. He was charged with the partial visitation of the archdiocese. In 1664, while fulfilling his visitorial duties, he was painfully impressed by the ignorance of the youth he met; and feeling the necessity of remedying so sad a state of affairs, he addressed a petition to the merchants and the magistrates upon the subject. The latter paid little attention to his remonstrances, but several charitably disposed persons enabled him to open a school in St. George's parish. This did not satisfy his zeal; he again addressed the magistrates, but this time so eloquently, that they were constrained to heed his appeal. His words were so striking, that it was thought proper to have them printed for general distribution throughout the country; among others, M. de La Salle received a copy. The city authorities then decided to appropriate a sufficient sum to found a school, where the children would be taught the catechism, reading and writing. In 1672, there were five such schools in Lyons; the children were taught gratuitously, and M. Demia was named inspector-general of these establishments. He immediately formulated the most precise instructions as to their direction. On certain days the children gave public exhibitions of their knowledge of the catechism, orthography, Christian politeness, and the method of mental prayer. Those who distinguished themselves were rewarded by the gift of clothes, or other necessary articles, for they were generally indigent. The direction and perpetuation of the schools required a body of teachers. To succeed in securing this necessary and vital element, M. Demia held quarterly meetings of priests and laymen, who consented to devote a certain time to the teaching of poor children. These masters placed themselves under the protection of the Blessed Virgin, each year, during the octave of the Nativity, and made a pilgrimage to Notre Dame de Fourvieres.

The Abbé Demia next gave his attention to the secular teachers in Lyons. A decree was issued on the seventh of May, 1674, by which all persons were forbidden to direct any primary schools without the authorization of the archbishop. They were, moreover, to promise faithful observance of the regulations established by the Abbé Demia. At fixed intervals these masters assembled to learn such new regulations as had been prepared for their guidance. The pastors of the various parishes were to give a strict account of the conduct of the teachers within their jurisdiction, and, from time to time, inspectors were delegated to report upon the condition of the schools. The reputation acquired by M. Demia's enterprise was such that numerous petitions were received, requesting his assistance for the establishment of similar institutions in other dioceses. The bishops of Grenoble, Agde, Toulon, and Chalons, wrote most pressingly, to obtain teachers; they even sent young men to be trained by M. Demia,

who was afterward to return these newly formed
teachers to their respective dioceses. He would
have desired to employ none save ecclesiastics,
and for this purpose he spent his private fortune in
establishing a seminary at Lyons. Its object was
twofold: to form country curates and primary
school-masters. The community thus established
was named St. Charles.' It was opened in 1672,
approved by the archbishop in 1676, and received
its legal status by letters-patent, under date of the
month of May, 1680. Without residing in the
seminary, M. Demia directed it by a school-board,
composed in part of ecclesiastics, and partly of laymen. In 1680, there were about twelve masters,
and as many assistant teachers, all ecclesiastics. M.
Demia died on the twenty-third of October, 1689,
being fifty-three years old. Despite the trouble he
had taken to establish his institute, the school for the
formation of teachers soon failed. Gradually the
institution for the training of country curates lost
its distinctive character, and became an ordinary
seminary.

However, previous to the Venerable de La Salle,
the founding of institutes, composed exclusively of
laymen who would devote themselves to the education of youth, had been thought of. Blessed
Peter Fourier Mattaincourt, founder of the Congregation of Our Lady, for the education of girls, had
also formed a community for the instruction of poor
boys in villages and cities. He could not obtain its
approval in Rome. Those who had joined in the
good work soon became disgusted, and returned

into the world. In 1654, Peter Tranchot, a lawyer, established a primary school, in which he was assisted by his nephew, but the undertaking did not find imitators. Toward 1600, Francis Perdouls founded schools of a similar kind in Blois, Tours, and in the villages, but his initiative was equally barren in perpetuators.

At Paris, in 1678, the Rev. Père Barré, founder of the Congregation of the Ladies of St. Maur, desired to establish seminaries for the training of lay teachers. The project failed. The young persons who entered, seemed to think much of themselves, and very little of the vocation they had embraced. They gradually looked upon their profession as one which they might render pecuniarily profitable, and thus the love of money lost them the grace of perseverance. At the end of a short trial they abandoned the schools, which forthwith were closed. Mgr. de Buzanvil, of Beauvais, attempted to form a seminary of school-masters, whom he would afterward have sent throughout his diocese, but he could not secure the funds needed to make his work permanent. At Rouen, a pious layman, M. Nyel, who was appointed by the city hospital to teach the poor children, endeavored to establish a body of teachers. He it was who, with a companion, was met at the door of the convent of the Holy Child Jesus by their future father, the Venerable de La Salle. They were sent by Madame Maillefer to establish a school in Rheims. Those who have read the lives of celebrated servants of God, may have noticed that, shortly before definitely calling them to a great work, He allowed them to see some special indication of His protection. Thus is St. Paul stricken with blindness, while on his way to persecute the Christians. He afterward receives spiritual and bodily sight at the same moment. St. Norbert, while riding a prancing steed, is suddenly thrown to the ground. His external appearance, while prone in the mud, is but an imperfect symbol of the doleful condition of his soul. Grace touches him at the moment; he sees the vanity of worldly pleasures, and forthwith becomes an apostle. St. Ignatius, a gay cavalier, lives as the world demands; he obeys the behest it gives its votaries, to demean themselves in pleasure-seeking. His heart is vain, yet it is good. A wound he receives gives him the retirement he needs. He asks for something romantic to read, and his nurses, having no other volumes at hand, give him the "Lives of the Saints," in which he finds truths stranger than fiction. Naturally noble-hearted, he asks why he cannot do what others have accomplished. In that moment was cast the seed which afterward bloomed into the Society of Jesus. St. Patrick is sent as a prisoner into the land which he is, in other days, to convert; St. Vincent de Paul is made a galley-slave, that he may fully know the misery he is afterward to relieve. The Abbé de Rancé is called to serve Christ, when he had least thought of his Master. M. Herman hears the sound of voices chanting matins. His soul is filled with a new harmony, and henceforth, instead of being the composer of secular songs and *pieces de salon*, he is to be the song-master of the most blessed sacrament. Thus God calls His own, by placing them under obligations that only a lifetime can partially repay.

So, too, was it with the Venerable de La Salle. About the year 1681, shortly before meeting M. Nyel, an accident befell him, from which he narrowly escaped with his life. Returning from the country one day, a fearful snow-storm overtook him. The roads were covered, leaving no trace by which travellers might be guided. An impetuous wind drove large quantities of drifting snow into the gulches along the roadsides. M. de La Salle lost his way, and, missing his footing, found himself precipitated into a deep ravine. In vain did he call for assistance: the wild winds drowned his voice. His struggles seemed only to render his position more precarious; each effort to regain his footing sank him deeper in this snowy grave. Nothing appeared left for him to do, save to recommend his soul to God, for, in a short while, he must inevitably be covered by the fast-falling flakes. After a fervent prayer he made another effort, which, fortunately, was successful, but it was accompanied by such physical exertion that a rupture, which then declared itself, ever afterward reminded him of his providential deliverance. He never could mention this merciful intervention of Providence, without the greatest tokens and expressions of gratitude.

When M. Nyel entered Rheims, he had left at Rouen the nucleus of a new religious community. There were twenty clerics attached to his work. These were known as Brothers; and M. Nyel came to the city of the early French kings, bearing the name of Brother Gabriel. His object in presenting himself at the Convent of the Child Jesus was to ask momentary hospitality; his instructions were to reside permanently with Madame Maillefer's father. M. Nyel was then about fifty-five years old. When the Venerable de La Salle had read the letter which M. Nyel and companion brought from Madame Maillefer, he offered to lodge the two strangers in his own house. " An inviolable secret," said he, " must be kept as to the essential object of your arrival in Rheims; your staying with M. Dubois, the father of your generous benefactress, might arouse suspicions, and seriously impair the success of your work; the least indiscretion on your part may create numerous obstacles, and cause you to fail, when you would feel most assured of success. Be prudent. Rather stay with me for a week or more; no one is ignorant that my house is open to receive all strange ecclesiastics. Your dress differs but little from ours; you will be taken for some country curate, and, in the meantime, we will be able to think over the best means to secure the realization of your object.* At the end of a week you will leave me, and make a pilgrimage to Notre Dame de Liesse, whither your devotion seems to call you. During your journey I shall do all in my power to prepare everything favorably; and, perhaps, when you return, you may be able to open a free school."† M. Nyel gratefully accepted the generous offer. M. de La Salle had at heart the

---

* F. Lucard.   † P. Garreau.

success of this good work, and consulted as to the best method of assuring its permanency. "The only means." said his counsellors, "that we see to establish these schools successfully, is to place them under the protection of some pastor with sufficient zeal to direct them, the required discretion not to betray the secret, and the generosity demanded to support the enterprise."

We shall see, later, the reasons which these discreet persons had for taking so many precautions. The writing-masters, as they were called, would naturally look upon such a public free school as M. Nyel sought to establish, as one likely to take away part of their patronage. M. de La Salle was encouraged to foster the work, and it was unanimously admitted that the Abbé Dorigny would be the one most likely to interest himself in this undertaking. His personal qualifications and his position enabled him to do so. Mild and conciliating in character, he also possessed the firmness required to direct this work, and was, moreover, extremely zealous for the spiritual and intellectual welfare of his parishioners. By a happy coincidence, this worthy pastor desired, at this time, to establish a public free school ; he was prevented from putting his intentions into immediate execution only by the difficulty he experienced in finding a suitable person to place at the head of the establishment, We may easily conceive the joy with which he accepted M. de La Salle's proposition. He agreed to lodge M. Nyel and companion in his own house, and to feed and clothe them for the modest sum of one hundred and fifty francs, which Madame de Maillefer had stipulated to pay annually for each. These wise precautions had the desired result. M. Nyel opened the school under the patronage of the pastor of St. Maurice: the writing-masters, seeing the protection under which the establishment was opened, made no resistance. The new teacher had a large number of children, and his school prospered.

Mme. de Croyères, a pious and wealthy lady, had watched the success of the modest enterprise with great interest; and being desirous that the parish of Saint-Jacques should enjoy the same blessing, she wrote to M. de La Salle, asking that a similar school be opened in her district, the expenses of which she agreed to defray. Providence manifested His will in the case, for three young men presented themselves at this time to M. Nyel, asking to be enrolled among the new teachers. After receiving some lessons in pedagogy, they were sent, under the direction of M. Nyel, to open the new school. It was found that the sum fixed for their sustenance was insufficient, and M. de La Salle generously agreed to defray the additional expense from his private fortune. Another link was thus attaching him to the new work. Still the ardor with which he devoted himself to these charitable undertakings, did not prevent him from pursuing his theological studies. In 1681 he received the doctor's cap from the faculty of Rheims. He sustained his thesis so successfully, that many persons gave him the expression of their fullest confidence; they were surprised to find that one so young should display so profound a knowledge of the human heart. The deep studies he had made, his recollection, his tender piety, and the daily practice of mental prayer, had enriched his mind with light that is usually the result of prolonged experience.

One would suppose that, by his studies, the Venerable de La Salle was unintentionally depriving himself of the taste which he manifested for the establishment and direction of these public free schools, in which none but the most elementary branches were taught. The contrary was the case. It is only littleness that finds itself above becoming a child for children, and a beginner for beginners in learning. True greatness never considers it very difficult to adapt itself to the capacity of youth. How far this was so with the Venerable de La Salle, we shall see farther on.

Till this time society had been divided chiefly into two classes: the ecclesiastical state and the professions on the one hand, and laborers and mechanics on the other. The rapid changes made in society since the invention of printing; the increased commercial facilities opened by the discovery of hitherto unknown worlds, the further distribution of labor, had altered the aspect of the middle classes, and demanded a wider range of intelligence among the masses. This it was the mission of La Salle to accomplish. He was to give a broader scope to the grade of instruction furnished the people, and, at the same time, establish a body of teachers who would prevent this instruction from becoming less Christian.

CHAPTER IV.

WITH all their success, the schools opened by
M. Nyel were far from being such as their founders, and especially La Salle, desired. The teachers had but few regulations, and those were scarcely
heeded. The lack of stability of character in M.
Nyel was in proportion to the goodness of his intentions. Père Garreau says of him and his
work at this period: "The schools were very
badly conducted, owing to the constant absence of
M. Nyel. Not only was order ignored, but the
masters, thus far, were subject to no rules of discipline. M. de La Salle had too large a share in
their establishment not to be interested in their
perfection. In order to repair, in part, the sad consequences of M. Nyel's constant absence, he determined to change the teachers' home, and to bring
it nearer his own residence. M. Nyel gladly consented to this proposition; he foresaw the benefit
that would accrue to his teachers by the vigilance

of their protector; and, moreover, this would give him greater opportunities of gratifying his erratic disposition. The masters left the house of the pastor of St. Maurice, and took their lodgings near the residence of M. de La Salle. They found themselves subject, in their new home, to regulations hitherto unknown to them. The hours for rising and for meals were determined. M. de La Salle indicated the time that should be employed in mental prayer. Each morning they assisted at the holy sacrifice of the Mass, and frequently communicated. In a word, these good masters found that, for the first time, they began to live a community life, and they were not slow in perceiving its advantages. But it was necessary to have a person of some authority to preserve the order thus established. This was **M. Nyel's** chief duty, but one which he proved utterly incompetent to realize. It is true that he could still be absent from time to time, at short intervals, but his itinerant disposition rendered the new *régime* irksome. On the other hand, M. de La Salle could not supply the deficiency caused by M. Nyel's repeated absence; thus, in spite of his zeal, the result obtained was meagre: even this threatened to perish. Yet the fruits of even the partial discipline that M. de La Salle succeeded in establishing, were such, that, when M. Nyel opened a third school in this house, its reputation drew to it a larger number of scholars than were to be found in the two others."

Apart from the general relation he had thus established between himself and these humble teachers, the Venerable had still no other thought than that of indirectly assisting them. " I imagined," he writes in his Memoirs, " that my relations with these masters required me simply to direct their external conduct, to provide for their wants, and to see that they fulfilled their duties faithfully ;" "whereas, Divine Providence," says Ravelet, "designed this to be the exclusive occupation of his life,—that to which all the others were to be subordinate. His deep theological studies, so far from proving fruitless, were to enable him to save his future disciples from the dangerous and subtle errors into which cunning sectaries would strive to ensnare them."

At this period M. de La Salle took another step in the work to which, insensibly, a divine but unseen will was leading him. Gradually he found himself more and more attached to his dear schoolmasters. It is true, he saw they were somewhat uncouth, but he admired their good-will, and looked upon them as instruments employed to draw souls to Christ. It was necessary, therefore, to form them upon this divine exemplar, and he devoted all his spare moments to the task. His occupations, however, did not give him the leisure that such an undertaking required. The canonical office took a portion of his hours. He had his time of study, together with his family duties ; and thus he found that he could give only a furtive hour to the masters. He then bethought him that, instead of sending them their meals, he might bring the teachers to his own table. The expense would be the same, and thus he might utilize the hours of meals to instruct them. The teachers would also, with the single exception of eating together, have all the freedom they had enjoyed. This project he realized, though not without opposition from his relatives and friends. The school-masters came, twice a day, to partake of the frugal meal offered by M. de La Salle; one read aloud, and the Venerable took occasion thus to instruct them in the duties of their position.

While circumstances thus developed themselves, the city of Guise, situated near Rheims, manifested a great desire to establish free schools. Mlle. de Guise had already founded three for poor girls, and asked Père Barré to send some of his spiritual daughters to direct them. The city magistrates desired similar advantages for the boys; and hearing of the schools of Rheims, they wrote to M. Nyel, asking him to come and establish such: a request that he knew not how to refuse. In vain did La Salle tell him that such a course was impracticable; that an uncertain good should not be preferred to one that was already in existence, and the continuance of which depended, in part, upon his assiduity. He told him, moreover, that a work undertaken under such imprudent circumstances could not be blessed by God. All to no avail were M. de La Salle's protestations. M. Nyel left for his new mission in the holy-week of 1681, relying upon the Venerable to replace him during his absence, which he said would be of short duration.

M. de La Salle could not, under the circumstances,

bear to see the young masters without a director, even for a few days; he therefore took them under his protection. They arose at five, made mental prayer, and then assisted at the holy Mass. He required them, after leaving the church, to repair to his residence, instead of going to their own lodgings. They spent the entire day with him, apart from the hours which they taught in school. They ate in the same refectory, each one receiving his portion of food; all the exercises were performed at the given hour till night-prayers; after prayer they returned to their own residence.

This mode of life lasted eight days, at the end of which time M. Nyel returned from Guise, covered with confusion, not having succeeded to found a school. During this short interval, the Venerable de La Salle had noticed many irregularities in the life of his disciples, and he resolved to correct them. M. Nyel's erratic course caused great inconvenience. He admitted this to be the case, but did not appear able to remedy the failing. He was happy to see the progress that had been made in so short a time by his companions, and urged upon M. de La Salle the necessity of taking these good people entirely under his immediate supervision, by removing them to his own residence, permanently.

The Venerable de La Salle was in the greatest perplexity. The lease of the other house was nearly expired. Should he renew it, or should he remove the teachers to his own dwelling, to have them always under his control? Such a determination was a serious question. Not only would it change his mode of life, but it would introduce into his formerly quiet existence a new occupation, that would involve great labor and annoyance ; one that would provoke the criticism of his friends, and the opposition of his family.

M. de La Salle, in this emergency, had recourse to prayer, and the advice of enlightened friends. He went to Paris, and consulted Père Barré, who had spent fifteen years at Rouen, and who had made great efforts, not without success, to establish schools there. Père Barré had also attempted to open schools for boys, but had failed. He had assembled a certain number of young people for the purpose ; but, through lack of preliminary discipline, and a rule with a sanction, they soon fell into various disorders, and finally abandoned their mission. La Salle explained the situation to this zealous priest, related what he had already done, and stated the success with which his efforts had been blessed. He then made known the difficulties of the position, his fears for the future, and the means by which he thought the work might best be saved. When Père Barré had heard all, he did not hesitate a moment in giving his reply. He saw why he had not succeeded in a similar undertaking. La Salle was the man destined to realize the sublime mission. The very trials to which the servant of God had been subjected, were so many means employed by Providence to strengthen the souls of His laborers. Père Barré omitted no argument to convince M. de

La Salle that his vocation was evident, his duty in the premises imperative. " God's greatest designs upon a soul," said he, " are accomplished only amid the fiercest contradictions. Trials, interior as well as exterior, crucify our nature, but they strengthen the soul. As wine cannot be extracted from the grape, unless this be placed in the press, so the soul can produce no lasting good, unless it has been passed through the press of trials, temptations, and contradictions. The perfect Christian must be like the weather-vane on the church-steeple : it turns in every direction, but never leaves the cross upon which it has been fixed." *   " Take your teachers," added he, " lodge them in your private residence, provide them with food and clothing : in a word, become their superior and their father."†

These counsels had their effects upon La Salle ; he left his adviser, fully determined as to the course he should pursue. On the twenty-fourth of June, 1681, feast of St. John the Baptist, his patron, he took the entire community into his own house.

This action brought down upon him a storm of abuse from his relatives. It even estranged some of them. Two of his brothers left him. The younger one was placed as a boarder with the regular canons of Senlis ; the second went to live with his brother-in-law ; but Louis, the one next in age to his guardian, resolutely determined to remain with him.

----

* "Spiritual Maxims of Père Barré," p. 26.
† F. Lucard, " Vie de M. de La Salle," p. 29.

About this time the magistrates of Rethel, learning the success which followed the establishments opened under the guidance of M. de La Salle, wrote to him, asking him for two or three of his teachers. Their petitions were strengthened by the influence of the Duke de Mazarin. M. Nyel was sent to settle the affair. Everything resulted to the fullest satisfaction of the zealous negotiator; the clergy and the poor families blessed M. Nyel and his work; charitable persons were anxious to provide all that was necessary for the new teachers. The Duke de Mazarin showed great generosity in this circumstance. "He did not limit himself to procuring temporal benefits for his dependents; he also sought to afford them the advantages of good and salutary instruction."* The duke, by his liberality, secured the opening of the schools, which, a short time previously, had failed at Guise. He gave the house and the furniture. Mlle. de Lorraine, Duchess of Guise, guaranteed the annual payment of a considerable sum, to defray the expenses of the two teachers. As this was not sufficient to cover the outlay, these teachers were authorized to receive half-boarders.†

Several magistrates, and parties distinguished for their zeal, solicited masters formed by La Salle. The authorities of Château-Porcien, and M. Guiart, pastor of St. Pierre-le-Vieux, at Laon, were first supplied. M. Nyel was sent to open these schools. Wherever he went, he was enthusiastic in his praises of the virtue of his noble

---

* F. Lucard, "Vie du V. de La Salle," p. 31. † Ibid., p. 31.

director.   During these voyages he induced several young men to join in the good work ; these he sent to be formed at Rheims.   Without their assistance, La Salle would have been unable to increase his establishments so rapidly.

When M. Nyel had seen the condition of the schools in Laon, he resolved to remain several months in that city.   These schools were then directed by parish chanters, who paid very little attention to them.   " It was heart-rending to see the ignorance and depravity in which these children lived." *   M. Nyel and companions were warmly welcomed by M. Guiart.   These instructors were already known to him, through M. de La Salle, with whom he had lived on the most intimate terms, and whom he had known through M. Roland, their common friend.   At his request, Mgr. d' Estrées took this school under his special protection.   The rapid progress made by the numerous scholars was the subject of public comment and congratulation.   The change effected in the morals of the children was not less noticeable ; and on the nineteenth of November, 1683, the municipal council declared that *M. Nyel had accomplished much good*, and granted to the new teachers an annual pension.   The Prémontrés de Saint Martin, a religious community, agreed to furnish them with dinner.

M. Nyel's prolonged absence, and the rapid increase of the work, had greatly augmented the Abbé de La Salle's responsibilities.   He could no

---

* Arch. du Régime—Les Frères de Laon, MS. 1728.

longer look upon the direction of the schools, and
the formation of the masters, as an accessory labor
to which it would suffice to devote his leisure
hours. The future of their schools was in his
hands. " I feared," said he, later, " that I had taken
too great a share in these good men's labors ; the
solicitude which their direction demanded, had
become incompatible with my duties as a canon."

What will the generous and faithful disciple of
Père Barré and Abbé Roland do under the circumstances? On the one hand, worldly preferments
are within his reach. Despite the course he has
thus far pursued, to acknowledge that he has been
mistaken, and to ask his friends once more to embrace him, would have been sufficient. All would
have been forgiven. But this is not his thought.
On the contrary, he seriously asks himself whether
he will exchange the canon's stall for the teacher's
stool. An all-important question ; a most decisive
moment! Upon it depend the creation of a new
religious order, and the vocations of thousands who
are to be known as Brothers of the Christian
Schools. " Faithful," says F. Lucard, " to a practice
that he will preserve till death, the Venerable de
La Salle seeks in prayer and meditation the solution
of his difficulties." For this purpose, he rented a
lonely garden, near the Augustinians. There, like
the son of Monica, he listened to the voice of God.
He took up the book of experience, in which so
many things had already been written for him ; he
pondered over its lessons ; in it he heard the will of
God, and he followed its behests." " In the choice I

am about to make," he writes, " what should determine my resolution? Certainly, the greater glory
of God, the service of the Church, my perfection,
and the salvation of souls. But if I consult these
motives, so befitting a priest of the Lord, I must
determine to renounce my canonry, to give myself
entirely to the care of the schools, and to form
good teachers." *   " Moreover," adds a manuscript,
now in the archives of the mother-house in Paris,
" God, who conducts all things wisely and gently,
who forces not the inclinations of men, wishes me to
devote myself entirely to the care of these schools;
He directs me toward this end, in an imperceptible
though rapid manner, so that one connection after
another has attached me to a vocation I had not
foreseen."

Upon his return from this retreat, M. Nyel and
companions found the Venerable de La Salle ready
to make any sacrifice for the welfare of their noble
undertaking.

Notwithstanding his assurances that their future
was in his hands, that he would see to their wants,
these poor masters, at times, gave way to thoughts
of despondency. Their task was a thankless one, in
many respects. Their best days were spent in the
service of an ungrateful class : what was to become
of them, when worn-out nature would be obliged to
seek rest? They addressed M. de La Salle in the
following terms : " If we attain an advanced age, if
sickness or infirmity overtake us, who will supply
our wants? Who will defray our expenses? What

---

* Père Blain, " Vie de J. B. de La Salle."

ϒand will pour the consolations of religion and of
friendship into our souls?"* The pious canon endeavored to allay their fears, by urging them to
rely upon Providence. He was promptly answered:
"You who are rich and honored, may look forward
with confidence; but what are we poor teachers
to expect? We will certainly die isolated and
abandoned!" †

Undismayed by such complaints, the servant of
God believed that herein he received another indication of the will of heaven. He wrote to R. Père
Barré, asking his advice. "Any other support
than Providence," replied this austere religious,
"is unsuited to the Christian schools." This was
equivalent to saying: "Renounce all your posses-
sions; give up your canonical dignity; forego all
idea of promotion in the Church; sacrifice the pleasures of wealth; become voluntarily poor. Your example will have greater effect upon your disciples
than the most eloquent and pathetic discourses." M.
de La Salle was nothing daunted at the great sacrifice that was proposed. He hastened to Paris,
hoping to meet there Mgr. Le Tellier. He arrived
just after the departure of this prelate for his archiepiscopal city. He then consulted R. Père Barré
and M. de La Barmondière, pastor of St. Sulpice.
Both advised him to carry out his intentions.
Several of his friends, his relatives, the members
of the chapter, even his superiors, endeavored to
dissuade him from such a step, but in vain. His
determination was fixed; a secret impulse of grace

---

* F. Lucard, "Vie du V. de La Salle," p. 34.　　　† Ibid.

gave him new strength to meet and reject every effort to withdraw him from the offering that was demanded.

As soon as he had reached Rheims he hastened to the archiepiscopal residence, and tendered his resignation.   M. Le Tellier refused his consent, but M. de La Salle, not in the least discouraged, consulted his advisers anew.   He particularly invoked the assistance of M. Philbert, canon and professor of theology, who had great influence with the archbishop.   After listening attentively to his reasons, all admitted that he was an instrument in the hands of God for the accomplishment of a much-needed work, and they unanimously declared it to be his duty to follow the impulse of grace.   Finally convinced, the archbishop agreed to receive his resignation, but, in common with many friends, especially M. de La Salle's relatives, his Grace expressed the hope that the Venerable would resign in favor of his younger brother.

It was evident that those who made such a request but partially knew the Abbé de La Salle.   He had labored, with all the zeal and earnestness of the most zealous suitor, that he might be allowed to divest himself of an honor which he found incompatible with the duties to which he felt himself irresistibly called.   Nothing but the greatest indifference to all purely human considerations could have induced such a resolution.   He was to change the company of learned and respected canons for that of a body of poor and partially illiterate men.   After determining upon so great a sacrifice, it would not be logical in so heroic a character to be found stooping to family considerations. in which nature would have the first place, duty the second. None could have shown more love for his relatives than the Venerable had manifested, particularly since the death of his parents. To watch over them more carefully, he had given up his studies at St. Sulpice, and pursued them as best he could, amid the distractions of household duties. But in all this, he felt that the will of God was manifest. He did so as a Christian brother ; as the administrator of an important stewardship. In all things he looked to the end he had in view ; and in consequence, when there was question of a successor to his canonry, he first consulted God, and next his neighbor. While he admitted that his brother had many excellent qualities, he claimed that there were others much more deserving of the position ; and, with him, merit had the first claim to the vacancy. His desire was to be worthy of the vocation to which he was now called, and he was aware that " he who loves father or mother, brother or sister," more than God, is unworthy of Him; hence, instead of giving his resignation in favor of Louis de La Salle, who had remained so faithful to him in the time of persecution, he caused it to revert to the Abbé Faubert, who was well known, and highly esteemed for his ability as . a preacher, and his zeal for the salvation of souls.

Louis de La Salle, whose nobility of character has already shown itself, did not take offence at the preference given to a comparative stranger. He approved the motives which directed his brother's selection, and was shortly afterward rewarded for his disinterested feelings. The archbishop availed himself of the first vacancy caused by the death of the incumbent, to prefer Louis to a canonry, and, in doing so, his Grace playfully remarked that he gave him the position, in order to repair M. de La Salle's folly in giving his benefice to another than his brother.

To judge by the Abbé de La Salle's acts, he was the only party who had been benefited by the exchange; for, no sooner had he witnessed the installation of his successor, than he assembled his disciples, whom he could now call his children, and with them chanted a *Te Deum*, in thanksgiving for this further preliminary step toward the establishment of the Brothers of the Christian Schools.

But still another sacrifice is required from this generous heart. He had given up the honors of a former position, he had selected an ungrateful task as his lifework, and still there was a great stream to cross. He had rendered himself humble with the little; it yet remained for him to become poor with the indigent. He was called to be the apostle of youth, and, as an apostle, he was asked by a conscience, to which he had never refused to listen, to sell all that he possessed, to give the price thereof to the poor, and then, having left all things, to follow Christ, who had not a stone whereon to lay His divine head. M. de La Salle had made too many sacrifices, had merited too many graces of strength and of courage, not to be equal to this draught of the chalice which he was to drink to the dregs.

Moreover, the circumstances of his newly accepted position demanded this offering. At this time we find him writing to a friend: "My mouth is closed, I have no right to speak the language of perfection to my teachers; nor can I tell them of poverty, while I am possessed of a rich patrimony, which precludes the possibility of want. How can I speak to them of abandonment to Providence, while I am provided against indigence?" The holy servant of God awaited but the favorable moment to divest himself of the last links which attached him to the world. Rarely have well-disposed persons to wait long to find objects upon which to lavish their alms. A special and pressing occasion presented itself, in which La Salle could dispense his wealth to advantage.

The year 1684 may justly be termed "the sad year," in the history of France. Several seasons of insufficient crops had rendered provisions as scarce as they were dear. From all the surrounding villages, hundreds of poor persons crowded into the cities, and Rheims had the appearance of a vast pauper-house. The greater number of the middle and lower classes were reduced to beggary, as all work had ceased. Even many rich persons were brought to the utmost state of misery. Religious communities, to whom want had hitherto been unknown, were forced to part with their most costly furniture, in exchange for bread. So afflicting a year was one in which the Abbé de La Salle

could part with his goods, without going far to
find ready receivers.   But, even here, an idea quite
natural under the circumstances, must have struck
him.   Was it prudent to become poor, when he had
a number of persons dependent upon him for the
necessaries of life?   The question was one difficult
to answer.   Still Père Barré's words resounded in
his soul: " No other reliance than Providence is
suited to the Christian Schools."   Moreover, he
believed with the apostle, that, " being poor, he
would possess all things," since he would thus purchase the blessing of God, called down upon him
by the prayers of those he would assist.   He had
long ago broken all ties of kinship.   He felt himself now as a member of the large family of the poor
and indigent.   What he called his was theirs.   To
them it belonged, and among them he resolved to
distribute it.

So he divided his patrimony into four parts: the
first purchased food for his poor scholars, and assisted the Sisters of the Child Jesus; the second was
given to the indigent, who were first taught catechism for a few moments each day, when they came
to receive their pittance; the third part was given
to females in distress, who were likewise instructed;
and the fourth was distributed among the poor who
were ashamed to make known their necessities.
" The good priest did all in his power," says Père
Barré, " to find these deserving poor, without being
discovered by them."   " Those among his adversaries," continued F. Lucard, " who had been most
bitter in their assaults against his character, were

the chief subjects of his liberalities." His disciples, affrighted at the number and extent of his charities, began to fear for their own future. Like the Israelites of old, they were in constant dread lest they should perish, never thinking of the manifestations already made by Providence in their favor. But, seeing their father reduced to the same poverty as themselves, these timorous teachers became more confident; the Venerable's instructions fell upon hearts that had been moved by the power of example to follow their master in all things. At this time he was thirty-three years old.

A distinguished writer has well said that no monastic institution has ever failed which had, for its corner-stone, faith; for its walls, poverty; and for its roof, modesty. These were the three virtues on which the Abbé de La Salle had centred his hopes. They were, therefore, built upon the strong foundation against which the winds and the waters strike without effect.

4

BOOK II.
THE VOCATION.

CHAPTER I.

Several Collegians enter the Society.—Removal to Rue Neuve.—
Incompetent Teachers requested to withdraw.—Retreat with twelve
Brothers.—They make triennial Vows.—The religious Habit.—M. de
La Salle establishes a Training-school.—Duke de Mazarin.—M. Nyel
retires to Rouen.—General Assembly of the Brothers in 1686.—The
Venerable resigns the Generalship.—Illness of several Brothers.—
Death of FF. Nicolas, Jean Paris, and Maurice.—M. de La Salle
receives Penitents, and is visited by distinguished Ecclesiastics.

THE last tie has been snapped. The Venerable de
La Salle has proved himself equal to the demands
imposed upon his generosity. His greatness of
soul begins to stand out in bold relief. But, as we
advance, we will get still better glimpses of it. He
is not a man of mere impulses; he is consistent in
all he does.

Having ceased to be rich, he believed himself entitled to no better treatment than the poor. He
placed himself among the mendicants, and begged
the morsel which was to preserve so precious a
life: this he did with all the humility his rare
virtue could command. "On one occasion," relates
Père Blain, "he had gone from house to house,
thus imploring the assistance that he had lately

so cheerfully given; many a rebuff, and no food, had been his fortune, when a good lady offered him a slice of bread. This he ate kneeling, and with an expression of joy upon his countenance, which none but those who knew of his virtue could understand." Providence seemed only to await this accomplishment of the final sacrifice, before manifesting His pleasure in the work to which M. de La Salle had unreservedly devoted himself. The teachers, who had thus far entered the new society, were of an inferior class. Some of them, discouraged at the perfection to which the Venerable wished them to attain in their profession, withdrew, leaving him with very poor material for the propagation of the schools. But this was of short duration; for several young men, who had already made part of their collegiate studies, struck by the example of the Canon of Rheims, and inwardly impelled to imitate his noble conduct, presented themselves to join the new army of the Lord.[*] The number soon became so considerable, that La Salle was obliged to seek for more spacious accommodations. He rented a large house in Rue Neuve, whither his numerous family retired. Already that family perceived that God does not allow Himself to be outdone in generosity.

M. de La Salle, possessing nothing, had still many friends; if what the world called his folly had lost him some admirers, his zeal and the success of his work had brought many others to his assistance. Thus several ecclesiastics, touched by the devoted-

---

[*] Maillefer—MS. *Vie.*

ness of their fellow-priests, collected a considerable
sum, with which he was enabled to purchase his
new residence. A flourishing school was opened
there, and the cradle of the work was the property
of the infant society. It was in 1700 that the deeds
were given to M. de La Salle.

Some of M. Nyel's first companions, whose good-
will was greater than their tact, were requested to
withdraw from the new institute; the others were
subjected to such a course as was most likely to
cultivate their talents. M. de La Salle, now fully
identified with his labor, desired to be united with
his adopted family by closer ties. His was one of
those characters that cannot make sacrifices by
halves. In 1684, on the feast of the Ascension, he
assembled twelve of his principal disciples; he
publicly announced that henceforth he would be
one of them; their trials would be his; their food
his nourishment, and their successes his sole earthly
reward. Together they made a ten days' retreat,
during which the disciples could not help admiring
the heroic efforts their father made to subject himself entirely to their simple method of living. At
the close of the exercises, several of the most zealous wished to unite themselves to the new society,
by perpetual vows. The prudent director did not
find them sufficiently prepared for so solemn an act;
still, he permitted twelve of the most ancient among
them to take the vows of obedience and stability
for three years. They were to renew these obligations each Trinity Sunday.

We need not be astonished that the Venerable's disciples should have been so pressing in their demands to join their fortunes with his. The examples he daily furnished, impelled them to present this petition. While they had something to suffer, in the humble nature of their employment, they saw their leader condemning himself to the most extraordinary and difficult mortifications. His body was enveloped in a thick hair-shirt, and a pointed girdle about his waist left his senses no repose. To these penances he added the severest disciplines, which he inflicted upon himself with leather thongs, tipped with iron. The marks of the blood which spurted from his body were visible upon the walls of his room; and by this means it was that the holy severities which he inflicted upon himself became known. Père Lacordaire has said that, when Frenchmen become monks, they become such " up to the neck." In this pithy sentence, he has expressed the spirit that actuated the Venerable de La Salle and his fervent disciples at this time.

Before separating, after the termination of the retreat, certain general measures of order and discipline were adopted. Among others, a costume was determined upon. The color and the form were left to the selection of the holy Founder. It was then decreed that the habit should be of coarse black cloth, closed in front with hooks and eyes; a white rabata, or collar, an ecclesiastical hat, with wide border, somewhat in the style of the old Continental hat of colonial days, and a mantle similar to

that then worn in Champagne, completed the prescribed outfit.*

The wisdom of such a measure is questioned only
by the superficial, as it is only the uneducated
and the rabble who find fault with the dress. It
is in keeping with the unchanging spirit of the
Church under whose sanction religious orders are
established, that their characteristic dress remain
unchanged. It is only in the world, where men pay
deference to the tyrannical caprices of fashion, that
the style of the hour is consulted. But religious
men are not of the world. Their thoughts are
above the cut of their coat. It suffices that their
dress be in keeping with their profession. In every
office there are certain external marks by which
its incumbent is distinguished. In the Church, also,
each position has its garb of dignity, its mantle, its
gown, to indicate the rank its occupant may claim.
As the veil worn by Sarah denoted that she was
a lawfully espoused wife, so the religious dress
indicates that the wearer has espoused a single
cause; that he is to reserve himself exclusively for
that cause, and that his energies are to bear all in
one direction. The pious Founder gave his followers a costume, not simply as teachers, but still
more as religious. When the judge has left his
official chair, he no longer wears his gown and wig,
for he ceases, temporarily, to be a magistrate; but
religious, wherever they go, in whatever company
they find themselves, are ever consecrated to God,
and must make open profession of their adherence

---

* This is still the dress of the Brothers of the Christian Schools.

to fixed principles. Countries or circumstances may require a temporary deviation from this rule, but the really courageous disciple will never, when possible, flinch from appearing in the garb of his religious profession.

The Venerable de La Salle was the first to clothe himself in the new habit. This costume, which is now respected throughout the world, was at first the cause of some insult and humiliation, but it gradually grew in favor, till to-day it is recognized as the symbol of true devotedness to the best interests of youth. It makes all appear equal, and does away with a thousand whims, fancies, and inconveniences. When the first disciples were insulted, so far from repining, they rejoiced "that they were accounted worthy to suffer reproach for the name of Jesus." The saintly Founder remarks on this subject: "Before the Brothers had taken the holy habit, they were considered as so many men working for pay; several who presented themselves even asked what wages they were to receive, like so many domestics. Since vesting them with the religious costume, no one has asked for pay, and each one enters with the intention of persevering until death; and those who are received deem themselves most happy. From that time seculars looked upon the teachers as men separated from the world. Their new costume produced the happiest results in every respect.

The Venerable likewise determined the name by which his sons were to be known. It is as touching as instructive. They are to be called the Brothers of the Christian Schools. Brothers,—men of one family in God. Brothers,—all laboring for the interests of God, their Father, and of the Church, their mother. Brothers of the Christian Schools,— men devoted to the work of evangelizing and of instructing the masses; men, who for two centuries, have been earnestly striving to do that which the late Holy Father, Pius IX, so urgently recommended, namely, "to make education more Christian." "They," says the Venerable de La Salle, "shall always address one another as our dear Brother." All family titles are to be unknown. If distinction is attained, it must be as Brothers that it will be acquired.* Shortly after the Venerable de La Salle had given this first impetus and form to his community, he proved, in a striking manner, the reality of his intention to become one in all things with his disciples. The Brother who taught the school of St. Jacques fell sick. The holy Founder immediately took his place. Then it was that Rheims beheld the former canon and doctor in theology leading little children to Mass, teaching them the first elements of reading and writing,

---

* A simple country lad enters the society. He has little means, but great talent. During twenty years he labors in its ranks, and for forty more, he directs its destiny. See that immense throng of people around the doors, surging up the aisles of St. Sulpice; watch those ten thousand children, who march in line with saddened countenance and measured step. What does all this mean? The world is paying its last respects to a man whose real name is unknown to one in a thousand of those who follow his remains. They weep the loss of a Brother of the Christian Schools, whose panegyric is written by Pius IX, and in whose honor France strikes a medal: his name is Brother Philippe.

Had the reader entered one of the poorest districts of Paris, on the sixth of February, 1856, he might have noticed a general gloom among

performing all the functions of the primary instructor. Even those who had most persecuted him could not help expressing their admiration at this conduct. Needless to say that his modest disciples were proud of their superior. In seeing him taking part in their simple functions, they felt, even humanly speaking, that their work was not to be despised. On his return from class, they flocked around him, asking him if he found teaching painful, or if the children were difficult to manage. He was cheerful and happy, and simply remarked: "Let us imitate St. Paul; let us make ourselves all to all, and we will find ourselves in our classes as a father in his family."*

The excellent results obtained by the Venerable de La Salle's children had already attracted public attention, and several parties desired their services. He told those who spoke to him on the subject, that he could not allow his disciples to live apart, as was requested, but he offered to establish a training, or normal school for village teachers, if the means were provided him. This school was accordingly opened at Rheims. Many of the clergy sent intelli-

---

the inhabitants. The merry song of the thrifty housewife is hushed. Little children look up into their mothers' faces, and strive to read the meaning of the strange sadness therein pictured. Old men shake their heads, and say, "We shall never see her like again." Who is this, whose name is so respected—whose influence has penetrated so deeply into those simple hearts? A woman who could scold princes, and command soldiers; who could stop the bloody carnage of the city mob, and obtain the pardon of thoughtless revolutionists; a woman who had the purse of the rich at her command, yet whose family ties were unknown. She was princess of her district, still her only title was that she was a daughter of St. Vincent, known as Sister Rosalie. This tells the secret magic of the religious dress—the charm of the titles, Brother, Sister.

* F. Lucard, "Vie," 2d ed., p. 74.

gent young men to be formed, and, after a certain length of time, which depended on their aptitude and application, they were sent to their various parishes, where, in their capacity as primary teachers, they did great good. Thus the holy Founder was widening the sphere of his influence far beyond his immediate action.

At the same time that this training-school was established, the Venerable de La Salle opened what he called the small, or preparatory, novitiate. " In this school," says the Venerable, " we train intelligent children, who are piously inclined, and who propose afterward to enter our society ; they are admited at the age of fourteen, and are formed to practise mental prayer, and other exercises of piety. They are also taught the catechism, and they learn to read and write perfectly. These scholars have a dormitory, a chapel, a refectory, and recreation grounds, apart. Even their exercises are different from those of the Brothers, and are proportioned to their strength of mind, and to the duties they are afterward destined to fulfil." The Venerable de La Salle devoted great attention to these boys: there were fourteen in this preparatory novitiate the first year.

The Duc de Mazarin, who had heard much of La Salle's work, was very desirous to form his acquaintance. For this purpose, he came to Rheims, and paid him visits. The duke's knowedge of human nature soon made him admire the charming simplicity, the brilliancy of talent, and the prudence and sweetness which were such characteristic traits in his new friend. The relations thus established between these two men were not to terminate in sterile formalities and mutual courtesies. Cardinal Mazarin, after having closed a brilliant but agitated career by the treaty of the Pyrenees, instructed his nephew, the Duc de Mazarin, to found several works that would be useful to religion and to society. Though twenty-five years had elapsed since the death of the cardinal-minister of state, during which time the good duke had endeavored to carry out his instructions as to pious foundations, there still remained something to be done. The wants of youth had not been sufficiently thought of. Meeting such a man as La Salle was an invitation to the duke to enter his name on a new list as benefactor. The latter advised him to found a school, similar to that of Rheims, in which he might train teachers for the many cities and villages in his vast domains.

On the twenty-second of September, 1685, the contract was drawn up, by which the duke agreed to furnish the means, and La Salle bound himself to direct the school. In this paper we find, among other items, "that the said duke has established a community of young men in the city of Mazarin, that he may draw from this institution, as from a nursery, a sufficient number of teachers to instruct the youth of the Duchy of Mazarin, and also other districts belonging to him; that this school shall be directed by two competent teachers, appointed by M. de La Salle."

The creation of this school had taken place on the

twentieth of April, 1685. The duke had established, in perpetuity, seventeen purses, to be given to the most intelligent young men of the Brothers' school in Rethel. These students were to be prepared to act as teachers. They were to learn to read and write perfectly, and also to sing, " that they might afterward instruct the youth of the lands, parishes, boroughs, and villages, in the said duchy of Mazarin."

It is characteristic of human intelligence that any attempt at going beyond what has already been done is sure to attract the criticism, if not the ridicule, of the world. The more this movement is directed to the moral amelioration of the race, the more certainly will abuse and vituperation follow. It seems as though it were a crime for any one to think or to see beyond the range within which previous ages have limited progress. Thus the Abbé de La Salle found that his intention of establishing a training-school, being something new, met with numerous opponents. Certain persons, not wiser than their generation, apprehensive of the results of the establishment of an institution which was without precedent, opposed the undertaking, and united their strength to stifle the attempt in its cradle. They influenced the archbishop and his vicar-general, and the contract entered into between the Duke de Mazarin and M. de La Salle was annulled. Such obstacles were not of a character to dismay either the Founder of the Christian Schools or his noble patron. Unable to obtain the approbation of the Archbishop of Rheims, they turned their attention elsewhere, and determined to found the school in the Marquisate of Montcornet, which was a part of the ducal domains which depended for spiritual ministration upon the Bishop of Laon, whose sympathies were in favor of the work.

Having cancelled the first agreement, the contracting parties prepared a second, the same day (twenty-second of September, 1685), in presence of M. Chopplet, notary-public. The stipulations were materially the same as in the former contract, but the number of teachers to be trained at a time was reduced to three. The Bishop of Laon was to be consulted in the choice of the young men to be educated. Besides the annual stipend for the training-masters, the duke was to furnish a convenient house, and all necessary furniture for the accommodation of six persons. Moreover, M. de La Salle solicited letters-patent for his establishment at Rheims, "that he might perpetuate the training-school."

In all these successes M. Nyel took no little pride. It made him young for the moment to see that, through the blessing attached to his labors, and the direction given them by M. de La Salle, so much good had been accomplished. But, with M. Nyel, there was no such thing as having a lasting dwelling. No sooner did he organize, or rather inaugurate, an undertaking, than his propensities hastened him to pastures new. He longed for the liberty of other days, and "did not feel," says Ravelet, "that he was called to join the new community;" for this had so changed since the incumbency of M. de La Salle, that the former head was but a simple laborer in the field. "He was likewise anxious," says F. Lucard, "to give the teachers he had left in Rouen the benefit of the experience he had acquired from the Venerable de La Salle."

"My mission," he said, "is accomplished in Champagne. Nothing now keeps me." He was then at Laon, and likewise had the supervision of the school at Guise. He had often pressed La Salle to take control of the schools, but the latter refused. M. Nyel knew the character of his protector too well, and determined to impose, in some sense, upon his good-nature. "He knew that, if he left," continues M. Ravelet, "M. de La Salle would act as he had always done: he would assume the increased responsibility." It was in some manner necessary that M. Nyel should withdraw from the new institute. It had taken too great an extension, and might, by his imprudent zeal, have been constrained to assume responsibilities which its holy Founder could not control.

Upon his return to Rouen, M. Nyel found his friend Madame de Maillefer. The touching narra-tive that he gave of the good accomplished by M. de La Salle and his companions, filled her heart with inexpressible joy. M. Nyel retired to the general hospital on the twenty-sixth of October, 1685, and received the title of "Superintendent of the city free schools," a title created for him, and which he alone ever bore. On the twenty-third of September, 1678, he had given a considerable sum to the poor, and to this he added another donation, *on condition that after his death they would pray for the repose of his soul.* He found his former colleagues sadly degenerated from their first fervor, and their schools very badly directed. Some biographers of the Venerable de La Salle think that it was M. Nyel's intention to unite these schools with those directed by the holy Founder, but, if such were his views, he did not live to realize them. Death brought him rest on the thirty-first of May, 1687, and, in his person, a useful though varied existence, one to which society is greatly indebted, had passed away. By none was his loss more seriously regretted than by the Venerable de La Salle.

The Venerable found that M. Nyel's departure from Laon had placed him in a very difficult position. The pastor, with whom he was closely united by ties of friendship, hastened to Rheims, and made the holy Founder understand that he could not allow such flourishing schools to disappear. Without his immediate attention the masters would become discouraged, and the children would be left without instruction. M. de La Salle could not resist such an appeal. To the direction of the schools of Rheims he added those of the neighboring cities. Thus he formed a congregation already spreading, and depending upon him for preservation.

Upon hearing of M. Nyel's death, the Venerable de La Salle celebrated a solemn service, in the chapel of the Sisters of the Child Jesus, for his eternal repose. Many of his disciples were present, and prayers were said in the various communities of Brothers, for the repose of this well-meaning and zealous pioneer.

So long as as M. Nyel lived, the Venerable de La Salle's humility might claim that he was but a secondary instrument. Now that the whole burden had directly fallen upon him, his modesty shrank from the honor. He convoked a general assembly of his disciples for the ninth of June, 1686. Herein he appealed, with all the eloquence that could have inspired the most ambitious, and his request was, that he might resign a responsibility he had never sought, and from which he wished to be freed. Accustomed to obey his simplest wishes, these good teachers were not prepared to resist so powerful and touching an appeal. To please their father, they consented to deprive themselves of the direction of their surest guide; but Providence did not require the sacrifice to be of long duration.

Frère Henri Lheureux was elected superior. This good young man had simply consented, in deference to the Venerable de La Salle, who had given many reasons suggestive of the absolute need of his resignation. He had assured them that the number of houses, as well as the increased responibility he had taken upon himself, in accepting their spiritual direction, was more than sufficient to occupy his time and attention. For a long while he had refused his disciples the happiness of having him for their confessor. These reasons, added to others, which the humility of M. de La Salle had mentioned, were the prevailing arguments in the victory which he had gained. It is true, as Père

Blain says, " that the disciples might have answered that he, being the shepherd, was bound to lead his sheep ; that, having promised to share their trials and bear their crosses, he should not seek to evade the largest portion." In his position as inferior, the Venerable was foremost in all acts of self-denial and humiliation. " One day while the brothers were in recreation, some one told the superior that there was a part of the house in a very filthy condition, and that some one should be sent to put it in order. The Venerable de La Salle at once threw himself upon his knees, begging to be allowed the privilege of performing this act of humility. The Brothers were pained at such marks of abnegation, and the superior had sufficient presence of mind not to permit the holy servant of God to perform this act. He answered that this was not in keeping with M. de La Salle's dignity. The latter understood quite the contrary, and hastened to do the work for which he believed himself appointed. He was followed by the superior, who refused to allow him to proceed. Frère Lheureux even reproached the Venerable, in presence of the Brothers, saying that he had acted contrary to instructions. Far from excusing himself, the Venerable once more cast himself upon his knees, publicly acknowledging a fault of which he had not been guilty, and humbly begged to be punished as a refractory subject."*

A simple circumstance ended this abnormal condition of affairs, and rescinded the effect of a vote that had been innocently imposed upon the

---

* Père Garreau, S. J.

good Brothers, and which none regretted more than the newly-elected superior. He felt the impropriety of placing so shining a light under a bushel, and, with the rest of the community, urged that the Venerable should resume his duty as superior. As M. de La Salle had engaged his subjects to preserve silence upon the result of the election, their sense of submission induced them to remain quiet, when Providence came to the assistance of his children, and publicly proclaimed the great virtue of His servant. Some time after the election of Frère Lheureux, several friends of M. de La Salle called to consult him. What was their surprise and astonishment when word was sent them by the servant of God, that he could not see them without having first obtained the permission from his superior! The Venerable might have asked this permission, and then met his friends, without making known the circumstances under which he was acting, but his love of humiliation and abasement knew no such subterfuge. His desire was to appear the least of men; and the Scriptures were here fulfilled, for he who sought to humble himself was again exalted. His visitors asked some general questions, the answers to which satisfied them that the resignation of M. de La Salle was already the cause of regret. Not that the Brothers were dissatisfied with their new superior; but they already acknowledged that it was the persuasions of M. de La Salle, not their convictions, that had prevailed. The ecclesiastical authorities, informed of the change, wisely attributed it to the

humility of the Founder, and to the simplicity of the
Brothers; they immediately ordered that matters
should be returned to their original condition.
Then was seen a holy contest. The joy of Frère
Lheureux, in beholding himself divested of an
authority his heart repelled, was only surpassed by
the humility, the holy sadness, manifested by M. de
La Salle, in seeing himself once more at the head
of the society.

The humble opinion which the Venerable de La
Salle entertained of himself, led him also to think
that Providence was chastising the little congregation because of his sins. He had sent two Brothers
to direct the school at Laon, which had been left
him by M. Nyel. After this, he had retired to the
solitude of Mount Carmel, near Louviers, a few
miles from Rouen. He had taken every precaution
not to be disturbed in his communings with God.
A Brother had been placed at the head of the
community at Rheims, and any urgent messages
for the Venerable were to be sent through a holy
religious, to whom the place of his retreat was
known. But Providence did not desire even this
momentary separation of His servant from the
important duties he had assumed. Scarcely had
he arrived at the mount when word was sent him
that both Brothers at Laon were dangerously ill.
They belonged to respectable families; and the
nobility of the one and the patience of the other
were manifested during the illness by which they
were attacked. Brother Gabriel Drolin first fell
ill, and was cared for with great charity by his

companion, Brother Nicholas Bourlette, who also endeavored, for a while, to keep both classes. In vain was he urged by the pastor to close the schools for a short time. Finally the latter said to him: "How can you manage under such difficulties?" "Why, my good pastor," replied the Brother, "my right foot is in one class, my left in the other; my mind is with the sick Brother, and my heart is in heaven." Brother Gabriel recovered his health, but Brother Nicholas soon was called to receive the reward of his charitable attentions. The fatigues incurred in watching his sick companion brought on a violent fever, from which he died on the sixteenth of September, 1686, being twenty-five years old.

His parents, who were wealthy traders at Rheims, had sorely tried his vocation, but his constancy was victorious. He was known at Laon as "the modest Brother." The entire city mourned his death as a public calamity. His burial-place afterward became a pilgrimage station; many went thither to implore the divine blessing, through his intercession. He was replaced by Brother Jean Paris, otherwise known as Brother Joseph, who faithfully followed in the footsteps of his predecessor. Previously, death had taken a victim in Brother Jean Francois, " the first of the disciples of the Venerable de La Salle who showed his Brothers the way to heaven." He also belonged to a distinguished family in Rheims; and by his talents he had obtained a very lucrative position, when grace called him to leave all things to follow Christ. In 1682 he joined the humble band which then looked upon M. Nyel as their leader. His last words breathed the joy of the exile whose eyes behold, in the distance, the borders of his true home. " Ah, beautiful Eternity ! " said he, " how charming is thy house ! Love, only love ! We go to heaven only to meet our love."

A third offering was demanded by death's stern decree. Brother Maurice was taken on the thirtieth of April, 1687. These were flowers nipped at the bud. From their earliest consecration they had exhaled the balmy odor of those rare virtues that add to the joys of heaven. " I do not know," said M. Dorigny, " which most to admire,—M. de La Salle or his disciples. I have already assisted several of them in their last moments; yet, despite their youth, they have left this earth with all the joy and resignation of persons eighty years of age."

For them, truly, death was

> " To close their eyes in silent prayer,
> And sleep, to waken in the skies." *

The severe character of the labor these good Brothers had undertaken was sufficient, in itself, to shorten life; but when we add to this that they practised austerities that would have almost eclipsed those of the ancient anchorites, we can conceive that death found them easy victims. The Venerable de La Salle tried to hide his mortification and his penitenial acts; but in vain. His disciples knew of them, and wished to imitate them. The reputation of his sanctity had gone abroad, and

---

* E. de Guerin.

many persons insisted upon having him as their
spiritual guide. Dom Francois E. Maillefer, in his
Life of the Holy Founder, says: " The Venerable
was now considered a man of extraordinary sanctity.
Many pious persons placed themselves under his
direction. He refused, as long as possible, and only
consented to receive a few penitents after he had,
by severe trials, determined that these were not
drawn to him by natural motives." The Abbé St.
Thierry, a Benedictine, and several other distinguished persons, came to see him, partially under
the impression that he was impelled by false zeal.
They retired, however, fully convinced that he was
directed by the spirit of God.

CHAPTER II.

De La Salle desires to establish a School in Paris.—Mgr. Le Tellier seeks to detain him in Rheims.—Pères Barré and de La Barmondière are consulted.—School in Rue Princesse.—M. Compagnon.—His Character.—Mme. de Maintenon.—Parish of St. Sulpice.—St. Vincent de Paul's Labors.—M. Olier.—The Venerable is persecuted.—M. Forbin-Janson investigates.—M. Baudrand succeeds M. de La Barmondière.—School in Rue du Bac.—M. de La Salle is called to Rheims.—He falls dangerously ill.—The Holy Viaticum.—M. Helvetius cures the holy Founder.—Death of Brother Henri-Lheureux.—Results for the Society.

"The Venerable de La Salle," says F. Lucard, "was not a man to take a backward step." Now that he felt the responsibility of his undertaking, and that his superiors assured him he could not do otherwise than remain at its head, he determined to seek its interest by a proceeding which marks his wisdom. M. Ayma tells us "that it was obedience alone that kept M. de La Salle in Rheims; but his heart was in Paris, and the good of the work he had engaged in urgently demanded the change. It was only from Paris, as a centre, that the new institute could extend its branches to all parts of the kingdom. Rheims had given the society its birth, but, if kept there alone, that city would also have been its burial-ground. Dependent upon the variable ideas of local ecclesiastical authorities, the new institute would have been obliged to change its regulations at every hour. The superior, subject to the caprices of particular individuals, would have found his authority weakened, and subordination lessened, among his disciples. Moreover, the city of Rheims could not be the tutor of an institute which was to extend over all Catholic countries. Paris alone could give M. de La Salle the assistance and the protection he needed. He was convinced of this, but, docile to the designs of Providence, he patiently awaited their manifestation before acting." The Venerable de La Salle was still more impressed with the necessity of making Paris the centre of his work, after finding that endeavors were made to detain him in Rheims,—endeavors which, while they were highly complimentary to himself and his institute, warned him that his greatest enemies, though unwittingly so, were those of his own household.

Mgr. Le Tellier, like many others, only learned the full value of the man he had known so long, when he found that he was about to quit his diocese. "Remain with us," said the prelate. "I will use my influence with the king to procure letters-patent for your institute, and I will give you money to found several establishments of your Brothers. I ask but one favor in return: that you will establish your schools exclusively in my archdiocese. The same condition has been accepted by the Sisters known as *Des Orphelines*." But the Venerable de La Salle had already received letters from Paris, urging him to establish his headquarters there. Louis, his brother, was then at St. Sulpice ; and M. de La Barmondière requested him to call M. de La Salle's attention to the promise he had made some time before, that he would take charge of the parish school of St. Sulpice at his earliest convenience.   M. Louis de La Salle, however, only asked for one Brother.   The Venerable Founder answered that the rule he had established forbade sending a Brother alone, and that, under the circumstances, he could not acquiesce in his desires and the desires of his friends.   He hoped, however, that arrangements might be made which would enable him to open the required establishment.   Having heard Mgr. Le Tellier's wishes, the servant of God wrote to Père Barré and to the pastor of St. Sulpice, asking their advice.   He was answered that his work bore the impress of general utility, and that he should not limit its beneficent results to the city of Rheims. His advisers, moreover, told him that, by establishing his institute in Paris, there would be greater likelihood of its approbation by the Holy See, and the securing of its canonical existence.   M. de La Salle made known these reasons to Mgr. Le Tellier, who agreed with them.   Left free to follow the direction of Providence, he started with two experienced teachers to establish himself in the capital.

A few years previously M. de La Barmondière had opened a school in Rue Princesse, which he had confided to Père Compagnon, a member of his community.   There were about two hundred children in regular attendance, and their time was divided between study and manual labor.

A linen factory had been connected with the school, and this was under the direction of an able workman, named Rafrond. M. Compagnon was a zealous gentleman, but narrow-minded, sensitive, and capricious. Such a teacher could produce but transient results, and his school presented a sad scene of tumult and disorder. This rendered M. de La Barmondière still more anxious for the arrival of La Salle and his companions. On the twenty-third of February, 1688, they started for their new and important mission.

Louis XIV had, at this time, just erected an establishment, which was known as St. Cyr. It was planned by Mansard, and was founded for the education of two hundred and fifty girls of noble families, with decayed fortunes. It is the brightest gem in the crown of glory that history has placed upon the brow of Madame de Maintenon. It was, in its day, a model school. Society was indebted to it for many a bright ornament of womanhood which it sent forth ; literature is eternally indebted to it for having been the occasion of the writing of the *Esther* and the *Athalie* of Racine. But the work of St. Cyr has passed, and there remains a work which, about the same time, was seeking shelter in the great metropolis of France. It is the work of the Venerable de La Salle, with the humble beginning we have recorded. This man of God had come to a parish well prepared for his reception. The district St. Germain, in which St. Sulpice is found, had been, not long previously, one of the most notorious portions of Paris. The number of monasteries and convents in the district was great. "But," says Ravelet, "in those abandoned streets, in those wide areas that divided the monasteries or convents, libertines and vagabonds could assemble unmolested: there they escaped the vigilance of the guardians of the peace. Thus, side by side with the pious population of the cloister, there was another element which had no sympathy with its neighbors; on the contrary, it was infected with every vice. It was in this parish that St. Vincent de Paul, struck by its great disorders, preached his only mission in Paris, and brought about so many and such great conversions that he changed its face. The following year M. Olier, St. Vincent's disciple and friend, took charge of these souls, and, aided by the zealous body of priests he had established, regenerated the character of the place. The parish soon acquired the reputation of being one of the most exemplary in Paris. We are told that it has not since lost its enviable reputation." Such was the soil in which was cast the first seed of the new society in Paris. Therein did M. de La Salle renew associations which his heart had always held dear. He there found his old superiors, MM. Tronson, Baüyn, and Lechassier. They continued to assist their former student, and gave him every mark of their sympathy and esteem. Protected by such powerful influences, and preceded by his own reputation, M. de La Salle was received with open arms by M. de La Barmondière. M. Compagnon also manifested great satisfaction in having for co-laborer a man already so well known, and whose virtue was so generally and so favorably spoken of.

Again the Venerable de La Salle was to learn how little we may count upon the protestations of men. Once more he was to find that, if he would only walk in the beaten path, allowing such disorders as were noticeable to continue, all would be well; the instant he attempted to go beyond this, the old battle began, fortunately with the same results in his case. The Brothers did their utmost to second the zeal of M. Compagnon; the latter, however, took offence at the many alterations that M. de La Salle wished to introduce in the direction of the school. The efficient management of the new teachers caused disagreeable comparisons; and this displeased him. His jealousy was aroused, and he endeavored to thwart their efforts. He even sought to discourage the Brothers, and thus to secure their withdrawal from Paris. M. de La Salle, thoroughly conversant with all that was attempted against him and his disciples, manifested not the least dismay. He said that, if his undertaking were the work of God, it would be sustained, despite the machinations of the ill-disposed. The Brothers, imitating the example of their father, worked silently, leaving their justification to the will and time of Providence.

The vigilant pastor of St. Sulpice, perceiving the nature of the difficulties, determined to strike the evil at its root. With this view he resolved to place complete control of the school in the hands of the Venerable Founder. Having determined to make the change, the pastor came one day to visit the schools, and finding the children noisy and inattentive,—for the Brothers, so far, were only assistants, and partially depended upon M. Compagnon for instructions,—he pretended to praise the results, in M. de La Salle's presence, but in such a tone that M. Compagnon understood quite well that the reverse of compliments was intended. His chagrin was greatly increased when he learned from the lips of his superior that henceforth the Abbé de La Salle was to have full direction of the school. "M. Compagnon," says F. Lucard, "had to content himself with the modest position of professor." The Venerable's success was to be bought at the price of personal sacrifices. One of the Brothers falling sick, the humble Founder immediately acted as he had formerly done at Rheims: taking the Brother's place, he taught the class with all the simplicity of the youngest novice.

"It was at this time,"* says M. de La Salle's biographers, "began to shine that remarkable talent in the servant of God which has placed him among the most illustrious educators. He found all the children assembled in one room, irrespective of their capacity, where each one received a lesson from the master." It was a custom sanctioned by ages ; but his genius suggested a better method. Having examined them, he divided them into three classes. Each was given a teacher, and was placed in a separate room. He established the same regulation in Paris that he had adopted at Rheims.

---

* April, 1688.

Each morning the children assisted at the holy sacrifice of the Mass. It was a touching and novel sight for all lovers of order and discipline to see several hundred children walking, two by two, in silence. Religious instruction was given morning and evening, for it was in this, especially, that the Venerable de La Salle desired his schools to be distinguished from others. The regulation determined exactly the time for each exercise. The masters were never to cease their vigilance; and it was by their example that M. de La Salle expected to induce the children to love order, and to acquire a taste for habits of industry.

The holy Founder would have desired to abolish the manual labor connected with the classes of St. Sulpice, but he felt that M. de La Barmondière was not prepared to make such a concession. Partially to remove the evil results arising from the distractions occasioned by this commingling of mental and manual work, he fixed the hours in which the children would be at the command of M. Rafrond in the factory, to the great disgust of this last-named gentleman. They were no longer looked upon as instruments of profit. While care was taken to make them skilful workmen, no less attention was paid to their intellectual progress. The happiest results crowned the Venerable de La Salle's regulations: the children became very assiduous, and their numbers increased. M. de La Barmondière begged the holy Founder to augment the number of Brothers, promising a modest compensation for each. The stipend was indeed small, but every one

knows that the Brothers did not then, as they do
not now, expect their reward here below.

The enemy of all good could not look undisturbed
upon a work so successfully carried on. He found
a suitable instrument of his malicious designs, says
Père Garreau, in the former director of the school.
In company with M. Rafrond, Compagnon determined to bring about the destruction of the classes.
The former complained that the children were not
given him for sufficient length of time, and that he
was losing money by the present system. He threatened to leave at once, if his demands were not
favorably met. M. de La Barmondière quietly told
him that, if the new order of things did not please
him, he might retire. Taken unawares, his self-
respect left him no choice: he resigned his position.
If the Venerable de La Salle were capable of spite-
ful feelings, he might easily gratify them; for the
grumbler, finding no work, agreed to initiate a
Brother in the difficulties of the trade. In a few
weeks the pupil was as expert as the master. Un-
happily, M. de La Salle was to suffer much more
from the other source.

One day, while the pastor held a meeting of ladies
in his parlors, M. Compagnon entered hastily, and,
with the most plausible air possible, told M. de La
Barmondière and his company that the new teachers,
and particularly their superior, should not be relied
upon. Like one whose conscience forced him to
make known the facts, the calumniator proceeded
to relate certain odious affairs, which he attributed
to M. de La Salle. The assembly appeared indig-

nant; even M. de La Barmondière, with all his passiveness of disposition, was made the dupe of the accuser. He said that he regretted having placed so much confidence in a man who deserved so little. M. de La Salle, meanwhile, had learned the occurrence, and went to see the friend he seemed about to lose. He was received with the utmost coolness, was thanked for his past services, and given to understand that he might prepare to retire to Rheims. M. Baudrand, his confessor, was intrusted with the formal declaration to M. de La Salle that his services were no longer needed. This worthy clergyman, who knew the heart of his penitent, was grieved at being made the bearer of such sad intelligence, and he mingled his message with so many words of appreciation and kindness, that the venerable servant of God understood that it was his confessor's wish that he should not leave Paris without having first paid a farewell visit to the pastor. This he did, and, to his surprise, was received with deep emotion by M. de La Barmondière. "Oh! do not leave us," said the father; "keep the direction of the school; do not deprive the parish of the blessings it begins to experience from your zeal and that of your disciples. I will think about your departure later." "He will think of it for three years, before talking again upon the subject," said M. Baudrand, who had assisted at the reception, and who had labored strenuously to disabuse his pastor of the false impression under which Compagnon's calumnies had placed him.

That the matter might be settled to the satisfac-

tion of all parties, M. de La Barmondière appointed
M. Forbin-Janson to make a strict examination of
the school, its methods, the teachers and their conduct.   The future Bishop of Arles entered into the
minutest details in this investigation.   The proceedings lasted several days, and all resulted in the
complete vindication of the Brothers.   "Too much
praise cannot be given," writes one of the Venerable's biographers, " to the patience and resignation
shown by M. de La Salle and his disciples during
this trying circumstance.   Abbé Forbin-Janson
could not detect a word or a sign that might indicate
discontent on the part of those thus subjected to
the humiliation of a research into their conduct
and its motives."   "What do you think of M.
Compagnon?" asked the investigator.   "I am not
charged with his conduct," answered the servant of
God.   "I have but one favor to ask: it is that you
will notify me and my Brothers of the faults you
perceive in our method or in our conduct, that we
may correct ourselves."   Does this not sound like
a trait borrowed from the life of the Prince-bishop
of Geneva, the amiable St. Francis de Sales?

This beautiful spirit of simplicity burst the bonds
that cunning and duplicity had been endeavoring
to ensnare it with.   La Salle triumphed.   M. de La
Barmondière determined to render full, though
tardy justice to him, by the removal of the source of
all his annoyance.   This, however, was left for his
successor to accomplish.   The good pastor had real
difficulties, as well as imaginary ones, to contend
with.   Previous to his incumbency, St. Sulpice had,

for pastor, M. de Pousse, one of M. Olier's first disciples. He had contracted a debt of five hundred thousand francs in the erection of the church, and M. de La Barmondière found it impossible to pay the interest. He then took the method of asking voluntary contributions from his parishioners; afterward he sought to make these contributions obligatory. Such was the discontent created by this measure, that the pastor was obliged to resign in favor of his assistant, M. Baudrand. This happened in 1689.

The new pastor had already proved himself the Brothers' friend. He further showed that he understood whence arose their previous difficulties in the parish, by forbidding M. Compagnon to have any future relations with the school. The number of pupils increasing, a new school was opened near Pont Royal, at the extremity of Rue du Bac. Everything in the new establishment was regulated according to M. de La Salle's wishes. He was beginning to breathe freely, when a storm arose from an unexpected quarter.

The Venerable at this time needed repose. His constant labor of mind and body had considerably weakened his health, but learning that difficulties were arising in his dear community of Rheims, he forgot his personal sufferings, to hasten to the assistance of his children. The director of the Brothers in that city had acted with such harshness, that he alienated the hearts of his inferiors. He had also allowed the normal school to fall into decay. A few days sufficed for the Venerable de La Salle to restore everything to its former condition. As the preparatory novitiate seemed threatened in its present location, he transferred the young plants, that he watched with such solicitude, to Paris, where they would be under his immediate supervision. He had barely arrived in the capital when his illness showed alarming symptoms. The Brothers were in dismay at the apparent proximity of their father's demise. "Alas, my children!" said he to them, "how much I regret that I am a burden upon your hands! Since I am poor, let me be treated like the poor. Take me to the hospital, where I will no longer be a source of disquietude." The Brothers could not think of such a proceeding. They answered him only through their sobs and tears. Heaven, their only resource, was appealed to, and not in vain.

While imploring mercy from above, they neglected nothing that could possibly be of service to their father. Dr. Helvetius, a celebrated physician from Holland, was called in, and he prescribed a remedy which, he said, would prove decisive as to life or death. The Venerable de La Salle accepted the medicine, but, previous to taking the draught, he wished to receive the holy viaticum. M. Baudrand, followed by the priests of St. Sulpice and many seminarians, came to his room. During the ceremony all the Brothers knelt around the couch on which lay their hearts' treasure. All were deeply moved when M. Baudrand asked the sufferer to bless his children, and to say some parting words which his disciples would treasure as a fond legacy. It was necessary for M. Baudrand to assist the

Venerable when he attempted to make the sign of the cross on the forehead of each of his disciples. "My children, my dear children," said he in a voice choked with pain and emotion, " I have but one advice to give you, that which the beloved disciple had constantly upon his lips : *Love one another, and be perfectly obedient.*"

Dr. Helvetius, who was deeply interested in his patient, asked Père Baudrand to bless the remedy he was about to employ, after which none but the Brothers and the physician remained in the room. The patient then swallowed the medicine, and the doctor watched the results with the utmost anxiety. The feelings of the Brothers in that crisis cannot easily be imagined. It were vain to attempt a description. But what was the joy of physician and disciples to find that the remedy was efficacious! In a short while the holy man could take some food. God had great designs upon M. de La Salle, and wished to preserve him for years to come. As soon as cured, he thought only of giving renewed thanks, and of consecrating himself more unreservedly to the sovereign Physician, the Master of life and death.

Heaven had spared the father ; it now demanded a holocaust in the person of one of his beloved sons. It struck the Brother in whom he had centred his hopes for the future of the society. A short, but painful, malady bore away Brother Henri Lheureux, who, in 1686, had been elected superior-general. God chose to immolate him by a premature death, at a time and under circumstances each of which was a thorn that cruelly tore the heart of this Abraham, who so loved one who might truly be called the Isaac of the institute. The Venerable de La Salle had appointed him director of the Brothers at St. Sulpice, and it was in this community that death took him, in 1690. It was La Salle's intention to have had him, in a little while, ordained priest. This unexpected reverse produced decided results as to the future of the society.

At this time it was the intention of La Salle to have in the new society a certain number of priests who would act as directors of the communities and confessors of the Brothers. But the death of Brother Henri Lheureux he regarded as a warning from heaven that this course was not in accordance with the will of God. As such he regarded it, and forthwith decreed that no clergyman be admitted as a member of the congregation, and that no Brother aspire to the dignity of the priesthood. Time has sanctioned the wisdom of this decision. It brings with it that true union and harmony arising from equality of condition. It secures to the society an order of talent that would, under other circumstances, make it simply a stepping-stone to another sphere of labor, as would inevitably be the case in missionary countries especially. The genius and the man of slender attainments,—each finds in it work to suit his capacity. There is no intelligence. how elevated soever it may be, that can say : " I am too learned to teach ; I know too much to impart my knowledge to others ; instruction is beneath me." Its saying so were proof enough that it was of an inferior grade. Neither Plato nor Aristotle thought so, and they were deeply learned ; neither Roger Bacon nor Thomas Aquinas thought so, and they knew all that their times could gather together; neither Fénelon nor Bossuet thought so, and they were superior geniuses, the glory of their age, their masterpieces inspired by the instructions they were imparting. The regulation thus made by the holy Founder was another breaking-off from old customs. Hitherto all primary and intermediate teaching had been confided chiefly to clerics. Attempts had been occasionally made to found orders of lay teachers, but with no permanent result. It remained for the Venerable de La Salle to be the successful organizer, on a large scale, of such an order. The Brother of the Christian Schools is the pioneer among the various lay teaching-orders by which he is now surrounded.

CHAPTER III.

Means adopted to firmly establish the Society.—The Venerable retires to meditate.—He secures a Novitiate in Vaugirard.—The Brothers make a three-months' Retreat.—The Normal School Teachers replace them —Brothers Jean-Paris and Jean-Henri.—The Venerable makes a special Vow with the Brothers Nicolas Vuyart and Gabriel. —The Formula.—Its Meaning.—M. Baudraud wishes the Brothers to change their Dress.—The Venerable refuses.—Vaugirard : its Poverty. —Famine in 1693.—Count du Charmel.

THE Venerable de La Salle was too keen-sighted not to perceive, despite the successes of the past, the horizon was laden with trouble for the future. Thus far he had opened schools which, owing to his personal supervision, had given great satisfaction. His individual worth was such, that any enterprise he sanctioned, found supporters among intelligent Christians. But the perpetuation and extension of the institute? There were children to be educated throughout France. He could not be everywhere. His teachers, to be successful, must be thoroughly formed. No just mind will hold the Venerable de La Salle responsible for the faults of M. Nyel's disciples. It was his charity that made him assume the management of the new work. But, now that he has identified himself with it, his genius will employ such means as could alone succeed in forming that intelligent class of men through whom he desired to perpetuate the task of the Christian education of youth. " It was not sufficient for him to have chosen intelligent co-laborers, and to have subjected them to a uniform rule : it was necessary to form them. A delicate and minute labor ; long, difficult, frequently thankless ; a labor that he could have begun himself in the novitiate and normal school, but which directors, perfectly initiated in the science of teaching, were to continue and complete."*

The regrettable occurrences which took place at Rheims, and some acts of insubordination in the community of Paris, had made the Venerable more freely understand the nature of the ground upon which he was building, and the character of the materials with which his work was being erected. Among his disciples were some whose time of probation had been but short, and who had not had the opportunity to acquire those virtues which distinguish the religious teacher. The exalted idea which he had of his duties; the qualities of mind and heart which he felt were necessary in those who entered his institute, which now embraced a course hitherto unknown in the schools of his day,—all these considerations rendered it necessary for him to adopt measures by which his disciples could be fully prepared for their position.

Fénelon, whose authority in matters of education none will question, pertinently asks : " How are men to be governed, if not well known ? How are they to be known, if we live not with them ? For this purpose it is necessary to see them closely, to draw from their hearts all that may there be lurking.

---

* F. Lucard, " Vie," etc., p. 63.

They must be examined in every light; their maxims need sifting; their talents must be exercised; the solidity of mind and the strength of virtue they have acquired must be determined."

God has allowed no order of things to exist opposed in itself to the success of His designs in favor of men, without giving at the same time a means by which all such obstacles may be overcome. This principle the holy Founder well understood; and perceiving the necessities of the hour, he took the surest methods to meet them. In prayer and meditation he sought their solution. He retired for a few days to a desolate retreat, where, alone with God, he studied the best way in which to accomplish the good he desired to effect. The retreat which he had made in 1684, had given him strength to renounce his patrimony, to become poor with the poorest; that which he made in 1690, was productive of no less important results for his institute. Ever distrustful of himself, his first care was to insure the continuance of his society, even should unforeseen circumstances take him away unexpectedly. For this purpose, during his seclusion, he resolved: first, to make, with two other Brothers, a vow to defend, and to sustain till death, the *Society of the Brothers of the Christian Schools;* secondly, to open a novitiate for his disciples; thirdly, to make it obligatory upon all the Brothers to write to him once a month upon their spiritual condition, fourthly, to make an annual visit to each of his communities. No mention is here made of the sick, the aged, or the infirm; but these were not forgotten by the charitable Founder. They were to find in the novitiate all the attention and care that could be suggested by the fondest charity and the most heartfelt gratitude.

It was necessary for the Venerable de La Salle to take some precautions at this time, for several of his Brothers had fallen sick, and others were so delicate as to be liable to become victims at any moment. Thus the servant of God found himself prevented, on one side, from extending his work, so limited were his means; on the other hand, if he did not adopt some immediate measures to form new subjects, it was only a question of time for his work to fall through. He, therefore, made search for some more suitable location: his desire was, if possible, to secure his new home in the vicinity of the grounds on which M. Olier had established his congregation of St. Sulpice. His happiness was at all times to designate the founder of the Sulpitians by the tender name of father. To St. Sulpice and its professors he held himself indebted for whatever of good there was in his character and in his enterprise. His humility still allowed the thought of escaping the superiorship to haunt him. He imagined that, by associating his society with that of St. Sulpice, it would be better protected, and he would thus be enabled to retire from an office that he felt unfit to occupy. Admirable as was the Society of St. Sulpice, much as its spirit was worthy of imitation, Providence had destined for the daughter institute an extension that St. Sulpice was never to attain. In proportion as M. de La Salle sought to evade the honors of direction, Almighty God so disposed events as to compel him to continue to receive them. The proposed union was not deemed expedient; but, as a partial consolation, M. de La Salle was assisted in his researches for a suitable location, and he soon secured for his residence a place in Vaugirard, which has since become historic in the annals of the institute. Here M. de La Salle found himself near his old-time souvenirs with opportunities to practise virtues dear to his heart. In September, 1691, he rented this spacious though impoverished house, and, the following month, called some Brothers from each community to meet him there.

We have seen that the Venerable had already shown his interest in the training of teachers who would take charge of village schools, where one person could do the required labor. In this he had manifested his breadth of view; and in the present circumstance, where several of his Brothers were to be taken from their duties for a while, these teachers proved their gratitude. Being requested to replace his disciples for a time, these good gentlemen readily consented, and demonstrated, not only their skill in successfully managing their classes, but their joy in being deemed worthy of confidence by M. de La Salle temporarily to replace his disciples.

If the Venerable had suffered anguish of mind as to the dispositions and the motives of his children, the pleasure he must have experienced in meeting them at Vaugirard can well be imagined. He found them true to their vocation; anxious to acquire its spirit; desirous only of knowing the wishes of their father, which they forthwith promised to consider as the will of God. All the Brothers manifested this same admirable spirit; yet, there are four whose names must be handed down to the admiration of their successors. We marvel at the zeal of the early missionaries, their intrepidity, their forgetfulness of themselves; well, in the early history of the lives and deeds of the first Brothers formed by M. de La Salle, there is all that the most exacting can require, more than the most reasonable would expect, both in matter of heroism and in point of interest. We can well conceive how, with such men, the Founder could build up a strong and permanent institution. Christ selected but twelve apostles to convert the world; the four Brothers of whom we are to speak would have been numerous enough, their faith and zeal considered, to establish the Institute of the Christian Schools.

The first we shall mention is Brother Jean-Paris, Director of Laon. Severely tried by an asthma that gave him little respite during the day, and none at night, this good Brother was in constant suffering, which, nevertheless, did not prevent him from attending to his duties as teacher and director. His pupils, seeing such devotedness, were careful to give him little trouble, while his Brothers lavished upon him every mark of affection and esteem. When called by the Venerable de La Salle to meet the others at Vaugirard, Brother Jean-Paris was also suffering great pain from a swelling of the knee. Now, it must be remembered that the orders sent

to the various Brothers required, according to the
rule, that the journey should be made, as much as
possible, on foot. What was the surprise and edification of the travellers, who had, according to instructions, stopped at a certain inn, near Soissons,
when they beheld Brother Jean-Paris painfully hob-
bling along as best he could, assisted by his companion! They might have then all returned home:
that sight was as good as a whole retreat. They
had example of how far a man could do violence
to human nature and triumph over its infirmities,
when totally absorbed in the spirit of his state. It
eloquently said to each of them: Do thou in the
same spirit; but they determined at least that the
sufferer should not go farther afoot. They required
him to take passage on a boat which was about to
depart, and which brought him within a short distance of Paris.

Though suffering from acute rheumatism, Brother
Jean-Henri was not less heroic than his fellow-in-
arms. He was director at Rheims when the sum-
mons to repair to Paris reached him. He might,
in all justice, have claimed exemption, but he had
been too long in the disciplined school over which
the Venerable de La Salle presided, to give any
excuse. Though warned of the risks he ran in
venturing afoot upon such a journey, he intrepidly,
we might say rashly, ventured to fulfil the orders
of his beloved father. Painfully he dragged himself
as far as Soissons, where he met the Brothers of
Rethel, Guise and Laon. In vain did his companions declare that he should also take passage by the

boat : when they started, he pretended to be cured, and went his way with them. His courage was not equalled by his strength. Weakness and excruciating pain compelled him to admit that he could proceed no farther. Then was seen a touching sight. The Brothers, two by two in turn, made a sort of chair of their clasped hands, and thus carried the brave but discomfited soldier till they reached the headquarters of his general. The sight of these two valiant religious was painful in one sense to the holy Founder, who never intended his instruction to be taken in their literal meaning by such sufferers : but at the same time his heart was overwhelmed with joy when he saw that his infant society already possessed men so far advanced in the love of mortification and forgetfulness of self. He received them with all the love and the esteem that his heart of a father and his knowledge of their merit suggested. To prevent the recurrence of the imprudence which he found these two Brothers had committed, he regulated that in future neither the aged nor the infirm should travel afoot. " As for the two heroes of the day, the one forgetting his asthma and swelling, the other his rheumatism, both vied with the youngest members of the retreat in the practice of every virtue, and the acquiring of that degree of perfection which they beheld in the person of their Venerable Founder."

During this retreat M. de La Salle was fully compensated for all his past troubles. But there were two Brothers whose dispositions were so remarkable, whose piety was of so pure a type, and whose judgment of men and things was so accurate, that the Venerable determined to place them as two pillars in the new society. They were Brothers Nicolas Vuyart and Gabriel Drolin. The retreat lasted three months, during which time he held frequent consultations and conferences with these two Brothers. These consultations filled them with inexpressible delight. The result of their combined opinions was, that they determined to perform a supreme act of consecration to the Almighty, on the anniversary of the day on which Mary Immaculate had been offered in the temple. When the daughter of Anna and Joachim offered herself to God, He looked with love on her in whom there was no stain. When the sun rose upon the day when the Venerable de La Salle and his two beloved disciples pronounced their perpetual consecration to Him, He beheld three chosen princes, whose life was to be spent in recovering for youth part of that purity and innocence which constituted Mary's glory. Children cherish and hoard up the last will and testament of a fond father or a loving mother. The Christian Brothers, with reason, look upon the parchment, whose contents we will here reproduce, as upon a relic of the past, which gives the most encouraging lesson to the children of the institute at present, and which will be treasured as an heirloom to be transmitted for the edification and the instruction of the Brothers of the future.

When the Mass of the day had been offered, and each had been fed with the Bread of Life, the three chosen ones knelt at the steps of the altar, and pronounced aloud the following vow: " Most Holy Trinity, Father, Son and Holy Ghost! prostrate with the most profound respect before Thy infinite and adorable majesty, we consecrate ourselves entirely to Thee, to procure, as far as possible, and as far as our efforts will permit, the establishment of the Society of the Christian Schools, in the manner that we will believe most agreeable to Thee, and most advantageous to the society. And for this purpose I, Jean-Baptiste de La Salle, I, Nicholas Vuyart, and I, Gabriel Drolin, from the present hour, and till the last moment of our lives, or till the final establishment of this society, do make vows of association and union, to procure and to maintain the establishment of the said society, without the power of withdrawing from it, even were but we three to remain therein, and that we were obliged to ask alms, and to live on bread only. For this purpose we promise to do together, and by common consent, all that we will believe, conscientiously and without any human consideration, to be for the best interests of the society.

" Done this twenty-first day of November, Feast of the Presentation of the Most Blessed Virgin, in the year of our Lord, 1691."

If the text of this vow be carefully studied, we shall, in some sense, obtain the key-note of the intentions of the courageous three. They positively promised but one thing : to establish the Institute of the Brothers of the Christian Schools. What the means to be employed in its establishment were, what the limit or sphere of action within which the society would act, what the extent to which the society was to be allowed to spread,—all these were so many questions which they wisely left to time and experience to decide. Thus the Venerable spared his successors the pain of even indirectly deviating from any practice he might have established. Principles, and severe ones also, he did leave, but their application he ventured not to decide beforehand. Not that either he or his two generous companions feared the future: their vow proves the contrary. They vow, if necessary, to live upon bread only, and even determine, if required, to beg that same, rather than abandon their purpose; but they demonstrate what so many saints had shown before them: that religious vows bind men to do a determined good without taking away a certain liberty in the manner of doing it. They did not fear the machinations of jealousy, for, in the text of their consecration, they state that they would "conscientiously, and free from all human consideration, do all that they would believe to be for the best interests of the society." The Venerable de La Salle had already formed his disciples, especially Brothers Nicholas and Gabriel, to seek only the will and glory of God in all things; thus justifying in their regard what a learned author has remarked of their Founder: "If," says Père Huguet, "we pay attention to each of his proceedings, we will remark, and not without astonishment, that he never did anything to procure himself the protection of worldly power." After this solemn act of consecration, the Venerable de La Salle called his disciples for the last time, before allowing them to return to their respective houses. He addressed them in words full of heavenly enthusiasm. All were anxious to return to their fields of labor, determined that they would show to angels and to men that they were worthy followers of their chosen and beloved head. They had learned so much of his hidden virtues, they had basked so long in the sunshine of his fervid example, that, though they felt it good to be there, they knew that it was their duty to go forth and to disseminate among the less favored disciples of M. de La Salle who had not heard his burning words, or seen his saintly example, the seed which had been so plentifully cast, and which, with a divine blessing, had produced such astonishing fruits in their hearts. As a tie by which the fruits of this three months' retreat were to be preserved and increased, it was unanimously promised that they would write once a month to their venerated chief, to obtain new lights, life, and aid in the work of their own perfection and the salvation of youth. The master is no less strengthened than his disciples ; he is prepared to begin the battle with renewed vigor. Nor has he long to wait. His is a continual warfare. Hitherto he had been accustomed to the buffets of his enemies ; now God permits him to be tried even by his friends, among whom few ranked higher than M. Baudrand. " Thus," says Père Garreau, " the saints help one another to reach heaven."

The pastor of St. Sulpice had obtained permission

from M. de La Salle to have the scholars of the preparatory novitiate to act as acolytes. This was for them a source of some distraction, which, however, their superior suffered, as he knew he could put a stop to it when the young men would enter the novitiate proper. But M. Baudrand then urged upon de La Salle to change the costume of the Brothers, saying that it should be made as nearly as possible like that of the clergy. M. de La Salle admitted that a priest should dress as one, and therefore consented to revest himself in the ecclesiastical habit. Farther than this he was unwilling to be led. He had vowed to do all in his power for the best interests of the society, conscientiously, and *without human consideration;* here was an opportunity to observe this solemn promise. In a modest but positive manner M. de La Salle refused to make any concession. Bossuet says that, "when Providence sends men a legislator, He fills him with the twofold spirit of wisdom and foresight." Both qualities are manifest in the memorial which M. de La Salle prepared in defence of his position. He submitted his views to MM. Tronson and Baüyn, and both warmly approved his reasons, and encouraged him to firmness in the position he had assumed.

" There are few things more prejudicial to religious communities," says the venerable servant of God, " than changes in matters of importance; and it is to the facility with which such alterations are permitted that we must attribute the greater part of the disorders which have crept into monasteries. . . . .

For religious, the change of costume is an important matter. During five years the Brothers have worn this habit in five principal cities in the dioceses of Rheims and Laon. It is there looked upon as a decent dress, and one that is likely to maintain the masters in the regularity and modesty proper to their state, and likewise to attract the respect of their scholars. For nearly two years it has been worn in Paris, and no one has thought of finding fault, save the pastor of St. Sulpice."* History repeats itself in the Church as well as in the world : the Venerable de La Salle had done his duty, and he was made to suffer for it. M. Baudrand refused to allow the novitiate to continue in his parish. "The Venerable de La Salle," says Ravelet, "could not accede, and did not wish to leave the parish. He had recourse to prayer and mortification. He implored heaven to change the dispositions of those with whom he had to deal. His patience was subjected to a severe and protracted trial. M. Baudrand was inflexible, and even told M. de La Salle that it was useless for him to do violence to heaven; that he would never give his consent. God," says the pious journalist, "is more easily moved than men, and is at the same time master of their hearts. He listens to the prayers of his servants." M. Baudrand concluded the struggle by giving his consent ; and the Venerable de La Salle, to prevent further difficulties in like directions, requested M. de Harlay, Archbishop of Paris, to

* "Mem. sur les Habits des Frères," par M. J. B. de La Salle. MS. Arch. of the Régime.

recognize the new establishment as a regular religious community.

His request was granted, and on the first of
November, 1692, the pious Founder had given the
habit to six novices.   To persevere in such poverty
as here surrounded the children of La Salle, demanded truly apostolic zeal and courage.   "M. de La
Salle," writes Père Blain, "having secured victory
from the throne of grace, now thought only of
taking full possession of his dear Bethlehem, for
this is the only name by which we can designate a
house whose poverty and solitude placed it in such
apposition to the poor grotto in which Christ gave
Himself to the world."   A few benches upon which
to sit, and a few miserable mattresses thrown upon
the ground, were its only furniture. The roof being
leaky, the windows badly closed, and the lights in
many cases being broken, we may imagine the
condition of the poor novices and their Founder,
when either rain, snow or cold prevailed.   " A sort
of holy rivalry," continues Père Blain, "was kept
up between the disciples and the master.   There
were too or three good mattresses intended for the
sick.   The Brothers each day put one of these
under the miserable hay-bag upon which M. de La
Salle slept, and each evening he was equally careful
to remove the little chance of comfort that had been
innocently given him by his children."   Their
poverty was so great that they were obliged to live
upon what other communities were pleased to give
them. One of the novices went each day to seek this
miserable repast, and more than once he was stopped

in the way as he returned, and partially deprived
of his scanty meal by vagrants, who robbed him of
the only resource by which life was to be preserved.
Badly nourished, poorly lodged, the Brothers bore
on their persons the marks of poverty. Patched
clothes, shoes that beggarmen would cast aside as
unworthy their notice, hats that had lost their shape
from long usage,—such constituted their only protection from the cold of winter and the heat of
summer. Still, beneath these rags there shone the
Christian gentleman. If their garments were poor,
their souls were pure ; if their bodies suffered, their
hearts rejoiced : and this joy was depicted on every
countenance. " Poverty repels only when it is the
fruit of, and accompanied by, vice and irregularity.
When, on the contrary, it is accepted as the better
part by Christians, it is at once transfigured, and
assumes a heavenly aspect. Such it is, as seen in
the saints ; such we see it in the Venerable de La
Salle and his disciples. Many of these had abandoned opulence and ease, to accept obloquy and the
portion of the poor. Their chief had given them
the example, and he found children worthy of being
his followers."* Vaugirard is therefore a cherished
chapter in the history of the Institute of the Brothers
of the Christian Schools. We need not be astonished,
then, that one of the most distinguished sons † of
La Salle should, in our own day, have made it his
watchword, and closed one of his most eloquent
pages with the words, "*Remember Vaugirard!*" The

---

* Ravelet, " Histoire du Ven. J. B. de La Salle," p. 204.
† Brother Philippe.

novices were there prepared for the sad days that were at hand. The Brothers of Paris, by visiting their solitude every holiday, likewise breathed the air of sanctity and self-denial which abounded therein; and now came the hour of trial.

In 1693 a terrible famine ravaged all France; it was felt with increased severity in the large cities. Paris was the scene of heart-rending misery, in which the novices of Vaugirard had a large share. Louis XIV did not prove unworthy of his reputation. Daily he had immense quantities of bread distributed. Madame de Maintenon gave a large portion of her fortune to the perishing; and Mgr. Godet des Marais, Bishop of Chartres, who was an ancient comrade of M. de La Salle, after having sold his gold and silver vessels, also gave his entire revenues to the sufferers. Such examples found many imitators, and thus the horrors of the situation were partially lessened. Withal, the misery was extreme. Gangs of starving men and women were seen wrangling over the possession of articles of food which, in other days, would have excited their disgust. The Brothers of Paris did not forget the novices at Vaugirard. From their own scanty pittance they saved a portion, which, however, did not always reach its destination. On the way it was sometimes taken from the carriers. On such occasions the young apostles of poverty rejoiced in their misery; but the Venerable de La Salle, unwilling to expose his children to increased suffering, brought them to live with the Brothers at St. Sulpice.

Notwithstanding the efforts thus made, his disci-

ples were at times on the verge of starvation. One
day the steward came to tell the holy Founder that
he had but four-pence to purchase food for the day.
"Go," said the holy man, "and make your purchases
as usual; God will provide you with the means."
The Brother obeyed, and, as he went his way, perceived a number of poor persons awaiting their turn
to receive the charity dispensed with a liberal hand
by a wealthy lady. The steward placed himself in
line with the others, and on seeing him, the good
lady exclaimed: "How is this, Brother? what brings
you here?" Having learned of the misery in which
the Brothers were, she at once sent them assistance,
and the same day went to intercede for them with
M. Baudrand. The latter had not forgotten them,
but surrounded as he was by an extensive parish, he
could not think of everybody. Touched by what
he had learned, the good pastor hastened to see the
Brothers, and was met on the way by M. de La
Salle, who told him in a few words the straits to
which they were reduced. "It is heaven that has
made us meet to-day," said M. Baudrand. "The
king has just sent me a large sum to divide among
my poor; here are two hundred francs: I will see
that your Brothers want nothing." A magnificent
promise; but historical justice compels us to add
that when, three months after, La Salle sent the
good pastor the baker's bill, he paid it, but with the
remark that he would deduct the amount from the
Brothers' salary. Whereupon the servant of God,
somewhat surprised at M. Baudrand's behavior, replied in these noble words: "He who sends our

Brothers among the poor children, will furnish them with the daily bread that they earn at the price of their strength and their health."*

Nor did the other communities of Brothers in various parts of France escape the general dearth, but Providence prevented them from being reduced to extremities. They all of them passed through the sad period without having to desist from teaching school. In 1694 better days shone upon France. The crops were abundant, the industries began to resume their wonted activity, and the terrors of the late famine became something to speak of in comfortable homes. The Venerable de La Salle hastened back to his loved retreat at Vaugirard.

The virtue practised there could not always remain unknown. M. Baüyn often retired thither in his spare moments, to be edified by the examples he met there. Even seculars found attractions in this new Thebaid. Each year the Brothers of the various communities came to Vaugirard for their vacations and their annual retreat. On one occasion three young Brothers reached the vicinity of Vaugirard during the night, and called upon the parish priest of the village for lodging. Struck by their modesty and their intelligence, the good priest at once spoke about them to Count du Charmel, who always spent the summer in his villa near Vaugirard. The count, who was a very pious gentleman, was surprised that he had not sooner known the nursery of piety situated so near his residence. He was so pleased with the three travellers, whom he insisted

---

* F. Lucard, "Vie M. de La Salle," 2ᵐᵉ Ed., p. 114.

upon seeing, that he offered their Founder, through them, his villa as a stopping-place for the Brothers in future. Not satisfied with this mark of kindness, he afterward called upon M. de La Salle, and presented him with several articles required for the altar service. He recognized the greatness of soul of the man of God. A close intimacy was afterward established between the two, which terminated only with the death of the count. The Venerable de La Salle pronounced the eulogy of his patron in four words, by saying that he was a man "whose prayer was continual." The count, be it remembered, was not always such. In the early part of his career he was the gayest among the gay that thronged the brilliant, bad court of Louis, in the first part of his reign, but meeting a pious book, he read it, and forthwith devoted himself to a life of piety and austerity. The outspoken St. Simon thus records his impression of him at this period of his life: " He was a man of the celice, of iron points, of all sorts of instruments of continual penance, an extreme faster, and otherwise sober to excess, though naturally a great eater." *

* "Mémoires," t. ii, p. 219.   See also t. v, p. 25.

CHAPTER IV.

EUGENIE DE GUERIN has said that "nothing is
better than faith for the soul, and friendship for the
heart." Indeed men are never more firmly united
than in sufferings borne in a spirit of faith, and in
submission to the principles taught by our holy
religion. The trials which seemed about to shat-
ter to pieces the new institute, did but settle it
more firmly upon the foundation of faith which had
been given it as its surest support. "Thus are the
works of God made. They live on what would
destroy worldly enterprises." * What was more
likely to dishearten these good teachers than famine, cold, misery of every description? Yet, so far
from being discouraged, they wished irrevocably
to dedicate themselves to the vocation they had

---

* Ravelet, p 210.

embraced. "Why should we act as mercenary laborers?" said these generous souls. "We give ourselves to God for a year or three, and when our time is expired, we are at liberty to change masters. Is this what God expects from us? Are we to have one foot in religion, and the other in the world? Surely, if we have the good-will to consecrate ourselves to God forever, He will strengthen our hearts." The Venerable de La Salle knew the earnestness of those who then wrote to him; but he was too prudent to take his disciples at their word, in what might possibly be, for some, only the heat of momentary fervor. Knowing that, while the spirit is willing, the flesh is still weak, M. de La Salle delayed answering their petition.

"Ten years had elapsed since the General Chapter, held in 1684; the wise Founder had taken time to study the character of his disciples, and to inspire them with the virile sentiments of abnegation by which he was animated."* In 1694 he chose twelve of the most virtuous among them, and notified them that they might prepare to contract perpetual vows of stability and obedience. Brothers Nicholas Vuyart and Gabriel were first selected. These had persevered in their holy dispositions, and had many times in their hearts promised what they were soon to vow. The other ten were, among the Brothers, what the chosen soldiers are to whom are given the defences which cover a city; they were the picked ten of the institute, of tried zeal and sincere piety.

---

* F. Lucard, p. 77.

Affianced youths never heard the sound of marriage-bell, nor soldier the trumpet that called to arms, with more joy than did this new college of apostles listen to the assurance given them by their venerated father, that at length he was to permit them to perform the solemn act that was to be the crowning glory of their lives. A retreat of some days was made, that, the lights of the Holy Ghost being more abundant, and the fire of charity burning still more brightly in their hearts, they might be holocausts worthy of the cause in which the offering was to be made, and of Him to whom it was to be presented.

It was determined that the vows should be pronounced on Trinity-Sunday. After the exercises of the retreat, the twelve chosen ones were more than ever impressed with the necessity of the act toward the performance of which they had looked forward with so much confidence and love. They felt, on that Trinity-Sunday, more than ever, their dependence on Him in whom they lived, moved, and had their being. They yearned to consecrate themselves unreservedly to Him who gives the lily of the field its brightness, to the flowers of our gardens their variegated hues, to the earth and all it contains that diversity of purpose and that oneness of end which make us acknowledge that God is love, and that those who wish to be His must love Him in return.

It was with sentiments of joyous solemnity that, after the Mass on Trinity-Sunday morning, all the other Brothers having retired, the Venerable de La

Salle first, and the others after him, pronounced the following formula: "Most Holy Trinity, Father, Son and Holy Ghost, prostrate with the most profound respect before Thy infinite and adorable Majesty, I consecrate myself entirely to thee, to procure Thy glory as far as possible, and as far as thou wilt require of me; and for this purpose I, J. B. de La Salle, priest, promise and make vow to unite myself, and to live in society, with Brothers Nicholas Vuyart, Gabriel Drolin, Jean Partois, Gabriel-Charles Résigade, Jean Henry, Jacques Compain, Jean Jacquot, Jean-Louis de Machéville, Michel-Barthélemy Jacquin, Edm. Léguillon, Gilles Pierre and Claude Roussel, to keep, together and by association, gratuitous schools, in whatever place it may be, even if I am obliged for this purpose to beg, and to live on bread only; or to do in the said society that at which I may be employed, whether by the body of the society, or the superiors who may have the guidance thereof. Therefore I promise and make vow of obedience, as well to the body of the society as to the superiors; which vows of association, as also of stability in the said society, and of obedience, I promise to keep inviolably all my lifetime."

The Venerable de La Salle had now constituted his disciples into a religious body, as far as was possible. Again the thought of his insufficiency recurred, and he determined to resign the position of general. His Brothers had just made vow to obey the superior who would be named by the institute, but he said that he was simply the originator of the new society; now that its existence was secured, he could easily give place to another. His good opinion of the Brothers also led him to believe that his will in this respect would be their pleasure ; he therefore called them together, and having disclosed his reasons, humbly besought them to accept his resignation, and to proceed to an election. His children could not refuse to listen ; they accordingly proceeded to an election, and the name of Jean Baptist de La Salle was unanimously given as that of the coming general. Pained at the result, and fearing that human motives had some share in the matter, he addressed them anew, adding many reasons why he ought not to be elected, which only his humility could suggest. He asked them to pass a half hour in prayer before taking the second vote. The Brothers were too good not to allow their father the pleasure of reviling himself by his humble statements of his supposed incapacity, his lack of virtue, and the like ; but they were too wise to deprive themselves of such a director, and the second vote gave the same result as the first. Not discouraged, though deeply grieved, the Venerble de La Salle, like Gideon of old, asked another proof that he was really to be the leader of the body that was to fight ignorance and vice, and for the third time his name was unanimously pronounced as that of the father, more than the superior, of the Brothers of the Christian Schools. Seeing no other alternative, he submitted ; yet his convictions were that the society should be governed by a Brother, and not by an ecclesiastic. To prevent the consequences that might afterward result from this election, he requested the twelve Brothers to sign the following document :

" We, the undersigned, Nicholas Vuyart, Gabriel Drolin, etc., after having associated ourselves with M. J. B. de La Salle, priest, to keep gratuitous schools according to the vows made the day before yesterday, acknowledge that, in consequence of these vows and of the association we have contracted, we have chosen M. J. B. de La Salle for superior, to whom we promise entire obedience and submission, as also to those who will be given us by him as superiors. We also declare that we do not intend that the present election shall be taken as a precedent in the future, it being our intention that after M. J. B. de La Salle there shall never be among us, nor shall there be chosen for superior, any priest or any person who has received sacred orders ; that we will have and will admit no superior who will not be associated with us, and who will not have made vows such as we have pronounced, and as will be made by those who will be associated with us hereafter.

" Done at Vaugirard, June 7th, 1694."

The Venerable Founder next sent these twelve chosen Brothers into different communities, where they became shining lights, giving bright examples to all who surrounded them.

The Brothers had shown their appreciation of their Founder's virtues by refusing to accept his resignation. Herein they were only asserting that their estimation of his worth equalled that placed upon it by learned and pious ecclesiastics.

M. de La Salle's influence could not be reserved
for the Brothers alone. The brilliancy of his virtues shone in every direction. Worthy ecclesiastics
came to make retreats in the novitiate of this great
master of the spiritual life. Hardened sinners were
sent to him, that he might bestow upon them the
care that his charity would suggest, and that he
might apply the remedy their spiritual ailments
demanded. He effected conversions where all hopes
had been abandoned, and which could be considered
as nothing less than so many miracles of divine
grace.   While laboring thus zealously, he was
suffering most cruel physical pain, which he could
but partially disguise. Among other trials he was
greatly afflicted with rheumatic pains, that he had
brought upon himself, the physician said, by sleep-
ing on the bare floor. A severe and somewhat
curious prescription was given him. He was told to
stretch himself upon supports, and to allow the
flame from a sort of pungent seed to penetrate the
afflicted parts. He cheerfully submitted, and, like
another Lawrence, stretched himself upon the
instrument of torture. Two pans filled with burning wood were placed beneath him, and the berries
or seed thrown into them. For several days in
succession he submitted to this painful remedy,
until he found relief.

When his cure was sufficiently determined to allow
him to walk about, he accepted the invitation given
him to spend some time in the retreat known as
Parmenié, where a holy nun named Sister Louise was
the object of much edification. No sooner had these

two servants of God met than they understood
each other. " We need not be surprised," says F.
Lucard, " that the Venerable should have found a
simple village girl who understood more of his
character than the most distinguished among his
clerical friends." Sister Louise listened with great
interest to the conversation of her newly-acquired
friend, whose humility made him take pleasure in
consulting one who desired only to hear his advice.
The Abbé de Saléon, who had made known this good
religious to the Venerable, felt that those two souls
would mutually appreciate each other's virtue.   It
was in the quiet home of this worthy abbé that M.
de La Salle spent the hours of repose which he so
much needed.   But who was this pious woman?

Sister Louise had been a shepherd girl.   As she
grew up in innocence, attending her flocks, grace
increased in her soul.   It happened that, near by the
field in which her flocks grazed, were the ruins of an
old chapel.   Thither went she daily to pray.   In the
solitude of the place, her imagination frequently
occupied itself in reconstructing the decayed splendors of the building, and peopling it once again with
devout pilgrims.   The desire grew upon her to accomplish the good work.   She obtained permission
from the proper authorities to beg for the requisite
funds, and finally succeeded in rebuilding the chapel.
Selecting two pious ladies to assist her, she devoted
the remainder of her life to the service of the
pilgrims who flocked thither to be refreshed by
prayer, or to obtain some signal favor from heaven.
But in the performance of this pious work she

grew in wisdom as well as in grace. Persons from far and near came to consult her on their spiritual welfare, and always left her presence enlightened and fortified. This was why the Abbé Saléon urged upon the Venerable de La Salle to recruit his strength at Parmenié.

As the Venerable de La Salle often walked along the beaten paths of his chosen retreat, he could see in the distance the cliff upon which was built the Grande Chartreuse, and he could not help thinking how calm and quiet would be his life, if he did but retire to this beautiful spot. Had not St. Bruno, a canon of Rheims, chosen this retreat as his own; and could he desire any better model than one who had given such renown to his cathedral chapter? Such thoughts gave him great uneasiness of mind. He believed that his presence created enemies for his disciples, where they might otherwise have only friends; but an interior voice told him that his vocation was not to abandon the task that Providence had given him, but rather to persevere in it till death, as he had vowed. Sister Louise, when consulted on the subject, answered humbly but promptly: "You must not think of any such change. God wishes you to persevere as you are, and to unite in your life the difficult but necessary duties of Martha and Mary." * The Venerable, renewed in courage, hastened to his beloved disciples who greatly needed him. Another difficulty presented itself. M. Baudrand, through motives of economy, wished to transfer the Brothers from

---

* Ayma, "Vie du Ven. de La Salle," pp. 158, 159.

their residence to an old and insalubrious dwelling. M. de La Salle was obliged to refuse his consent, and thus found himself again in opposition to one who, with some reason, had considered himself a benefactor.

Seeing that he could not succeed by argument, M. Baudrand had recourse to means which he considered more likely to be effective: he therefore retained the Brothers' stipend during six months, and even refused to renew the lease of the house then occupied.* After consultation with M. Lechasier, of St. Sulpice, the Venerable Founder determined to take the responsibility of the rent upon himself, and thus remove the difficulties, as far as M. Baudrand was concerned. Moreover, he had made so favorable an impression upon the proprietor of the house, that neither written agreement nor security was required. The Venerable's word was accepted; but, in return, says Abbé de Montis, he had to suffer from the ill-will of M. Baudrand, who became more irritated.†

Having settled this difficulty, he determined to make a visitation of his communities. He had already given some general rules, the observance of which he wished to examine. He also hoped, by the experience that he would thus acquire, to be in a better condition to establish such fixed regulations as would tend to the preservation and development of his society. Wherever he went he

---

* It was on Rue Princesse.

† "Vie de M. de La Salle," p. 83.

It will interest our readers to know that M. de Montis, when he prepared this "Life" was blind, and dictated the subject-matter to an amanuensis.

was received with the utmost expressions of delight.
His children vied as to who would show him the
greatest marks of submission and love. Each one
had some special word of welcome to pronounce,
some counsel to ask, some assurance to give, that
he was not forgotten, and that, on the contrary, his
name was on every lip, his love in every heart.

How consoled the Venerable Founder must have
been, seeing at every step the blessings God had
been pleased to shower upon his institute! Not a
single complaint came to lessen his joy. Shielded
by the faithful observance of their rules, the
Brothers everywhere found themselves honored and
protected. What zeal, patience, devotedness, what
lights, had been necessary for the pious Founder
to give such an impulse to his society since 1684!
Under his wise but firm government the Brothers
each day realized the happiness of their vocation.
Speaking of this period in the history of the institute, Père Garreau says: "Up to this time the
observances that had been introduced among the
Brothers had not the force of law. *Fervor rather
than authority had secured their fulfilment.*"

"Returning from his visitations," relates Père
Maillefer, "the Venerable de La Salle met a young
gentleman whose countenance and general expression pleased him very much. Addressing him in
Latin, he asked the young man who he was, and
whither he was going. In reply, the youthful
traveller said, in the same tongue, that he was from
Holland, and was on his way to Paris, where he intended to seek his fortune. As the conversation

proceeded, M. de La Salle perceived with sorrow that his companion was a victim of the Calvinistic heresy. He so far 'won the confidence of the young gentleman, that they agreed to finish the journey together. M. de La Salle paid all expenses on the way. As the young man had no fixed place of residence, M. de La Salle offered him a safe harbor, for the time being, at Vaugirard. There he endeavored to bring his guest to a sense of his errors; but, for a time, his efforts were vain. Having exhausted arguments, he had recourse to prayer and mortification, and in the course of a few weeks had the happiness of presenting the young man for baptism to the pastor of Vaugirard. Upon examining him, the father found him thoroughly instructed. After some delay in the capital, the convert returned to his home, bringing with him the warmest affection for his protector. Upon learning of his conversion, his parents and friends expressed great dissatisfaction; but they were no more able to resist his arguments, supported by fervent prayer, than he had been able to refuse his assent to the words of M. de La Salle." What was the Venerable's delight upon learning that his young neophyte not only persevered in his own good disposition, but had, moreover, brought his parents and friends into the bosom of the one, holy, Catholic and Apostolic Church! Thus did this holy man do good wherever he went. His great mind, that could accommodate itself to the limited intelligence of children, was, at the same time, adequate to command the respect of trained intellectual athletes.

The Venerable de La Salle availed himself of the leisure at his command at Vaugirard, to revise the rules of his infant society. According to the holy practice of all the saints, founders of religious orders, he had recourse to prayer.* He implored the lights of the Holy Ghost, and begged the assistance of his powerful protectress, the Mother of God.† To this he added the most extraordinary fasts and macerations,‡ that heaven might inspire him with the proper spirit. When the fruits of his vigils and his fasts were complete, he submitted them to the Brothers assembled in annual retreat. "He had them publicly read, and each one was free to make his remarks. Availing themselves of this privilege, some Brothers complained of the extreme severity of certain chapters. The Venerable religious legislator replied that he would submit the points in question to the decision of three distinguished spiritual directors, then well known in Paris. The Brothers accepted this proposition. Thus the rules were prepared, such as they exist at the present day."§

The Venerable de La Salle met with a severe loss for his society at this time, in the person of Mgr. de Harlay, who was suddenly called away by a stroke of apoplexy. There was a general desire expressed that the polished and pious Fénelon should succeed him. Had this taken place, the Venerable, who already, at St. Sulpice, had known the author of "Letters on the Education of Daugh-

---

ters," would have had a warm friend and powerful protector ; but the adviser of Madame de Maintenon had already been raised to the See of Cambrai, and Mgr. de Noailles, Bishop of Chalons sur Marne, was selected as incumbent for the capital. Though Mgr. de Harlay had directed the affairs of the arch-diocese with great ability, his natural kindness of heart had led him to be too lenient in some mat-ters: these Mgr. de Noailles felt obliged to correct. During this change of pastors the Venerable de La Salle took no part in the discussions which were held as to the respective merits of candidates. His only desire was to see a worthy successor to Mgr. de Harlay, and such he hoped would be found in Louis Antoine de Noailles.

" At this time the Abbé de La Salle and his insti-tute enjoyed comparative tranquillity ; but in 1696 contradictions were renewed. Cardinal de Noailles applied himself to correct certain abuses ; among others the multiplicity of private chapels." * " Not only every community, but every person of suffi-cient means, endeavored to have a private chapel, in which the holy sacrifice might be offered up ; so that the parish churches were almost deserted, or at least only the middle and lower classes assisted at the public services. Those who should have been present, to give good example by their influ-ence, were absent. Divine service should be offered publicly, that no irregularities may creep in, and that all the parishioners, assembled under the eye

* " Vie de M. de La Salle," by a Member of the University, p. 68.

of their pastor, may encourage one another, and receive the advice which the Church may deem necessary to give." *   Mgr. de Noailles, therefore, interdicted the continuance of these private chapels. " In his novitiate of Vaugirard, the Venerable, to celebrate Mass, was obliged to take his novices to the next house, in which a wealthy friend gave him the use of his private altar.   This chapel was interdicted like the others, and M. de La Salle found himself constrained to take his disciples to the parochial church, which was at a great distance, and without beaten paths in winter.   Besides, the populace crowded into Paris early in the morning, on festivals ; and the indecent and worldly spectacles which met the eyes of the young Brothers or postulants, could have no other than a very pernicious effect upon them.   This last consideration made a deep impression upon the holy man : he spoke to the archbishop, who, hearing his reason, and being already favorably disposed toward his society, gave him the desired dispensation to celebrate Mass, and to give benediction of the Most Blessed Sacrament, in his novitiate.   Moreover, he gave him a written renewal of the verbal approbation with which Mgr. de Harlay had favored his community." †   The Venerable de La Salle immediately erected a modest chapel in the most respectable part of the house ; he personally helped to carry the materials to construct the various parts of the altar ; but " the joy which the Brothers and their Founder felt at the concession which had been made

---

* Ravelet, pp. 213, 214.
† "Vie de M. de La Salle," by a Member of the University, pp. 68,69.

them, was soon disturbed by the efforts of the pastor of Vaugirard, hitherto a warm friend of M. de La Salle, to oblige them to assist at the public services. ' I can never consent,' said he, ' to be separated from religious who are so great a source of edification for my parish.' " * The Venerable de La Salle, who always sought to deserve the blessing promised to the meek, endeavored to reason with the good pastor, and as a compromise, says Abbé de Montis, " promised that he and his community would go the first Thursday of each month, and sing a solemn Mass in honor of the Most Blessed Sacrament." † After some time a complete understanding was arrived at, and the curate of Vaugirard admitted that the Venerable de La Salle was right in insisting t at his children should be kept in the solitude and r treat so strongly urged upon all novices by Clement VIII. The young Brothers also went to the parochial church on the feast of St. Lambert, the patron of the parish. The best proof that these two ecclesiastics were in harmony, is found in the fact that, at the request of the Venerable de La Salle, Mgr. de Noailles deputed the pastor of Vaugirard to bless the new chapel. It was opened March 27th, 1697.‡

" It is not easy to imagine how the Venerable de La Salle could meet the expenses connected with such works of charity and zeal. It is true that he found several pious and wealthy persons whose pleasure it was to assist him, yet he was so reserved about his personal wants that only such as could

---

* F. Lucard, p. 82.   † De Montis, p. 90.   ‡ F. Lucard, p. 83.

not be concealed came to the knowledge of his patrons. Some of the Brothers, however, who did not think it necessary to be as mortified as their Founder, occasionally made known the extreme poverty of their establishment; and thus they were provided with the few comforts of life which were allowed them. M. de La Salle, who placed all his confidence in Providence, rejected such diffidence, and preferred his state of poverty to all the abundance of the earth. Nevertheless, God, who always cares for those who rely upon Him, did not permit him to be deprived of the merit of his faith, or his hope to be confounded; for, while he was in extreme indigence, he found a powerful ally in the person of M. de la Chétardie, who had succeeded M. Baudrand as parish priest of St. Sulpice. This new pastor's first care was to determine the condition of the poor in his parish: how could the Venerable Founder and his children escape when such a census was taken? M. de La Chétardie knew the great utility of the society, and desired to perpetuate the good work. He visited the schools, which he found filled to repletion; he admired the order and regularity reigning therein; everything was done in the most satisfactory manner. From that moment the Brothers and their labors were the special objects of the new pastor's solicitude. He was so attentive to his duty in this respect, that he seemed to place it first among his pleasures, and everywhere among his obligations. Each month he visited the schools, examined the pupils, distributed recompenses to the deserving, and encouraged the Brothers by every means in his power. Thus a close friendship was established between the pastor and the Venerable de La Salle,—a friendship which produced immediate results in favor of the new institute." *

"The reputation of the society continued to spread with such rapidity," says an anonymous biographer,† that, though poverty was its chief riches, and mortification its only pleasure, the number of novices became so considerable, that Vaugirard could not accommodate them."

"M. de La Chétardie determined to transfer the novitiate to his parish, that he might have their good example continually before him. M. de La Salle, who referred all things to God, believed that this change was in the order of His designs, and might contribute to His greater honor. He acceded to the wishes of the pastor of St. Sulpice, though he had not yet been told whence would come the large amount required to meet the expenses of a new establishment. M. de La Chétardie agreed to furnish all. He secured a spacious dwelling, which, in 1638, had served as a convent for the Sisters of *Notre Dame des Vertus.* When all was ready, the novices were transferred to their new and more commodious home. It was never seen better than on that occasion how simply and economically the Venerable and his children had lived. The furniture was so common and so small in quantity, that it was difficult to conceive how so many persons had managed to do with so little. The pastor generally

---

* Père Maillefer, "Vie de M. de La Salle," pp. 83, 84.
† A Member of the University, "Vie de M. de La Salle," p. 70.

supplied what was wanting, and added to the joy of the occasion by enabling M. de La Salle to open a beautiful chapel. In the house there was an oratory, which for years had not served its original purpose. It was small, but means were found to add an adjoining apartment. When all was prepared, M. de La Salle requested the Bishop of Chartres, who was then in Paris, to bless the new chapel. It was dedicated to St. Cassian. This saint was a schoolmaster; he had refused to worship the gods of the pagans, and in consequence was condemned to be stabbed to death by his pupils with their styluses and knives. It will easily be perceived why the Venerable de La Salle selected the saint as one of the patrons of his society."*

In the same year two schools were opened through the zealous efforts of M. de La Chétardie: one in Rue Placide; the other, in Rue des Fossés—Monsieur-le-Prince. The first was no sooner started than it was so crowded with children of all classes, that the second was needed. Six Brothers were unable to meet the requirements of the former, which continued to prosper. The projectors of the second patronized it liberally; but after their death, subscriptions failing, it was closed. M. de le Chétardie not only visited the schools himself, he also took pride in bringing others to be witnesses of the regularity, peace and application that reigned in them. Nor would he content himself on such occasions with merely looking on; he examined the pupils; he spoke words of encouragement to them; he dilated

---

* Père Maillefer, pp. 84, 85.

upon the great good the Brothers were doing.
Once he took Madame Voisin, a great patroness of
the school, to see it working. She was struck with
the discipline of the classes ; she noticed the beam-
ing countenances of the children ; she observed
the alacrity and content with which the Brothers
labored to instruct them. The good pastor saw
how touched she was with all she witnessed. He,
too, became moved, and exclaimed to the Venerable
Founder : " Ah ! M. de La Salle, what a great
work ! Where would all these children be to-day
if they were not gathered together in this place ?
We would see them roaming the streets, corrupting
one another, and living in ignorance of every principle of morality and religion. What a work !" said
he with still greater emotion. " What an admirable
work !" Is not this the feeling of every pastor
visiting his parochial school, when it is under the
management of religious teachers, be they Christian
Brothers or others with a kindred object ? As for
Madame Voisin, that visit formed an epoch in her
life. She never forgot it. Ever after, she took the
deepest interest in the school ; she used to watch
the children walking in procession to the parish
Church ; and when a drought occurred some time
subsequently, she had a small loaf of bread distributed to each child in the school.

But to have friends is also to have enemies.
Therefore, it is not to be expected that so much
good was to continue without opposition. M.
Compagnon had not forgotten the humiliation to
which his intrigues had exposed him. No longer

able to blacken the character of M. de La Salle with the clergy, he addressed himself to the writing-masters, and gave them to understand that the Brothers were not only powerful, but dangerous rivals, who, if left unmolested, would soon destroy their profession. He suggested that, since the Brothers took children who were not poor, they could not claim the privileges attached to " charity schools."

These writing-masters—*maitres-écrivains*—were a guild of teachers, who pretended to have the exclusive privilege of teaching writing. They had their special rules, which had been approved. These rules exacted a very high standard of proficiency in the branches the members were to teach, and this fact gave them influence. But the day of their usefulness had long past; they had grown into an insolent monopoly. Seeing that the Brothers taught the same branches as they, and with great success, they naturally looked upon them as rivals who should, at any cost, be removed. The establishments so far founded by the Venerable de La Salle in Paris were strictly parish schools, and did not depend upon the city authorities; moreover, they were open to all, rich or poor, who wished to avail themselves of the advantages they offered.

The writing-masters received M. Compagnon's suggestions with marked satisfaction. Throwing aside the mask of friendship or neutrality they had hitherto worn, they assailed the school in Rue du Bac, chased the scholars, and seized the school furniture, which they triumphantly carried away. Far from blaming them, the officer to whom appeal was made, gave a verdict in their favor. But the "iron will" which M. Droz, of the French Academy, says was the distinctive feature of M. de La Salle, here manifested itself. Strong, because he had justice on his side, and encouraged by M. de La Chétardie, he appealed to parliament. On the eve of the day upon which his argument was to be heard, the Venerable, with his disciples, made a pilgrimage to one of the most venerated sanctuaries of the Most Blessed Virgin, to solicit the powerful protection of this benign Queen. The day following, the case was heard. Unwilling to risk the result in other hands, and free from all false modesty, the Venerable de La Salle pleaded himself, and with such eloquence and logic, that the decision of the subordinate officer was reversed. The Brothers were allowed to proceed in their good work. Then, as later, it might be said of them what Ravelet has written: "They asked no monopoly, not even that of doing good," but they expected to be left in the peaceful pursuit of a work which had charity and justice in its favor.

The success which attended the new school of St. Placide, again aroused the ire of the writing-masters; they caused its classes to be closed for three months. Again the man of peace and good-will to all is compelled to go to court. When the day of trial came, he was barely able to leave his sickroom to plead the cause so dear to his heart. The importance of the case gave him unexpected strength; before his logic and earnestness the quibbles of the writing-masters vanished. Again opened, the

school became, more than ever, the favorite resort
of M. de La Chétardie, who took pleasure in bringing with him the many eminent personages whom
he had interested in the enterprise.

Madame de Maintenon could not have been an
uninterested witness of all these proceedings. Her
charity was too far-seeing for them to escape her
notice. We even have reason to believe "that she
induced Louis XIV to interest himself in the schools
taught by the new society." "The Brothers," says
F. Lucard, "were frequently the object of this great
king's generosity." *

The training-school established by the Venerable
de La Salle had obtained but partial success. He
ardently desired to establish one on a firmer basis.
Soon the opportunity presented itself. Struck by
the excellent results obtained by the disciples of
M. de La Salle, the pastor of St. Hippolyte desired
to secure their services. After consultation with
the Founder, it was agreed to establish a training-
school in this parish. One of the pastor's friends
gave him a suitable house ; another offered an annual
sum with which to support the students ; other
well-disposed persons wished to join in the good
work ; the pastor agreed to pay the teachers, and to
procure the furniture. The normal-school was soon
opened. The Venerable Founder was resolved to
regulate it according to the dictates of his genius.
Now that he could have it under his own supervision, he was going to make it conform to the ideal
in his mind. The school was the conception of his

* F. Lucard, "Vie de M. de La Salle," p. 89.

brain ; only he could realize the design he had formed. He began with basing the admission of the young men upon a severe examination. None were received except such as came to him with the approbation of their pastors, with acquired habits of order, and possessed of sufficient mental capacity.* Writing on the subject, the originator said : " The house which these young men occupy is called a seminary. They remain a certain number of years, till they have acquired not only piety, but likewise the instruction needed for their employment. They are instructed and fed, and their washing is furnished gratuitously. Afterward they are sent into villages or districts, where they act as teachers. When they are thus placed, they have no longer any relations with the institute, save such as friendship or gratitude may suggest. Nevertheless, they are received to make retreats. Their dress is the same as that usually worn in society, but it is black, and they are distinguished from other laymen by the rabat, and their hair is somewhat shorter." † A parochial school was attached to this establishment, that the poor might not be deprived of the advantages of religious education. The normal students taught in this parochial school, under the supervision of an experienced Brother, and thus prepared themselves for their future labors.

It will be surprising to many to learn that the programme of obligatory studies prepared by M. de La Salle, in 1697, is equal in extent to that pro-

* F. Lucard, "Vie de M. de La Salle," p. 89.
† Arch. of the Régime.

mulgated as law by France, in 1851. But such is the fact; we are not inventing, we are only narrating. Both are matters of history; let us compare them. The course of 1851 runs as follows: *religious and moral instruction*, reading, writing, elements of the French language, arithmetic, system of legal weights and measures, and religious music. This course, coming a century and a half after that of 1697, has had the experience of all that time to perfect it, and yet it has not added a single item to that laid down by the Venerable de La Salle for his normal-school of St. Hippolyte. It included: catechism, reading, writing (which in those days included orthography, elements of the French language, and the knowledge of accounts), arithmetic, the system of weights and measures in use, and, finally, plain chant. The Venerable de La Salle took special pride in this last branch, and with no slight pleasure did he write to a friend : " The students in our seminary learn to sing perfectly." St. Paul's, London, Trinity Church and the Paulist Fathers in New York, and many others, who have done well in establishing ecclesiastical singing-schools, are repeating what was a success nearly two hundred years ago. We admire their success; we may rest assured that those conducted by La Salle were equally admirable. He was not given to boasting, and he was a good judge; for we have seen that his own musical tastes had been cultivated in his younger days. The pupil and successor of M. Bourdoise, a most competent person to form an opinion on the subject, bears this testimony to the young men formed for teachers:—" M. de La Salle," he writes, " has been so good as to educate four young men for me. They went forth from him so well formed and so zealous, that, if they had received proper encouragement, and the good dispositions with which he inspired them had been cultivated, they might have established a community that would have proved most useful in the provinces." * We can form some conception of the proficiency of these young men when we remember that they attended the normal-school, not for a few months, or even a single year,—as is so frequently the case in modern institutions bearing the name,—but for years; and the Venerable Founder, when speaking on the subject, seems to think even that not sufficient time: " The students," he says, "remain there but a few years." * The parochial schools taught by the Brothers reached a proportionately elevated standard. Ravelet says of them, some years later: " Boys who had spent two or three years with the Brothers of 1720, were able to prepare a deed, or to draw up a contract. *How many college graduates of the present day can do as much?*" The age was not accustomed to see educational work so thoroughly and efficiently done. La Salle was already spoken of as one of the greatest educators in France. His schools attracted the attention of princes in Church and State. One of the greatest marks of the esteem in which he was held, is furnished in the history of the establishment of his first boarding-school.

---

* Letter of the Director of St. Nicholas-des-Chardonnet to Brother Barthélemy.　　　† " *Les élèves n'y demeurent que quelques années.*" MS. in Arch. of the Régime.

CHAPTER V.

The Venerable's Friends.—Louis XIV and the Irish Exiles.—M. de La Salle opens a Boarding-School.—Gratitude of James II.—Memorial of the Clergy of Chartres to their Bishop.—Religious Orders true Republics.—Mgr. des Marais and the Jansenists.—The Venerable visits his Communities.—His Reception in Chartres.—The Bishop offers to secure Letters-Patent for the Society.—The Venerable declines.—His Forethought.—He changes the Method of teaching Reading.—Mortifications practised by the Brothers in Chartres.

THAT which was an object of admiration to others seemed to La Salle something ordinary. He and his Brothers had only done their duty. That fact interested him most. He did as he knew how: he could not have done otherwise. It is ever so with genius. It embodies an idea in a poem or in action; the world applauds; it recognizes a new power upon earth; but the genius is surprised; he did not mean to be great, he only did as it was given him to do; if he possesses virtue and modesty, he shrinks from the fame that is thrust upon him. So it was with La Salle. He found himself the centre of an ever-widening circle of admiration, and it brought him confusion. But the greater the efforts made by him to remain hidden from the world and its praises, the higher he found himself in the estimation of his ecclesiastical superiors, and of all appreciative persons who learned of his virtues, as a priest, a spiritual director, and an educator. M. de La Chétardie, who had so many opportunities to judge of

his worth, never tired speaking of him to his friends.
An opportunity presented itself in which he was
enabled to give M. de La Salle an introduction and
a recommendation that were of great service to the
institute. One of the greatest glories of the reign
of Louis XIV is the princely manner in which he
treated the exiled king, James II, after the battle of
the Boyne. Among those who followed the dethron-
ed king into his retreat were several noblemen, who
sought in Catholic France that freedom of religious
worship they were deprived of in their native land,
and who preferred to cling to the fallen fortunes of
their rightful sovereign, rather than sacrifice their
faith for the favor of the new ruler. Their children
were to be provided for. The occasion sufficed to
suggest to Louis XIV the course to pursue. He
acted with all the delicacy that was inherent in his
noble nature. The daughters he placed in the convent of the Nuns of St. Thomas. He might have
given the sons positions in the army, but this
would have been only partially to do his duty by
them. They were in a strange country, unacquainted
with its habits and manners, and only imperfectly,
if at all, knowing its language. They required to
be polished and instructed, and made presentable
to society and the court. But who is competent
to fulfil this important task in a manner worthy
of France and royalty? These fifty youths must be
placed in the hands of none but the best educators
in the land. The king consults Cardinal de Noailles
upon the selection; the cardinal makes inquiries;
he especially relies upon M. de La Chétardie to find

the proper persons. "The pastor of St. Sulpice," says Ravelet, "knew no one who could better assume the responsibility of educating these youths than M. de La Salle. The servant of God was therefore, requested to admit them into his own house, and the Venerable, who never refused to accomplish the good presented to his zeal, hastened to open a boarding-school." This act did honor to the judgment of M. de La Chétardie, at the same time that it did honor to La Salle. " It was," says Garreau, "a mark of confidence that did great honor to the venerable man; it was rendering generous testimony to the regularity that reigned in his seminary." *   It was another occasion for doing a great good, and promoting the glory of God : for this reason it was not to be let slip. Accordingly, La Salle received these hopeful young Irishmen with joy, and cared for them with a truly fatherly love. † It is of the utmost importance to understand that in the present instance the man of God was sacrificing no jot or tittle of principle in taking charge of these young men. " The object pursued by the Institute of the Brothers of the Christian Schools," says a competent authority on this point, " was not exclusively the direction of free schools. The zealous Founder already had occasion to make known his real intentions in regard to this matter; he had created a preparatory novitiate; he had established four normal-schools, and he had directed the school of technology of St. Sulpice." ‡ The proposition

---

* Père Garreau, vol. ii, pp. 19, 20.   † P. Jos. Aloys Krebs, "Leben," § 105.   ‡ In the narrative we have deemed proper to pursue, this school of technology is mentioned later.

made by the archbishop was for him an invitation
from Providence to walk in the logical and sure path
that he had traced out for himself, in order to dif-
fuse the benefits of a Christian education among a
greater number of families. As soon as Notre-Dame-
des-Vertus was prepared for their accommodation,
Louis XIV sent these noble strangers to him, re-
commending them to his solicitude.* There was
no need of such a recommendation. It sufficed
that **La Salle** had consented to take charge of them.
All the rest would follow. With him, to know his
duty was to perform it at every risk; and therefore
Maillefer, a relative of the Venerable, and intimately
acquainted with the history of this important movement in his life, tells us : " He lodged these young
gentlemen in his own house, and took particular
care of their education. *He selected Brothers to watch
over them, and to give them all the instruction suited
to their age and their position in society*, so that, in a
short while, they were able to fill the various offices
to which they were appointed." † This is a valuabe
piece of testimony ; it contradicts a popular version
given by later biographers, not at all in keeping
with La Salle's character. By them we are told
that, not satisfied with intrusting them to any of the
Brothers, he took sole charge of them himself.‡

---

* " Vie de M. de La Salle," t. i, p. 137, 2ᵐᵉ edition.   † Ibid., p. 89.
‡ This is the version of it put in the popular life, in German, by P.
Jos. Aloys Krebs. His words are : "*Nicht zufrieden damit, einem eig-
enen Bruder diese kleine Gemeinde anvertraut zu haben, wollte er sich
auch noch selbst mit ihrer Erziehung beschäftigen.*" " Leben," drittes
Buch, 4tes kap., § 105. And the English version, based upon Garreau,
says : "Through respect for the persons who confided to him these exiles,
he charged himself, in a great measure, with their education." " Life,"
c. vi, p. 95.

To give these fifty youths all the accomplishments required, would have absorbed his whole attention. And, in the meantime, who would foster the young society, and guard its interests? Under the circumstances, the zealous Founder could in no sense be justified in abandoning the care of his order, and laying aside so many more urgent and immediate duties for the sake of these young strangers. It would have been a blot on his character. But we are glad to find history rectify the false impression. He who was so efficient in moulding competent secular teachers, could not have allowed his own Brothers to remain incompetent to prepare these young men for the posts they were to occupy. His educational standard was too elevated to admit of any such supposition; his sense of justice too keen to undertake to do anything he felt himself unequal to, or to allow others to do the same.

Under the care of the Brothers the young men made rapid progress. M. de La Chétardie frequently visited them; so did Madame de Maintenon and the Bishop of Chartres. They spoke to the archbishop and to the monarch of their advancement in studies, of their order and regularity, of the consideration with which they were cared for, of the ability and modesty of the Brothers, and, above all, of the saintly life and the various accomplishments of La Salle. As the young exiles had made the cause of James II their own, he was not indifferent to anything concerning them. The recitals of Madame de Maintenon or of the archbishop interested him. No doubt his first intention was not to see them

till their studies were completed, and to find more
pleasure and satisfaction in the first surprise occasioned by their polished behavior. A sense of deference toward his royal host would suggest as much ;
it would be a compliment to his judgment to take it
for granted that they were well cared for. But his
curiosity is excited by all he hears. He must see
these admirable educators ; he must behold with his
own eyes their discipline, their new methods of
teaching, and their behavior. So, one day, in company with the Archbishop of Paris, he pays a visit
to Notre-Dame-des-Vertus. History has recorded
the result of that visit. James was pleased with
everything. His heart overflowed with joy on
seeing these young men so well cared for ; he expressed his satisfaction at all he beheld ; he con-
gratulated the Venerable de La Salle upon his
success, "and testified his gratitude to him in the
most honorable terms."*

What were the methods which the great educator
used in this, his first boarding-school, and which so
elicited the admiration of all ? What was the course
he pursued ? We do not know ; and here we must
reëcho the regret of F. Lucard : " It is to be regretted that the plan of studies then followed by
the Venerable de La Salle has not been preserved ;
but we are assured by his earliest biographers
that he retained for himself the direction both of
masters and pupils, that he took personal direction

* *"Il parut tres-satisfait, sous tous les rapports et en temoigna, dans
les termes les plus honorables, sa gratitude, au M. de La Salle."* "Vie
de M. de La Salle," (1733) t. i, p. 369.

of the principal courses, and that he earnestly endeavored to develop the noble qualities with which heaven had endowed these students."* It must not be supposed that La Salle had opened this school simply to meet the present urgency; nothing was further from his idea. Shortly after, he extended its benefits to other students. Sometimes there were presented to him wild young men, who had resisted the influences of the most experienced masters. By his gentleness, the penetrating unction of his words, and, above all, by the efficacy of his own example, he won them to his person, and afterward to the practice of virtue. They returned to their families as edifying as they had been previously troublesome. Thus it was that he extended to the wealthy, as he had previously done, and was still doing, to the poor, the fruits of his educational genius; and in Notre-Dame-des-Vertus he inaugurated a system of education which, later, carried out on a large scale at St. Yon, was to produce the most beneficial results for society.

Such successes could not long remain a secret from the public. In 1691, Mgr. Godet des Marais had most earnestly begged his friend, the Venerable Founder, to give him some of his subjects, but the scarcity of Brothers prevented the granting of his request at the time. Five years later, the pastors of his diocese requested him to renew his petition. In the letter which they addressed the bishop on the subject, they said : " We have heard that there is in Paris a priest distinguished for his piety, who

---

* "Vie de M. de La Salle," t. i, p. 137, 2ᵐᵉ edition.

educates young men to become teachers, and tnat
he succeeds in making them acquire the qualities
necessary for their profession. It is an obligation for
us to appeal to your lordship, and to humbly solicit
that you will use your influence, and even your
means, to procure for Chartres so powerful an
agency for the amelioration of the morals of the
people."

The bishop made known the substance of this
letter to the Venerable de La Salle. This was
highly honorable to the servant of God; but the
praises of which he thus found himself the recipient,
made him hesitate before giving a definite answer.
He wished to consult some of his principal disciples.
In this he showed a wisdom which can scarcely
be overrated. To govern men well, they must be
ruled intelligently.

The petition presented by the Bishop of Chartres
was more than usually important. Jansenism was
then making fearful havoc among the faithful in
France, and Mgr. des Marais was considered one
of its most powerful and learned adversaries. That
he should select the Venerable de La Salle's disciples to instruct the youth of his flock, was equivalent to saying that he looked upon their Founder
as a priest, the purity of whose doctrine enabled
him to spread healthy instruction among minds so
easily led astray as are those of children. It was
also acknowledging that his disciples were actuated
by the same spirit, since their ministration was to be
"a powerful assistance in reforming the morals of
his people." The good prelate was certainly taking

the speediest method for bettering his people.   The shortest and easiest way to reach them is through the children.

With the unanimous consent of his community, he determined to accept the new mission.   He selected seven Brothers, and they were welcomed in the kindest and most enthusiastic manner by the clergy and laity of Chartres.   " No one appeared more happy than the prelate himself, who received the Brothers as so many angels sent him by heaven." *   The Sisters of Providence were installed in a former convent of Benedictines, and their establishment was suitably prepared for the reception of the Brothers, under the personal supervision of Mgr. des Marais.   The Duc d'Orleans promised a considerable sum for the annual expense of the community, and the Canon de Bangy contributed largely toward their maintenance.

Mgr. des Marais did not wish the Brothers, as teachers, even to have the trouble of gaining the confidence of the parents.   He prepared a circular-letter, addressed to his faithful people, in which he eloquently spoke of the necessity of Christian education.   In convincing words he showed that the evils from which society suffered are, in great part, owing to the imperfect religious training received in youth.   He presented the Brothers to his diocesans as men whose life and whose doctrine, he doubted not, would be of great service, morally and intellectually, to the most cherished portion of his charge, the youth of Chartres.   In conclusion, he

---

* F. Lucard, p. 95.

quoted the words of the great and good Jerome :
" I know not if there be anything more noble, or
more agreeable to God, than the education of youth,
and to water those young plants in the Lord's garden with the heavenly doctrine of truth and justice."
As guarantee to such as might doubt the capacity
of the new teachers, Mgr. des Marais said : " To
second our pious intentions, we have secured masters
who are well formed in the art of teaching, and who
will give our children all necessary instruction."

On the twelfth of October, 1699, the school was
opened. The day was one of universal jubilation.
Parents and children came in large numbers; the
former to see, the latter to be instructed by the
Brothers. Everything that could make the new
teachers feel at home, was cheerfully done by the
good people of Chartres. The Brothers, thus encouraged, entered zealously into their new field of
labor, in which they reaped an immense harvest
among souls.

In the visit which M. de La Salle made to all his
houses in 1700, he stopped for some days at Chartres.
His first care was to call upon the generous prelate
who had taken so lively an interest in his disciples.
Nothing touched the heart of M. de La Salle more
promptly than the love manifested for his children.
He also wished to consult this learned bishop upon
certain matters relating to the institute.

Their meeting was that of two friends. The
bishop would allow no formality to his former college companion. He regarded him as a companion-
in-arms, who, in his own modest but noble way, was

doing great service in preserving the purity of Catholic doctrine among the rising generations. He asked many questions about the society and its prospects, and was delighted to learn that the former student under M. Tronson and M. Baüyn had been made an instrument in the hands of Providence for the realization of so much good. The amiability shown by La Salle in conversation, the modesty with which he related the success with which his work had been blessed, the clearness with which he traced his plans for the further development of his infant society,—all struck the worthy prelate with admiration, bordering upon astonishment. "Upon his features," says F. Lucard, "Mgr. des Marais read the marks of the most austere penance ; his dress was so poor that even the seraphic St. Francis would not have found it too good for a covering. The prelate hid his emotion under the cloak of familiarity, and playfully twitted the former canon of Rheims upon the style of his mantle, and the thickness of the soles of his shoes; his hat also called for remark. Before allowing his visitor to retire, the bishop offered him a new mantle, which the servant of God accepted as an alms, with many marks of gratitude."*

Mgr. des Marais had great influence with Louis XIV ; he was also Madame de Maintenon's director, and his advice was often sought in reference to the management of St. Cyr. Bossuet, Fénelon and Cardinal de Noailles also consulted him. Louis XIV wished to raise him to the cardinalate, but

---

* "Vie de M. de La Salle," t. i, pp. 141, 142, 2ᵐᵉ edition.

could not overcome his humility. St. Simon says that " his disinterested conduct, his learning, piety, and his rare probity, were to be his only lustre."

This worthy prelate was anxious to show the Venerable de La Salle the deep interest he took in the future of the new institute, and for this reason offered to use his influence with the king to secure it letters-patent. This was an offer which one would suppose the Venerable would have accepted with alacrity. He certainly desired to give his institute a legal status which would prevent it from being attacked at any moment, and which would likewise give it a public character it thus far had not acquired. In this way he might have silenced clamorous rivals, and have shown them, in the words of an official document, that their ire was as useless as impotent. " How, then," ask his biographers, " are we to account for his polite but positive refusal to accept what seemed so necessary and so desirable a protection?" If we look more closely into the question, we shall find that his determination was marked by that rare foresight, wisdom and discretion which are always ingrafted in those who do a lasting work. All such undertakings are to be built upon the rock which allows no agreeable but useless cover-ing of grass or flower, but which withstands the storm and defies the waves. Now, the order of La Salle differed materially from any other, both in the character of its organization, and in the objects of its creation. Hitherto schools had been divided into two classes: the university for the rich or the ad-vanced student, and the parish school for the poor.

It was the aim of the Venerable Founder, in establishing his congregation, at the same time that he was embracing all classes of the poor, to cover a middle ground between the parochial school and the university. He was, therefore, reasonably to expect opposition. No man can go out of the beaten track without meeting with difficulties. This is in the nature of things. If the writing-masters attacked him because he taught the poor gratuitously, those whose interests were centred in higher education might be his enemies, because he trenched upon part of their domain. And, as such a twofold opposition would place among his opponents persons of rank in Church and state, he preferred to establish his work only under the protection of Providence, fearing lest, if he asked official recognition, clauses might be inserted in the approbation which would be opposed in principle to the course he wished to follow. The future determined the wisdom of this policy. Relying for the time being upon the intrinsic merit of the methods pursued by his disciples, and which gave success to their teaching, he awaited the hour when, under more favorable circumstances, he might appeal to the state for the approval of an institute which would then be recognized as already having done much for society at large. Moreover, his great desire was to teach his disciples self-reliance and self-government. The future he had marked out for them was such that his relations to them as an ecclesiastic could not stand for precedent. To have their legal recognition established under those relations, might give color of plausibility to any ill-designed efforts made to reëstablish similar relations afterward. And this, in our opinion, seems to have been the chief motive actuating the far-seeing Founder in deferring to take this important step.

Mgr. des Marais held frequent conversations with his friend, whom he styled a public benefactor. On one occasion he determined to detain the servant of God for dinner. To succeed was no easy task. He gave orders that the doors by which La Salle might retire be closed. In vain did the latter beg to be excused; in vain did he allege the rules and customs which had been established among the Brothers in this respect: the prelate would hear of no other alternative than that of his dining with him. He was obliged to receive such warmly-pressed hospitality. After the repast a prolonged conversation took place, in which M. d'Aubigné, Vicar-General, and afterward Archbishop of Rouen, participated. The rules and constitution of the new society were discussed; the plans according to which it was to be established, formed the matter of close study for the bishop, who felt that he owed it to his friend to take an abiding interest in all that concerned him. The knowledge which the prelate had acquired in revising the regulations of St. Cyr, gave him experience respecting the rules of an order devoted to education. After mature reflection he returned the manuscript to the Venerable Founder, without an erasure or mark. He had found nothing except what was worthy of the highest commendation. To the approbations of De Harlay and Noailles was added a third, that of Mgr. des Marais.

The good prelate took the liberty of making but two critical remarks. The first was, that he did not think the method adopted by La Salle, *to make children learn to read French before having learned to read Latin, was judicious.* He founded his objections upon the general practice followed till then. It is difficult for one at present to understand any other course. Not so at that day. In the "Methodical Instruction in Parochial Schools," published in 1669, it was said that "the children must first be taught to read Latin well before attempting to read French, for the former language is the basis of the latter." Fénelon, as well as La Salle, saw through the absurdity of such a process; he ridicules the idea of keeping children three or four years in mastering the reading of a tongue they understand nothing about. So did the gentlemen of Port Royal. They had begun to introduce the new method into their primary schools; but to La Salle it is due that it became generally adopted soon afterward. It was evidently the rational method, yet the bishop censured it; but, after some discussion upon the matter, he bowed before the genius of La Salle, and acknowledged the correctness of his views.

The second remark made by Mgr. des Marais referred to the penances and austerities practised by the Brothers. The good bishop had learned what human nature could endure, for he was known as one of the most mortified prelates of his time. "To the fatigues and responsibilities of the episcopate he added the austerities of the religious state; he was the imitator of the Basils and the Chrysostoms, and gave honor to France by the antique type of his sanctity." * He had already written to the Abbé de Rancé in the spirit in which he addressed the Venerable de La Salle. In his letter to the great Trappist reformer, he had written: "Your chanting, your labor, and the moist air in which you live, exhaust the body, apart from the silence, solitude and discipline you practise. I have always thought that half a flask of wine would serve to nourish the stomach. In the same way a couple of eggs at dinner, with a portion of vegetables, would warm languishing bosoms, and, as the repast is over some hours before retiring, this can produce none of the pernicious effects that might otherwise be feared; and as for your patron saint's day, and the four great feasts of the year, were you to give some little fish to your community, you would do nothing more than what was in vogue in the earliest days of the existence of the Order of Chartreux. These little things which seem to be nothing, and which cannot cause intemperance or relaxation, are a wonderful means by which to cheer the mind, to strengthen the body, and to encourage the religious afterward to pursue their exercises of penance with more zeal and fervor." The Abbé de Rancé replied to this good-natured advice, that he could not change anything in the rule he had adopted,

---

* "Histoire de La Trappe," par M. Gaillardain.

and gave reasons which fully satisfied the prelate.
As for the Venerable de La Salle, he knew, long
before Montalembert had written it, that no order
had ever perished from want of subjects, so long as
the rule was strictly observed ; * and he was able to
assure Mgr. des Marais that what was required of
his subjects could hurt no one.   The mortifications
which the Brothers of Chartres had imposed upon
themselves were not included in the regulations:
the good prelate had not seen them there.   But he
did not stand aloof from the Brothers; he had
frequently visited them; he had watched by their
bedside when they were sick : he therefore spoke
from personal experience.   He had found that the
illness of some of these Brothers was the result of
indiscreet zeal.   He had noticed disciplines and
hair-shirts in their cells.   These he removed, saying,
in all justice, "that the use of such instruments of
penance was not compatible with the laborious and
self-sacrificing life of a teacher."   The holy Founder
had made the same remark during his visitation.
While he was moved with deepest emotion at the
fervor of his children, he was compelled to tell
them that their life as teachers and as Brothers
already offered them sufficient sources of mortification, without adding these to the practices which
could only be followed by recluses.   Such were the
principal events that transpired upon the occasion
of La Salle's sojourn at Chartres.   The visit brought
sunshine to his heart.   When with the bishops, he
was frequently reminded of the happy days they

---

* "Monks of the West."

had spent together in the seminary ; when with
his Brothers, he was edified by their zeal and piety ;
when with the clergy, his words were received as
the utterances of a great servant of God : everywhere he did good.

CHAPTER VI.

The Venerable establishes Sunday Lecture Courses for Artisans and Tradesmen.—Success of the Enterprise.—Schools in Calais and Troyes.—Brother Gabriel and a Companion sent to Rome.—Avignon and Marseilles obtain Brothers.—Envy and Discontent in Paris.—La Salle unjustly held responsible.—M. Pirot, Vicar-General, investigates the Complaints.—Patience and Humility shown by La Salle.—Cardinal de Noailles appoints a new Superior.—The attempted Installation.—Scenes.—M. Bricot refuses to accept the Position as Superior.—La Salle threatened with Exile.—M. de La Chétardie interferes.—The Director of Novices and his Companion abandon the Institute.

GREAT diversity of opinion prevails between Protestant and Catholic concerning the observance of the Sunday. The former attempts to revive the Judaic strictness of the Sabbath; the latter takes the idea of rest in a broader signification than that of mere bodily repose. The Puritanical idea is, that listening to a sermon and reading the Bible shall occupy the Sunday; there must be no recreation, no innocent amusements; a Christian household must live throughout the day in the gloom and silence of the tomb. The better-instructed Christian believes that after divine services the son of labor may amuse himself rationally, or devote his spare hours to mental improvement. These were the views entertained by the Venerable de La Salle. Certain Flemish priests, in obedience to a decree of the Council of Malines, had opened Sunday-schools, in which reading and writing were taught for a couple of hours; this was followed by religious instruction. This was an idea according to the bent of La Salle's genius. Ever on the look-out for a new means of doing good to youth, he consulted with the Archbishop of Paris, and obtained his consent for the opening of such a school in St. Sulpice parish. M. de La Chétardie coöperated as far as possible, and in the month of October, 1699, the classes were opened to all young men of twenty or thereabouts, who had good-will and some talent to acquire the knowledge suited to their avocations. Thus we see that, as early as the close of the seventeenth century, La Salle had understood and more completely provided for the instruction and improvement of tradesmen than the associations and trades-unions of our own day. Always systematic in his undertakings, he submitted the young men to an examination, after which they were placed in classes or sections suited to their capacity. " M. de La Salle," says F. Lucard, " who created training-schools in France, is also the first to inaugurate public lessons in mathematics and the fine-arts."* " Three hours were devoted to the sciences or arts suited to each one's profession or avocation. Special stress was laid upon geography, bookkeeping, architecture, geometry and drawing; this was followed by a religious instruction. We cannot express the good produced by this school. It caused an entire change in the morals of these young men, who had at first been

---

*" Vie de M. de La Salle," t. i, p. 147, 2ᵐᵉ edition.

attracted only by the desire of improvement in secular studies."* The fame of the school spread throughout Paris. Soon it passed into the provinces.

" Ponthon, a student of theology in the seminary of Bons Enfants, gave so glowing a description of the good effected by the Brothers in St. Sulpice, that his uncle, the Dean of Calais, determined to secure the services of such excellent masters."† He said that the occasion was a favorable one, as the teacher had died a short time previously. La Salle wished time to study the means by which to found a permanent establishment; nevertheless, he stated that it was his earnest desire to comply with the wishes of the pastor. Delay only increased the desire of the latter. As soon as the vacation time set in, he once more urged upon the Venerable Founder the opening of the new community. Not satisfied with his own repeated request, he secured the influence of the city officials. They wrote to the governor of Calais, Duc de Bethune, to interest him in the project ; and so favorable were the accounts he received of the great work done by La Salle and his disciples, that he was pleased to join his voice with the others to obtain Brothers for the new field of labor. The Venerable Founder called upon the duke, and was surprised to find him the same commander who had attracted his attention that very morning by the piety and modesty with which he had communicated. Two such souls were not long coming to an understanding. La Salle sent

---

* " Vie," by a Member of the University, p. 78.
† F. Lucard, p. 104.

two Brothers to Calais. They found everything in readiness for their reception. They declined, however, to assume their duties without having first obtained the blessing and the consent of Mgr. de Langle, the Bishop of Calais. His lordship received them very kindly, gave them the necessary powers, and issued a circular-letter to his people, encouraging them to send their children to the new teachers. The school was immediately opened, to the great satisfaction of the good pastor.

The same zealous priest was partially instrumental in securing the establishment of a school for sailors' children. After his death, which occurred too soon for the good of the schools, Louis XIV appropriated a considerable sum for the continuance of these good works which he had inaugurated. His liberalities were largely increased by the generosity of prominent persons in Calais.

The city of Troyes was the next to welcome the Brothers. Two were sent to open a school in M. De Bé's parish. Their expenses were partially defrayed by Madame de Galmet ; the balance was supplied by Mgr. de Chavigny and M. Bouillerot. The attendance was so large, that two classes were found totally inadequate. Père Chantereau, a celebrated Oratorian, insisted that five extra Brothers should be secured. In the pulpit and in private he spoke pathetically of the good which the disciples of M. de La Salle were effecting.* After the death of M. De Bé, the bishop purchased a home for the Brothers ; previously they had been installed in the

---

* "Histoire de la ville et du diocèse de Troyes."

vestry.   The city authorities, to show their appreciation of the services rendered by the Brothers, voted an annual sum in their behalf.

We have already seen that the Venerable de La Salle was considered as a priest the purity of whose doctrine was beyond suspicion.   He was devoted to the Papacy.   It had long been his desire to see some of his children in the eternal city.   The position of teacher was not in great repute at the time in Rome, for the Italians thought such labor beneath them.   District schools were generally taught by strangers.   The most ancient schools of this class were known as *régionnaires*, probably because there was one for each region or section of a city.   The first gratuitous school was founded in Rome by St. Joseph Calasanzio.   The masters already established thought that the field should be left entirely in their hands, and it was only after a protracted struggle that the holy man succeeded in founding a prosperous institution.   The Venerable de La Salle was ignorant of the existence of St. Joseph Calasanzio's schools when he sent his disciples thither.   This fact is established by his correspondence with Brother Gabriel, Director of Laon, whom he had sent to Rome.

This Brother, whose name will be mentioned several times in the remaining pages of our narrative, was one of those souls who do not bargain with God, and who, after having labored much, consider themselves useless servants.   His rare piety as a religious rendered his merits as a teacher much greater.   His school at Laon was in a most flourishing condition; his scholars remained with him several years: many of them were from sixteen to eighteen years old. The reputation of his school brought to it such crowds, that it was found absolutely necessary to request the Venerable de La Salle to send two additional Brothers. The bishop, Mgr. Louis de Clermont, promised to supply their wants from his private purse. Such was the esteem which the wise direction and cultivated talents of Brother Gabriel brought upon the good work in his charge. His past success, and an intimate knowledge of his character and ability, induced his superior to make him the representative of the institute at Rome. M. de La Salle and his friend, M. Guiart, pastor of Saint-Pierre-le-Vieux, recommended him to the kind attention of Cardinal César d'Estrées, former Bishop of Laon, and for a considerable time *Chargé-d'Affaires* for France at the court of Rome. Brother Gabriel had as companion one whose name is now unknown.

Thanks to the influence of Cardinal d'Estrées, these two Brothers received a private audience of the Holy Father, Innocent XII, who treated them with great kindness, and promised to protect them. His death prevented him from realizing his generous intentions. It is, therefore, about the end of the seventeenth century that Brother Gabriel and his assistant settled in the capital of the Christian world, for Innocent XII died in 1700.

Cardinal d'Estrées had already assisted at the election of three popes. Before returning to France, he labored earnestly, and with success, to secure the election of Cardinal Albani, consecrated pope

under the name of Clement XI. In 1703 he left
the Eternal City, never to return, for Louis XIV
sent him for a time to the court of Philip V of
Spain, and afterward gave him the abbey of Saint-
Germain-des-Prés, where he remained till 1714, the
year in which he died. Before quitting Rome, he
recommended the Brothers to the kind offices of M.
Claude de La Bussière, who was afterward to prove
a warm friend and protector of the children of La
Salle. Brother Gabriel always found him ready at
a moment's notice to render any service, and after
his companion had returned to France, M. de La
Bussière's home often gave him hospitality. A few
months after, the Venerable Founder was called
upon to open another school, which was a source of
consolation for him. It happened that Brother
Gabriel's companion, on his return from Rome,
stopped at Avignon, where he gave so flattering an
account of the work accomplished by the Brothers,
that M. de Castel-Bianco, papal treasurer, who
desired a teacher for a district school which his wife
had established, wrote to M. de La Salle, asking for
two of his disciples. They were immediately sent,
and, while awaiting the arranging of the house in
which they were to dwell, they became the guests of
the worthy treasurer, who lavished upon them every
mark of esteem and sympathy. " Faithful to the instructions received from their holy Founder, the two
Brothers first presented themselves to the Archbishop of Avignon, Mgr. Fieschi, who received them
most cordially. Under his auspices the school was
opened in 1703." * Heaven blessed the new mission

---

* F. Lucard, p. 119.

to such an extent, that M. Castel-Bianco was obliged to ask for two additional Brothers. This gave great consolation to M. de La Salle, who wrote as follows to Brother Gabriel: "We have four Brothers at Avignon; their schools are doing very well; a house is to be built for them, sufficiently spacious for twenty persons. I introduced these Brothers to the Archbishop of Avignon, nuncio-extraordinary to France; he received them very kindly, and was pleased to give them his blessing, with many marks of good-will."

The Brothers were next established in Marseilles, where a number of merchants, and other persons of means, subscribed a sufficient sum for the proper maintenance of a public school under the patronage of St. Lawrence. "It is to be desired," said these generous persons, "that there should be a sufficient capital assured for the continuance of St. Lawrence's school. This will come with time; Providence will not allow His work to remain incomplete; some one will be found to finish it. In the meantime we will create an association of subscribers, who shall have the charity to contribute, each year, to support the school, and to pay the teachers." This association was established, and received the approbation of the ordinary, who headed the list with a generous subscription. The city authorities promised to aid the good work by an annual contribution.

The school was first placed in charge of Baron, a deacon of Castellane, who, in the committee, had received the greatest number of votes.

" Père Croiset, S. J., who had been decorated by
Clement IX, and whose piety and talents gave him
great influence in Marseilles, induced Mgr. de Vinti-
mille to replace Deacon Baron by the Brothers of
the Christian Schools. The bishop knew little of
them at the time, and, before coming to any decision,
resolved to examine into their methods of teaching. Such open-handed dealing must have been
not a little gratifying to La Salle, and prepossessed
him in favor of acceding to the request of the good
citizens of Marseilles, headed as it was by their
bishop. He accepted the school. The success
which blessed the Brothers elsewhere followed
them hither. Their classes were unable to accommodate the number of scholars that hastened to
be instructed, and they were obliged to secure
more spacious apartments. In the minutes of the
association we read that the two Brothers opened
the school " with much piety and prudence, and to
the great gratification of the parishioners." We are
further told that two of the citizens " bought the
furniture for them, provided for their wants, and
paid all the expenses they underwent in establishing themselves." *

The first Brothers in Marseilles proved worthy
of the reception they had received. Their holy
Founder, writing to Brother Gabriel on the sixteenth of April, 1706, told him, with great satisfaction, that the establishment in Marseilles, " though
opened but one month, already counted over two

---

* Séance, 6 avril, 1706. F. Lucard, " Vie de M. de La Salle," t. i, p.
157, 2ᵐᵉ edition.

hundred scholars."*　Year after year the merchants of Marseilles proved that their old affection for the Brothers had not grown lukewarm.

After one of those social upheavals to which France is subject when religious institutions were reëstablished, it was concluded that the Brothers might be dispensed with ; but the merchants and principal business men, who had been educated by the Brothers, thought otherwise, and by protest and petition so influenced the government of Louis Philippe, that the Brothers' college was reëstablished.

The work of genius is not allowed to pass unchallenged by the world ; when it is the work of genius and saintliness combined, the ordeal through which it passes is still more severe. That of the Venerable de La Salle combines both ; it cannot always continue in this prosperous condition. We must look for the hour of adversity. It is at hand. While we have been recording its rapid growth, the storm has been gathering, and will soon burst. Such a good work could not live without adversaries. They were not at this time numerous, but they were powerful. " Some," remarks Rohrbacher, " were probably instigated by their Jansenistic proclivities ; others obeyed only personal passions."

The immediate cause of this serious and prolonged trouble to which La Salle was subjected at this time, was the conduct of the director who governed the Brothers of Paris ; the severity of the novice-master was the culmination of the difficulty.

---

* F. Lucard, p. 115.

With a growing multiplicity of houses, there devolved upon the Venerable Founder a corresponding amount of responsibility. This drew him off more and more from entering into the minute details of each house. He relied in a great measure upon directing them during the greater part of the year by the monthly correspondence which he had established. And then he knew no favoritism in the governing of the various communities of the institute. He supervised his houses in Paris no more attentively than he did those in Chartres or Rouen. He placed implicit confidence in the men at the head of affairs. Their regularity satisfied him. He knew them to be exact; but he did not know them to be extremely exacting. They were so to harshness, and this precipitated upon his head the storm that had been brewing.

In the month of November, 1702, two young novices, one of whom was employed in school, the other being yet in the novitiate, were harshly treated by their superiors. The holy Founder was then absent, visiting his communities. The novices, instead of waiting for his return, laid their grievances before M. de la Chétardie. The uniform kindness which this pastor had shown the Brothers and their Founder was, perhaps, an extenuating circumstance in the conduct of these young men. They were led to think that his influence would be brought to bear in their favor: it is not to be believed that they thought in any way of injuring M. de La Salle, from whom they had received none but the greatest marks of kindness. The part of prudence, and even of justice, would have been for M. de La Chétardie to advise the young Brothers to submit, for the time being, to the local directors, awaiting the return of the only person who could rightfully hear and remedy their complaints; but, strange as it may appear, he took the opposite course: he encouraged the novices, by not refusing to flatter their insubordination, and conceived a prepossession against M. de La Salle, which was removed only partially after several years. The trouble, once made known, became public property; and La Salle's enemies were but too glad that so favorable an opportunity was given them to vent their spleen against him. For this purpose they held conversations with the two young Brothers, and induced them to give a written statement of their grievances, which their interlocutors made the basis of a memorial they shortly afterward presented to the archbishop.

"Cardinal de Noailles then occupied the archiepiscopal chair of Paris. He was learned and charitable, but of a weak and vacillating character. As Bishop of Chalons, he had approved the Moral Reflections of Quesnel; as Archbishop of Paris, he had condemned the Jansenistic work of the Abbé Borcas; later, he combated the Jesuits, and, in 1700, caused several propositions, drawn from their works, to be condemned. In 1713 he refused to receive the bull *Unigenitus;* some months after, he revoked his approbation of Quesnel's works. In 1717 he headed the appellants, and published a pastoral, which was condemned at Rome; afterward he repented, wrote

a touching letter of submission to the Holy Father,
retracted his appeal, and kept all the promises
made to the Holy See." *   With such a man first
impressions are often decisive. Though originally
well-disposed toward the Venerable de La Salle, to
whom he had given extensive powers, he allowed
himself to be influenced by the apparent sincerity
of those who presented the memorial.

"His eminence," says Garreau, "read the memorial with great surprise, and could not discover in it
any resemblance to the spirit of moderation and mild-
ness that he had always remarked in M. de La Salle;
but the facts were so circumstantially stated, that
they at least created suspicion. Consequently, he
resolved that investigations should be made quietly,
and with as little publicity as possible."†   Another
biographer, with great pertinency, remarks: "Certainly, as superior, M. de La Salle might be held
responsible for the excessive severity of his subor-
dinates, if he had authorized it either by word, example or toleration : but the second occurrence, like
the first, had taken place in his absence. If his conduct had never encouraged such rigor, was it just to
blame him? Nevertheless, this was done. It was
believed that, because a second Brother-Director
had acted like the first, it could only be through
nstructions received from the Founder. *A system
was built upon two accidents.*" ‡   His eminence never
thought of looking at the affair in this light. He
treated the whole as one of great moment.

<hr>

* Ravelet, p. 287.   † "Vie de M. de La Salle," vol. ii, p. 51.
‡ Ayma, "Vie de M. de La Salle," p. 213.

" Some days after, the cardinal sent M. Edme Pérot, his vicar-general, to the Brothers' community, under pretext of a visit, but really to obtain information as to the complaints that had been made, and to discover the true sentiments of the Brothers toward M. de La Salle."* And, after all, what did the specific accusations amount to? Was there in them any shade of Jansenism or Quietism? By no means. It was simply a question of severity in governing. Be it remembered that the men at the bottom of the whole trouble are straining every nerve, are making a mountain out of every mole-hill, in order to carry their ultimate aim; and still they can only accuse him of being severe toward his subjects, as though it was the first time it was heard that religious superiors ruled their subjects with severity! " We must confess," says a worthy son of this suffering Founder, " that the reproaches addressed to him bear only on the nature of his dealings with his disciples. The noble Jean Baptiste de La Salle, so well known by his education and amiable character ; the Sulpitian, who, according to his superior, *never gave trouble to anybody*, was represented as a man hard, even brutal, pushing to cruelty his tyrannical exactions with regard to religious austerities. They dare not incriminate either his acts or his words; all were compelled to praise his doctrine, and to admire his private conduct: they attacked in him only the superior."† " M. Pérot, who was empowered to make the investigation,

---

* Père Maillefer, " Vie de M. de La Salle," p. 92.
† F. Lucard, " Vie de M. de La Salle," t. i, p. 162, 2ᵐᵉ edition.

was doctor of divinity, professor in the Sorbonne, chancellor and canon of the Metropolitan Church. Being seventy-one years of age, it was supposed that he possessed the prudence required in so delicate a mission. For an entire month he came each week to the novitiate, and obliged all the Brothers, under oath, to make known their grievances. The Venerable de La Salle was then absent, establishing a school in Troyes. Upon his return, he found the investigation proceeding, but refused to learn anything of its character, made no defence, and awaited with patience the good pleasure of Providence. The examination proved in his favor. All the Brothers loved him tenderly; they lived in peace, happy in their vocation, attached to their rule, save three, who were displeased with others because they were not pleased with themselves. No complaint was made."* His friends began to breathe freely. They found the complaints of the novices a mere cloaking for deeper malice.

M. Guiart, pastor at Laon, learning from the Brothers of that city of the difficulties in which the imprudence of his children had placed the holy Founder, wrote to one of his friends, a doctor in theology, asking him to use his influence with the cardinal. The answer he received throws light on the subject: "I have seen Mgr. the Cardinal and M. Paulet. I trust that, with time, his eminence will cast aside the unfavorable impressions which he has allowed himself to entertain against M. de La Salle, *whose great crime, as far as I can see, is that he refuses*

---

* Ravelet, p. 288.

*to be led by his enemies, who wish to interfere in the
direction of the spiritual affairs of the community.*
So far, M. de La Salle has refused to allow this." *

Despite these powerful influences brought to
bear in his favor, the good Founder was destined to
feel the keenest humiliation. "M. de La Salle,"
says Maillefer, "who did not know the object of
this visit, deemed it his duty to thank his eminence
for the interest he had taken in the good order and
discipline of his community." The cardinal had
his mind made up concerning the affair. "He
received him with his usual politeness. After a few
moments' conversation, without making any complaint or reproach, without making known the
motives of his decision, he quietly said: 'Sir, you
are no longer superior of your community; I have
appointed another.' The Venerable de La Salle
felt the severity of the blow which had been entirely
unforeseen. He asked no explanation, sought not
to avoid the stroke, but retired in silence, blessing
God who had allowed him to be humbled. He
had often wished to be relieved of the great burden
which weighed upon him. He was now heard." †
Returning to his community, he said nothing of
what had happened. His confidence in God made
him calmly await the course of events.

M. Pérot was appointed to introduce the new superior. He had previously notified M. de La Salle
to have all prepared for the installation. It was
something unusual for the Venerable to invite all his

---

* Père Blain, "Vie de M. de La Salle," vol. i, p. 418.
† Ravelet, p. 288.

children, in an urgent manner, to meet him ; and when the Brothers of Paris received the notice that they were to assemble on the first Sunday in Advent, at a somewhat late hour in the afternoon, they supposed an agreeable surprise to be in store for them. Accordingly they assembled, and all appeared delighted to be with their father, who on the occasion was more than usually kind and gracious toward them. At about six in the afternoon the vicar-general was announced. With him came M. Bricot, a young priest from Lyons, who was warmly attached to M. de La Chétardie. The Founder received them with great respect, and conducted them to the places of honor which had been prepared for them in the neatly decorated hall.

When silence had been restored, and all the Brothers assembled, M. Pérot addressed his somewhat surprised audience. He began by paying a very warm tribute to the worth of M. de La Salle, who, he said, had been destined by Providence to bring the rising institute to its present degree of prosperity. He next proceeded to speak of obedience to ecclesiastical authority, and, by a dexterous use of words, finally introduced the delicate part of his mission, by presenting them M. Bricot as their future superior. There was no doubt, M. Pérot said, that they would all prove docile children to their new father, and thus give great pleasure to the cardinal, who had manifested such deep interest in their welfare by the rare choice he had made of the new superior.

While the speaker had contented himself with a

mere enumeration of M. Bricot's qualities, the
Brothers listened with surprise; but their suprise
changed to indignation when he said : "I regret to
announce to you that M. de La Salle is no longer
the superior of your community: he has been replaced by M. Bricot."

The tumult that followed, say M. de La Salle's
earliest biographers, can more easily be imagined
than described. Among the entire community there
was but one calm person, and that was the deposed
superior. He urged that the wishes of the cardinal
should be obeyed, and, in the name of the power
he still held, since they continued to protest that
he was their superior, he commanded them to
submit in all things to the new general. The
Venerable de La Salle, fortunately for his institute,
had instructed his disciples too well in the meaning
of the obligations they had taken, and the import of
the document that had been signed, in reference to
future superiors. The Brothers humbly, but positively, protested that they recognized no superior,
except "one of their own choosing:" in fine, they
declared that a decision which had been extorted
from the cardinal by false representations was, of
itself, null and void ; and as this introduction of a new
superior, even if he were one of themselves, could
not be legal, unless approved by the body of the
institute, they refused, under the circumstances, to
accept M. Bricot as their future guide.

"This resistance proved how false were the reports that had been spread against M. de La Salle.
Had he been the hard taskmaster that he was

represented, he would never have been so warmly defended by his disciples. M. Pérot should have by this time seen the imprudence of the step which he had taken. Policy would have dictated a prudent retreat, but he was now determined to go through with his undertaking. He did not wish to continue a discussion in which he had no valid reasons to advance, and in which he was obliged to limit himself to the assertion that he acted under authority. He took the sentence of the cardinal, signed by him and sealed with the archiepiscopal seal, and read it aloud. This instrument, in which the pretended wrongs committed by the Venerable de La Salle were enumerated, increased the opposition. The Brothers could no longer contain their indignation, and they appealed from the archbishop to the archbishop better informed." *

The imprudent director of novices was present, and appeared disconsolate at seeing the difficulties that his severity had caused. He attempted to defend his superiors, but was told by M. Pérot that he at least should be silent. It was not for him to speak who had given rise in part, said the vicar-general, to the scandalous spirit which was manifested on the occasion. Another person, continues Ravelet, who was greatly disconcerted, was M. Bricot, who felt the awkwardness of his position, and who desired to terminate the painful scene, by declaring that he wished the Brothers to be left in the keeping of the person for whom they expressed so much love and attachment. He further declared

----

* Ravelet, p. 290.

that he would never accept the direction of a house whose keys could open its doors, but could not give him free entrance to the hearts of its inmates. The archbishop, on learning what had occurred, was highly incensed, and vented his anger upon M. Pérot, whose want of tact he blamed for his non-success. And yet, for a moment, the clouds that enveloped the servant of God in their folds, were rent by the light of truth which flashed from M. Pérot in these words: " If religious in every community were as attached to their superior as the Brothers are to M. de La Salle, we would not witness so many disorders in Paris." But the light was only momentary, and left no impression upon the cardinal. To him, the superior's conduct, his actions, his motives, his saintliness of life, his noble genius, were shrouded in impenetrable darkness; he saw nothing of them; he only saw in their stead a tyrannical superior, who would cloak his harshness in the garb of simplicity. This accounts for the manner of the next reception he gave him. The humble Founder, whose heart bled at the very appearance of insubordination, hastened to the archiepiscopal residence, and throwing himself upon his knees before the cardinal, implored his pardon for the scandal which, he said, his disciples had given. Mgr. de Noailles, without even noticing the servant of God so humbly prostrate before him, left the room. Crushed in the keenest feelings of his heart, M. de La Salle returned, offering to God this draught which had not yet filled the cup of his sorrow. Soon was noised abroad the scene of his humiliation. La Salle seemed, to all intents and purposes, a man doomed to fall a victim to popular prejudice. Daily, wild stories were scattered in certain circles, tending to incriminate him still more deeply, and each succeeding one wilder than its predecessor. Finally, the popular mind became so worked up, that it began to deliberate whether such an execrable character should not be forbidden the city. Men began to talk of having an act of parliament passed, exiling him. The Brothers grew alarmed. They went to M. Chétardie, and told him plainly that, if their superior were obliged to quit Paris, they would not remain behind him. "They wish to exile him in spite of his innocence," said they; "but, should they go to this sad extremity, we are determined to abandon all the schools we direct in Paris, to follow him. We will go and establish ourselves in some diocese where, under the impartial and enlightened protection of the ordinary, we will be permitted to live according to the rules of our institute." M. Chétardie read determination in their words, and, however indifferent he might be concerning the Founder, he was not so concerning his schools. Moreover, notwithstanding the prejudices under which he labored, he could not help admiring the love which the Brothers expressed for their Venerable Founder. He therefore set about reconciling the latter with the archbishop. But, fearing lest he might not succeed in fully settling a difficulty he had helped to create, he requested Abbé Madot, who had great influence with the cardinal, to endeavor to secure a peaceful solution of the pending troubles. So far, La Salle had one consolation in this persecution: those who had been foremost in condemning the shepherd, pitied the sheep. But there were those who struck at the shepherd only that they might scatter the sheep. Theirs was a deeper game; it was none other than the destruction of the institute. They took advantage of the present troubles to go among the Brothers, and make them dissatisfied with their state. They reflected upon their scanty meals, their meagre fare, their poor dress, their life of constant mortification. But the good Brothers retorted upon them their remarks with a noble indignation. Especially did these malicious people look with an envious eye upon the brilliant success of the Sunday lecture-course. To break that down, they made use of all their address. They plied the good Brothers in every direction; they spoke to their vanity, by letting them know their ability; they tempted their cupidity, by showing them the riches they might acquire in giving such courses upon their own responsibility. The Brothers wavered, La Salle rushed to their rescue; but they heeded not his words, self spoke too loud in their hearts: they finally abandoned their vocations, to learn soon enough that they had been deceived. This was the greatest pang to the holy Founder in the midst of all his trials. In the meanwhile, the sky began to clear; men were seeing things once more in their true light.

Shortly after his interview with the Brothers, M. de La Chétardie took pleasure in telling them that the proceedings against their Founder had

been quashed in parliament. He was not without
his reward for this needed intervention. Several
Brothers, after some scruples, caused by the late
desertion from their ranks, had been removed by
the advice of their Founder, anxiously devoted
themselves to the study of linear-drawing, that
the Sunday lecture-course might be reopened.
After three months' interruption it was again inaugurated, and over three hundred young men
availed themselves of its advantages. At the request
of M. de La Chétardie, drawing was made a study
in all the schools of Paris. It were well to bear in
mind that this was a step far in advance of the times,
for drawing was unknown in other schools than
such as were directed by the Brothers. Before
calling upon his eminence, M. Madot called upon
the Brothers, but found that their resolution was
fixed; they wished no other superior than him
whom they had themselves elected, according to
rules which had already been approved by several
prelates. When told that their resistance was an
insult to the archbishop, they replied that they
were willing to make any reparation required, if in
fault; but they could recognize no one save M. de
La Salle as their superior. They agreed, finally, to
allow M. Bricot to preach once in their presence,
and to make another visit at the end of three months.
The sermon and the visit were accepted; and the
good M. Bricot, to whose credit it must be said
that he had been led into the false position, requested the cardinal to give him another duty:
which petition was at once granted. And now

that the storm has subsided, let us cast a glance at those too exacting directors who had brought it on.

As is often the case, those who had been so exacting with others, were unable to bear humiliation themselves. When warned by the Venerable de La Salle that their conduct was not in keeping with the maxims of the Gospel, those would-be saints left the community in their religious dress, and applied at La Trappe to be received as penitents. The prudent superior inquired the particulars, which were given by M. de La Salle, and the deserters were refused admission. Returning to their sorely-tried superior, they implored forgiveness, which he was so charitable as to grant. The director of novices was sent to a community, where he died, after a short time, of a frightful disease. The other's inconstancy made him again abandon his state. Cardinal de Noailles, who was as generous in reparing as he was hasty in judging, ever afterward honored the Venerable de La Salle as a person of the greatest worth, and whose virtue was of a character that no future calumnies could injure in his estimation.

CHAPTER VII.

The Venerable removes from Notre-Dame-des-Vertus.—The Sisters of
St. Dominic.—The Sunday Lecture-Course closed.—St. Roch.—Dar-
netal and Rouen receive Brothers.—Difficulties of the last Mission.—
Novitiate at St. Yon.—Madame de Louvois and the Benedictine Nuns.
—The Boarding-School at St. Yon.—Its Character and Regulations.—
The Abbé Hecquet.—La Salle opens a parochial School at his own
Expense.—Schools for Delinquents and Culprits.

LA SALLE had barely succeeded in reopening the
Sunday lecture-course, when the lease of Notre-
Dame-des-Dix-Vertus expired. The building was
offered at public sale for forty thousand francs,
which sum, though small in itself, was quite beyond
his control.   He was therefore obliged to seek other
accommodations, which he found in Rue Charonne.
The new dwelling was rented for a year; the consent of the pastor of St. Paul having been first obtained, for it was in his parish. The holy Founder
and his novices took possession of their new home
on the twentieth of August, 1730. Every day he
went with them to the chapel of the Sisters of St.
Dominic, which was close by, and he offered the
holy sacrifice for the two communities.

It was not long till these good religious appreciated the worth of the holy priest. " I know," said
one of the prioresses of this convent, " that the very
appearance of the saintly Founder inspired the

Sisters with so much confidence, that they desired
to speak with him and receive his counsels." The
superiors, always on their guard against the abuses
which may arise under such circumstances, at first
objected ; but no sooner had they seen the servant
of God and appreciated his merit, than they wiil-
ingly gave the dispensation requested." The Venerable de La Salle thus became the spiritual director
of the Sisters of St. Dominic. The admiration
which his virtues had acquired him, daily increased.
The Brothers in Paris ever after found in these
Sisters generous and disinterested benefactresses.

In leaving Notre-Dame-des-Vertus, La Salle did
not wish the Sunday lecture-course to be discon-
tinued. He therefore invited the students to his
new residence, where the studies were continued,
till the writing-masters interfered and caused the
lecture-course to be closed. In 1705 this important
undertaking was suspended. "But it is not less true
to say," remarks a judicious historian, "that it is a
glory for religion to have given birth to, and realized
the idea of, an establishment so advantageous to the
progress of art, *the first of its kind seen in Paris or
known in France.*" *

In the midst of his trials, the good work progressed
in other directions. Thanks to the liberality of M.
de Blaisey and Claude Rigoley, the Brothers were
enabled to open a school at Dijon. But the discon-
tinuance of the Sunday lecture-course rendered it
once more necessary for La Salle to change his
domiciliary residence. He scarcely knew whither to

---

* "Histoire des Catechismes de St. Sulpice."

turn, when Providence inspired M. Louis Coignet
to establish a school in his parish of St. Roch.
This was very favorable to the Venerable, as M.
Coignet was the senior pastor of Paris.   He sent his
novices to the Brothers of St. Sulpice, while he,
with Brothers Ponce, Jean and Joseph Tenant, established themselves in Rue St. Honoré.   The school
succeeded beyond the pastor's expectations, and
he did all in his power to make it continue prosperous.   Such dispositions proved him worthy of the
position to which he was shortly afterward called.

In 1704 Abbé Deshayes, who had intimately
known La Salle in Paris, encouraged the citizens of
Darnetal to call his disciples to direct their schools.
" I urge you," he said, " to call the disciples of M.
de La Salle to direct our parish school.   They are
virtuous, well instructed, devoted and methodical."
His proposition was unanimously accepted.   He
received the following letter from the Venerable
Founder: "I have learned, through M. Chardon,
that you have written to obtain our Brothers for
Rouen, and that you ask for two ; you also request
to know what is required to found the establishment.   I am quite willing to send you the two
Brothers.   As far as the stipend is concerned, you
know that we are not difficult to please, but we
cannot send one Brother.   If you will please to let
me know for what quarter they are required, and
what it is proposed to pay them, you will oblige me
greatly.   I think we will arrange matters easily,
and that you will be pleased with the Brothers I
shall send."

These teachers were not asked for Rouen ; but Darnetal, being a thriving place and within a short distance of that city, was a locality in which La Salle felt that his disciples could accomplish much good.

Its proximity to the city of Rouen made him hope that the success his children there obtained, might be the means by which he would afterward be requested to establish a community in the city in which M. Nyel had commenced his labors, encouraged by P. Barré and Madame Maillefer.

Blain says that the amount offered by M. Deshayes was not sufficient to support one person, yet the Venerable de La Salle felt that God would come to his rescue ; and in sending his Brothers to Darnetal, he was adding another to the many responsibilities his zeal for the salvation of souls had already made him assume. He did not hope in vain. The good done by the Brothers drew numerous assistants to their support ; and the slender stipend which he accepted for their maintenance was fully supplemented by the generosity of the good citizens of Darnetal.

The Venerable Founder, though fully confident in Providence for the future of his schools, took the necessary precautions that the buildings appropriated for the purpose should be suited to their destination. He sent Brother Ponce to supervise the necessary improvements in the home offered in Darnetal ; and this good Brother also obtained assurances that the teachers were highly esteemed by the Archbishop of Rouen. In an audience which the two masters in Darnetal secured, shortly after, from his grace, they were convinced of his generous intentions, and they naïvely told him that the desire he then expressed of seeing Brothers in his archiepiscopal city was shared by their father, M. de La Salle ; and that they even believed that, if authorized, the holy servant of God would transfer his novitiate to that city. Delighted to know that Providence thus offered him the opportunity of securing Christian education for his children, and desirous of seeing the Venerable de La Salle, he wrote, inviting his future friend to meet him before Easter. It was then the Lenten season, and the good prelate wished to have a personal interview with a man of whom he had formed so favorable an impression through the reports of his disciples.

Nothing could have given M. de La Salle greater joy than the reception of this letter. We have seen that he was compelled to change the location of his novitiate several times ; and the Jansenistic atmosphere by which he found himself surrounded rendered Paris more and more unsuited to the purposes of a retreat in which young masters were to breathe the pure doctrine of which he was so earnest a supporter. Moreover, the constant annoyances to which he found himself and his disciples exposed, induced him most earnestly to beg that God would be pleased to offer him an asylum for his young novices, in whom he was so deeply interested. After consultation with the Archbishop of Rouen, it was determined that a school should be opened there ; but, as in all his enterprises, where a great result was at stake, the venerable found the

entrance to Rouen hedged about with so many
difficulties that he might have despaired of success, had he not been assured that the proposed
conditions would not long be kept in force. The
Brothers were required to live in the public hospital, where they were to serve the patients before
and after school-hours. The time occupied in
going to, and coming from, the classes which were
at some distance, and the distractions inseparable from such multifarious duties, convinced the
prudent Founder that it was not possible to continue
such services, and he notified the authorities that
he could only retain charge of the schools. The
directors of the hospital answered that, in this
case, they could only give half the stipend that the
Brothers had previously been receiving. They believed that this would induce him to withdraw his
teachers entirely, which was the ardent desire of the
writing-masters, who, even in Rouen, made war upon
their successful, though modest, rivals. M. de La
Salle, contrary to their expectations, accepted these
conditions. Apparently he had acted rashly, for, in
a short time, the Brothers were reduced to great
misery. At the moment when they seemed most
abandoned, a considerable sum was sent them, with
a note, which read : " Do not seek to discover the
donor ; place your confidence in God alone ; be
careful to serve Him faithfully, and He will provide
for you."

The schools of Rouen soon attracted the attention of several well-disposed persons, among others,
Colbert and de Pontcarré. These two generous

gentlemen urged the Venerable de La Salle to transfer his novitiate to their city, promising that they
would defray all the expenses for the journey of the
novices and the transport of the furniture.   The
next question was to secure a proper location,—
one which would be left him for some years, and
which he might thus adapt to his purposes.   .

At a short distance from the city at the extremity
of the district Saint-Sever, there was an ancient
mansion, to which vast gardens were attached ; it
was enclosed with walls, around which large trees
were planted.   The busy hum of worldly affairs
seemed to die away in this sweet solitude.   No
sooner had the traveller placed his foot upon this
secluded spot, than he believed himself in another
sphere, so sudden and agreeable was the change.
The high, towering trees and their thick foliage hid
even the tops of the walls, and nothing of the outer
world looked upon this chosen retreat.   The blue
sky above was the only witness of the acts of those
who inhabited St. Yon, for this was the name by
which the villa was known.   One of the last pro-
prietors of this delightful spot had erected a chapel
there : later, the property had been rented by the
Benedictine Nuns, who occupied it in 1691, and
enlarged the chapel.

When the Venerable de La Salle visited this
estate secretly lest his enemies should discover
and frustrate his intentions, he found it admirably
suited to his purpose; and as the ladies then in
possession were quite willing to abandon it to
him, he at once entered into negotiations with

the proprietress, Madame de Louvois, to whom he made known his intentions, and the little means he had to realize them. The good lady, whose heart Providence had already prepared, agreed to rent him the establishment at a very moderate figure.

St. Yon was all that could be desired in point of accommodation ; its sanitary conditions were such that the Benedictine Nuns had principally secured it for the benefit of their sick and invalid sisters. The kindness with which they treated the Venerable de La Salle, should not be forgotten. Anxious to manifest their esteem for a servant of God who was held in such veneration by Mgr. Colbert, their bishop, they left the paintings and carpets of the chapel for the use of the good Brothers, who had long since forgotten such luxuries.

A few days after, the lease was signed for a term of six years, and M. de La Salle transferred his novices to their new and spacious home. The work which had commenced in Vaugirard, with no other crown than that which encircled the head of the divine Master, in whose name such sufferings had been endured, was now installed in a home where the roses that are found accompanying the thorn, clustered about it, resembling in their delicious odor the sweet perfume of virtue which has rendered Vaugirard a household name among the Brothers. Mgr. Colbert, with some influential friends, often visited La Salle in his new home, and was pleased to give him full powers in his archdiocese. Needless to say, the latter was overwhelmed with holy joy. He was a captain who, after having been buffeted by the waves of persecution, had finally brought his devoted crew to a safe harbor. There, in breathing the air of peace and quiet, they might pursue, undisturbed, the work of their own sanctification and of their intellectual improvement, thus preparing themselves for the double duties and obligations of the good religious and the intelligent teacher. St. Yon also served as an asylum to which the Venerable's disciples could from time to time retire to renew their fervor, and to strengthen themselves by the examples of their holy Founder.

This new establishment was also to offer the Venerable the opportunity of realizing an idea which he had long cherished, but which, in obedience to a law he had prescribed himself, he deferred till the will of God would manifestly indicate that he should undertake its accomplishment. In establishing training-schools, the Venerable had supplied the smaller districts with competent teachers; his preparatory novitiate had furnished him some of his best subjects, and the Sunday lecture-course in Paris had been of incalculable service to intelligent and industrious young men. He was now to organize a fourth class of institutions, which, in its results, has been most beneficial to French society.

He had scarcely been settled at St. Yon when many of the principal families of Rouen and Darnetal requested him to admit their sons as boarders, and to take full control of their education. The proposition was acceptable in more than one sense. La Salle had long entertained the desire of establishing such a school: moreover, the expenses under which he was placed rendered it necessary to realize his idea at an early day. Besides, the location was all that could be desired for such an institution, and he had had his disciples long enough under his care and instruction to enable him justly to undertake the higher education of young men. The boarding-school established to receive the fifty young Irish gentlemen had already given him considerable experience, which he now sought to employ for the benefit of others. St. Yon was such a spot as the Seraphic St. Francis or the dear Saint Mary Magdalen de Pazzi would have delighted to frequent. There they would have found flowers in abundance which they might gently caress, telling them not to cease preaching the love of God. The Venerable de La Salle too was an ardent admirer of nature, and he often spent an agreeable hour in trimming the trees that guarded the enclosure. His children also found innocent amusement in the healthy exercise of gardening. The vast grounds attached to the villa rendered it quite easy to admit students, without fearing that they would interfere in any way with the recollection in which he desired his novices to live: for this was his first consideration.

Such reasons were decisive. The Venerable de La Salle therefore wrote to those who applied, expressing his willingness to accept the care of their sons. "It was quite agreeable to him," says Blain, " and he opened his home with pleasure to all those who were sent to be educated." Maillefer adds that the number of boarders sent was so great, that he was obliged to form a college apart from the novitiate. " In the ideas of the holy Founder this establishment was also to be pecuniarily beneficial to the Brothers of St. Yon. " You complain," he writes to the procurator-general, " that the novitiate is very poor : I believe that the means which God wishes us to employ is to take youths as boarders, to instruct and educate them properly." * How well this idea of his was realized, his biographers have proved. They all agree in representing the institution he established as a most efficient and successful undertaking.

" Whatever may be the humility of the saints, the good they do cannot long remain hidden. The reputation which the Venerable man and his disciples had acquired, spread abroad, and it was correctly thought that such men should not limit themselves to the direction of parish schools. It was therefore proposed that they take charge of boarders. M. de La Salle never refused to do any good within his sphere, when proposed to him. He received such youths as were sent him by parents who could not conveniently keep them at home. He placed them under the direction of a skilful and learned Brother, and gave them regulations suited to their age and capacity. In a short time such results were obtained as astonished the parents and their friends." † The idea was new in France. The course of studies was novel. Everything that this educational genius inaugurated bore the impress of his originality. He always found a

---

* " Lettres de M. de La Salle."　　　　† Ravelet, p. 361.

means of placing things on a new basis. There
were numerous educational establishments in which
the higher branches were taught in his day, but
no one saw through their real character better than
he. Perceiving that every grade of school, from
the primary up, laid undue stress upon the study
of Latin, he resolved to inaugurate a system better
calculated to fit young men for the higher business
pursuits. For this purpose, he established a course,
which, reversing this order of things, and laying
no stress upon the ancient classics, gave undivided
attention to the literature of the vernacular, the
fine arts and the sciences. "The servant of
God," says F. Lucard, "proposed, by a course of
serious study, to prepare young men who would
frequent these boarding-schools for all careers and
professions in which the knowledge of Latin was
not requisite. With this view, he prepared for his
disciples a course of studies such as had not existed
in France thus far. We have been enabled to form
a correct idea of the extent to which these studies
were pursued, by an attentive reading of the regulations and of the manuscripts of some of the
professors in the earliest boarding-schools." *

---

*And in support of this assertion, he refers to the following documents :

1. Regulation for the boarding-schools of St. Yon and Marseilles.
(*Archives of the Régime.*)

2. Notes on the daily regulation of St. Yon in 1742. (*Archives of
the Department of the Seine-Inférieure.*)

3. Papers concerning the course of hydrography in the boarding-
school of Nantes. (*Archives of the Department of the Loire-Inférieure.*)

4. Course of Literature in MS. by Brother Olivier. (*Archives of the
Régime.*)

"In establishing this new department in his society, the Venerable de La Salle was directed by those broad and intelligent views which had inspired him in the founding of the training and Sunday lecture-schools," * and his first care was to make the students good and intelligent Christians. He began by instructing them thoroughly in the catechism, and in the principal events of sacred history, which two branches were a subject of daily explanation. While anxious to form intelligent scholars in secular sciences, he was aware that religion is the warmth which gives life and light in the use of all other instruction, and without which learning becomes a danger rather than a blessing. We are recording, and not inventing. We are speaking of the beginning of the eighteenth century. At that time this great educator and man of broad views had not only allowed the reading of the sacred text, with proper safeguards, but had required it to be committed to memory, and then explained by competent teachers. So true it is that, in looking to the example of the intelligent thinkers of the past, we find many questions solved which worry our leaders of the present.

"Secular education at St. Yon was divided into two parts: the first comprised the course usually followed in the parish schools,"† as founded by the Brothers, for even these were far in advance of what were then **known** as free schools, throughout France. "This comprised the reading of French, Latin, and of manuscripts or registers containing

---

all classes and styles of writing, grammar, orthography, arithmetic and drawing. The second course embraced, besides these, history, geography, general notions of literature and of style, bookkeeping, natural history, and, in certain cases, hydrography ; also music and some of the living languages. For these courses the parents were obliged to pay, *but a botanical garden and a large library were free for the use of the scholars."* * The method was successful ; the school became known as one of the most thorough in France. Records testifying as much are still extant. "At St. Yon," says an ancient record still preserved at Rouen, "they teach all that relates to commerce, finance, enginery, architecture, mathematics ; in a word, all that a young man can learn, with the exception of Latin." † It has been seen why this last was omitted. Even in the manner of conducting these studies, La Salle anticipated modern times : that manner was eclectic. Each student applied himself to those branches best suited to his talents, his inclinations, and his pursuits in life, as is the present custom of the University of Virginia.

"All the studies of the second programme were not obligatory. 'The prefect of the boarding-school,' say the regulations of St. Yon, ' will consult the parents ; he will make known to his colleagues the special studies to be pursued by their students, and shall agree with them as to the time that will be given thereto.' The Venerable de La Salle, therefore, had the double merit of having conceived and realized the project of special courses, wherein the

---

* F. Lucard.   † "Arch. dep. de la Seine Inf."

instruction given would be in harmony with the wants of certain localities, and the true needs of the students.

" His was also the honor of surrounding these courses with such conditions as were proper to secure their success, under the twofold relations of morality and intelligence. Celebrated thinkers in Germany have complained that their gymnasiums or lyceums have become hotbeds of irreligion and servility. The boarding-schools established by the Venerable de La Salle have multiplied in the hands of his disciples, but all were in the last century, and have continued since to be, schools wherein respect is prominent, order a requisite, and religion the mistress. The cause is easily determined. Instruction was not a dead letter with the Venerable de La Salle. He employed it as a means to do good, but gave his disciples the full right to harmonize this instruction with the needs of special times and places, causing it to progress with the onward march of science and industry; but his essential aim was to create, in the boarding-schools directed by his disciples, as well as in their parish schools, establishments wherein Christian education would be imparted. To be convinced of what is here advanced, it is only necessary to read the regulations established for the proper direction of St. Yon. Several contain wise prescriptions proper to make the studies flourish; in others we perceive that all has been foreseen to protect the innocence of youth, through the influence of a watchful and attentive discipline. Thus evil was prevented, or cured upon its earliest appearance." * We here republish a few of these regulations :—

" At the extremity of each dormitory there is a little oratory dedicated to the Most Blessed Virgin, which one of the most pious scholars decorates on the principal feasts. Each morning, before leaving the dormitory, the scholars shall kneel and say the *Sub tuum*, and the invocation, *Sancta Maria Immaculata*.

" When the morning prayer is concluded, the students will proceed to the reading of manuscripts the recitation of catechism and of grammar: if any scholar, through his fault, shall not have given satisfaction in these branches, before Mass, he shall be deprived of recreation. This correction is imposed upon all those who will voluntarily have omitted, or badly performed, their class duties. On certain days the rules of politeness will be explained. One master will have control of this department.

" All the general evolutions of the scholars must be executed with order and in silence ; the students will walk one after the other ; a Brother will be placed at the head of the rank, and another at the end. If needed, a third or a fourth Brother may be employed in securing order.

" In public promenades the students shall be ranged three by three, which is much wiser and more prudent than placing them two by two.

" When the scholars have reached the play-ground, they shall be divided into three sections, the young men, the juniors, and the small children. The Brother in charge of the last class will be very

---

* F. Lucard, *Vie*, p. 151.

vigilant, owing to their giddiness and exposure to accidents.

" In winter, if the weather be disagreeable on the holidays or during evening recreations, the students will amuse themselves in the class-rooms. They will be required to speak in a low tone of voice, and they may play dominos, checkers, or other games that are not noisy. They may also read interesting and instructive books.

" On promenade days a conference will be made to the students instead of spiritual reading. Those who appear inattentive or distracted must be particularly questioned.

" As the principal duty of the masters is to form the students to the Christian virtues, they will be careful to give them the example of perfect union among themselves; and piety, justice, evenness of temper and zeal must be manifest among them, to form their students to the virtues necessary in society, and likewise to develop their talents according to the state which they are to embrace.

" The masters will in vain strive to gain the esteem and the good-will of their students, unless these latter perceive that religion, justice and kindness direct all their teachers' actions, and render them irreproachable.

" Every Wednesday and Saturday the prefect and the professors will meet to exchange ideas in regard to the studies, and also to determine the names of such as may have deserved to be kept from recreation the following days." *

---

* Règlement de St. Yon.

In reading these regulations, without giving the date of their publication, one would suppose that they were the production of some director who had examined a number of similar programmes, and had extracted what was best in each.

They are replete with good sense. They show rare insight into human nature. They speak of a fatherly care, and a tender respect for youth. They leave nothing untouched. The direction of the outward deportment is attended to, as well as that of the moral sentiments. All this forethought and accuracy is the more remarkable when we remember that we are quoting, not from a regulation of to-day or yesterday, but from an original document of nearly two hundred years ago.

Religion presided at all the exercises. Pious confraternities kept up the fire of devotion, and the example of earnest professors made up the sum of influences which enabled the student to leave St. Yon fully prepared to meet the world and its varied obligations and responsibilities.

Each year's experience has confirmed the wisdom of these regulations, and the superiors-general who have succeeded La Salle have been careful to preserve them intact. Brother Agathon, one of the most distinguished among these generals, says : " After having examined these regulations of the boarding-school at St. Yon, we hereby approve them, and wish that they be continued in force without alteration, addition or abridgment, for they have been established by M. de La Salle, and continued by our predecessors, as fit to produce great

good.   We therefore wish that they be preserved
in their entirety, and that no change be made save
by our written authority or that of our successors,
who, for good reasons, may deem proper to alter
something therein."

The success which attended St. Yon naturally
called for similar establishments elsewhere.   Prior
to the French Revolution of 1798, they were very
numerous.   Contemporaneous testimony to the fact
is on record.   "Boarding-schools," says a writer
in 1792, "have always been numerous among the
Brothers.   They have been approved, protected and
patronized, as useful to all branches of commerce." *
The fact had a legal recognition in France.   In the
letters-patent granted the institute by Louis XV, it
is formally stipulated: "We permit the Brothers,"
says this document, "to receive such boarders as
present themselves of their own accord."   The manuscript Rules, bearing date of 1717, two years prior
to the death of their saintly framer, contain this
clause: "The Brothers may open boarding-schools
in the buildings attached to the novitiate, or in a
structure destined for the purpose, when the superior, with the advice of his assistants, shall judge
this necessary." ‡   As early as 1751, they had become so numerous that it was decreed in General
Chapter that no others should be opened without
grave reasons.†   With the Revolution came the dis-
solving of the society, the scattering of documents,

---

* "Idée générale de l'Institut des Frères des Ecoles Chrétiennes,"
p. 34.   Imprimé à Angers, 1792.
† *Archives du Régime. Règles MS.*, 1717.
‡ Ibid. *Chap. Gén. de* 1751, 7ᵉ *séance. Art.* 1ᵉʳ.

the breaking off from the old traditions, and the subsequent misunderstandings in reference to this important subject.*

The interest which La Salle felt in this important enterprise did not prevent him from devoting proper and constant attention to his other communities. Brother Barthélemy was placed at the head of the novitiate; another learned and experienced Brother was given charge of the boarding-school; Brother Ponce took the direction of the parochial schools in Rouen. He had already distinguished himself in the management of the classes in Paris. Occasionally the holy Founder supervised their work; and his counsels enabled his sons to prosper beyond their fondest anticipations.

St. Yon had quite a number of students as early as 1706, and the pastor of the parish, Abbé Hecquet, desired to exercise his parochial duties in their behalf. We shall learn in another chapter of the agreement which was concluded in this respect. Gratitude was one of the most shining qualities in the character of M. de La Salle. He never felt that he had done enough for any favor that had been shown him. He naturally was more than gratified with the result of the institution at St. Yon, and, to mark his appreciation, he opened a parochial school at the expense of the Brothers. The funds which had previously been employed in

---

* After speaking of the Brothers' College at Passy, a great authority on educational matters says: "France enjoyed these beneficial institutions before the Revolution. Rouen, Rheims, Saint-Omer, Nancy, Carcassonne, Montpelier, and many other cities, had similar colleges, and were indebted for them to the zeal and devotedness of the Brothers." (Mgr. Dupanloup, *De l'Education*, t. i, p. 283.)

paying lay teachers, were now given to the city to
be distributed in charity.   The school was opened
in the same populous quarter in which a grateful
people has recently erected the beautiful statue of
this benefactor of society.

During a certain number of years the college of St.
Yon received only such scholars as were morally
beyond reproach ; but the reputation the institution
had acquired was such, that many parents requested
the holy Founder to admit young men whose conduct had not been satisfactory. La Salle consented,
but kept these young people's apartments separate
from the boarding-school proper. These were subjected to severer discipline; and as their derelic-
tions had often been the result of thoughtless levity
and bad example rather than of ill-will, a few months
under the influence of virtuous masters, in an atmosphere of piety, with no sights save the green fields
and the smiling gardens about them, sufficed to
work a complete change in their character.

M. de Pontcarré, president of the parliament of
Rouen, continued his warm friendship to the
Brothers of St. Yon. After the fatigues of parliament, he found rest in the solitude of the place,
away from the agitating scenes of political life.
He was wont to walk in the garden, where his
Venerable friend had appropriated a certain alley
for his sole use. There he matured his plans,
and strengthened that wisdom that made him
the chosen leader of men. Seeing the influence
which M. de La Salle's sons had upon the giddy
young people who were confided to them, he

bethought him of asking the servant of God to take a certain number of persons who had even been condemned to some term of punishment. He saw that there was also room for another class of persons in St. Yon. Much has been said of the *lettres de cachet*. They were secret orders for privately withdrawing from society a dangerous member, on whom the law might take hold, and more effectually destroy. They were intended to save the honor of families of distinction, by silently placing members belonging to them beyond the power of sullying their name by a criminal record. As they depended solely upon the will of the king, they were subject to great abuse. " Undoubtedly," says Beaurepaire, " they were greatly abused ; but in the generality of cases the letters of the king were directed against the insane, or they struck, in their personal interest, or in that of a name or an order whose honor they sought to save, parties whom ordinary justice might have treated much more severely than did the good pleasure of the king." * The objects of these letters M. Pontcarré proposed to La Salle also to accommodate. This could not well be done by creating an establishment distinct from that founded for young men of dissipated lives, but both might be merged in one, by dividing that one into two distinct divisions, namely : those who were decidedly vicious, and those who showed simply weakness of character, but at the same time gave evidence of serious efforts to reform. The former were confined in separate rooms, while

---

* *Notice sur les Maisons de Force*, p. 4.

the latter were permitted to work and recreate themselves together during several hours of the day. The plan worked admirably. On their first entrance all were subjected to the severest discipline, but it relaxed in proportion to their reform. They were given good books to read; they were instructed in the French language and literature, and in mathematics; the younger members whose means were not independent were taught trades, and workshops were set up for them on the grounds; all were encouraged in the innocent amusement of rearing singing-birds and trailing flowers upon their window railings. This institution flourished till toward the end of the eighteenth century. In 1777 it numbered seventy-seven, twenty-nine of whom were placed there for mental derangement. "These gentlemen," says an ancient manuscript of St. Yon, "were in a great measure persons of quality; some of them members of eminent families, officers, lawyers, priests, religious, merchants, and some giddy youths. There were also several insane." But La Salle did not have these men merely instructed in letters and trades; he did not establish schools and workshops simply for their own sake: these were only means to a higher aim. Those men were to be reclaimed. To this point he bent all his energies. Exhortations and conferences, spiritual readings made every evening after recreation,* the sacraments and prayer, were all resorted to, in order to elevate the thoughts and aspirations of those unfortunate ones. Nor did they remain

---

* *Coutumier de la Pension de Force de St. Yon.*

unsuccessful. "It is inconceivable," says an eye-witness, "how many perverted people became converted in this manner: how many rebellious or unruly youths learned to become modest and submissive; how many returned to duty and virtue. The most of those who were confined therein proved, in their subsequent conduct, the power and the goodness of the education they had received."*

Thus do we find St. Yon the most complete, and, in the diversity of work done, the most general institution in France. In one part is the novitiate; in another is the college; in a third place the prisoners' home; in a fourth the workshops; outside, a free school for poor children.† With one other establishment it would have embodied all the kinds of institutions that the genius of La Salle created: there was still wanting the normal school. His earliest and most authentic biographer tells us that, in concert with the first Brothers, he conceived the project of endowing St. Yon with a normal school for the education of lay teachers, but unknown obstacles interfered with the generous project.‡ As it was, the institution had become famous. Tourists spoke of entering the famous house of St. Yon.§ And now that St. Yon has established an enviable reputation, envy and jealousy begin to buzz abroad strange reports of its management.

It was in 1708 that these rumors came to a crisis.

---

* Père Blain, "Vie de M. de La Salle."
† See the plan of S.. Yon in the Appendix.
‡ Père Blain, "Vie de M. de La Salle," p. 279.
§ *Notes et Remarques sur toutes les Villes de la Haute Normandie.* (MS. Bibl. Rouen.)

La Salle was then sick in bed. The grumblers on this occasion were old-time people, who regarded with a suspicious eye all the innovations which this educational genius was making upon their traditional notions of matters pertaining to youth. They deposed before the mayor that the whole management was wrong. The mayor was both timid and prudent. He did not wish to act without advice. The first person to whom he communicated the late deposition, happened fortunately to be President Pontcarré. The latter immediately told him : " Instead of charging others to make an inquiry, let us both go there together ; you will then be able to verify for yourself the facts charged against the institution, and inform yourself of the wise government and prudent economy of the new establishment." They proceeded to the house together, and found the Venerable in his bed, in the most uncomfortable room in the building. It was damp and bare. The only furniture it contained was the bed on which he lay, a table made of deal boards, two chairs and a crucifix. President Pontcarré announced the object of their visit. "You have been deceived, sir," said the Venerable de La Salle to the mayor; "our house is not as badly managed as is represented. All our Brothers are occupied ; but we assign each the office suited to his capacity." After entering into details of the workings of the various departments, he told the mayor to go and see for himself, and judge of the spirit animating pupils and professors. Both visitors went through all parts of the house, and when they returned to the room of the superior, the mayor expressed both astonishment and satisfaction at the order and efficiency with which every part of the varied system was carried out. On their leaving, M. Pontcarré remarked: "Did not I tell you, Mr. Mayor, that you would return from St. Yon much more satisfied than you went there?" * Complaints, thereafter, broke at the feet of this good mayor like waves upon the rock. He had learned more than hearsay : he had seen.

* F. Lucard, " Vie de M. de La Salle," t. ii, p. 5, 2me edition.

St. Yon, even after two centuries, possesses all the traits we give it in the description. During the great Revolution it was confiscated from the Brothers, and is now (1876) used as an insane asylum for women. The Sisters of St. Joseph are in charge, and preserve, as far as possible, the marks of its ancient purposes. The Novices' Chapel is still in a fair state of identity, and the main buildings are intact. The chapel planned by the Venerable, and built by the Brothers, is still in existence.

See plan of the establishment on the following page.

CHAPTER VIII.

Troubles in Paris.—The Writing-Masters.—Parliament refuses to sustain the Venerable's Appeal.—St. Sulpice Schools temporarily closed.—The Brothers return.—Schools in Mende and Alais.—Protestant Scholars received.—Foundations in Grenoble, Valréas and St. Denis.—Brother Joseph named Visitor.—The Venerable visits his Communities.—Assembly at St. Yon.—Brother Gabriel and the Roman Mission.—Famine in 1709.—The Novitiate brought to Paris.—M. Helvetius and the sick Brothers at St. Sulpice.—Brother Barthélemy.—The Brothers in Moulins and Boulogne.—The Abbe-Clement Difficulty.—The Bishop of Avignon.—The Venerable ill at Vans.—FF. Henri and Nicolas.—M. de La Salle returns to Marseilles.

WHILE the Brothers of Rouen, and those of St. Yon in particular, were thus enjoying the most profound peace, their companions in Paris were again the objects of persecution. It was evident that the evil genius of all baleful influences had determined to drive the new teachers from their strongholds in the capital. The more anxious M. de La Salle appeared to secure the perpetuity of these schools, the more unstable seemed the ground upon which they were erected. The reputation which these parochial schools had won, especially that of St. Sulpice, was the great crime for which they were attacked. The writing-masters and their sympathizers believed that it was useless to strive longer in their profession, if the Brothers continued to receive scholars whose parents were not poor, and who otherwise would have been obliged to patronize the secular establishments.

The Brothers' great fault was their success. This the writing-masters could no longer quietly endure. They had recourse to their usual methods, and availing themselves of the plea that the Brothers were not legally recognized, summoned them before the court. La Salle refused to appear, and even disregarded the sentence which had been pronounced against him by the lower court. He instructed his Brothers to continue their classes as usual. This was made an additional crime, and we find the following memorial prepared by the plaintiffs: "They (the Brothers) continued, from the first of September, 1704, to receive the children of the wealthy in various quarters of the city, where they taught these children publicly. The masters of the primary schools declare that this is very prejudicial to their interests; they thus see themselves deprived of their best scholars, the children of distinguished families, which prevents them from earning a livelihood: and this they are willing to declare in open court."

The sympathy which the Brothers had already acquired gave this trial a certain notoriety abroad, and the attorney-general at Paris prepared a paper on such communities as had not received letters-patent. This he presented to Louis XIV.

The enemies of La Salle spoke of him in their memoir as the "so-called superior of the would-be Brothers of the Christian Schools." When Louis XIV asked for information on this point, Cardinal de Noailles was happy to inform the prince that, so far from being an intruder, M. de La Salle had been recognized as superior of a regularly constituted community, since he and his predecessor, Mgr. de Harlay, had approved the society. The appeal which La Salle made to parliament was left for two years without being acted upon, and this gave his disciples some repose. It was during this interval that he set on foot the college and schools of Rouen. But his enemies, fearing that further delay would prove detrimental to their cause, took measures similar to those which they had previously pursued. In the August of 1705 they proceeded in a body to the schools of St. Sulpice; they insulted the Brothers, they drove away every child having an appearance of being possessed of home comforts; they carried away the school furniture, and would even have sold it, were it not for the energetic opposition of the school of St. Placide.* When the Venerable de La Salle, who was then in St. Yon, had read the letter detailing these injuries, he said: "God be blessed. If our work be of men, it will fall; but if it be of God, the world will league against it in vain. Their attacks will but strengthen the foundations, and render its services more durable and efficacious." As soon as he could possibly leave, he hastened to Paris, where his children impatiently awaited him. No sooner had he seen the condition of affairs than he perceived that there was no hope under the circumstances. He had relied upon the pastor of St. Sulpice, as it was from him alone that the Brothers

---

* F. Lucard, "Vie de M. de La Salle," t. i, 2ᵐᵉ edition, p. 221.

held their contested rights; but his efforts in this direction were of no avail. "The Brothers," says F. Lucard, "had for their defence but the affection of their pupils and the confidence of families: glorious and blessed arms, but powerless before the law to deliver them from the hands of enemies thirsting for their destruction."* On the fifth of February, 1706, parliament refused to entertain La Salle's appeal, and forbade him or his disciples to hold any school without the authorization of the inspector of charity schools; thus preventing him from carrying out his intentions, and 'threatening to place the schools, even if continued, under the direction of persons who understood neither the Brothers nor their method, and who were not disposed to understand the one or the other. The Venerable de La Salle had made every sacrifice except that of principle: this he refused to yield. It would have been a violation of the promise he had made never to do anything merely to secure the protection of human authority. The schools of St. Sulpice were therefore closed, over a thousand children were reluctantly sent adrift, and the masters distributed among the various communities, where they were much needed, and in which their assistance was productive of great good.

That the Brothers might not easily return to St. Sulpice, other teachers were sought; but their number was so small, and among these so few gave proof of the zeal and intelligence of those who had a few months previously been allowed to retire, that

---

* F. Lucard, "Vie de M. de La Salle," t. i, 2me edition, p. 222.

a spirit of discontent soon became manifest among
the people. God was also pleased to touch the
heart of M. Chétardie, who had not defended the
Brothers in their late difficulties with all the zeal
that his former energy would have given reason to
expect. He wrote to the Venerable Founder, asking
that all past differences be forgotten, and that the
Brothers be returned to his parish. The latter
was too humble to ask for any further apology, and
he hastened to return the twelve teachers who had
been taken from St. Sulpice. An arrangement was
made by which any further disturbance was prevented. This reopening took place in the month
of October, 1706; and the marks of affection and
gratitude shown by the pupils and their parents
more than compensated for the Brothers' past sufferings. Far from seeking to avoid meeting M. de
La Chétardie, La Salle took the earliest opportunity
to show that he entertained toward him no harsh
feelings. He assisted the Brothers in reorganizing
the classes, and thus proved himself superior to
those little piques and jealousies upon which small
minds feed.

As usual, the Brothers received all scholars that
presented themselves, without asking any questions
as to their position.

" We cannot too highly praise the wise and intelligent firmness displayed by the Venerable in this
delicate affair. It contributed not only to establish
the liberal principle upon which parochial schools
were henceforth to be founded, but, by bringing

about a settlement between the conflicting rights
of pastors and private teachers, constant litigation
was thus brought to a satisfactory termination.
The settlement arrived at was, that in all that referred to parochial schools the masters were to
depend solely upon the pastor." During this time
the institute was establishing itself firmly in other
parts of France. The novitiate at St. Yon received
a large number of postulants, and thus the Venerable Founder was enabled to accede to some of the
many requests he received to send his children into
other dioceses. Among the earliest to receive his
attention was the city of Mende. Mgr. de Piencourt,
bishop of that city, was already in the decline of a
life which had been spent in doing good. Among
the charities that distinguished his administration,
was the foundation of a public hospital. His intelligence and his faith taught him, however, that he had
other obligations, perhaps more pressing than the
care of the bodily wants of his poor. Thus far his
schools had not been a success, and, before leaving
this world, he desired to place them upon a satisfactory basis. He wrote to the Venerable de La Salle,
and in a few days had the happiness of raising his
hands in benediction over the kneeling form of good
Brother Ponce, who was sent to prepare the mission.
Soon after the venerable prelate wrote to the servant
of God in the following terms: " I cannot bless God
too much for having inspired you to train school-
masters to instruct youth, and to form them to
Christian piety. It is impossible to be more contented than we are with the Brother you have sent

us. We would be very grateful if you could send us another, who will be expert in arithmetic and penmanship, for it is thus we hope to attract all the children, and be enabled to give them the first impressions of Christian piety. On my part, they will find all the protection that I can possible give them, so that they will have reason to be quite happy in this city." Two Brothers were sent, and M. de Piencourt had the consolation of seeing his work fairly inaugurated. Fearing that unforeseen circumstances might interfere with the prosperity of the schools after his death, he gave the Brothers a house, and established a fund for their maintenance.

The Brothers were next urgently solicited to establish a school in Alais. This city had been, till within a short time, included in the jurisdiction of the Bishop of Nimes; but Louis XIV, seeing that it was one of the strongholds of heresy, as the best way to counteract the evil, made it an episcopal see. M. Maurice de Saulx, superior of the royal missions, was consecrated its first bishop. It was Innocent XII who sent the Bulls. M. Merez, vicar-general of the new diocese, ably assisted his zealous prelate, and knowing that evil, to be counteracted, must be attacked in its source, resolved to begin with the instruction of the children. After consultation, it was determined to invite M. de La Salle to send some of his disciples. M. Merez had been a college companion of the Venerable Founder, and believed that this would be in his favor. From the letter he sent, we extract this passage: " I do not know if my name is still familiar to you, or if you at all remember me, but I have not forgotten you; and I recollect quite well having seen you at St. Sulpice. You were then a canon of Rheims; this was in 1671. I have learned that you have since resigned your canonry, and that you devote yourself to every good work; and, among others, that you have formed a community of teachers who do much good wherever they are established. They are greatly needed here, where we can scarcely find Catholics to whom we may confide the direction of youth. We desire some sent immediately to Alais. We wish to destroy heresy, and to reëstablish the Catholic religion. The task is great, and we need good laborers. I have recourse to you, and ask for some of your disciples. Père Beauchamp has greatly praised those he has seen in Avignon and in Marseilles."

This letter gave great joy to the Venerable Founder. He perceived that he was still remembered by his schoolmates; and his heart exulted at the thought that his children were invited to take part in the conversion of those who had strayed from the one true fold. He sent two experienced teachers, who were received by M. Saulx, who presided at the opening of the school, in the month of October, 1707. He obtained an annual stipend for them from Louis XIV, and named the humble beginning "The Royal School." In a few months the number of Brothers was increased, and M. Saulx addressed the Venerable de La Salle the following letter: "Your teachers give us every satisfaction. I have the pleasure to thank you for having sent

them, and I wish you to give us a greater number.
I am doing, and will do, all in my power in their
favor, for they are accomplishing incalculable good."

The Brothers of Alais were also given, in their
mission, a very delicate part to perform. The authorities required Calvinist parents to send their
children to the "Christian Schools." The spirit of
the children thus forced to attend classes to which
they and their parents were opposed, may easily be
imagined. The Brothers did all in their power to
lessen the difficulty for their little Protestant friends,
and in a short time had the gratification to learn from
the lips of their former enemies, the Calvinistic
parents, how pleased they were at the progress
their children were making, and with the mild
manner in which they had been treated.

The city of Grenoble was the next field in which
the disciples of La Salle displayed their zeal. An
association, consisting of the principal ecclesiastics
and laymen of the city, determined to secure the
services of the new masters. MM. de Saléon and
Canel were appointed to select the teachers. "We
are certain," said they in reply, "that none will
answer our purposes as well as the Brothers of the
Christian Schools. We have seen the results of
their work at St. Sulpice." Instead of writing,
these two ecclesiastics took the wiser part of seeing
the Venerable de La Salle, who received them very
kindly, gave them a plan for the building which
they agreed to erect, and the two Brothers were
sent in the month of September, 1707, to the great
joy of the parents. As the number of pupils

became too considerable for this establishment, two Brothers were shortly sent to open a school in a different part of the city.

A community was established about the same time at Valréas, and the bishop gave his own residence for the use of the Brothers.* The following year, after reiterated demands, two Brothers were sent to open a school at Saint Denis. Mlle. de Poignant left an annual income in their favor.

To prevent the evils which might arise from so rapid an extension of his society, the Venerable de La Salle appointed Brother Joseph, with the title of Visitor, to inspect the communities of Guise, Rethel, Laon and Rheims. "This Brother loved regularity, good order, the advancement of the Brothers, and the progress of the congregation. Nothing cost him a thought where the glory of God and the good of his Brothers were in question. In 1708, the Venerable de La Salle made the general visitation of his communities of the North. Wherever he went, he was received with the greatest demonstrations of respect and affection. His heart was inundated with holy joy in seeing the virtues of which his disciples gave the example. The servant of God was not satisfied with seeing his disciples in their communities. He profited of the establishment at St. Yon to renew the spirit of fervor and retirement which the troubles in Paris might have disturbed. During the vacations he assembled his Brothers, and for eight days, assisted by several priests who accompanied him, he renewed

---

* Lettre de M. de La Salle à Frère Gabriel.

their fervor by his exhortations, his examples, and the faithful observance of the rule." *

" When the Brothers told him that they feared such great strictness could not be continued in the future, the Venerable replied that he was not responsible for the future, but for the present, and that he was determined to remain faithful till the end. Full of these pious sentiments, he continued his penances and austerities to such an extent, that he was confined to his room with a swelling in the knee. After trying several remedies, it was at length determined to make several incisions, during which operation the courageous sufferer quietly read his breviary as though nothing were taking place." † Brother Gabriel Drolin was the only Thomas in the institute, when the annual retreats occurred ; but his Venerable father did not forget his son in the Eternal City. He kept up frequent correspondence with him, and ever acted as the kindest of fathers toward him. For some time Brother Gabriel had been tutor in the family of M. de La Bussière, but La Salle wished to see him at the head of a numerous class. He wrote, saying that, "after two years spent in Rome," it was time to have established a school. " I will be responsible for the rental of the house which you will occupy as a school till such time as Providence will otherwise provide for you," wrote the solicitous superior. At the same time he sent a sufficient sum to enable his distant disciple to carry out his instructions. In 1705, Brother Gabriel received the direction of a district school,

---

* Ravelet, p. 361.   † P. Maillefer, p. 109.

and the holy Founder, on learning of this, wrote : " Your letter, my very dear Brother, has given me great joy, because it is some time since I have heard from you, and because I find you at length exercising the duties of your vocation. How delighted I am to learn that you have a good number of scholars." * This man of prayer and retiring disposition also found fault with Brother Gabriel for spending the evenings with M. de La Bussière. This, he said, could only tend to keep alive a spirit of vanity and worldliness. In obedience to the remarks thus made, the humble disciple rented a modest little dwelling near the school of which he had charge, and, as usual, he had recourse to the Venerable for the funds to pay the rent. " Though I am far from having money," La Salle replied, " I will do all I can for you, for it grieves me to know that you are obliged to live so poorly. Tell me what I can do to remedy your impoverished condition."

To encourage the somewhat disheartened Brother, his holy father sent him frequent letters, containing intelligence relative to the institute. " They have purchased a very fine house for our Brothers at Avignon, large enough to accommodate twenty persons. The vice-legate is our friend, and sends his page to the Brothers' school. Mgr. the Archbishop of Avignon, nuncio-extraordinary to France, and whom I know very well, has been appointed Archbishop of Genoa, and is to leave immediately for Rome, where he is to receive the cardinal's hat. He has promised me to protect our institute as far

* Arch. du Régime.

as possible." But of all the items of news he sent
his dear friend in Rome, none did he pen with more
real pleasure than the following : " Brother Albert
informs me, from Avignon, that the Father Inquisitor
has returned all our books, after having approved
of them." That, of all things, was a chief cause of
his solicitude. To teach sound doctrine by tongue
and pen was an object of the most scrupulous care
with him. Thus encouraged by the paternal watch-
fulness of the Venerable, Brother Gabriel persevered
in his trying isolation, and ardently sighed for the
day when he might be of service to his society with
the authorities of the Eternal City.

Poor as the Venerable Founder was when he
wrote to Brother Gabriel, he was to experience
not only the want of money, but to see around him
a renewal of the terrible days of famine through
which he and his had passed, when he found so
favorable an opportunity to dispose of his patrimony in behalf of starving thousands.

In 1709, France was visited by one of the heaviest
frosts which, till that time, had been known. The
largest trees were rent asunder ; the most rapid
streams were stopped in their course ; the very sea
was ice-bound for miles along the coasts, and the
fall wheat was killed in its growth. Whole families
were found frozen to death in their dwellings, where,
even beside the brightest fires, the purest liquors
were changed into ice. A terrible famine was the
result ; for, when the spring months came with
their warmth, the sun's rays could not revivify con-
gealed nature. The belligerent forces which then

occupied the frontiers of France, prevented the importation of cereals from the overstocked markets of Holland and Germany; and to add to the distress, many who had laid in a stock previous to the intense colds, refused to dispose of their stores at any price. They hid their treasures, and resisted even the power of Louis XIV, who ordered that all such grain should be disposed of. To allay in part the intense character of the sufferings of the people, the king imported grain from Barbary and the Archipelago. He converted some of his finest dwellings into public bakeries, and sent his costly service to the Bourse. Madame de Maintenon and the ladies of St. Cyr gave a noble example. They contented themselves with the poorest kind of bread, while many rich persons, to imitate the illustrious directress, gave largely of their means. All these efforts, however, were but so many drops taken from the ocean of misery which inundated France. Nobles, even, were seen going through the streets of Paris, pale and famine-stricken, asking an alms, and sometimes, driven by hunger, desperately menacing those from whom they demanded the morsel that was to increase suffering by prolonging life.

In the midst of such heartrending scenes the Venerable de La Salle neither lost his own confidence, nor permitted his disciples to abandon themselves to useless, though well-founded doubts. " Blessed be God, my Brothers!" he cried out. " Is it not His hand that afflicts us? Let our confidence be placed in Him ; we are the children of Providence.

He who cares for the little birds, and who protects the lily of the field, did not abandon us in those other similar days through which we have passed. It is from His divine hands that we will receive our daily bread." In this difficult occasion La Salle thought it prudent to recall his novices to Paris, where he hoped that his old friends would think of them. M. de la Chétardie had procured a suitable dwelling for the Brothers, in 1707, and the holy Founder, after preparing this properly, called Brother Barthélemy and his interesting family to the capital. Several young men asked to be admitted : many through sincere motives, but some, doubtless, to escape the famine. The servant of God admitted them all; and when blamed for this conduct, he exclaimed : " Would it not be cruel to send them away in such calamitous times? If they do not all persevere, they will at least make a good retreat." It was on one of those sad days that he wrote this touching epistle to one of his children who asked him for some little articles to distribute among the best boys of his class :—" I cannot send you any pictures. I have not wherewith to buy bread for forty persons who are now in our house of St. Sulpice !" " Whither are you going?" said a friend who met the man of God one day in the streets of Paris. " Alas ! " said the good priest, " our Brothers have no bread, and we are without money to purchase any. The baker refuses to give us credit : I am going to say Mass, that the good God may take pity upon us." Touched by such a simple and pathetic statement, the generous friend handed him wherewith to meet the wants of the house for a few days. Other alms followed, often from unknown hands, and thus they were saved from perishing. " How could we be abandoned?" he would ask. " Are we not the children of Providence?"

Even in such distress he did not wish the directors to practise a narrow-minded economy. He wrote to one : " I do not think it necessary to retrench the Brothers' breakfast. Here, in Paris, we eat the bread that is given us. The Brothers have half a pound at each meal, and four ounces at breakfast. I am told that in Avignon all the inhabitants are reduced to one pound per day. This allows the Brothers two ounces at breakfast, and five at the other meals. Brother Hubert, the Director of Chartres, kept up his courage till the death of Mgr. de Marais led him to believe that there was no longer possibility of procuring subsistence. He hastened to La Salle, to make known his distressing condition. " Do you believe in the Gospel?" said the holy Founder. " I would willingly give my life to attest my belief," replied the Brother. " Well, then, does the Gospel not say, 'Be not solicitous about the morrow. Seek first the kingdom of God, and all the rest shall be added thereto'?" At these words Brother Hubert felt new confidence revive within him, and he hastened back to his field of labor; and when he arrived, he found that charitable persons had already amply provided what was needed. He afterward remarked that from that time forth his community did not lack the necessaries of life.*

---

*Arch. Com. des Frères de Chartres.

The famine had scarcely ceased to be felt when the Venerable Founder met with a more trying cross in his path. Several of the Brothers of St. Sulpice were attacked with a species of scurvy, which completely disabled them. He hastened to their assistance. Dr. Helvetius again proved himself a warm friend, and the Brothers were soon able to resume their duties.

The joy which their cure caused was soon changed into sadness, for Brother Barthélemy, the Venerable's right arm in the establishment of the rising congregation, was taken seriously ill. This good Brother deserves more than a passing notice here. Born in 1678, at Cambrai, where his father was a schoolmaster, Brother Barthélemy, previously known as Joseph Truffet, at an early age showed that he was destined for some important mission. He made his studies under the Jesuits at Douai, and when he had completed the course, felt himself called to the religious, rather than to the ecclesiastical state. Yet, to give himself time for reflection, he pursued his theology, which he had almost concluded, when he determined to apply for admission to the Trappists. Abbé de Rancé, who was then in charge, received the postulant, but after some trial was obliged to tell him that, though he certainly had a religious vocation, he was not destined to be a Trappist. " You are called," said the reformer of La Trappe, "to do great good in another sphere." It is probable that M. de Rancé advised his young friend to enter the congregation of La Salle; yet, when he was about to apply for admission, he tells us that he felt an almost irresistible antipathy for his future vocation. Finally he overcame himself, entered, and gave such satisfaction that he was named Director of Novices. It was the zeal with which he had cared for the sick that brought upon him the disease under which he was then suffering. Its progress was watched with painful suspense by all the Brothers; and La Salle implored heaven to spare this promising subject to the work that so sorely needed the services of intelligent and true religious.

In the meantime Brother Barthélemy's father died, and his place was offered the son. The physicians advised that the position be accepted. The day had already been fixed for his departure. The evening previous the Venerable de La Salle spent several hours in prayer before the crucifix, and the next day, when the good Brother came, as he thought, to say good-by, what was his agreeable surprise when the Venerable Father said to him: "O my son! remain with us, you will be useful! Heaven wishes you to be a Brother of the Christian Schools." Brother Barthélemy found himself clasped in the arms of the holy Founder, and both shed tears of joy.

Shortly after he entirely recovered his health, and, as the future will show, fully realized the predictions of the Venerable superior. Madame de Maintenon, as we learn from one of de La Salle's letters, occasionally asked him to visit St. Cyr. She could have selected no better adviser. She even wished to confide to him the care of a private school she had opened; but he refused, because the regulation he had then introduced required that at least three Brothers should be sent in each mission. "Communities of two Brothers would destroy our institute," wrote he to the director of Chartres.

The Fathers of the Society of Jesus had, on several occasions, been instrumental in bringing the good done by the Brothers to public attention. Other religious orders were not less generous. In 1710, M. l'Abbé Huchon, Lazarist, and pastor at Versailles, desired to have Brothers. Three were sent, but the number proving insufficient, as many more were obtained. M. Huchon could not be a true disciple of St. Vincent without admiring the spirit and the work of the Venerable de La Salle. He often took occasion to say that he deemed the foundation of the Brothers' school as among the best works of his pastorship. M. Louis Aubery, a zealous abbé, procured similar advantages for the city of Moulins. He gave a very commodious house, which was enlarged; and the generosity of other persons enabled the citizens to open their school on the 8th of May, 1708. The good Abbé Aubery, whose device was "V. J. en M." (*Vive Jesus en Moi*), " Live Jesus in me," undertook the management of the school, but finding that his pastoral duties were incompatible with those of a teacher, he secured the Brothers to succeed him.

L'Abbé Languet de Gery took particular pleasure in listening to the catechism taught by the Brothers, and at his request one of the new teachers consented to give a public instruction to the Sunday-school masters, that these might learn the Brothers' method. Though somewhat out of his proper sphere in a pulpit, and before such a large audience, the good Brother acquitted himself with modest assurance and complete success, and his system was rendered obligatory upon the teachers.

M. de La Cocherie, a gentleman whose large fortune had been almost entirely given to the poor, still possessed wherewith to do some good, and promised that, if Brothers were sent to Boulogne, he would leave an annual rental in their favor. The bishop was then known only by his charities.* He, too, had given his wealth, even his service of silver, to the poor. Under the patronage of these gentlemen and a certain number of friends, the Brothers established a house in Boulogne, which has since been the means of rendering important services to religion. About this time the Abbé Jean Baptiste Clément, son of a distinguished surgeon of Paris, called upon the Venerable, and asked him to take charge of special courses of study which he wished to establish. La Salle received the abbé very kindly, but told him that more good might be done by establishing a training-school for lay teachers. This was an idea he had constantly at heart. It possessed him on all occasions. He was on the continual look-out for an opportunity to realize it on a scale as grand as that on which he had realized his college course. " M. de La Salle never lost sight of this great design, nor despaired of making it a success. He always believed that

---

* He afterward became involved in the meshes of Jansenism.

something would be wanting to his institute, or that it would fail in rendering the Church all the services it should, while it was not raising, for county and city, masters pious and capable of giving youth the instruction and the education necessary for salvation."* At last the pious educator thought his views would be realized beyond all expectation; but Providence had otherwise disposed matters.

The Abbé Clément was at that time about twenty-three years of age; his youth rendered M. de La Salle more than usually prudent, though till this time the abbé had been known as an exemplary person. Of all the benefices attached to his position he accepted but a small sum, instructing his father to dispose of the rest in good works, according to his discretion. But La Salle's deep insight into human nature detected in the abbé's anxiety a certain restlessness of character which was hidden from the latter's own knowledge, as well as from that of the world. He therefore counselled the abbé to wait and pray, and take no step without having calculated the consequences. In the vocabulary of the too zealous abbé there was no such word as calculation. His fancy was all aglow with the project. Already he saw it a grand success; weekly he sent letters to La Salle, urging him to accept the bequest, but he always received the same reply: "Wait, pray, consult."

Thinking that M. de La Salle was unwilling to transact so important an affair with a young man, Abbé Clément sought and obtained the approbation

* Père Blain (1733), "Vie de M. de La Salle," t. ii. p. 56.

of Cardinal de Noailles, who not only approved, but offered a house outside of Paris, in which to open the school. M. Clément preferred one nearer the city, which he purchased; and the Venerable de La Salle, believing that an enterprise approved by his ecclesiastical superiors might be undertaken without further delay, signed an agreement by which the training-school known as St. Denis was opened. Three distinguished teachers were selected by the holy Founder, and the new school was regulated according to the rules in force in other institutions directed by the Brothers. Cardinal de Noailles expressed his great satisfaction at the success this school was attaining; and Abbé Clément was proud of his part in the good work when, quite unexpectedly, a storm came which the passions of the envious had aroused.

The reputation acquired by M. Clément as surgeon had merited for him titles of nobility from Louis XIV. When he consented to receive the honor, the king made but one condition: that he would not abandon his profession. The dignity thus acquired seemed to tell the recipient that he should live in greater splendor than previously; and when he found that his son, the abbé, had appropriated part of the revenues of his benefices to the purposes of a training-school, he broke out into invectives against La Salle. Abbé Clément, far from telling the true condition of matters, pretended that he had been led into the negotiation by La Salle.

Severe laws existed against those who, by dole, fraud or violence, extorted an assignment from beneficiaries, whether these were minors or persons of age : Abbé Clément and his father invoked the force of these laws against M. de La Salle.

The Venerable Founder, equally pained and astonished, prepared a memoir, to which he added thirteen letters that had been written him by the Abbé Clément. These papers he confided to persons in whose good faith and zeal he had confidence, and they promised to protect his interests. He then went upon a visitation of his communities, intending to return to Paris in time for the trial. Though proofs were furnished in these papers that the cardinal had given his approbation, the letters were disregarded, and La Salle, by a strange injustice, which the spirit of Jansenism could alone explain, was condemned to lose a large sum that he had advanced to assist in the founding of the training-school, whereas another party, Rogier by name, was refunded all that he had lent to start the establishment.

When the Abbé de La Salle heard of the monstrous sentence that had been pronounced, he raised his eyes to heaven, and saying, "God be praised!" he continued his labors, leaving to Him who saves the flower from the force of the winds, to dispose of all things as would best please His holy will.

Finding that he was the subject of so many contradictions in Paris, the Venerable Founder had already named Brother Barthélemy as director of the establishments in that city ; and he deemed it better for his institute that he should, for a while, hide himself from enemies who, in attacking him, caused his children also to suffer. He instructed

the new superior to write often, and to let him
know the particulars of whatever might relate to
the communities. Brother Ponce and his *confrères*
received their holy Founder on the 27th of July, 1711.
Marseilles opened its doors to welcome him on the
3d of August, and gave him hospitality till the 1st
of September. Next he visited Avignon, and the
houses of Alais, Vans and Mende.

The Venerable's observations led him to believe
that a novitiate was needed in the south of France,
similar to that of St. Yon. The deliberations and
negotiations for this enterprise, and his projected
voyage to Rome, kept him some time from visiting
Paris. That the institute might not suffer there, he
gave Brother Barthélemy full power to administer
its affairs, and appointed Brother Ponce to visit all
the houses he could not personally inspect.

In 1712 he again visited the Brothers of Avignon.
The visit brought him consolation. He heard
nothing but eulogies of the Brothers. The archbishop used to visit the schools himself, and to spend
whole hours in listening to the lessons that were
given, and watching the orderly manœuvrings of
the scholars. At other times he would invite the
children to his residence, to compete for the rewards
he took pleasure in distributing. As the Brothers
narrated all these incidents to their venerated general, his countenance beamed with joy, and the sight
was more encouraging to them than his words of
unction.

While in Avignon, a young Brother who taught
the primary class fell sick. " Rest yourself," said the

charitable superior; "I will teach your class:" which he did, to the great edification of all the Brothers and of several ecclesiastics. And the Brother of Avignon, who transmitted to us this edifying trait, adds that each time a Brother fell sick the Venerable Founder taught his class.*

In spite of the fears expressed by the Brothers, M. de La Salle departed, to expose himself to the insults and even personal injury frequently inflicted by the maurauding bands that then infested the roads and by-ways between the large cities.

"God be blessed!" said he. "Providence, that protected me against the wicked last year, will again take me safely to our good Brothers of Alais, Vans and Mende."

When he arrived at Vans he was quite ill; his feet were greatly swollen, for he had passed through a hilly country, whose roads at best were extremely severe upon pedestrians. The regularity and piety which he found at Vans repaid the pain incurred in the visitation. Mgr. Poncet, the Bishop of Uzes, was so pleased with the Brothers that he desired their Founder to attach them irrevocably to the school of Vans. This he could not promise to do. It was contrary to the spirit of the religious order of which these good Brothers were worthy members. It would be doing them an injustice. La Salle showed the good bishop that the event of a change was not calculated to injure the schools as much as his fears represented. "Formed," said he, "in the same spirit, initiated from the novitiate in the knowledge

---

* *Rép. à un Memoire, etc. (Arch. Dép. de Vaucluse.)*

and practice of the same method, the Brothers, in succeeding one another in class, will offer, as masters, no other essential difference than that resulting from their personal character. Their dealings with the pupils, the programme of teaching, and the means of emulation, are the same; the real differences might occur in their mode of application; but these are so merged in identity of mind and views that they often escape the observation of the scholars. A few days suffice to accustom them to a new master." The bishop was satisfied with this reasoning. At the request of his lordship, the Venerable taught school a few days at Uzes, to initiate the young ecclesiastic who was then in charge of the children into his method. The zealous educator gladly complied. The tradition of his teaching still exists at its scene.

Brothers Henri and Nicolas. who directed the Christian School of Mende, next were favored with their holy superior's company. These disciples deserved to have it recorded of them that "they were the most famous teachers, and those under whom the children made greatest progress." At Mende each worthy person vied with his neighbor in the honors paid to the Founder of the Brothers of the Christian Schools. While enjoying the quiet hospitality of the good people of Mende, he was unexpectedly called to Marseilles. He promised to return soon. A school had been lately established for young Protestant converts, and he was consulted upon the rules and methods best calculated to make it succeed.

CHAPTER IX.

Mgr. de Belzunce.—The Jansenists seek to bribe the Venerable.—Brother
Timothy.—Novitiate in Marseilles.—M. de La Salle persecuted.— He
prepares a Memoir.—Desires to visit Rome.—Love for the Holy
Father.—A Jesuit defends the Venerable's Cause.—Charity for the
Fallen.—The Dominicans welcome the Venerable.—The City of Mende
calls the holy Founder.—The Brothers of Grenoble.—Brother
Hilarion.—Père Blain, Chaplain at St. Yon.—M. de Brou interferes
with the Brothers in Paris.—The Venerable teaches School.—He
revises School-books.—Frère Irénée.

In Marseilles the Venerable de La Salle was also
edified and delighted with the good his Brothers
were effecting. Mgr. de Belzunce, whom Pope calls
" Marseilles' good bishop," * directed the church of
this ancient city, and under his zealous administration heresy, which had made such sad ravages
elsewhere, found little opportunity to spread. He
received La Salle with affection and respect, recog-
nizing in him a saint and an educational genius. It
was then that the Jansenists, seeing the influence
which M. de La Salle possessed, thought of ensnar-
ing him. But they proceeded so stealthily that their
intentions were for some time concealed from him.
They protested that the time had come for the
establishment of a novitiate in Provence, in order

---

* " Why drew Marseilles' good bishop purer breath,
　　When nature sickened, and each gale was death? "
　　　　　　　　　　　　　Essay on Man, iv, 107-8.

that subjects for the order might be educated, who, knowing the manners of the Provençal youth, would all the more easily succeed in instructing them. This was a sentiment in accordance with the Venerable Founder's own desires. He sent for Brother Timothy, one of his most experienced disciples, who was then director of Chartres, to govern the new establishment. This Brother was a man of lively faith and sterling virtue. The circumstances under which he went to Chartres were characteristic of the man. Having suffered for some time from a gathering at the knee, the surgeon opened it, but seeing the irritated condition of the flesh, gave little hopes of a cure. La Salle wished to send his ailing disciple as director to Chartres. He expressed his regret to Brother Timothy that his sore knee prevented him from going, whereupon the latter, in his childlike faith, said : "Bless my knee, and I shall start for my new destination." Though confused at the remark, the holy Founder consented, and the Brother left for his mission. When he reached Chartres he uncovered the knee to dress the wound, and to his surprise found the wound no longer existed. There was not the slightest trace of infirmity upon the left knee; it was quite as strong and free from pain as the right. "Then," adds Brother Timothy, in his account of this occurrence, "I was convinced that God had healed me through the touch, the blessing and the prayers of my worthy superior." * Called to Marseilles, he devoted his whole time and attention to the formation of the

* "Vie M. de La Salle," t. ii, p. 496. (1733.)

postulants, many of whom were sent by the secret partisans of Jansenism.

He explained the spirit in which they should strive to become good Brothers of the Christian Schools, and also fully dilated upon the questions they would be required to answer before receiving the holy habit. They were to state that they had entered of their own free-will; that no constraint had been used; that they believed themselves called to the Brotherhood; that they knew the rules, understood them, and were resolved to fulfil them. Apparently all went well. As La Salle became known, he was all the more appreciated by the people. They flocked around him for advice. The good bishop requested him to exercise the priestly functions in Marseilles. He even gave him power to absolve reserved cases. The saintly servant of God devoted what remained of his time not required by the duties incident upon the governing of his congregation, to the work of preaching, hearing confessions, and giving spiritual advice to the people. He everywhere did good. No one seemed more ardent admirers of the new apostle than those who sought to ensnare him. In proportion to the secret hate that rankled in their hearts, was their praise loud. Finally they grow weary of concealing their motives, and resolve to show their true colors. They agree to hold a conference, in which the disputed points of doctrine are to form the principal theme. At first guarded in their expressions, these disciples of error gradually unmasked themselves; they openly derided what they were pleased to call the blind zeal of the good bishop, and, to give coloring and effect to their arguments, they presented the Founder of the Brothers of the Christian Schools as one of their number: "For," said they, "does he not admit as much by assisting at our solemn discussions?" This was insulting, but not surprising, to the servant of God. Without a moment's hesitation he arose, and in language borrowed from the purest sources, and an eloquence that the occasion created, he proved the fallacy of the position which he had just heard assumed. Never had he felt the importance of not being misunderstood more than on the present occasion, and never were his enemies worse confounded. They were surprised at his manly defence. He did honor to the title of which he was so proud, and with which he always gloried in signing documents, namely, that of *Roman Priest.*

Then it was that his would-be friends thought of bribing the man they could not deceive. This goes to show how little they knew of his character. He who had voluntarily left a canonry to condemn himself to a life of labor among children, was not likely to be bought with the promise of dignity. He rejected with holy disdain the offer of a mitre, which, had he accepted in this case, would have crowned a traitor's head.*

M. de Bonald, one of the greatest thinkers of this

* "I certify to all whom it concerns that in the year 1712 our most Venerated father, M. J. B. de La Salle, Founder of the Brothers of the Christian Schools, assured me, from his own mouth, that it only depended upon himself to be bishop, which he generously refused, because those who made this offer were entirely opposed to the Constitution, and thereby wished to enlist his sentiments in their favor."—*Attestation du F. Bernard, 6 Mai,* 1742.

age, in speaking of the congregation founded by M. de La Salle, has said : " The Institute of the Brothers of the Christian Schools is a masterpiece of wisdom and of the knowledge of men." * The Jansenists thought otherwise as soon as they ceased to hope that M. de La Salle could be secured to their party. They did all in their power to destroy the schools; but they directed their attacks principally against the novitiate. They sought to withdraw the young men from it ; they told them that they had deceived them at first; they said they did not like to see them subject to a man whose ideas were so narrow, and whose will was so perverse. " Your novitiate," they added, " is only a cold grave; you ought not to bury in it your youth, without profit for yourself and utility for your neighbor." † When such proceedings failed of their full effect, they had recourse to calumny. Never was printing put to a more infamous purpose. They prepared a libellous pamphlet, in which the faith and even the character of M. de La Salle were misrepresented. This they circulated far and wide. They hoped to be able to force him to quit the city : his retirement they would have regarded as equivalent to a victory. The Venerable de La Salle would willingly have suffered his character to be maligned, and said nothing about it, but he owed it to the faith he professed, to the institute he directed, and to the Brothers who composed it, to defend himself and his doctrine. He therefore prepared a memoir, in which, while speaking mildly

---

* *Théorie de l'Ordre Social*, l. i, c. xx.
† F. Lucard, " Vie de M. de La Salle," t. ii, p. 17, 2ᵐᵉ edition.

of the character of his maligners, he tore their doctrinal errors to shreds. His victory was complete. His friends, who had known him principally because of his virtues, now found, to their great delight, that he was one of the ablest, though most modest champions of the Church against the errors of Jansenism and its hypocritical followers.

Rather than betray his faith, the Venerable preferred to forego the permanency of his novitiate, the opening of many schools, and the friendship of unfortunate but powerful persons who were either to be his masters or his persecutors. But the scene of all these sufferings afterward became the theatre of brilliant success for the Brothers. "Future years," says a biographer, "repaid the ill-treatment of the Venerable's early trials in Marseilles: few cities have since done more for the institute."*

Such difficulties as we have been narrating are the food upon which great men, in a Christian sense, live : this being admitted, great indeed must have been the force of character possessed by the Venerable de La Salle. But while he was prepared to suffer without a murmur so long as persecution touched but his own person, his tender love for the Brothers, the desire he had to see them in the enjoyment of that peace which was so necessary for them,—all these sentiments made him wish to shield his children from further persecution by removing what, in his humility, he believed was the cause of all their trials. He had already said that his children, like the subjects of David, were punished for the

---

* De Montis, p. 137.

sins of their master. He now felt that, if he would retire for a time, the storm might pass over, and, forgetting the chief object of attack, his enemies would cease to annoy the disciples. Moreover, the Venerable's heart was constantly turned toward Rome. Where could he better pour forth the anguish of his soul than at the tomb of the apostles? Who would give him better advice and encouragement than the supreme shepherd, the vicar of Christ upon earth? As early as 1694 he had taken counsel with the principal members of the society, and had determined that the benefits already conferred upon religion, and the results to be hoped for in the future, justified the Brothers in the hope that the Holy Father would deem the institute worthy of official recognition. It had, indeed, been approved by several bishops, but this was limited to the extent of the dioceses over which these prelates presided. The law of the Church, moreover, allowed none save the Sovereign Pontiff to give an absolute recognition: such as might be accorded by individual prelates was always subject to the revisal and sanction of his Holiness.* The Brothers and their holy Founder had also decided, in this assembly of 1694, to establish a school in Rome: thus they hoped to impregnate the entire institute with that vigorous sap that is drawn from the source and root of all religious communities.

"I wished," said the holy Founder, "to plant the tree of our society, and to make it take root; to graft

---

* This was decreed in the Council of Lateran, held under Innocent III. It was renewed by Gregory X.

it at the centre of unity, under the shadow and the auspices of the successor of the Prince of the Apostles. I also desired to open a path by which I might be led to the feet of the Sovereign Pontiff, to ask the approbation of our rules and constitutions; to obtain for our Brothers the privilege of making the three vows of religion ; to beg the representative of Jesus Christ to bless our institute, and to give it, in his own words, the mission to teach Christian doctrine, according to the good pleasure, and with the permission, of the bishops." *

Brother Gabriel had already spent several years alone near the tombs of the apostles. The Venerable de La Salle felt that so faithful a son should be allowed once more to embrace his father; and his kindness of heart suggested that he should rather go to his child than call him from the field of his labor. Age was beginning to tell upon this pioneer of the institute. He had proved his fidelity in time of trial. He became known in Rome as " a learned and serious man." Some priests who knew his ability urged him to continue the theological studies he had commenced before entering the society, but he refused ; and his conduct, while left alone in his distant mission, had added to the love which his Venerable superior already entertained for him. It was natural that two hearts, knowing how to love as they knew how to suffer, should desire to interchange the varied experiences of their respective careers. These and similar considerations impelled the Venerable de La Salle toward Rome.

---

* " Vie," par Père Blain, t. i, p. 392.

When it was suggested to the Venerable de La Salle that he might use certain influences in the Eternal City to secure the approbation of his society, he promptly replied: "I do not like such human views; they are not the means which the saints would employ."

He had prayed long, before deciding upon this journey, and he took passage in a vessel then bound for Civita Vecchia. This was in 1712. He had taken leave of the archbishop, and proceeded to the boat, happy as a child going to throw himself into the arms of a long-absent father. Scarcely had he arrived at the quay when he perceived Mgr. de Belzunce coming toward him. "Do not go," said this prelate; "there is a certain person who desires to establish a school, and to place its direction in your hands. I desire you to remain to set it going, and place good masters at the head." La Salle was a man to do the good that offered itself at the moment, and leave to the future to deal with possible prospective good. He was emphatically a doer, and not a dreamer. In the present instance he adhered to his principle of action. "God be blessed!" said he, turning to the Brothers who had come to see him off; and he remarked, to their great surprise: "Behold me back from Rome! It is not God's will that I should go there, since He wishes to employ me at something else." He forthwith allowed the Brother whom he was taking to assist Brother Gabriel, to go alone, while he quietly returned to his community, and thought no more, for the time being, of his projected voyage.

" I wished to visit you," he wrote afterward to Brother Gabriel ; " I was even ready to depart with a M. Ricordeau, Canon of Troyes, who left for Rome a month ago. But I was detained by a pressing affair which, nevertheless, has not since prospered."*

The Venerable had made a great sacrifice in not visiting Rome, but his reward was in the contentment of a will freely resigned to that of God. The new mission which the Archbishop of Marseilles wished to confide to him was to have been opened through the generosity of a rich lady, who, influenced by the enemies of M. de La Salle, suddenly declared that she had changed her intentions. A learned Jesuit preacher determined to remedy this defection. He eloquently pleaded the cause of Christian education, and succeeded in bringing together quite a number of subscribers to the praiseworthy cause. But it sufficed that a Jesuit should have espoused the undertaking, to arouse the hatred of the Jansenists. By their artful deception and their seductive manners they sowed dissension among the subscribers, and the enterprise failed. It was the greatest praise for any society, in those days, to find its sons opposed by the followers of

---

* *Lettres du Venerable.*—Providence seems to delight in those contrasts that show how different are His ways from those of men. Brother Gabriel, in the days of which we write, was scarcely able to procure the bread that preserved his devoted life ; the society of which he was a member seemed to be the only one that was unnoticed by the Holy Father. In our day, while the Divine will has permitted the most solidly established communities to be driven from their retreat, and their properties turned into values wherewith to swell the public revenues, the Brothers have been spared their five schools in Rome, while a sixth is on the point of being opened at the private expense of the Holy Father, whose predecessors, in 1731, had founded a Brothers' school in Avignon.

Jansenism. The good Jesuit had the honor of dividing the contumely of the enemies of the Church with the Abbé de La Salle.

While at Marseilles, the Venerable Founder gave a striking proof of his goodness of heart and his charity for the fallen. A young Brother who had taught school with great success at Calais for five years, having been sent to Grenoble, became disgusted with his state, and when called upon to remove to another community, set out apparently with the intention of complying with the demands of his superior. On the way, he threw off his religious dress, and reëntered the world, which delayed not to make him feel the bitterness of the cup of pleasure that he had placed to his lips. Stung with remorse, and with the falsity of human enjoyments, he came to Marseilles, where, casting himself at the feet of his injured father, he begged to be again received. Touched with his contrition, the good superior took back this prodigal, and, having made him pass through some months of trial, sent him to Mende, where he fully realized the expectations that had been entertained of him.

The Venerable de La Salle having taken all necessary precautions to secure the work that had been so painfully, though successfully, begun in Marseilles, desired to visit his other communities; but, before doing so, he determined to pass some days in retreat in the very spot rendered famous by the thirty-three years' penance of Mary Magdalen. He was received with much kindness by the Dominican fathers who then had charge of the pilgrimage, and from them he received examples of silence and regularity which he often afterward spoke of with many marks of admiration.

While he was thus enjoying the sweets of contemplation, his children in Marseilles were attacked with renewed fury by the Jansenists, who pretended that the Venerable had abandoned his Brothers. Pilgrims, who returned about that time from Sainte-Baume, dispelled the impression which such reports were likely to produce. They declared that he was spending some days in prayer, and that his presence in the midst of his disciples, within a very short time, would prove that his heart and his hand were still in the good work. In confirmation of their words, M. de La Salle's speedy return silenced the calumniators, and prevented any further injury being done his character.

These continued persecutions made the Venerable think for a time it would be necessary to withdraw the Brothers from Marseilles. Before doing so, he determined to consult M. Baumer. This learned and holy priest was then spiritual director of a pious young girl who had received special favors from God. When he was consulted by M. de La Salle he asked for time to deliberate, and in the meanwhile consulted his holy penitent. " How can I tell you anything about M. de La Salle?" said she to her confessor. " I have never seen him." " You will see him to-morrow," M. Baumer replied. " Go to the Mass said for the school-children; you will receive holy communion from the hands of M. de La Salle, who says that Mass, and afterward you will tell me what God shall make known to you concerning him." She did so, and on her return said to her director: "Tell M. de La Salle not to think of withdrawing his Brothers from Marseilles: they are now as an imperceptible grain of mustard-seed, but they will become very numerous, and will produce abundant fruits." Encouraged by such words, La Salle told his disciples to be patient and confident. Brother Timothy continued the novitiate, and he proceeded on his tour of visitation.

Mende at this time was the scene of a very interesting work, which the Venerable de La Salle had promised to encourage. A number of good ladies had established a school for the instruction of young converts. Mlle. de Saint Denis was the directress. This work, in which La Salle took great interest, occupied his attention for some weeks. He drew up for the teachers a rule of life which the bishop approved and praised. He saw it practised by the ladies who were assisting Mlle. de St. Denis, and was witness of the fruits produced in the school by the new rule of order and regularity. This was to him a source of gratification. But he was soon to find cause for other feelings. One day, as he was about to leave Mende, Brother Timothy arrived there most unexpectedly. His sad expression of countenance foreboded unwelcome intelligence from Marseilles. "Where are your novices? Does our work still stand?" said the superior all at once. The answer of Brother Timothy confirmed his suspicions: "These men you know of," said he sorrowfully, "snatched from the threshold of the novitiate the young men who came to us with a sincere vocation. . . . Seduced by their protectors, those you left are no longer your disciples." " God be blessed!" replied the Founder; and after having detained Brother Timothy for some days with him, he sent him to Avignon, to replace Brother Ponce. He himself set out for Rouen. When leaving Mende, Mlle. de St. Denis presented him with a horse to pursue his journey with, as he was at this time in feeble health. He accepted the present with gratitude, as a means of sooner reaching his dear St. Yon. However, he found some inconvenience in taking care of the horse. Once he alighted to say his Office, and allowed the animal to graze in an open field. The latter strayed into the garden of a rough farmer, who, coming out, overwhelmed La Salle with abuse, and gave him a blow. The man of God immediately threw himself on his knees, and asked pardon of his brutal assailant for having involuntarily caused him pain. Astonished at this humility, the farmer muttered some words of excuse, and went off as confused as he was edified.* Upon his return to St. Yon, the Venerable sent Brother Barthélemy to visit many of the communities.

In 1714 the Brothers of Grenoble, who were supported by contributions annually given by certain intelligent and pious persons, began to feel the result of a falling-off of the interest which had, at first, been shown by some of their patrons. The bishop, to remedy this, took the committee of subscribers under his special protection, and knowing

---

* F. Lucard, "Vie de M. de La Salle," t. ii, p. 98, 2ᵐᵉ edition.

the eloquence and piety of M. de La Salle, invited
him to be present at one of the public meetings.
The latter acquiesced ; and the result of the address
which he made was the rekindling of the enthusiasm
that had previously marked the zeal of the founders.

While in Grenoble the Venerable was consoled,
also, by the intelligence that peace had been
restored to his children in Provence. Though he
would have desired to rejoice with them, he felt
that prudence required him to abstain from seeing
them.*   It was on this occasion that he appointed
Brother Timothy visitor.   Brother Bernardin succeeded him as director at Alais.

At this time, also, he received a very touching
proof of the love entertained for him by the
Brothers of St. Yon. Knowing the poverty of the
houses, and that their holy Founder needed many
little attentions and comforts, rendered necessary
by the enfeebled condition of his health, they sent
him a considerable sum with which to provide himself with what might be necessary in his journeys.
However, he would accept of no such immunity, but
deposited the amount with reliable parties in Rouen,
till called for. " Perhaps," adds F. Lucard, " he was
already thinking of acquiring for his novitiate and
college the vast property of St. Yon."† The thought
was worthy of his generous soul, ever leaving itself
out of consideration, ever mindful of others. Thus
he renounced the means of rendering himself necessary cares and attentions, that he might purchase a
home for the young and a retreat for the aged.

* Vie P. Maillefer.   † Loc. cit., p. 106.

Père Blain, afterward the historian of the Venerable de La Salle, was appointed spiritual director of the boarding-school and of the community, in the absence of the Founder. He was a man of rare prudence, and acquired the confidence of all the Brothers by the wisdom shown in his acts. He had been renowned in his day as being an able preacher. On every great occasion he was the orator of the day. But that for which he is especially remembered with esteem by the Brothers, is the perfect manner in which he understood his real relations toward the community as its spiritual director. " He never meddled in the government of the Brothers of St. Yon ; he made to their institutions only those visits authorized by his charge; his relations with the community always took the character of a discreet and prudent sympathy."* A little incident is told, that shows his good-natured disposition. One day, as he entered the garden, Brother Hilarion, who had been porter for several years, noticed that the good abbé was about to enter the walk known as the president's. " You must not go there," said the Brother ; " our superior has reserved that for M. Pont-Carré, who will be here shortly, and I have orders to see that no one disturbs him." Far from being offended at this prohibition, M. Blain said with a smile : " Do not be afraid ; the president and I are good friends. My company will not be disagreeable to him."

Brother Hilarion was one of those noble characters who find no sacrifice too great when there

* F. Lucard, "Vie de M. de La Salle," t. ii, p. 108, 2ᵐᵉ edition.

is question of saving their souls.   At first the father
of a numerous family, he entered the society shortly
after the death of his wife.   His oldest son had
already preceded him, and now another followed
his example.   A daughter of his also received the
grace of a religious vocation, and was placed by
the Venerable de La Salle in a convent in Paris,
where she led a most edifying life.

In entering religion, Frère Hilarion found himself
under the direction of his own child, Brother Dominic.   After his novitiate, he was, in 1708, named
porter of St. Yon.   He had been there till 1713,
when Brother Barthélemy sent him an order to
proceed to Guise.   Though he might have claimed
exemption from this change, he started afoot for his
new mission.   He remained but one day in Paris, to
receive Brother Barthélemy's instructions.   When
he had nearly reached his new home, he was taken
ill; a sudden weakness took possession of all his
members; he asked for the last sacraments, which
he received with a rare piety, and died, repeating
these beautiful words: "I die happy, since I leave
this world in the very act of accomplishing the will
of God."   The death of this edifying old man was a
source of grief to the Venerable de La Salle.   He
reproved Brother Barthélemy for what he considered his imprudence; but the latter replied that the
Brother had given no indications of fatigue when at
Paris.   "His death," added he, "was the fruit of
a heroic virtue, of which the saints themselves offer
few examples."   Another loss distressing to La Salle
was that of Brother Placide.   He died at the early

age of twenty-three.   Brother Barthélemy says of him : " Our good Brother died as he had lived.   His peculiar virtues were : great horror of the world, love of retirement, openness of heart to his superiors, admirable obedience and regularity, modesty, patience, and most edifying union with the Brothers."

Intelligence of a more grievous nature reached the Venerable from Paris.   The deaths of an aged saint and of a young martyr to the cause of Christian education were rather subjects of joy than of sadness; but M. de La Salle now learned that his dear disciples were again the object of persecution from the numerous enemies he had left there.   The writing-masters had once more attacked the schools ; they reiterated the calumnies which the Venerable de La Salle had so triumphantly refuted.   The lieutenant-general of police sent a subordinate to Brother Barthélemy, empowered to make inquiry into the facts alleged.   " The wisdom of Brother Director's replies, and the admirable management of the schools, turned these proceedings to the glory of the Institute of the Brothers."*   But another complication arose which was not so easily unravelled.   During La Salle's absence M. de La Chétardie had obtained the appointment of M. de Brou as the spiritual director of the community. Cardinal de Noailles, in making the nomination, had no idea of interfering with the authority of M. de La Salle, who was always recognized by the ecclesiastical powers as the lawful and only superior. It was not long previously that the cardinal had

---

‡ F. Lucard, " Vie de M. de La Salle," t. ii, p. 110, 2ᵐᵉ edition.

expressed his sympathy and good-will toward the Brothers, at a time, too, when he was surrounded by clergy, some of whom he knew had little good to say of them or their superior. After the Brothers had spoken some words of respect and esteem, he delivered a eulogy, within hearing of all present, upon the life and virtues of La Salle. "Say to him," he added, "that he always has my esteem; he is a holy man; I recommend myself to his prayers." This was at St. Denis, on the occasion of a confirmation. The croakers and buzzers frowned, and the Brothers retired, glad at heart. La Chétardie, who still felt somewhat ill-disposed against the holy Founder, encouraged de Brou to go further than the cardinal had intended, and even succeeded in having priests appointed over several communities, notably those of Rouen, Chartres and Moulins.

M. de La Salle was written to on the subject, but many of the letters did not reach him. In these he was accused of having abandoned his Brothers, and his motives of inaction questioned, when such a crisis was going on. The fact was, he knew nothing whatever of the matter.

The cardinal, who had received one lesson, did not desire another. "He blamed M. de Brou's temerity, and he showed his esteem for M. de La Salle by declaring that he wished nothing changed in the order which the servant of God had established." * As soon as Brother Barthélemy had learned the real nature of M. de Brou's mission, he was urgent upon the Founder's returning to Paris. Instead of

---

* Père Maillefer, "Vie de M. de La Salle."

adding to the difficulty by appearing upon the scene of trouble, the latter sent the director of Grenoble, a pious, learned and experienced Brother. His instructions being faithfully followed, the clouds dispersed, and peace again reigned among the children of the holy Founder.

The attempt to weaken authority in the society was strangled in its birth, and the integrity of the institute was preserved.

As the Venerable had frequently done before, he took charge of the class taught by the Brothers he had sent to Paris. When the new master took his children to Mass, the people were heard to say : " Let us go to church ; the holy priest is going to say Mass." " These words," says a venerable Brother who had learned the circumstances,—" these words were repeated to me by old men who had been pupils of M. de La Salle." *

On the days that the Venerable did not teach class there was a holy rivalry between the Sisters of the Visitation and the canons of the church in Grenoble, as to who would have the happiness of hearing his Mass. As often as duty would permit, the holy servant of God gratified the pious wishes of the daughters of St. Francis de Sales.

As soon as the director of Grenoble had returned, the Venerable de La Salle hastened to steep his soul in the delights of solitude, by retiring for some time to the Grande Chartreuse, which had been rendered

---

Déposition du Frère Patrice. This worthy Brother was born in 1760; he was educated in the Brothers' College of Montpelier, and entered the Novitiate of Avignon in 1777.

illustrious by the life and virtues of the sons of St Bruno.   Some of the good fathers of that monastery who had been witnesses of his austerities, and appreciated his virtue, solicited him to take up his abode with them.   But his mission was elsewhere. Still, long after his death, the tradition of his visit to the Grande Chartreuse remained.   When Brother Patrick and his director went there to spend a few days in retreat, they were told that the lapse of sixty-six years had not dimmed the lustre of the good name their Venerable Founder had left among them.

Upon his return to the community of Grenoble, the Venerable de La Salle spent some time in revising the books he had prepared for his schools.

It was about this time also that the servant of God received a subject who was afterward to give lustre to his name as a Brother, and to the society that received him.

Abbé de Saléon, whose name has already occurred in these pages, was quietly pursuing the duties of his pastorate at Parmenie, when he one day noticed a noble-looking pilgrim approaching.   Under the simple garb of a traveller, the young man evidently hid a proud title and a checkered career.   He recognized the pilgrim as Dulac, son of Claude Lancelot de Montisambert.   This young man had entered the army at the age of fifteen, and had added to the risks of a career dangerous in itself by giving full bridle to all his passions.   His love of gambling had already caused serious losses, when his parents placed him in a regiment, the officers of which were special friends of the family. The battle of Malplaquet was the occasion that Providence took to recall the young soldier to a sense of duty. Severely, though not fatally, wounded, he was tenderly cared for, and during his illness was given the " Lives of the Saints " to read. Like another Ignatius, he asked himself why he could not be a Christian hero. Grace spoke the answer to him; the young officer became a changed man; he daily grew more and more disgusted with the world. Dulac, after eight years' service, and without notifying his parents, retired from the army. He sold his horse, left his uniform in his bedroom, and with a single suit, which on the way he exchanged with a beggar, departed for Grenoble. Away from all who knew him, he began a life which was the astonishment of the beholders, so severe were its austerities, so numerous its acts of humiliation. Visiting the sick was his chief delight. At the foot of the altar he acquired the strength necessary for his new career. He afterward applied for admission among the children of St. Bruno, and again among those of St. Francis. In both houses he was told that his vocation was elsewhere. He had just made a pilgrimage to Rome, having begged his bread both in going and returning, when, on reaching Parmenie, he was to learn the long-sought object of his life.

When the Venerable de La Salle was told by the Abbé de Saléon that he believed Dulac called to become a Brother of the Christian Schools, the holy Founder feared that the erratic life previously led by the young convert should prevent him from persevering. However, after conversing some time with the pilgrim, and having explained the principal duties of the life of a Brother. he told him to retire to a cell for some days, and to pray that divine light might lead him out of darkness.

The generous penitent, prostrating himself before a crucifix, begged his Saviour to give him strength to imitate his pious aunt, who had devoted " the flower of her youth" * entirely to the instruction of the poor and the ignorant. As soon as the Venerable de La Salle entered his cell, Dulac, in a most imploring and sincere petition, begged to be admitted as a member of the society. " It is to labor with you in your institute that I am called by heaven; I wish to do penance for my sins, and to prevent children from becoming victims to passions which, alas! have had such sway over me." La Salle was touched with his tears and urgent solicitations.

" God's holy name be blessed !" said he ; " you will be a Brother of the Christian Schools. Heaven wishes you amongst us : you will do much good."

The director of Grenoble was charged with the formation of the new disciple. The long and beautiful curls that had been so much admired, were cut off; Dulac was vested in the habit of the Christian Brother, and edified the people of Grenoble by a most mortified life, under the name of Brother Irénée. His great request was "to pray for him." The Venerable assured him that the Brothers would not

* Inscription over Françoise Dulac de Montisambert. She died 1704, in the thirtieth year of her age, " distinguished by the ancient nobility of her family, her grace and beauty, but still more recommendable by her intelligence and rare piety."

fail in this religious duty. "By his fidelity in following the advices of the holy Founder, Brother Irénée became one of the most useful members of the Society;" from the day of his admission he had been among the most edifying.

CHAPTER X.

The Bull *Unigenitus.*—The Venerable recalled to Paris.—His Reception.—Death of M. de La Chétardie.—Louis XIV and his Age.—The Novices return to St. Yon.—Chevalier d'Armstadt.—His Trials.—The Venerable returns to St. Yon.—Visited by distinguished Persons.—He Visits Calais.—Devotion to Mary Immaculate.—His Portrait secured.—Resigns the Generalship.—Brother Barthélemy elected.—Assistant Superiors named.—The School's Conduct.—Method introduced by the Venerable de La Salle.—His views.—How to direct and to interest Children.

WE have seen the zeal with which the Venerable de La Salle defended Catholic doctrines, and the magnificent offers he so promptly rejected when they were to be obtained at the price of infidelity. His conduct, when the Bull *Unigenitus* was published, is another striking proof of his attachment to the See of Peter.

M. de Montmartin, whose orthodoxy thus far was beyond suspicion, issued a pastoral in connection with the Bull *Unigenitus;* and the Venerable de La Salle, who was celebrating the feast of St. Joseph with his Brothers of Grenoble, received a copy. He immediately assembled his community, read the two documents, and added such explanations as he deemed necessary under the circumstances. Moreover, not satisfied with this manifestation of loyalty, he published several articles in defence of the true doctrine. This irritated the Jansenists anew, but their opposition only served to give greater lustre to the purity and zeal of their opponent.

While thus employed in defending the Church, his disciples in Paris, St. Yon and Rheims, were anxious for his return. Brother Barthélemy, who knew the great virtue of his superior, availed himself of an innocent device to secure his presence in the capital. He prepared a document in which, in the name of the Brothers, he called upon the Venerable Founder to return to Paris, where he was needed to look after the interests of the institute. " Sir," said the good Brother, " we humbly beseech you, and we ordain in the name and on the part of the body of the society to which you have promised obedience, that you immediately take upon yourself the general direction of the society. In testimony of which we have signed. Done at Paris, April 1st, 1714." *

The Venerable de La Salle was still governing the society through Brothers Barthélemy, Joseph, and Timothy, visitors. Hence the form of command taken by Brother Barthélemy was merely a fiction which he employed more certainly to secure the attention of the holy Founder, who, in his humility, thus had the pleasure of obeying his own children.

His departure from Grenoble was a triumph. Every one sought to give him renewed marks of appreciation. Before leaving for Paris, he resolved to visit his Brothers of Marseilles and Avignon. Next he went to Lyons, remained there a few days, and then made a pilgrimage to the tomb of St.

---

* Père Blain.

Francis de Sales. At Dijon he met several friends, whose delight it was to manifest their esteem for his disciples. At Rheims he stopped some time to consult with Brother Joseph, whose wisdom was afterward to secure his appointment as assistant-general. Here he spent many hours before the altars that had been the witnesses of his first steps in the path of virtue.

On the tenth of August, 1714, M. de La Salle entered Paris, and his humility was shown in the first words he spoke. "What do you desire? I am here to obey," said he to the Brothers, who were more than confused at such an address. But their hearts were too full of filial emotion to mention their past difficulties. At the sight of their beloved father all was forgotten.

The Venerable de La Salle would have considered it a duty to further show his humility by presenting his respects to M. de La Chétardie; but that zealous, though changeable, clergyman had been called to the reward of his labors. In dying, he asked that his heart might be placed in a leaden casket, and buried at the feet of the priests of St. Sulpice who had gone before him, "that," he said, "he might thus render them homage, and by this act repair the faults he might have commited while in their holy society." He expired on the twenty-ninth of June, 1714.

M. Langnet de Gergey, his successor, was well known for his zeal; and the Brothers had reason to believe that an abbé who had distributed his patrimony among the poor would be a friend to

them, whose Founder had been equally heroic.
They were not disappointed. The new pastor gave
every proof of his generous intentions, and through
his advice M. Brou refrained from any interference
with the Brothers, whom he afterward frequently
helped by his alms. The Venerable, in gaining a
friend of some importance, was losing his most generous patron, one who had always acted and spoken in
favor of the new institute. Louis XIV, after a reign
which had many critics, but which all must admit
was exceptional in its brilliancy, was called to the
bar of the Supreme Ruler, before whom all men are
equal, each being judged according to his works. A
reign which produced Bossuet and Corneille, Fénelon and Racine, Bourdaloue and Boileau, Moliere
and Lafontaine, Descartes and Pascal, Turenne and
Condé, needs no comment. Madame de Maintenon
was now the only courtly friend left to the Venerable. In her death, which occurred not long after,
the holy Founder lost a benefactress as kind as she
was intelligent, and whose charities were all the
more praiseworthy, as they had the first requisite
of goodness: that of being done in silence.

The altered circumstances rendered it necessary
to remove the novices to St. Yon. Brother Barthé
lemy continued as director, while Brother Irénée,
recalled from Avignon, was appointed assistant
master of novices. Before leaving Paris, the novitiate received a notable acquisition in the person of
Chevalier d'Armstadt, a German convert of illustrious birth. He had served under Prince Eugene,
and was several times wounded. After the battle

of Denain he quitted the army and came to France. One day, as he passed through Lyons, he heard that a possessed person was to be exorcised. Being a confirmed sceptic, the chevalier determined to see the mock ceremony, as he called it. He had scarcely entered the church when the possessed woman, looking fiercely at him, exclaimed: "Ah! you do not believe in devils: well, one day you shall feel their power." Struck by the strange prophecy, he left the church, filled with emotion: the woman had never seen him before. Some months later, through instructions received in Lyons, he renounced Lutheranism, and became a sincere Catholic. By the advice of his spiritual director, a priest of St. Sulpice, he entered the Brothers' novitiate. Here it was that the prediction was fulfilled. His wounds, which had been healed by a charm, soon reopened, and when the novice-master went to his cell, he found the poor postulant insensible, weltering in his blood. The last sacraments were given him, and he became better, only to fall again into like sufferings. In this paroxysm he seemed anxious to address a crucifix placed before him, and his arms were constantly in motion, as if parrying invisible assailants. He beheld immense numbers of evil spirits, who were suddenly driven from his room by a supposed apparition of the Most Blessed Virgin.

Strange to say, after this attack he asked for the habit of the Brothers with such unceasing perseverance that the Venerable de La Salle gratified him. This was the signal for new terrors. He had no sooner taken the holy habit than he appeared to be strangled; his face became black, and he imagined that M. de La Salle, Brother Barthélemy, and the priest who had received him into the Church, were so many executioners who tortured him. Convinced that it was a true case of possession, La Salle remained alone with the novice, and performed all the ceremonies prescribed by the Church in similar cases. The poor young man was relieved, and from that moment was no longer disturbed. However, with the passing away of all his troubles, and his restoration to health, he began to grow negligent in the service of God, and lost the grace of his vocation.

M. de La Salle remained in Paris about a month after the departure of the novices. He desired to leave without seeing Cardinal de Noailles, for the latter refused to receive the Bull *Unigenitus*. After two days' reflection he decided not to call upon his eminence: he contented himself with taking leave of M. Brou. The abbé, fearing that the absence of M. de La Salle would give him extra labor in connection with the schools, requested him to wait some time, which he did; but he hastened as soon as possible to St. Yon, where his services were needed in the reorganization of the novitiate. In 1716 the Venerable had the pleasure of receiving M. Gense, the principal benefactor of the Brothers of Calais, at St. Yon. M. de La Cocherie accompanied him. They undertook this voyage solely to see the great educator, of whom they had formed an exalted idea. He showed them the boarding-school, and, say his biographers, " spent several hours with them among the flowers, in a little retreat he had built himself, in imitation of Parmenie." He promised to visit Calais. This he did soon after, and his entry there bore all the marks of an ovation. The Brothers had feared that their stipend, paid in part by Louis XIV, would be lessened after the death of that prince; but Louis XV promised the same amount, which was further increased by the city authorities. By special invitation, the servant of God officiated on the feast of the Assumption. The pastor preached, but said not a word about the Most Blessed Virgin. This was more than the Venerable had imagined possible, and he took the liberty to call his host's attention to the fact. The pastor acknowledged his mistake, and repaired it the following Sunday.

M. Gense was desirous to secure the portrait of his friend, but he could not prevail upon him to sit for the purpose. He therefore invited him to dinner, and placing him in a proper position, an artist labored so industriously during the meal, which was designedly prolonged, that the portrait was sufficiently advanced to assure its correctness. M. de La Salle made no remark when he learned of the occurrence, but never could be induced to honor his friend's table again.

During his sojourn in Boulogne, which he next visited, the holy Founder had the pleasure of seeing his children better lodged. By public proclamation the masons and laborers of the city were called upon to erect a dwelling for the Brothers. M. de La Cocherie furnished the materials, and the number who willingly presented themselves to help in the good work made it speedy. " We are happy," said these honest workmen, " to do something for Brothers who give their lives for our children."

The declining health of the Venerable warned him that it was time to think of placing the helm in other hands. During the past few years he had kept aloof as much as possible, in order to accustom his children to govern themselves. He assembled the Brothers of Rouen and Darnetal at St. Yon, and, after some touching details upon his late voyage, he told them that his age and his infirmities, which each day increased, rendered it absolutely necessary for him to resign. He did not refuse to labor, but he loved his institute too well, and knew that it was necessary, during his lifetime, for another to direct its interests.

" Many say that you cannot govern yourselves," he continued, " but it is because they desire to place a stranger at your head ; not understanding that a superior who would not have been trained to your spirit, who would not follow your manner of living, could not serve your true interests with intelligence and devotedness. Such a project, if realized, would bring ruin upon our society. Now is the time to elect a superior, and to prove the contrary : thus, when I am called away, there will be no vacancy made." These and many other arguments which the Venerable employed, were at first answered by sobs and tears ; but finally, accepting the reasons advanced, they agreed that Brother Barthélemy should act as general visitor, and perform the other functions of the superior, it being understood, however, that the Venerable Founder should remain with them, and at their head, giving his advice whenever asked or needed. The following document was then drawn up:—

" We, the undersigned, Brothers of the Christian Schools, assembled in our house of St. Yon to consult upon important questions relative to the welfare of the institute, having recognized that for the past year M. de La Salle, our Founder, on account of his infirmities, has been unable to perform the duties of his office, have judged it proper, and even necessary, that Brother Barthélemy, who for some years has been at the head of our institute, shall forthwith visit all the houses which depend upon it, to see what is therein done, and the manner in which the Brothers conduct themselves, that we may afterward, in council of the principal Brothers, regulate what may be necessary to preserve union and uniformity in the society, to determine and to establish our government, and, at the same time, to provide for the general administration of our institute, in an assembly which Brother Barthélemy will convoke in our house of St. Yon, from the feast of the Ascension to that of Pentecost. In testimony whereof we have signed. Done at St. Yon, this 4th of December, 1716.

" F. FRANÇOIS,   F. CHARLES,

F. DOSITHÉE,   F. AMBROISE,

F. ETIENNE."

Underneath these signatures we read:

" I approve and think well of what the Brothers have resolved, as per above.

      (Signed)   " DE LA SALLE."

The only one out of reach of the visits of the new superior was Brother Gabriel. It had been so with his dear father and bosom friend. But he was not forgotten. Next day, the Venerable Founder, among other things, wrote as follows: " For the past ten months I have been ill in this house, where I have been for about a year. Your last letter has consoled me greatly, and your continued affection and goodness of heart give me much pleasure. Let me know, I pray you, how you are succeeding. This vacation I had hoped to send you a very good Brother, who has spent some time in Italy, and who knows some Italian; but we have employed him elsewhere, believing it very important to supply the place he occupies.

" The Brothers intend to hold an assembly between Ascension and Pentecost, to regulate many things regarding the rules and the administration of the institute. I beg you to send your assent to all that will be determined therein by the chief Brothers in the society. I believe your schools are always open ; let me know how many scholars you have. Your nephew told me that he wished to become a Brother. As he is rather giddy, I deferred his request ; since then I have heard nothing of him."

Though Brother Barthélemy trembled, and could not refrain from shedding tears, when he received notice of his appointment, still, overcoming his natural feelings, he at once left for Chartres, where he placed his visitations under the protection of the Mother of God. The Brothers of that city welcomed him warmly, and promised him implicit obedience. They prepared a document to this effect, which was signed by Brothers Hubert, Sebastien, Cyprien and Pierre. The other houses were visited in turn, and everywhere the same spirit of union was manifest. All signed the document by which the proposed assembly was approved, and obedience promised to its regulations. Several times in his journey Brother Barthélemy was visibly protected; especially on one occasion when, falling from his horse, his foot caught in the stirrup, and he was dragged for some distance without any injury. Another time he lost his way in a snow-fall, and dreading to be benighted in so lonely a by-road, he earnestly recommended himself to his guardian angel. He immediately saw several persons, who made signs to him to follow them. No sooner had he reached the open road than his guides suddenly disappeared.

Six days after the arrival of Brother Barthélemy, sixteen professed Brothers were assembled at St. Yon. That their discussions might be entirely free, the Venerable refused to be present. " I will remain in my cell," said he, "and pray the Holy Ghost to enlighten you. I shall see you only during the conferences." By his orders they proceeded to the election of a president, and Brother Barthélemy received a full vote. The next thing in order was the election of a superior-general; but the holy

Founder first required them to make a three days'
retreat, during which they frequently recited a
prayer he had expressly composed for the occasion.
In his conferences he insisted upon the qualities of
a good superior, and advised them to choose the
man most capable of fulfilling the onerous position.
" Name him among you," he said, " whom you
know to be the most enlightened, wise, virtuous and
firm. . . . Look not to talents, or birth, or age of
community, or personal appearance ; in a word,
look not to the man, but to God, whom he is to
represent. . . . Give your vote to him whom your
conscience designates as the most meritorious, and.
whom, at the hour of your death, you would choose
to govern the institute, maintain it in regularity, and
cause fervor, devotedness and charity to reign in it."

On the eighth of May, 1717, after having heard
Mass and received holy communion, the capitulants retired to the conference-room, where, the
light and assistance of the Holy Ghost having been
again implored, Brother Barthélemy, by a large
majority of votes, was elected superior-general of
the Brothers of the Christian Schools. " God be
praised!" said the holy Founder, to whom this
intelligence was at once brought, " he has already
exercised the functions of the office for some time."

In vain did the new general beg to be excused
from carrying a burden which his humility made
him feel unable to bear ; but, after struggling to no
purpose, he calmly resigned himself to the cares
and the honors of the first place.

The capitulants next prepared a document, in

which they declare that, of their own free choice, and without any constraint, they had elected Joseph Truffet, known in religion as Frère Barthélemy, as general and perpetual superior. By the advice of the Venerable Founder, the chapter elected Brother Jean, director of the Paris community, and Brother Joseph, visitor, as assistants to the superior-general. Their duties were to aid Brother Barthélemy by their wise councils, and to divide with him the labors of the general administration.

Brother Fiacre, director of Boulogne, replaced Brother Joseph as visitor, and Brother Irénée was appointed director of the novitiate, and also of that part of the establishment of St. Yon in which culprits were detained. The former soldier introduced the strict discipline to which, in early days, he had been subjected, and for thirty-three years rendered important services in this position.

Brother Irénée, when called upon by the most honored superior-general to address the novices, on the occasion of his installation, had but a few moments to prepare. However, meditation had already given him a fund from which he immediately drew with such effect, that all who heard him were struck with the justness of his remarks, and the insight they indicated in all that related to spiritual things.

His confidence in the holy Mother of God induced him to implore her blessing upon the novitiate, in a manner which at once shows his simple faith and Christian humility. Seeing that the number of postulants continued small, he knelt before a favorite painting of the Immaculate Conception, and, with a halter about his neck, deposited the keys of the novitiate at the feet of his Queen. So eloquent and pathetic a petition produced happy results ; and after the death of the holy Founder the novices rarely numbered less than thirty.

Brother Gabriel was informed by Brother Barthélemy of the changes that had taken place. " In the assembly held last month," says the most honored superior-general, " our dear Brothers, despite my unworthiness, elected me superior-general of our institute. Our dear Brothers, John and Joseph, were also elected, by secret ballot, as assistants."

The " Brother Director's Rule " next occupied the attention of the chapter ; the " Government of Schools " likewise called for several sessions. All was decided "after mature reflection, according to the majority of votes ; and in all things the greatest good of the society was considered." *

The chapter was closed on the twenty-third of May—Trinity-Sunday. The capitulants presented the verbal process of their deliberations to the Venerable Founder, asking that he would examine and advise according to his best judgment. Delighted at the result of their labors, and seeing himself at length freed from the burden of governing, he promised to do all in his power to carry out their intentions.

Before retiring to their various communities, the Venerable de La Salle invited the capitulants to the chapel, where they celebrated the new departure of the institute in pious hymns and canticles.

* * *

* *Arch. du Régime, Chapitre de* 1717.

Those who do not know the spirit of religious communities, can understand but little of the joy experienced in such meetings of childlike devotion. The hymns and canticles then sung are the battle-song at the bivouac, before the departure of the soldiers of Christ against man's greatest enemies, ignorance and incredulity. The Venerable de La Salle availed himself of the repose that had been given him, to review the rules and constitutions of the society. When he had completed his work, he submitted it to the most honored brother superior, who sent a copy to each community. The following document certified the correctness of the text :

" We the undersigned, Superior of the Brothers of the Christian Schools, send to our dear Brother of——— the rules found hereto attached. They are divided into thirty-two chapters, and contain a para-graphed formula of the vows prepared by us. We send them as determined and decreed by us and by the Brothers Directors of our society, in the general assembly held in our house of St. Yon, *Faubourg de Rouen,* in the month of May, last year, 1717. They are to be put in force and observed by all our Brothers. Therefore we declare null and void any other rule which may be found in any of our houses. In attestation of which we have signed. Done at our house of St. Yon, this thirty-first of October, 1718.

" Joseph Truffet,

"(*Otherwise*) Brother Barthélemy."

A similar declaration was made in reference to

the " Brother Director's Rule," and each page was verified and countersigned by the superior.

" The Government of Schools," a work urgently demanded by the Brothers, and imperatively necessary in a teaching body that was tracing a new path in its methods, occupied many hours in the Venerable's attention. " God alone knows with what persistency and charity our Venerable Founder sought, with the best experienced of the Brothers, the most efficacious method by which to attain success in school." *

To the method developed in the admirable work generally known as " The School's Conduct," we owe the introduction of the simultaneous-mutual method. Previously, the individual method, in which each scholar received a special lesson from the teacher, was in general usage. The universality of its practice rendered the change the more difficult. Yet it seems evident in our day that this system must have been productive of very poor results. The shortness of time devoted to each pupil, the absence of emulation, and the throwing the young learner entirely on his own resources for the greater part of the day,—rendered progress difficult for the more gifted, and almost impossible for the less favored.

The simultaneous method, likewise, had its serious disadvantages. While a section was taught together, the other scholars were left to themselves, thus inviting disorder, and often creating it.

---

* " Circular Letters," 1720.—A commission appointed by the English government to examine the system invented by the Venerable de La Salle, summed up their report by saying: " If we had known the Christian Brothers, we would not have had Lancasterian schools."

The simultaneous-mutual method, which the Venerable de La Salle introduced, removes these difficulties. Two or three of the most intelligent scholars oversee the sections that are not under the immediate care of the Brother, and thus all are kept busy. In this way, also, many young men acquire a taste for teaching, and become the most successful of masters. This appears extremely simple to those who have not seen the less perfect methods. It is so with all important innovations: we naturally say: " The wonder is that the change was not sooner made." This, however, derogates nothing from the honor due to the successful innovator. Moreover, it is characteristic of genius that it simplifies. The method thus inaugurated by the Venerable and his first disciples is that which, at the present day, is followed by the Brothers of the Christian Schools throughout the world. The success which everywhere appears to crown their labors is due in great part to the rules and regulations dictated by experience, and followed as a Christian and religious duty. Lancaster, Uhland, Pestalozzi. and Jacotot deserve well of the people ; but the Venerable de La Salle, in his method as expounded in his " Government of Schools," will be found to have introduced, before them, all that is good in their systems, and much that their experience had not discovered. The insight which the holy Founder had obtained into the human heart is visible in every page of the part of his system which treats of the moral and intellectual training of youth :—

" Children must be induced to love school, and to

consider it a recompense to be allowed the privilege of attending it. . . . Parents being usually worshippers of their children, if these ask to attend school, fathers and mothers will be but too glad to send them. . . . Children usually become disgusted at school when the teachers have no tact, or display no energy. . . . You must take courage, and speak without fear," said the Venerable to a young Brother; " we must begin boldly by blundering, for at first we can be skilful in nothing. Be persuaded that authority is secured and preserved rather by firmness, gravity and silence, than by blows and severity."* "Your schools and your community," said the Venerable to the director of Chartres, " must be your whole care. If you meddle in anything else, you oppose the will of God. Your duty is to direct the Brothers, and to make the schools prosper."

Thus the holy servant of God touches the vital part of every question, and places responsibility where it really rests. Teachers often blame their scholars, when their own want of tact, or their inexperience or lack of interest, is the true cause of failure. Schools are such as masters make them. Children or youths are the same the world over. " We need not, then, be surprised at the success which the Venerable de La Salle, attained as an educator. His name, through the work of his disciples, was revered, before his death, in twenty-nine cities of France. They were abundantly blessed, because they were extremely careful to follow his advices."†

---

* *Lettres*, etc., *Arch. du Régime.*   † F. Lucard, p. 371.

CHAPTER XI.

The Venerable de La Salle as an Inferior.—His Humility.—He visits Paris to receive a Legacy.—Love of Truth.—St. Yon to be sold.—Death of Madame de Louvois.—Generosity of her Son.—St. Yon the Property of the Institute.—The Venerable plans new Buildings.—Fervor of the Novices.—M. de La Salle's Recollection in Prayer.—Brothers asked for Canada.—Illness of the Holy Founder.—Temporary Cure.— Mass on St. Joseph's Day.—Was the Venerable interdicted?—He follows St. Vincent de Paul.—He receives the last Sacraments.—Last Will and Testament.—He advises Retirement from the World.—His Prophecy.—Last Words.—"The Saint is dead!"—Brother Barthélemy's Letters.—Brother Gabriel.—The Funeral.

THE Venerable de La Salle, in his retirement at St. Yon, might look upon his work, and truthfully say of it, "It is good." His mission as superior was complete : it remained for him to manifest that he had been worthy to govern, since he so well knew how to obey. When written to about the success of his schools, after his resignation as general, he took occasion to say : "It is true that I began to form Brothers to direct gratuitous schools, but it is some time since I have been relieved from directing them. *It is one of the Brothers, named Brother Barthélemy, who now conducts them, and all the Brothers acknowledge him as superior."* When requested by Brother Barthélemy to add some words to a letter which he was sending to a distinguished person, the Venerable said in his postscript : " Permit me, though a poor priest of St. Yon, to send these few lines with the letter which is written you by Brother Barthélemy, superior of the Brothers. I request you to do that which is asked; and I am quite certain that your zeal is such that my worthless suffrage is not necessary to induce you to listen favorably to the brother superior."

When some persons expressed their astonishment that he, a priest and doctor of divinity, should submit to a layman, he said: "Well, shall not the ministers of Him who has said, 'Learn of me, for I am meek and humble of heart,' humiliate themselves? Can they, without prevarication, limit themselves to teaching by word? Are they not obliged to teach by example?" In his letters to Brother Barthélemy, he constantly professed obedience and submission. "You know," he says, "that I am willing to obey in all things, for I am now a simple subject; and I have not made vows of obedience, that I may do my own will."

His choice would have been the last place at all the exercises. Several times he was seen mending his clothing, and it required an absolute order to prevent him from sweeping his cell. and from making his bed. Brother Barthélemy gave this office to a novice. Forthwith the older members complained that such an honor was given to a novice rather than to a professed Brother! The holy Founder attributed these attentions to the sympathy which the Brothers felt for an infirm old man. His humility was to be pained by a much greater mark of esteem,—one that he thought threatened to deprive

him of the merit attached to one of the greatest
trials he had passed through in his earlier days.
M. Rogier, who had been one of the chief abettors
of the Abbé Clement, was taken dangerously ill at
Paris. The sight of death gave renewed strength
to a remorse which had long pursued him, and
he wished to leave an annual income in M. de La
Salle's favor.

Brother Barthélemy was obliged to give an order
to that effect, before the servant of God would
consent to visit Paris, whither he was called by
the attorneys. His love for the Brothers of a city
in which he had suffered so much, would have
induced him to stay with them; but the dread of
such honors as he knew would be paid him by his
dear children, induced him rather to stop with the
successors of Père Bourdoise.

In the testament made in his favor he was styled
" Superior of the Brothers of the Christian Schools."
This the Venerable refused to permit, and even
went so far as to state that he would rather renounce
the legacy than accept it at the price of a seeming
prevarication. His humility triumphed, and the
papers named him simply as M. de La Salle.

During this transaction, Madame la Marquise de
Louvois was called to eternity. The Brothers were
notified that St. Yon was to be sold. Brother
Barthélemy considered himself obliged to seek
another home for his novices. Notice was issued
that no more boarders could be received. When
Brother Thomas, procurator-general, according to
the superior's instructions, called upon M. de La

Salle for advice as to the future, the holy man replied: "What do you fear? Have I not already told you that St. Yon shall be yours?"

To encourage them still more, he gave them his library and his vestments, which had been kept at St. Sulpice. When consulted by Brother Barthélemy as to the means by which to secure the property, he replied: "I do not advise you to borrow money to purchase, yet I do not positively say that you should not do so. You can consult others on this subject. I believe that all you do will be well. It is not proper that I should interfere in these matters: for I am nothing, and you, as superior, are the master." In regard to the persons you wish me to see, I will call upon them if you say so. In this case deign, as my superior, to send me an order to this effect. I will go immediately, or the first holiday, and I shall tell them that you have sent me. I wish you and all the Brothers a prosperous and happy year."

Providence soon realized the promise made by His servant. The annual income left to M. de La Salle, but which he had not used, was converted into the sum of five thousand two hundred livres. The money which had been sent him, when making his visitation, was withdrawn from Rouen, and amounted, with the interests, to six thousand six hundred livres. To this was added what the communities of Paris, Rheims, Versailles, Guise, Boulogne and Calais, sent him through the brother director of St. Sulpice. In all they had but fifteen thousand livres: an amount quite inadequate for the purchase of the coveted retreat, already so dear to all the Brothers.

Again the hand of God was manifested in the goodness of heart shown by His servant. The pious Abbé de Louvois, executor of his mother's will and testament, did not offer the property at public sale. He was satisfied with what the Brothers could give him, and only asked that he might be remembered in the prayers that would be said in a house that the Brothers so gladly called their own from that moment. The deeds were made in the names of Joseph Truffet (Brother Barthélemy) and Charles Frapet (Brother Thomas).

Thus far Moulins was the only city in which the institute had obtained letters-patent. On the thirtieth of March, 1717, M. Auberg, a special friend of the Brothers, obtained permission from the bishop of Autun to secure this favor for the new teachers. His request was granted in June of the same year.

But the absence of the Venerable Founder from among his children was to them a source of great sorrow. He wished, now more than ever, to accustom them to self-government, as he saw his zealous career rapidly coming to a close. The Brothers, for the same reason, felt that, as their father's days were few, they should be spent among those whose delight it would be to treasure up his examples, and to keep all his words in their hearts. At the pressing invitation of Brother Barthélemy, the holy Founder returned to St. Yon, not without a struggle on the part of the Brothers of Paris, who also claimed that, if their father left St. Nicholas, he should rather spend the remaining days of his life among those who, with him, had suffered most in the founding of the society. Brother Barthélemy induced the Venerable Founder to spend two days with his children in the capital, after which both returned to St. Yon on the seventh of March, the eve of the day upon which all the papers transferring the property were to be signed.

Momentarily rejuvenated when again among his own, the Venerable, at Brother Barthélemy's request, drew up the plan of the chapel, still at St. Yon; also for structures that surround the principal courtyard of the establishment. The holy Founder had the consolation to bless the beginning of these various works. But in the midst of these distracting duties he forgot not the spiritual wants of his flock. He heard their confessions, said Mass each morning for them, and gave daily conferences to the novices.

A single instance will give an idea of the piety which at that time reigned in the novitiate. Among the novices, none was more distinguished for his rare virtue than Brother Stanislaus. One morning, immediately after holy Mass, the good Brother left the ranks without permission, and approaching a postulant who had been received but a short time previously, he embraced him with many marks of affection, and professed himself ready at any moment to render him service. Brother Irénée, astonished at this strange proceeding, asked the novice for an explanation. "Well," said Brother Stanislaus, "I do not know why, but I feel an extreme repugnance to this postulant, and I have asked our Lord to give me grace to overcome it. I have even begged our Saviour to give him part of the graces destined for me, as a remuneration for my lack of charity." Another time, appearing quite sad, he was asked the reason. " Why, dear Brother Director, you neglect me : I am truly happy only in the midst of humiliation, and you refuse to try my weak virtue," replied Brother Stanislaus. In the students' recreation the Venerable, despite his old age, was often seen encouraging the young people to enjoy themselves. He took great interest in their games, and knew from experience that there are few sins in students' play-grounds when there is great noise.

In 1718, Charron, one of the founders of the hospital in Canada, came to St. Yon, and asked for four Brothers. The Venerable, being consulted, at first advised that they should be given. All arrangements were made, when, unexpectedly, the holy Founder returned from prolonged prayer, and begged Brother Barthélemy to withdraw the promise. " But," said the superior, " we have followed your advice." " If the Brothers go, they will not succeed," replied M. de La Salle. The negotiations were annulled, and Charron afterward admitted that he intended to send them separately into the villages as teachers.*

---

* One hundred years later (1817) four Brothers were sent to New Orleans (La.), where, contrary to agreement, they were separated, and sent to various missions. Deprived of the graces of community life, they soon tired, and withdrew from the institute. Thus the previsions of the Venerable de La Salle were confirmed. In 1853 one of these former Brothers asked to make a spiritual retreat in the Christian Brothers' College, St. Louis, Missouri.

An occurrence at this time shows the piety with which the Venerable recited the divine office. The bakery attached to the establishment having taken fire, the Brothers, novices, and postulants hastened to the threatened locality. In the noise and tumult that ensued, all these persons were obliged to pass and repass before the door of the room in which La Salle was engaged in prayer. Still he heard nothing of it all. Finally, seeing that they could not control the spreading flames, Brother Barthélemy called upon the holy Founder, and requested him to pray that the disaster which threatened them might be averted. The servant of God, through obedience, went with his superior, and had scarcely commenced his prayer when the flames ceased, and St. Yon was saved, all admitted, through the intercession of its first father.

With all the care that the Brothers could bestow upon the Venerable, his health rapidly declined. Then it was that the affection of his children was displayed in its brightest colors. They spoke in an undertone when near his apartments, and often walked some distance, rather than make any noise by passing before his door. When they did give themselves the privilege of going the shortest way, it was that they might, unseen, salute their venerated father, and offer a prayer for his preservation.

One day Brother Barthélemy was heard speaking in a loud tone in the holy Founder's apartment. A Brother took the liberty of entering, to tell him that he should strive to speak in a lower voice, as the Venerable was suffering so much. The superior said : " What! can I be patient when M. de La Salle tells me that his sickness is ruining the house, and that we are spending too much upon him? He wishes us to send him to the hospital." *

Toward the end of January, 1719, a severe attack of asthma was added to his already excruciating rheumatic pains. Brother Barthélemy was then visiting some of his communities, and the Venerable, despite his age and sufferings, wished to renew and increase his austerities. He resumed the last place, and would have been taken for a country curate, who was making a retreat at St. Yon, he was so modest and simple in his appearance. The lenten season had begun, and M. de La Salle could not be induced to accept the privileges required by his suffering condition. " The victim will soon be immolated : let it be as pure as possible," was his reply.

When Brother Barthélemy returned, he requested the servant of God to retake the place of honor due him, and he also forbade him the use of the severe penances and fasts he had been practising. Docile to the voice of obedience, M. de La Salle humbly submitted to all the cares that were bestowed upon him.

As he never spoke of his sufferings except to the physician, and as he had acquired such command over himself that he could conceal his pains, the Brothers loved to believe that he might yet be preserved some years in their midst.

In the month of February his illness increased ;

* The hospitals are, in France, what the poorhouses are in England.

the nervousness caused by the falling upon him of a heavy door augmented his headaches, while a severe pain in his side added to the difficulties of the position. The physician still anticipated a favorable turn in the patient's condition till, toward the end of the month, he was constrained to make the sad announcement that he no longer had any hopes. Then, as though heaven would consent to be taken by violence, the Brothers implored the divine mercy not to strike them so soon and so painfully. Their prayers were continual, their promises numerous, their faith unbounded. God seemed to listen to their cries, in the first days of the month of March : their *Te Deums* resounded in honor of the merciful God who allowed them to see their father once more at the altar.

Their joy had scarcely reached its height when their beloved chief was once more a victim to sufferings more cruel than any he had hitherto experienced. The Brothers were to have but one more consolation.

On the eighteenth of March the Venerable expressed the great desire he felt to offer the holy sacrifice on the feast-day of St. Joseph, to whom he always had a special devotion. Late in the night the servant of God felt a sudden change for the better, and, to the intense delight of the Brothers, —a delight mingled with the deepest sympathy, they saw him painfully approaching the foot of the altar, on the beautiful feast of the patron of their society, since named universal protector of the Church.

Several hours were spent in the celebration of the day, and the Venerable was able even to talk quite freely with his dear children. The joy was but momentary, for he was retaken with the acute pains that had so suddenly disappeared. He was borne in a sad procession, in the arms of those he loved, to his couch of suffering.

Several biographers have declared that the Venerable de La Salle, pursued by the malignity of his enemies, spent the last days of his life under the censure of his bishop. A close research has not enabled us to give this assertion the weight of documental authority.

These biographers state that the cause of this penalty was the refusal of M. de La Salle to take the "culprits" of St. Yon to the public services on Sunday.

On the twenty-second of March, 1706, an agreement had been entered into between La Salle and the Abbé Hecquet, then pastor of St. Sever. The chief points in this document were: 1, that the boarders of St. Yon should assist at the parochial Mass; 2, that the feast of Easter should not be celebrated in the chapel of the institution; 3, that the Brothers and their scholars should receive paschal communion in the parish church.

In 1715, the Venerable Founder consented to open a reformatory school, and in this were to be received the sons of distinguished persons. St. Vincent de Paul had already established an institution in which young men made retreats, and were offered opportunities to reform. Both the holy founder of the Sisters of Charity and the Venerable knew that charity as well as prudence required that these young persons should remain unknown, and therefore they could not be required to attend public services. Moreover, the law required the most rigorous secrecy to be observed as to the history, and even the names, of these young libertines. "Each reformatory had its private chapel, served by chaplains appointed by the king." * M. de Pontcarré gave St. Yon all the rights attached to chapels of reformatory schools." † Necessarily, from this moment the agreement of twenty-second March, 1706, was no longer in force.

During this change of plan, or rather its extension, at St. Yon, Abbé Hecquet was called to a better world. M. Dujarrier-Bresnard became the incumbent of St. Sever. One of his first movements was to demand that the reform scholars should be brought to public services.

Abbé Robinet was appointed to examine the disputed question, and after a full hearing declared that, "although the Brothers were mere laymen, without letters-patent, they might have Mass said in their chapel during the two weeks following Easter, *and the boarders might make their first communion therein.*"

In 1719, M. Dujarrier-Bresnard renewed his claim, and appealed to the archbishopric. He failed in his efforts to oblige the boarders to attend public services, though Easter was made an exception. "Moreover, M. de Pontcarré would never have

---

* F. Lucard, p. 420. † Ibid.

permitted the rights attached to the chapel of St. Yon to be tampered with." *

At this juncture the severest trial of M. de La Salle was to take place. The vicar-general accused the Venerable Founder of lack of sincerity to the archbishop. This irritated the latter. It was also cause of much indignation to a clergyman present at hearing an old man of such irreproachable character so lightly spoken of, and at a time, too, when stricken with sickness, and unable to defend himself. He thereupon took the liberty of saying to Mgr. d'Aubigné: "Either M. de La Salle has but ill expressed himself, or the vicar-general has but ill understood. The accused ought to be heard before being condemned." The archbishop regarded the remark as ill-timed, and expressed his determination of placing La Salle under an interdict. The peacemaker, in all probability Père Blain, immediately hastened to St. Yon, and, without informing the accused of what had happened, asked him to repeat the substance of his last interview with the vicar. It was as he had anticipated: La Salle had been misunderstood. He hastened to the archbishop, and gave him a true statement of the case, and protested against the injustice ; but his remonstrances were in vain. Mgr. d'Aubigné preferred the testimony of M. du Bresnard, who had already been in litigation with his parishioners, and likewise had several lawsuits with the Jesuits, and whose disposition was of such a quarrelsome nature as to render

---

* M. Alibrandi, advocate for beatification and canonization of the Venerable de La Salle. Rome, 1869.

his assertions deserving of but partial credence. M. de La Chétardie had also been instrumental in ill-disposing the archbishop toward the Venerable de La Salle.

Père Blain refused to be the bearer of so unjust a sentence, but another priest agreed to do so. The Venerable listened with patience to the messenger. " May God's holy name be blessed! I die like Jesus, on the cross," said the holy Founder, in reply. The man who had refused a legacy rather than sign a title he no longer could claim, was thus interdicted, because of a supposed falsehood.

The above, which is an abbreviated recital of the supposed censure, is not sustained by the determined facts in the case. " Neither M. Hecquet nor M. Dujarrier-Bresnard had any interest in securing the censure of M. de La Salle, for he could have engaged another priest to say Mass. The interdict, requiring that Mass should not be said in the chapel on Easter-day, was simply a restriction made upon a previously-granted privilege. Moreover, the Brothers soon reëntered into the full possession of their rights. The Prince de Croy, Cardinal-Archbishop of Rouen, declared, in 1835, that his predecessors had exempted the Brothers of St. Yon from the jurisdiction of the pastors of St. Sever."*

" However this may have been," continued the same authority, " notwithstanding the most obstinate researches in the archives of Rouen, of the parish of St. Sever and of St. Yon, we have been unable to find any document containing the pre-

---

* F. Lucard, p. 426.

tended interdict against M. de La Salle ; . . . neither does the necrological article, published in 1720, in the *Flambeau Astronomique*, mention it, though this publication was under the auspices of the Archbishop of Rouen." *

The Venerable de La Salle was nearing his final hour. M. Dujarrier-Bresnard called upon him : " Do you know," said he, " that your days are numbered ? The physicians have despaired of your recovery ; soon you will appear before your Maker." " Yes," replied the servant of God, " I know this : soon I shall see my Saviour. I am resigned to His will my end is in His hands. May His holy will be done !" A conversation of some moments followed, in which the Abbé Dujarrier-Bresnard was allowed to read the heart of the Venerable servant of God, and to perceive the injustices that had been committed against him. He wished to hasten at once to the archbishopric, and to repair the injury he had done. As he retired, he was recalled by the Venerable, who said : " I feel that I shall soon be no more ; do not delay to bring the holy viaticum." The pastor of St. Sever did not think the danger so imminent, and he wished to publicly declare how changed his sentiments were. Under instructions from the Venerable, the walks through which Père Bresnard was to carry the most blessed sacrament were decorated.

---

* His Eminence, Cardinal Bonnechose, says that long and minute researches in the archives of the archbishopric have been unable to reveal anything of this reputed interdict, " although," he adds, " the registers of administration of Mgr. d'Aubigné seem to present no *lacuna* " (*Declaration*, fifteenth November, 1868.)

Like a valiant soldier, the saintly Founder wished to die arms in hand. His faith gave him supernatural courage. What was the astonishment of the pastor, his fellow-priests, and many persons distinguished for their piety, when they beheld the dying man, not in his bed of suffering, but prostrate on the floor to receive his God! A short thanksgiving, made in the same posture, was more than the patient could bear; he was again placed in his bed, where he continued his secret conversation with the Spouse of his heart. He had already received the bread of angels; he was soon to hear their songs.

Profiting of a few moments of strength, the Venerable dictated the following testament: "I recommend, in the first place, my soul to God, and, next, all the Brothers of the Society of the Christian Schools, to which He has united me; and to them I recommend, above all things, to have an entire submission to the Church at all times, and particularly in these troublous days; never in any manner to have a disagreement with our Holy Father the Pope and the Church of Rome; ever remembering that I have sent two Brothers to Rome, to beg grace from God that our society may be ever submissive to him. I also recommend them to have great devotion to our Lord; to have great love for the holy communion and the exercise of mental prayer; to have a particular devotion for the Most Blessed Virgin, and toward St. Joseph, the patron and protector of our society; to discharge the duties of their station with zeal and disinterestedness; to preserve an intimate union among themselves, and a blind obedience to their superiors, which is the foundation and prop of every perfection in the community."

On Holy-Thursday night, after prayer, the most honored superior, with the Brothers of the community and the members of the novitiate, assembled around the bed of the dying patriarch. "We are your children," sobbed the superior; "we come to implore a father's blessing." "May God bless you all!" said the Venerable, in reply. Like Jacob of old, he beheld the Joseph of his heart at his feet. He had not lands to divide, nor wealth to distribute; but, like the divine Master he had so faithfully imitated, he gave his children the whole world as the field of their labors; they were to teach all nations that "sweet is the yoke and light the burden" of those who truly serve God.

After some moments of delirium, the holy Founder recovered his presence of mind. His zeal, which still burned brightly, urged him to say something more to his children, who can never forget his parting words without ceasing to be his disciples. He said: "If you wish to persevere and to die in your holy state, have no transactions with persons of the world; for, insensibly, you will acquire a liking for their manners, and you will enter so deeply into their conversation that you cannot help praising their language, however pernicious it may be. This will cause you to fall into infidelity to your rules. Being no longer faithful, you will become disgusted with your state, and will finally abandon it."

It was not a time to think of worldly affairs, yet one of the Brothers expressed some fears for the future of St. Yon.   In six months they had received but three postulants, two of whom had proved ripe for heaven already.   "In a few years," said the Venerable, "there will be a great change in St. Yon; this establishment will acquire a great reputation, and will render important services to the whole kingdom.   Brother N——— will see this."   He did not promise that happiness to Brother Barthélemy, and this was noticed.   A short while served to verify the prophecy.   The superior soon followed the Founder, who was fast sinking.   Toward midnight he entered into his death-agony.   At two in the morning he rallied for a moment, and murmured : " Mary, Mother of grace, of sweetness and of clemency ! protect us against our enemies, and receive us at the hour of death!"

For many years these words had closed each day for the Venerable; they were among the last he uttered.   A moment before his death he was asked if he willingly accepted all the sufferings he was then enduring.   "Oh! yes," he replied, "in all things I adore the will of God in my regard."

With this profession of faith, the last embers of life were faintly glimmering.   Making an effort as if to rise and meet one whom he wished to embrace, Jean-Baptiste de La Salle breathed his soul into the hands of his Creator.   The world had lost one of its greatest benefactors, the Church one of her most faithful sons, and the Institute of the Christian Schools its Founder.   Heaven had welcomed the

valiant warrior, who had fought the good fight.
The steward who had been at first faithful in few
things, and was afterward placed over many, had
entered the joy of the Lord. It was Good-Friday
morning.

" The saint is dead," was heard on every side.
' Yes; the saint is dead, the holy priest is no more,"
replied Urbain Robinet,* when the Brothers informed him of the sad event. From every part of
France where the Brothers were established, or in
which the Venerable Founder had spent any time,
the same testimony was received.

It was Brother Barthélemy's sad duty, while overcome with emotion, to appear brave, and to console
his numerous family. The letters which he wrote
bespoke his sorrow and his resignation. The epistle
which he sent to a director who said that "he
wished life to close," will amply repay perusal. In
it he says :—

" My dear Brother, may the grace and peace of
our Lord Jesus Christ be always with us!

" It is not without reason that you shed tears in
learning the death of our very dear father. I do
not think that a single Brother could forbear from
weeping, it was so natural to do so. But, all things
considered, I do not know if we should give ourselves up to sterile regrets. We must adore the will
of God. He left us our father as long as He
thought well; He then took him to Himself to
receive the reward of his holy life and labors. We

* Secretary to the Archbishop of Paris.

must submit, and conform ourselves to His divine will.

" The holy apostles were very sad at the thought of being deprived of the sensible presence of their divine Master. To console them, Jesus said : ' It is expedient for you that I go, for, if I go not, the Paraclete will not come to you ; but if I go, I will send Him to you. Our very dear father is not lost to us : he is, according to all appearances, with the angels and saints. He must have great power in heaven, since on earth he obtained so many graces for himself, and for others whom he helped to be converted and to give themselves to God.

" We now admire his great virtues : his evangelical poverty ; his zeal for the divine worship ; his great taste in all that related to the ornaments of the Church and the sacerdotal vestments, for which he spared no expense ; his great charity toward the poor, though he was extremely needy in living with the Brothers ; his zeal for the salvation of souls, which inspired him to resign his canonry to accept a pastorship ; his humility, patience, obedience, and abandonment to the will of Divine Providence, and many other heroic virtues. I believe he is among the virgins, from what I can learn of his chaste demeanor.

" No, no, my dear Brother, I will not ask God to take you out of this world ; I will pray Him to preserve you, as long as He may deem proper, for His glory, your own good, and the salvation of souls. Do not be unduly sad, for he whom you weep as dead liveth. He is in the possession of that peace of which no man can deprive him. Preserve yourself in the practice of the charity and other virtues which he so recommended you. Do not sadden the Holy Spirit within you by unmeasured grief at the death of our dear father. I cannot, indeed, tell you my own feelings. I am sad and joyful at the same time. Be not cast down; for the sadness which arises not from a movement of the Holy Ghost is dangerous, and productive of much evil. When inclined to be thus sad, pray. I trust in the Lord that He will not abandon us, and that, so long as we serve Him according to the spirit of our institute, He will bless us."

Brother Barthélemy had previously written a letter to Brother Gabriel, at Rome, in which he said :—

" May the grace and peace of our Lord Jesus Christ be always with us!

" It is with great cause for sadness that I write you this second letter, to inform you of the death of our very dear father, which occurred on Good-Friday morning, at four o'clock. He had previously received the last sacraments in a very edifying manner. He had been sick the entire Lent. All Rouen regrets his death, and looks upon him as a saint. His remains were visited by large numbers. His grace the archbishop, the vicar-general and the president, favor us with their protection. I fulfil a duty by sending you the first article of our holy father's testament, which relates to all the Brothers of our society.   This we must look upon as the last instruction and order he has given us.   He has also written several letters in favor of the Holy Father which have done much good."

The funeral ceremonies took place the afternoon of Holy-Saturday.   Many members of religious orders, and other persons of every rank, assisted. M. Dujarrier-Bresnard presided.   Six Brothers bore the body to its resting-place; the others followed: their tears and sobs mingled as a strange but fitting harmony with the solemn chant of the psalms.   The pastor insisted that the remains should be entombed in the church, in the chapel of St. Susanna.   He also placed the following inscription over the sepulchre :—

" Here awaits the resurrection to life Jean-Baptiste de La Salle, priest, doctor in theology, ancient canon of the Metropolitan Church of Rheims, Founder of the Christian Schools ; illustrious by his birth, more illustrious by his virtues.   He died on the sixth day of Holy Week, the seventh of April, in the year 1719, in the house of the Brothers of St. Yon, of this parish, aged sixty-eight years.   May the Lord grant him to find rest in this day !

" This monument of pious gratitude has been erected to his most pious parishioner by Louis Dujarrier-Bresnard, pastor of this parish."

D. O. M.

Hic,

Expectat Resurrectionem
Vitæ Venerabilis
Joannes-Baptista de La Salle,
Rhemus Presbyter, Doctor Theologus,
Ex-Canonicus Ecclesiæ Metropolitanæ Rhemensis,
Institutor Fratrum Scholæ Christianæ,
Natalibus clarus, Virtutibus clarior.
Obiit Feria Sexta Parasceves,
Die septimâ Aprilis, Anno MDCCXIX.
In Ædibus Fratrum Sancti Yonii hujusce Parochiæ,
Annum agens LXVIII.

———

Det illi Dominus invenire Requiem in illa Die.

———

Hoc Pietatis et grati Animi Monumentum
Opposuit tam piissimo Parochiano
Ludovicus Dujarrier-Bresnard, Ecclesiæ Rector.

BOOK III.

THE WORK CARRIED ON.

CHAPTER I.

State of the Institute at the Death of the Venerable.—Brother Barthélemy's Demise.—Brother Timothy elected Superior.—Letters-patent
secured for St. Yon.—Pope Benedict XIII approves the Society.—
A General Chapter receives the Bull. —The Venerable's Remains trans-
ferred to St. Yon.—Imposing Ceremonies.—Brother Gabriel returns
to France.—His Death.—Brother Timothy resigns.— Brother Claude
elected.—Literary Character of those Days.—Election of Brother
Florence.—His Resignation.—Brother Agathon.—His Career and
Sufferings.—The Revolution.—Martyrs.—Brother Frumence named
Vicar-General.—School in Lyons.—Pius VII visits the Community.—
Napoleon I.—Cardinal Fesch.—Brother Gerbaud elected Superior.—
His sudden Death.—Brother William of Jesus succeeds him.—School
Books prepared.—Brother Anaclet elected Superior.—The Prepara-
tory Novitiate.—Evening Schools.

AT the death of the Venerable de La Salle, the
institute comprised twenty-seven houses, two hundred and seventy-four Brothers, nine thousand
eight hundred and eighty-five scholars. This was
the legacy left to the intelligent care of Brother
Barthélemy. Fortunately for the society, the most
honored superior's worth was equalled by his
modesty. His amiable disposition, which his plain
appearance did not at first indicate, gained him all
hearts. "I saw," wrote the Bishop of Macon, "the
superior of the Brothers when he passed through

our episcopal city; he is not handsome-visaged, but he wrote me so nice a letter that it deserves to be printed : it has attached me forever to the Brothers of the Christian Schools." The Brothers gathered about him with their submission and their sympathies. They rendered his task as light as possible. He visited the communities, and deserves special gratitude for the prudence and zeal with which he preserved himself and his inferiors from the foul taint of Jansenism. He opened several schools; among others, that of St. Omer. In the colds of winter and the heats of summer he travelled on foot.

Though in the prime of life, this holy religious felt that his end was near at hand. Moreover, his heart was with the Venerable Founder; his body alone remained on earth. He wished, if possible, to visit all his communities once more before going to the home of his father. In the first months of 1720 he began his visitations, and the Brothers noticed the force with which their venerated chief spoke of eternal things. In May he was with Brother Jean, at Paris. One evening, in recreation, he took a handful of earth, and turning to the Brother, he said : " Behold, this is all we are; to this we shall soon be reduced!" Toward the end of May he returned to St. Yon, and feeling his end at hand, called for a reverend father in whom he had great confidence, and made a general confession.

Brothers John and Joseph were sent for, but, despite their haste, they arrived only to take part in the sad ceremony of his burial.

In dying, the departing general exclaimed : "O, how happy I am! I see the Most Blessed Virgin and our Venerable father, M. de La Salle: they are coming to receive me." His remains were placed beside those of the holy Founder. On the seventh of August, 1720, the Brothers, assembled in general chapter at St. Yon, elected Brother Timothy to the position of superior-general.

In his election, the institute was paying a fitting tribute to one who had had a large share in the love and esteem of the Venerable Founder. He had rendered important services in Chartres, Marseilles and Avignon. The institute rejoiced in its new chief, but no one seemed so pleased as Brother Irénée who saw his former director of novices in a position for which nature and grace had prepared him. After the election, sessions were held, to collect a statement of such practices as had been introduced into the institute, but were not found in the "Common Rules." These formed the matter of what are known as "Rules of Government." In this chapter the capitulants also gave the assistants charge of the most honored Brother Superior's health. This was necessary, for it was generally believed that Brother Barthélemy had shortened his days by excessive austerities. Brothers Timothy, John and Joseph were worthy guardians of the interests and honor of the society over which they presided.

The death of Brother Barthélemy, and the old age of Brother Thomas, rendered the possession of St. Yon very precarious. It was necessary, therefore, either to transfer the property to other names, or to obtain letters-patent for the society. The latter course was selected.

Pontcarré, who still continued his friendly relations with the Brothers, took charge of the matter, and presented the memoir prepared by Brother Timothy, under date of January, 1721, to Louis XV. He also obtained the influence of Mgr. Bezons, Archbishop of Rouen, then in Paris.

The papers were on the point of being issued, when the archbishop was prematurely called to give an account of his stewardship.

Brother Thomas, the surviving member in whose name the property was held, went to see M. de Tressan, a special admirer of the Venerable de La Salle's work. At the sight of this pale and venerable old man, the prelate understood the necessity of speedily procuring the desired letters.

They were accordingly issued, through the influence of his grace. in the month of September, 1724. It was also to be the glory of Brother Timothy's administration that he was to obtain the papal recognition of the Brothers of the Christian Schools. Many negotiations were necessary, and two popes, Clement XI and Innocent XIII, were to have been addressed, but it was only under Benedict XIII that the favor was granted.*

That pope, in honoring whose memory history does honor to itself, considered it one of his grandest acts that he had approved of the Brothers of the

---

* Benedict XIII was elected May twenty-seventh, 1724, while the Bull bears date of the seventh of the Kalends of February, 1724. This apparent discrepancy is due to the mode of computing the year. The Roman Court, in dating Bulls, began the year with March twenty-fifth. Therefore every document issued between that day and the first of the January previous would bear for date a year less than that ordinarily laid down. So what, in the language of the Roman Court, was the seventh of the Kalends of February, 1724, in civil computation is to be regarded as the twenty-sixth of January, 1725.

Christian Schools: " He was rejoiced that he could thus give another proof of the incessant fecundity of the Church."

In nothing could Benedict have better shown his esteem for the work in which the Brothers are engaged than by stating, in the conclusion of the Bull of Approbation, that the members were not to leave the society to enter a more austere order, without the express permission of the superior. A general chapter, opened at St. Yon on the ninth of August, 1725, received the Bull of Approbation. Rev. P. Bodin, S. J., and two assistants, preached the retreat which the capitulants made before considering the election of a superior, for Brother Timothy insisted upon resigning. His wishes were disregarded, however, and the thirty delegates unanimously continued him in his office. Brother John, whose age and services entitled him to an honorable retreat, was relieved from the position of assistant, at his own request. Brother Joseph was continued in his office, and Brother Irénée replaced the retiring member. The chapter was closed by the benediction of the Most Blessed Sacrament, during which the most beautiful vestments, presented to the society by the Venerable de La Salle, were used.

In 1734, the Brothers had the great happiness of receiving the body of their Venerable father in their chapel of St. Yon.

Sixteen ecclesiastics bore the remains in triumph, while four others acted as pallbearers. Over thirty thousand persons went before or followed the relics of the Venerable servant of God. Many Brothers from various cities were also present, and followed the body, each bearing a lighted taper in hand. Ladies of the highest nobility and rank had already taken their places in the chapel.

Places were also reserved for the president of the parliament of Rouen, the chancellor and the attorney-general, who honored the procession by their presence. The dean of the chapter, the pastors of the four city churches and their assistant priests, were also among the grateful public that paid a fitting tribute to the Venerable de La Salle. It was not an hour in which a panegyric could be pronounced. The people had spoken by their love and appreciation: a less eloquent tribute would have been inappropriate.

The ceremonies were to have been presided over by his grace, the most reverend archbishop, but M. Bridelle, archdeacon of the metropolitan church and vicar-general of the diocese, replaced him. The prelate, whose occupations did not permit him to assist two days in succession, dedicated the chapel on the following day. It had only been completed in time to receive the mortal remains of its architect.

The Roman rite, which had been introduced by the Venerable de La Salle at St. Yon, was continued by Brothers Barthélemy and Timothy. By special permission, the Brothers were allowed to continue this rite, though the missals were not according to the text used in the archdiocese.

Brother Gabriel, who had been instrumental in giving the Brothers so favorable a character in the Eternal City, was permitted to return to France, shortly after these joyful occurrences. He was

received by the most honored superior, Brother
Timothy, and by all the Brothers, as the last of M.
Nyel's disciples, and as one who had been known
for a time in Rome as the second Joseph Labre.
His first request was to pronounce his vows according to the form approved by Benedict XIII. The
good Brother, in 1691, had vowed "to sustain the
Christian Schools, even if he were obliged to beg his
bread;" now, with Brother Timothy as witness, and
the Brothers of St. Yon as a delighted audience, he
pronounces the new formula, which he had already
so faithfully observed. It was a matter of pious
discussion as to what community would have the
happiness to welcome the veteran into its hospitable
bosom. All wished to honor the man whom the
Venerable had selected as "Roman envoy." In
exchange for the charity and affection by which he
found himself surrounded, he gave the brightest
examples of simplicity and obedience. It was the
delight of the young and the pleasure of the old to
hear his impressions of the City of the Seven Hills,
and of its numerous consecrated spots. He died at
Auxonne, in 1733, full of virtues and merits.

Brother Timothy governed the institute during
thirty-one years. His firmness of character and
knowledge of men entitled him to the continued
confidence of the society. During his administration were opened no less than seventy establishments. Such services endeared him to the institute
at large, and it was only after repeated solicitations
that his resignation was accepted August third,
1751. Death overtook, but did not surprise him,
January seventh, 1752. He was seventy years old.

The general chapter which received Brother Timothy's resignation elected Brother Claude, Director of Avignon, as his successor. In the chapter held at St. Yon, July tenth, 1761, he sought to resign, but he found his appeals in vain. He referred to the growing infirmities of his age; yet the capitulants still refused, and he was obliged to continue till the ninth general chapter, held May, 1767. In this he was relieved, but lived eight years, preparing for his final rest, which he entered at the age of eighty-five, being the last Brother, probably, who had known the Venerable de La Salle.

At this time infamous writers, under the direction of Voltaire, were doing all in their power to destroy the mind of youth, by polluting the sources whence it was to drink. History was falsified, a superficial philosophy attacked truth, and libertinism kept pace with the march of new ideas. In the midst of such sad scenes and times the Church proved her strength. The religious life was the chief object attacked; its spirit was decried as one of abasement, which deprived man of his free-will and liberty. God came to the rescue, and religious houses, especially the novitiates of the Brothers, were crowded. It was in the midst of such occurrences that Brother Florence took the reins of government. He served for ten years, after which neither the tears of his Brothers, nor their supplications, could induce him to continue in office. He had fixed his residence at Paris, in 1770, and some years later at Melun. His comparative youth had made the society hope for many years of his government, but his determination to resign having prevailed, he was given the direction of Avignon. He was but fifty-two years old. During the latter years of his life he suffered imprisonment and many other trials, but remained unshaken in his adhesion to religion and his vocation. He died in 1800, when France was beginning to breathe freely after the horrors of revolution.

To Brother Agathon, one of the most distinguished generals, is due the credit of having made special regulations for the welfare of the sick and infirm. He had been professor of hydrography at Brest, and had been director of the boarding-school of Angers. To scientific qualities of a high order he added virtues of the purest type. Much was expected of his administration, and these hopes were realized. He established a normal-school at Melun, and prescribed special rules for the direction of the novitiates. His explanation of the "Twelve Virtues of a Good Master" founded upon the draught of a manuscript prepared by the holy Founder, and greatly appreciated by his first disciples, has given this confessor of the faith his greatest renown. Though a slender volume, it has been pronounced a masterpiece by the most competent judges. It created so favorable an impression, and was at once so fully appreciated, that, within the lifetime of its author, almost every living language had its translation. The superior-general of another religious order, having examined it, was so struck by its accuracy and depth of thought, that he presented a copy to the Censor of Books in Rome. This learned

critic, having carefully read it, not only approved
its publication and translation, but added expressions showing the exalted idea he had formed of the
work and its author.

Treatises on arithmetic and the French language
also show how faithfully he employed his leisure
moments. He governed the institute with rare
prudence and ability. He went around visiting the
various communities, and it gave him great pleasure
to find "that everywhere the primitive fervor was
kept in its vigor."

"Brother Agathon," says an anonymous biographer, "was at once a cabinet officer and a business
man. Under his vigilant administration the Brothers' colleges attained a very great reputation. The
institute had one hundred and twenty-one communities and one thousand Brothers, when the decree of
February thirteenth, 1790, ordered the suppression
of orders and congregations of both sexes. The teaching bodies were not directly attacked then, but their
respite was of short duration. Brother Agathon
was not a man to submit quietly to an unjust decree,
and he appealed to the assembly, stating that,
relying upon the faith of the government, many
Brothers had grown old in the service of youth,
and that the decree of suppression deprived such of
the home they had looked forward to for their old
age. Moreover, he said that the Society of the
Brothers could not be included in the "exterminating
law," since it devoted all its energies for the benefit
of the people, in whose name it was pretended the
onerous decree was published. "Reason and jus-

tice," says Poujoulat, " would have listened to such
arguments, but these had been driven from our midst
in those days ; his remonstrances were of no avail with
an unreasoning mob, that ruled the hour in the name
of liberty." All the Brothers resolutely refused to
take the oath required, and protested against leading
their children to services presided over by schismatical priests : thereupon Brother Agathon issued a circular-letter permitting his inferiors to retire to their
homes till such time as Providence would be pleased
to take pity upon their unfortunate country.* The
decree of August eighteenth declared that "a free
state should not suffer the existence of any corpora-
tion, *not even of those which, being devoted to public instruction, had merited well of the country.*" Thus, in
striking these institutions, the state could not refuse
to compliment them. This decree was illegal in itself, for it had not received the sanction of the king.

The reign of blood commenced ; the prisons were
filled : they were so many vestibules to the scaffold
Brother Salomon. secretary to the superior-general, had gone out with the latter, and, in the confusion then reigning, lost his companion. While
seeking to retrace his steps to St. Sulpice, he was
taken by the revolutionary mob, and conducted to
the convent of the Carmelites, Rue Vaugirard,
where, having refused to take the oath, he met
death in the massacres of the second and third of
September.

" Brother Abraham was already in the hands of
the executioners, when a national guard cried out:

---

* He had received special powers to this effect from the Holy See.

'I know that Brother; he taught school till the moment of his arrest. He has done no harm : I shall be his security.' The poor Brother, forthwith released, hastened to the bosom of his family."*

Brother Florence, former superior, and Brother Agathon, were incarcerated ; the latter escaped death only through the interference of Bourdon de l'Oise, member of the Convention. Many Brothers lost their lives under the guillotine; among others, Brother Martin, whose courageous words are still remembered. When called before the revolutionary tribunal at Avignon, he said : " I am a teacher, vowed to instruct the poor. If your expressions of love for the people are sincere, my position entitles me to your consideration; if your principles of fraternity are not vain formula, I may claim your gratitude." Such words were a direct passport to the block. " In those days courts condemned; they did not judge."†

After eighteen months of imprisonment, Brother Agathon was released. He hastened from Paris to Tours, where he spent his remaining days in prayer and affliction. In the month of August, 1797, he expired, and had the consolation, in his last moments, of seeing two Brothers, who recited the prayers, and assisted him in his preparation for the last sacraments. He was seventy-six years old, and had proved his attachment to the institute by corresponding, as often as circumstances would permit, with the Brothers of the three communities in Italy : two at Rome, and one at Ferrara. He had also

---

* " Vie du Frère Philippe," par Poujoulat, p. 24.   † Ibid., p. 25.

given his consent to the appointment of Brother
Frumence by the Holy Father, Pius VI, as administrator, or vicar-general, of the society. When the
French entered Rome, in 1798, the two communities were closed, and only those of Ferrara and Or-
vieto remained. The latter had been established a
short time previously. In 1800, Napoleon permitted
the Roman houses to be reopened.

In the midst of these trials the Brothers received
special marks of esteem wherever they could continue their ministry, even indirectly. In 1797, they
had been imprisoned in Laon, upon the report of a
schismatical priest; but the mothers of the children
assembled in such numbers, and in their own way
gave such positive marks of indignation at the imprisonment of such men, that they were forthwith
released. A banquet was immediately prepared in
the schoolyard, at which the Brothers and pupils
assisted, while the mothers waited upon them. It
was a proud day for the teachers, one that cannot
be forgotten. In this city, also, a Brother, whose
writing had secured him a position as secretary in
the military bureau, saved the original of the Bull
of Approbation of the society, as well as several
relics of the Venerable de La Salle. These are
now piously preserved, and are in the keeping of
the Régime.

On the second of May, 1802, after the signing of
the Concordat, the Brothers were permitted to reunite, and their first establishment was opened in
Lyons on the feast of the Exaltation of the Holy
Cross. A venerable old Brother, Francis of Jesus,

who had taught as a secular, was the instrument
of this happy revival. His children were so well
formed, that many asked where the teacher had
acquired his method. Upon declaring himself a
Christian Brother, he was encouraged by Abbé
Girard, Vicar-General, to seek some other members
of the disbanded society, to form a community.

Brother Francis knew but one, Frère Pigmenion,
who was employed as teacher at Condrieu. He
wrote for him ; but the good Brother, so happy in
being recalled to his holy state, arrived only in
time to witness the last moments of Brother Francis,
who died on Good-Friday, 1802. He was sixty-nine
years old. Left alone, but not discouraged, Brother
Pigmenion opened a school. Three postulants
presented themselves, of whom but one persevered,
Brother Augustin, who died in Paris, in 1869, aged
ninety-three years.

Napoleon's attention was called by Cardinal
Fesch to the good that had been done by these
Christian teachers. Brother Frumence, with three
companions, returned to France. It was in the
former college of the Jesuits, in Lyons, occupied
by the Brothers after the Revolution, that the vicar-
general and his associates were welcomed on
October twenty-first, 1804. In 1805, Pius VII, who
had returned from the consecration of the emperor
who was to dethrone him three years later, passed
through Lyons, and honored the Brothers' community by his paternal visit. He was accompanied
by four cardinals. He blessed the renovated chapel
and the re-born institute. His words were considered as the harbingers of brighter days.

The Mayor of Orleans, in welcoming back the Brothers, said : " It is time that justice should be done to men who lost their positions in the disastrous days through which we have passed, only because they filled them too well."

When some individuals complained that Napoleon wished to exempt the Brothers from military service, he pointedly remarked : " I do not know what sort of fanaticism some persons manifest against the Brothers: everywhere I am asked to reëstablish them : this general cry shows their utility. The least that Catholics can expect is equality ; and, certainly, thirty millions of men deserve as much consideration as three millions."* Cardinal Fesch had already written a circular-letter to all the disbanded Brothers, in which he said : " Brothers are asked for in many cities, and they are offered all that is needed. In several places their former houses await their return. Brother Frumence, your superior, is inconsolable at not being able to meet all the pious demands made upon him. Subjects are needed. The harvest is abundant, but the laborers are few. I invite you, my dear Brother, and conjure you by the zeal with which you are animated for the glory of God, the salvation of souls and your own duty, to hasten, at the earliest moment, to place yourself at the command of Brother Frumence, to be employed according to the obligations of your pious institute. In so doing, you will give me a gratification that I shall never forget. Permit me to assure

* Poujoulat, " Vie du Frère Philippe."

you that my desire is to protect your congregation, and to propagate it. I can also assure you of the favorable intentions of his imperial and royal majesty in your regard. I salute you cordially."

This same cardinal, in a letter addressed, in 1808, to Mgr. de Villaret, Bishop of Casal, and chancellor of the university, said, "that to the Brothers the French people owed the regeneration of their morals, and the faith of their fathers." *   His eminence was endeavoring to procure a large and suitable house from the chancellor in which the Brothers might open a novitiate and receive the aged and infirm, "who would have deserved well of religion and of the state." June twenty-eighth, 1810, the society was recognized, with all the power and privilege of bodies admitted as of public utility. M. Emery, superior of St. Sulpice,† was among the Brothers' best friends and most powerful agents in the university council. "No one," said he, "esteems the Brothers more than I ; and it is a mark of the blessing of Divine Providence that they have been attached to the university."

It was a great consolation for Brother Frumence to see that the society was so favorably regarded everywhere, and that, before his death, it would have regained part of its ancient splendor, and have grown even more vigorous, because of the trials through which it had passed. He departed from a world in which he had seen so much misery, in the sixty-third year of his age, on the twenty-seventh of January, 1810.

---

* Poujoulat, " Vie du Frère Philippe," p. 34.
† This was the editor of Leibnitz' *Systema Theologicum.*

On the eighth of September, of the same year, the twelfth general chapter was held in Lyons, and Brother Gerbaud, already favorably known as the Director of Gros-Caillou, Paris, was elected superior-general.

At his installation the institute comprised about thirty-six communities. During the last years of the Napoleonic dynasty and the first of the Restoration, Brother Gerbaud was in constant anxiety, and was constrained to use every lawful means to save the young Brothers from military service. After many consultations, and through the influence of MM. MacCarty, de Villeville and de Bonald, a favorable solution of the vexed question was obtained. The most honored superior, who had learned in the midst of these difficulties to appreciate, to its fullest extent, the peace and quiet of humble positions, sought to resign, in the thirteenth general chapter. But his firmness of character joined to his affability of manner had created too favorable an impression, and he was obliged to continue in office.

In 1819, Louis XVIII expressed the desire that so useful and important a congregation should have its headquarters or mother-house in Paris. Brother Gerbaud assented to the change. A royal ordinance of May thirtieth, 1821, approved the municipal deliberation which gave the Brothers possession of a large establishment, Rue du Faubourg-Saint-Martin, which was called "the house of the Infant Jesus." The principal portions of this institution had been erected by St. Vincent de Paul, and had been named in honor of the Infant Saviour of the world. The Father of the poor had prepared a home for the children of the true friend of youth.

Brother Gerbaud continued to direct the affairs of the institute with that rare prudence and firmness to which was owing so much of the success that blessed it. He had already given twelve years to the difficult task of generalship, when a stroke of apoplexy called him suddenly away on the night of the tenth of August, 1822. He was sixty-two years old. One hundred and eighty houses, with twelve hundred subjects, attested the zeal with which he had labored, and the success which had crowned his efforts. It was a noble legacy left to the intelligence and piety of Brother William of Jesus, who was elected superior-general in the fourteenth general chapter. He was then seventy-five years old : " It is time for me to think of death. Do you not know that seventy-five grenadiers pursue me?" he said to the capitulants, who heeded not his remonstrances, for they saw a bright soul in a somewhat enfeebled body. His career proved the justness of the hopes that had been placed in him. His activity and zeal were surprising in one of his years ; and the life and vim with which he impregnated the schools served greatly to augment their reputation. The youngest Brother was as much an object of his solicitude as the one more advanced in years. " You do not know your happiness," wrote he to a young Brother who has since grown grey in the institute, " in entering religion so young. . . . Take care of your health ; do not speak so loud as to injure your breast." He himself had experienced this happiness of entering young. "He brought with him his primitive innocence, and never did his soul know evil." *   In consequence, he was always cheerful, and never lost the boyish activity of youth.   To his intelligence the society owes an improved edition of the "Schools' Conduct," and he employed Brothers of culture and talent in the preparation of works suited to the wants of the Christian Schools.† He already counted two hundred and ten establishments, over two hundred and fifty novices and postulants, eight hundred teachers in active service, and an attendance of sixty-four thousand scholars, when, in 1830, God called him to a better world. He was in his eighty-third year, and barely escaped the horrors of the Revolution of July.

While thrones were tottering and falling, and princely heads were being uncrowned, Brother William of Jesus received as successor, in the fifteenth general chapter, Brother Anaclet.   He was a worthy descendant of so illustrious a body of generals.   From the time of his entrance into the institute, he possessed the modesty and humility that are characteristic of the Christian Brothers.   "He knew how to keep in the background for a long time his penetrating mind, the accuracy of his judgment, and the polished culture which he had acquired in the world.'‡   God's works stand not in need of the protection of men: the new superior, despite the character of the times in which he governed. directed

---

* *Relations Mortuaires*, 10 Juin, 1830.
† Most honored Brother William of Jesus requested Brother Philip to prepare a Practical Geometry.   The work is still a standard in France.
‡ *Relations Mortuaires*, 25 Sept., 1838, t. i, p. 305.

the interests of the institute with unlooked-for prosperity.   Speaking of the difficulties that surrounded
his administration, the   circular, announcing his
death, says: " The task was difficult, the burdens
heavy; but the most honorable Brother Anaclet was
rich in resources: he knew how to place them in
action, and he triumphed. His profound genius suggested the means to employ; his piety drew down
upon them the blessings of heaven."* During his administration public night-schools were opened ; and
Guizot, the minister of public instruction, was so
much pleased with their success, that he did all in his
power to secure their perpetuation and increase.
Under his family name of Louis Constantine, Brother
Anaclet prepared several works for the use of the
schools.   In the October of 1835, he established a
preparatory novitiate in the mother-house. He was
greatly, in all these works, aided by Brother Philip.
Services, so many and so great, rendered to France
in the name of religion, called forth the generous
admiration of Guizot. He tendered Brother Anaclet
the Cross of the Legion of Honor.   But the humble
superior declined the distinction.

Such multiplied and constant labors told on his
health. On the sixth of September, 1838, in the
fiftieth year of his age, he breathed his soul into the
hands of his Creator.   The institute then numbered
two thousand three hundred Brothers, seven novitiates, one hundred and seventy-two novices, and
one hundred and forty thousand scholars.

In dying, Brother Anaclet must have been greatly

---

* *Relations Mortuaires,* p. 306.

consoled at the thought that there was amongst his assistants a man whose soul was made to rule, and who, as the ninth superior-general, would not only continue the good work with a new and magic energy, but whose personal ability would give him a world-wide name. Upon his memory we will dwell a few minutes.

CHAPTER II.

Brother Philip.—His Character as portrayed some weeks after his death.—The World unites in honoring his Memory.—His Works, charitable and literary.—Letter of the Cardinal Archbishop of Paris.—The Holy Father writes the Panegyric of the deceased General.—Brother Jean-Olympe.—Success of his Government.—A Year's Administration.—The Society again in Tears.—Most honored Brother Irlide to continue the Work.

BROTHER PHILIP is justly considered the second Founder of the Institute of the Christian Schools. The difficult periods in which his wisdom saved not only his own society, but similar organizations that depended for existence upon the success of his endeavors; the universal sympathy created by the modesty of his conduct and the fruits of his labors, have placed his name, with that of the Venerable de La Salle, foremost in the affection of his subjects. *

The world would have us believe that to enter a religious house is equivalent to becoming worthless; it is burying, say they, in the obscurity of the convent, those talents given for the benefit of mankind at large. Such examples as that of Brother Philip tell the falsity of this assertion. They show us the obligation under which youth is to pray for light in the choice of a state of life, and for grace to

---

* This chapter is partly made up from an article of the writer's in *Brownson's Quarterly Review* for April, 1873. The fact will account for the coincidences in whole pages.

follow the voice of conscience when its dictates have been made known to him. God, who wishes that all men should come to the knowledge of the truth, undoubtedly gives religious vocations to many young persons. In refusing to follow such, when discovered, or in failing to ask for direction needed under such circumstances, do they not render themselves more or less responsible for the good that may remain uneffected? This question presents itself with twofold force in our own day, when there are no longer such difficulties encountered in embracing a religious life as were surmounted by Brother Philip in the prime of his manhood, amid dangers which threatened not only such as ventured to embrace a religious vocation, but even those who dared to profess their belief in Christ.

"Such men as Brother Philip belong to no country; they are a gift of a beneficent Providence to the world at large. Hence we shall say little about his youth, save that he was born at Gachat (Loire), on the first of November, 1792. About this time France was in the throes of one of those upheavals of her society which seem a periodical occurrence. Amid such horrors and difficulties were the early days of young Bransiet spent. Divine Providence, no doubt, was thus filling the heart of His future soldier with the dread of the spirit of the world against which he was afterward to wage so spirited a warfare. In looking around him with that keen perception that even in his early years he possessed, he learned that the great evil of the day was the forgetfulness of the Lord. In the language of the child of Monica, he cried out : ' Lord, teach me, in the midst of this world that forgets Thy name,—teach me to know Thee, and likewise to know myself.' " His father's home was made the refuge of fugitive priests, who preferred their faith to their positions in a schismatical Church. At the feet of these good and incorruptible men did young Bransiet learn the worth of virtue and the price of duty. At this time, also, the institute being still scattered, Brother Laure kept a small boarding and day-school near Gachat. Thither our youth was sent ; there he imbibed his vocation for the Brotherhood. When Brother Laure had read the appeal of Cardinal Fesch to the members of his order to reunite, he called his pupils together, and said to them : " My dear children, I was, before the Revolution, a Brother of the Christian Schools, and I always regretted having been constrained to abandon my vocation. But I learn, thank God, that our society is being reëstablished in France, and I hasten to become one of it again in Lyons.. If any among you desire to enter it, also, and to consecrate yourselves to God and the education of youth, I will endeavor to have you received and formed."* Several of the students then and there formed the resolution to follow this good Brother. An older companion of Matthew Bransiet entered the novitiate in 1807, and was afterward known as Brother Anselm.† Several others followed at considerable intervals of time.

---

* *Circulaire Nécrologique et Biographique sur le T. H. Frère Philippe,* 1874, p. 10.　　　　　　† He died in 1857.

Aware that, when God calls to-day, He may not wait for us till the morrow, young Bransiet entered the novitiate of the Brothers of the Christian Schools on the sixth of November, 1809. His first years were spent in the faithful discharge of the humble functions that are the ordinary lot of young religious teachers. However, even in these early days, he gave indications of future usefulness of a high order. His aptitude for mathematics developed itself at the outset, and at Auray he was charged with a special class of coast navigation. His clearness of thought, his assiduity in all the exercises, joined to a keen perception of the wants of his day, in educational questions, raised him rapidly in the estimation of his superiors. M. Deshayes, the parish priest, a man of great insight into character, used to call him a young ancient: *un jeune vieillard.* What lasting and beneficial impressions he left in the classes he taught, may best be testified to by the numerous vocations that were fostered by him, both for the religious and the clerical life. His pupils loved him, and he loved them with no less affection. "I often think of him," wrote an old pupil of his, forty years afterward, "standing on the platform of his desk, governing his pupils, and singing with them this Christian and beautiful hymn, '*Tout n'est que vanité!*'* His intelligent features still remain in my memory; they were so animated, and his eyes so darted upon us a kind of magnetic fluid, that it was impossible to withdraw from their attraction. So much was I

---

* "All is but vanity."

under his sway, that I often kissed his garments without his perceiving it; and I have always remained passionately and respectfully attached to him." * This is the unanimous expression of all who ever had the happiness of holding relations with Brother Philip.

A few years,—eight or nine we are told,—after Brother Philip had joined the institute, he was placed at the head of one of the principal houses of his order. He corresponded so well with the expectations of his superiors, and became so generally known to the Brothers, that he was shortly afterward elected to represent his district in the councils of the institute; and in presence of the assembled wisdom of the society evidenced so rare a knowledge of its future, that he was marked as one who would have a large share in the influence it was to wield. Honors rapidly followed; he was elected assistant-general in 1836. He created so favorable an impression in this new post that he was finally called to the position of superior-general, after the death of the much-respected Brother Anaclet.

The new superior-general had not the labor of making a name. He had already been so long in the public service of the institute, that all expected the greatest results from his administration. Nor were they to be disappointed.

There was nothing left undone to cause the institute to prosper, both in its spiritual and temporal

---

* Letter of the pastor of Chantillon-sur-Loire to the Brother-President of the College of Orleans, dated March 3d, 1858. The clergyman was Brother Philip's pupil in 1817.

affairs. He had to contend at intervals with the enemies of Christian education in the French legislative councils. Whatever may have been the faults of the late emperor,—and his best friends admit he had many,—one redeeming quality in him was his deference to religious persons. He always expressed and manifested the highest esteem for Brother Philip, and more than once discountenanced educational schemes that seemed indirectly aimed at the work which Brother Philip represented. Still, in 1861, there occurred a serious difficulty between the latter and the minister of public instruction. Up to that time the Brothers had given the children of the public schools in France under their charge gratuitous teaching. The small salaries required to support them, they received from the municipal authorities. But, as early as 1833, a law had been established requiring them to receive compensation from every child able to pay : this they resisted, as being contrary to the customs of their institute. They were generally shielded by the various ministers who came into power, till 1861, when a letter addressed to Brother Philip, from the minister, declared that, in case of longer resistance, "the government would be obliged to refuse a continuance of its good-will." * There was no mistaking the import of these words. Prompt action was required. "He acknowledged, with the members of the general chapter, that longer resistance would have been suicidal to the institute ; it became necessary to cede the point, and take measures to limit,

* *Lettre datée du* 10 *Juin,* 1861.

at least for the time being, the practical extent of gratuity to what was required by the formula of vows and the Bull of Approbation of the institute."* Gratuitous teaching he recognized as a means the more effectually to accomplish the great end of Christian education: as soon as it became an obstacle, rather than a facility, it was the part of wisdom to set it aside. Seldom did Brother Philip's rare business tact appear to more advantage than in the negotiation of this delicate affair. Not only had he to disarm the hostility of those in power, but he had also to reconcile to the new order of things Brothers who feared it might interfere with the keeping of their vow of teaching gratuitously. In both ways he succeeded.

But other difficulties, still more embarrassing, pressed upon the order, and were removed only by the consummate tact of Brother Philip. From time to time it became a question of no small importance as to whether teachers ought to be exempt from military service. In 1850 a law was passed, in a great measure through Brother Philip's influence, exempting from military service all teachers who were pledged to devote themselves for ten years to the education of youth. In 1866 it was attempted to force the interpretation of this law in such a manner that "all the Brothers dispensed should accomplish their engagements in the public schools." This would have interfered materially with the workings of the institute, so far as its boarding-schools and colleges were concerned. But again

---

* *Circulaire Nécrologique,* p. 34.

the indomitable energy of Brother Philip overcame all obstacles. Finally, in 1872, he achieved a triumph, not only for the institute of which he is so bright a glory, but for all the religious teaching-bodies in France. At this time the whole country seemed disorganized; the surrender of Sedan had humiliated the nation; men learned that in the new empire there was more glitter than gold; the communists had made a desperate struggle to take in hands the reins of government: thanks to the genius of Mac-Mahon they were unsuccessful: the army was to be reorganized; again the Brothers were to be pressed into military service; every Frenchman was to become a soldier. How evade the difficulty which threatened the very existence of every religious body in France? Nobly and well did the champions of religion fight for them in the national assembly; eloquently did they speak their praises. M. Chesnelong, especially, pleaded their cause with warmth. "They proved," said he, "in the last war, that they were men to brave it, and that in their religious breasts beat hearts of patriots and Frenchmen." (*A voice from the left :*) "Ah, well, make soldiers out of them."* This was turning his own argument upon him. But Brother Philip had tried the efficacy of prayer, as well as his own diplomatic skill. While he went round among the members, encouraging them in the almost hopeless contest, he had the whole institute to pray. Heaven blessed his efforts. At the end of a stormy debate, it was concluded, by a majority of three hundred and

---

* *Journal Officiel de l'Assemblée Nationale, du* 13 *Juin,* 1872.

thirty-seven votes, that the law referring to teachers remain as it had formerly stood. Thus it was that this great general was ever foremost in the hour of peril; ever on the alert to notice the threatening dangers; ever active to ward them off from his dear institute, which he cherished with as strong affection as a mother loves her children.

To continue the good work begun by himself and Brother Anaclet, he had several Brothers prepare a series of text-books on all subjects taught in the Christian Schools. The result was a series of books that are used extensively throughout France. "They are among the best," said an eminent educational authority, "as was recently declared in the municipal council of Paris. And that which goes to prove it is the use that is made of them by many secular teachers, in preference to other works." * He kept pace with all the educational schemes of the day; where he saw progress, he recommended it. He revised the "Schools' Conduct," bringing it up to the present strides made in primary teaching. A new idea or a new method was not rejected because of its novelty, if reason and experience combined in approving it. In the letter placed at the head of the "Conduct" of 1863, he wrote to his dear Brothers: "Teaching has assumed in these latter days a particular character, which we must take into consideration. Proposing to itself, as principal aim, to form the judgment, it gives less importance than it formerly did to the cultivation of the memory; it prefers making use of methods

---

* *Le Correspondant du* 25 *Janvier,* 1874, p. 408.

which exercise the intelligence, and lead the child
to reflect, to account to itself for facts, and to leave
the domain of words, in order to enter that of ideas."
Here, in a nutshell, is the embodiment of all that
is genuine in the modern improvements in teaching.
To pass from words to things and thoughts, is certainly a step in the right direction.

But he was too enlightened a superior not to
know that religious men are successful teachers only
according as they are fervent religious. He therefore took every possible means to revive the zeal
and pious sentiments of the Brothers. He wrote,
and caused to be written, books of meditation suited
to the tastes and occupations of the Brothers.
They cover the whole ground of the spiritual life.
All devotions consistent with the spirit of his institute, and that had received the approbation of the
Church, were very dear to him. As the result of
experience, he found that teachers, more than others,
need that the conscience, the heart and the religious feelings be kept tender, while the mind pro-
gresses in scientific pursuits. It was his opinion, in
common with many saints, that no subject is more
likely to produce this tenderness than the contemplation of the Man of Sorrows. So we have a book
of meditations upon the " Passion of our Lord."
" Should we not," he asks, " as religious, meditate
especially on the sacred passion? All in the life
we have embraced speaks to us of Jesus suffering ;
His image is constantly before our eyes ; we have
in hand, and even carry always about us. the sacred
book which contains the recital of His sorrows."

In harmony with this work, and in similar sentiment, are the treatises on " The Holy Eucharist " and on " The Sacred Heart."

The love of Christ is so closely allied to that of His holy Mother, that the author whose devotion induces him to write upon the love displayed by the Son in the " banquet of charity," will also feel pleasure in relating the wonderful prerogatives of her from whose pure substance was taken the sacred body which is our portion in the feast of the Lamb. One of the freshest of the series is that on the Most Blessed Virgin. It deserves a careful reading from all those who seek new lights by which to learn the beauties of the " Vessel of Singular Devotion."

Not satisfied with inspiring love for Mary, he would also promote an ardent attachment to the holy patron and protector of the Brothers' Institute. His zeal induced him to prepare a work in which to utter the praises of the man whom the Scriptures call the Just. What the sacred text has not recorded, nor tradition handed down to us, his enlightened piety suggests. His views were founded on the strictly devotional aspects of the subject, and, as a critic has remarked, in all Brother Philip's works on such subjects there is scarcely one, if one, reference to miraculous events, piously believed to have occurred, or those commonly accepted but unapproved relations that form so large a portion of even the best works of this nature. From this it must not be imagined that he was tainted with the " liberalism " that condescends to discard so much that is edifying. The " Catechism in Examples " which he caused to be prepared, wherein each sacrament, commandment or dogma is illustrated by several historical relations, would disprove the charge; but he seems to have felt that, in speaking to religious who, as various authors have remarked, are slowest to believe, though strongest in their convictions, he should avoid any assertion or proposition, historical, traditional, or of pious acceptance, unless founded upon the authority of some recognized leader in the Church. His practical good sense and experience also taught him that all true devotion must be founded on the knowledge and love of God, and our acquaintance with, and detestation of, the lurking passions of our hearts. Under such impressions he undertook to prepare the "Particular Examen." Herein are found three hundred and seventeen subjects, bearing on the whole range of the duties of the man, the Christian, and the religious. These chapters include subjects from "The Creation" to that of "Study." This book shows the powers of his searching mind in a special manner. It proves him to have understood the folds of heart and intellect in an eminent degree. But there was one form of composition in which Brother Philip's pen was particularly facile and efficient: it is the writing of circular-letters. In these he poured out his whole soul. His iron resolve, his virtuous heart, his fatherly care, his tender piety, his love for the institute,—all speak with inspiring eloquence from the pages of these letters; all proclaim the broad-viewed intellect, and the large, loving heart that embraced the whole world in its charity.

Amid the preoccupations of a life so busily employed, good Brother Philip still found time to think over, and give expression to, his feelings on the sufferings of our Holy Father, Pius IX. There was between these two characters close affinity. They loved each other dearly. Their hearts beat in perfect unison. Therefore, the late injustices of which the Sovereign Pontiff was a victim, were a source of great anguish to the noble-hearted superior. In the circular he issued upon the occasion of his last visit to his Holiness, he uses the following language, in reference to the gratitude manifested by the Supreme Pontiff upon receiving through him a donation from the institute.

"Thanks," said the Holy Father, " for this filial souvenir."

" Yes, my dear Brothers," says the superior, " it is sad, it is lamentable, it is heart-rending, to see the Vicar of Christ, heretofore a powerful sovereign, needing an alms from his own children, and obliged to say ' Thank you.'

" This word will touch you, I am certain, my dear Brothers, as it has equally touched us; it will inspire you with the noble thought of renewing this offering; you will have, once more, the merit of relieving Jesus Christ in the person of His worthy, elevated, illustrious, but sorely-tried representative."

In thus showing his devotion to the Holy See, he faithfully imitated the Venerable Founder of the institute, who sent special orders to the Brothers in Rome to make a visit to the tombs of SS. Peter

and Paul, there to pray that his Brothers might
ever remain faithful to the visible head of the
Church.

Brother Philip took a holy pride in his institute,
because he saw in it the means of doing so much
good. He experienced great pleasure in seeing
others having a similar interest in it. Though very
reticent, as a rule, he never failed to give public
recognition of esteem to such as had, within their
sphere, done or said something complimentary to
the institute. On the occasion of the holding of a
general chapter, the delegates from America paid
a visit to the college of Passy, and one of their
number, after an entertainment, spoke of "Our
holy Institute, the model republic." The fact was
repeated to the venerable superior, and when he met
the Brother, he embraced him, and said : "Thanks
for your filial sentiment : we are all members of this
republic, and we must all labor to preserve its demo-
cracy of spirit."

It was this love and solicitude for his institute
that led him to desire that some one less unworthy,
as he thought, should be placed in the position he
had honored during so many years. A powerful
appeal, in which the recital of his labors was
corroborated by his careworn and delicate appearance, could not induce the chapter to accept a
resignation which they felt it would be nothing
more than justice to entertain, under other circumstances. He was thus continued in office, and
constrained to keep, till the end, a burden he had

never sought,—one which his virtues and talents had imposed upon him, and which his immense experience rendered it advisable to insist that he should not relinquish.

Some few months after the close of the general chapter, Brother Philip was called to Rome, as heretofore narrated, and upon his return felt greatly fatigued. His health, which had previously been sustained only through the greatest care, gave way under the strain that had been given it, and he retired, one morning, after Holy Mass and communion, never to rise from his modest couch.

He had now received the highest rewards which Divine Providence, the Church, and society can bestow in this world. He had witnessed the first halo of glory placed around the brow of his Venerable Father and Founder; through the medium of the electric current, the blessing of the common father of the faithful was sent him, to soothe the last hours of a well-spent life; and the Cardinal-Archbishop of Paris came, on the sixth of January, to pay the debt of gratitude due to one who had done so much for Catholicity in France.

The gay capital was not aware that so powerful an interest was centred in a simple *Frère des Ecoles Chrétiennes;* still the hand of death was scarcely fixed upon him in the early hours of the seventh, when thousands called for a public expression of the nation's gratitude to the nation's servant. The humility of the superior had led him to prescribe that the simplicity of his rule should be observed in the last obsequies; but Brother Philip, as has been remarked, belonged not only to the Christian Brothers, but to the Christian world, and the latter insisted upon doing him homage when he could no longer resist or escape it. His modesty had required that the Cross of the Legion of Honor,. received during the time of the nation's greatest humiliation, should not be placed upon his breast. Gratitude was not to be cheated, however; as an officer, equally decorated, taking his cross from his bosom, and placing it upon the noble but pulseless heart of the great general, exclaimed: " If I have deserved this decoration, I owe it to the sentiments of religion and patriotism with which Brother Philip inspired me."

The people had spoken. Nor was the Church silent. His Eminence, Cardinal Guibert, of Paris, issued a letter to all the clergy in his archdiocese upon the death of the Brother. " What he has done," says this good successor of martyrs, " need not be repeated here; the whole world has been a witness thereof. He has restored and renewed, in some sort, the work of the Venerable de La Salle. He understood the nature of his mission with rare superiority of intelligence, and, without leaving the bounds of modesty, governed his society with a power of will not less remarkable. By the extension and development which he gave his work, he proved how fruitful was the charitable thought that had inspired the holy Founder.

"Brother Philip consecrated himself entirely to the service of the people, and he might well say that his mission was to teach the poor : *Evangelizare pauperibus misit me.* In addressing youth, he could say to them, in the words of St. Paul to the Corinthians : 'For, if you have ten thousand instructors in Christ, yet not many fathers who love you as I :' *Nam si decem millia pædagogorum habeatis, sed non multos patres.* Four hundred thousand children learned from him and his to become good Christians, and citizens fit to fulfil all the duties of their future professions. While others spend their zeal in spreading false ideas, that lead away the souls of youth, excite their wicked passions, and inspire the ignorant with thoughts of pride and presumption, he labored to make the sons of the people honest, and wanting neither in requisite instruction, nor in the virtues which are still more necessary.

"Placed by Providence at the head of one of the most important enterprises that have been undertaken for the good of humanity, in spite of his modesty and the simplicity of his life, he became one of the most useful, the most popular, and we may even say, one of the most distinguished men of our day. No ordinary capacity, zeal and perseverance were required to administer, during so many years, the affairs of a society spread throughout the world. Indeed, all those who became acquainted with him were struck by his rare wisdom, as much as by his virtue.

"The death of Brother Philip has given rise to a public mourning in the capital. The aisles of the great church of St. Sulpice could not contain the crowds that gathered around his modest coffin. There were persons of every class, who represented all that was noble, respected and religious in society. Two cardinals, several bishops, and a great number of the clergy, were among the assembly. Their presence testified the gratitude of the Church to this 'good and faithful servant,' and spoke of the value placed upon the services of the Brothers of the Christian Schools."

Not only in France were such honors paid his memory; throughout the entire world, in eleven hundred and sixty-one communities, containing two thousand one hundred and forty-four schools, numbering seven thousand four hundred and twelve classes, prayers were offered for the departed general. Where the children of two hemispheres manifested such sorrow, their common father could not remain silent. The crowning glory of Brother Philip's career will be found in the testimony borne in his favor by his Holiness, Pius IX, who said:—

" God, who, for the accomplishment and the progress of His works, employs fitting instruments, who assists by opportune help, and distinguishes by His gifts men chosen for this purpose, granted you for many years the excellent superior you have just lost. To him did He give a sound mind in a sound body ; him did He enrich with the spirit of faith and charity. And, that he might not be seduced by the wind of unsound doctrines that blows in every direction, He attached his heart and his mind to this chair of truth which your superior always surrounded with the worship of an humble veneration and an

ardent love. Such is the source whence he derived the virtue of fecundity, by which he quintupled
the family of which he had received the direction,
and which permitted him to offer its beneficent
ministrations to the most distant countries. And
as by a careful and religious training, by the exercises
of a regular life, through his frequent exhortations,
and a diligent vigilance over all things, as also by
his pious writings, your superior had filled the
members of his congregation with his own sentiments, they have become most useful, not only to
religion, but likewise to their country, to which they
rendered admirable services of charity during its
reverses. It is, therefore, with reason that you weep
his loss; but, as his spirit lives and flourishes among
you, we doubt not that there are many more besides,
from whom you will elect a man able to preserve
and to advance the work which your deceased
superior has developed, perfected, and propagated
by his prolonged and incessant labors. This we
desire, and for the purpose we implore the blessing
of heaven upon you."

Eleven thousand loving hearts thrilled with gratitude at this mark of affection bestowed upon their
departed chief, and of sympathy to themselves, by
the Vicar of Christ. It was not without a holy dread
that Brother Jean-Olympe took the reins of government, as successor of the great and good Brother
Philip. He was elected on the ninth of April, 1874.
His long-continued services as novice-master, and
the general esteem in which he had been held as
assistant, gave the fondest hopes for his administra-

tion. The love he constantly manifested for the aged, and his kindness to the young, gained him all hearts. In the first twelve months of his generalship he had opened no less than thirty communities; but all the cherished hopes of his children were chilled at the unexpected intelligence that cast a gloom over the institute, when its members learned that, on the seventeenth of April, 1875, their venerated general had gone to receive his reward, after an illness which had declared itself on the anniversary of his election. During his generalship, he had shown many marks of special confidence to his fifth assistant, Brother Irlide, in whose zeal and intelligence he had great reliance. In this confidence the entire council concurred; and when the Brothers from the four quarters of the globe had again assembled, to Brother Irlide was given the task of continuing the work of the Venerable de La Salle. The prayer of his numerous children is that he may be long left to them.

CHAPTER III.

IN the scope of the work established by the
Venerable de La Salle, every form of intellectual
want finds its fitting place; the success that has
blessed the work is due to a method which has
deserved the praise of men whose greatest satisfaction would be to chronicle its failure. But this Venerable Founder could scarcely have foreseen the full
extent of the magnitude of the work he had begun.
That were not in keeping with the greatness of his
soul. Few great men die in splendor. When saintliness of life is combined with greatness of action,
they leave the field of their labors with an air of dis-
appointment, accounting themselves unprofitable
servants, whose efforts failed because of their unworthiness. Only the Master of action could say,
" It is consummated." Only He could compass the
whole length and breadth, and depth and height, of
His work. To all others is it given but to approach

more or less proximately the ideal of action in their minds; and looking rather to what they have not done than to what they have done, they count their lives of small worth, and wonder why men applaud such failures. But this weakness of their nature is the source of their strength. They do so much, because they think they are doing so little: the Venerable de La Salle was no exception to the rule. The guiding principle of his life was such as to foster these sentiments of humility and self-depreciation. That principle was the spirit of faith. He was so impregnated with it, that he infused it into his institute, and it has also become the secret of its success. "The spirit of this order," says he, in the Rules and Constitution of the Brothers, "is, firstly, a spirit of faith, which should engage those who compose it to look upon everything with the eye of faith, to do all their actions for God, and to attribute all to him. *Those who have not this spirit, those who have lost it, should be regarded as dead members, and they should look upon themselves as such,* because they are deprived of the life and grace of their state."* What a grand protest against the scepticism of the age is not the life of a Brother so actuated!

The Comtist may deny the existence of God; the Cosmist may relegate Him to the unknowable; the Pantheist may identify Him with nature; but the Christian Brother lives under His eye, confessing His name, proclaiming His threefold personality, adoring His holiness, thinking of His presence. A life so actuated must needs be a holy life.

---

* Rules, p. 22.

16

The Venerable Founder's letters breathe the same holy spirit of implicit faith. It was his heart's desire to see the Brothers looking upon everything as God considered it, free from all human motives. The confidence which this sublime and heroic faith produced was equally remarkable. In the midst of danger and trial he was calm and hopeful. When others hoard up their treasures for days that threaten to be sad, he gives his whole substance to the poor, relying upon Him who feeds the birds of the air. Where good is to be done, he never hesitates; once the will of God is manifested, he begins to act; he does his share, satisfied that God, who never allows Himself to be outdone in generosity, will supply the rest. His charity likewise led him to sacrifice himself for the little ones of Christ. For these he relinquishes position and emoluments; he becomes poor with the indigent, and breaks to hitherto famishing souls the bread of the word of God. In every circumstance he cried out: " Lord, what wilt Thou have me to do? Speak, Lord, Thy servant heareth." He is called to form a body of teachers, and his charity induces him to instruct the smallest children in the simplest elements; his love of his neighbor makes him desire to succor all who suffer, to console all who mourn, to bear the burdens of all who are heavily laden. What humility, joined to Christian independence, do we see in all his undertakings! *He never did anything to secure the favor of men.* In all things he vows to do what will be for the best, without regarding human motives, or what men may say. But there is one thing he prefers: it is to obey rather than command. The good child is not more docile than he. His whole life is a struggle to avoid honors and responsibilities, which pursue him all the more earnestly. He looks upon himself as a worm of the earth, and the least of men; he is nothing in his own eyes; if success crown his efforts, to God is given the glory. "Praised be His holy name," he says in his greatest afflictions, as in his most prosperous hours. His spirit of simplicity leads him to entertain extraordinary devotion to the Divine Infancy, which appears in all his writings. He places his institute under the special protection of the Holy Infant, and rejoices most amid the poverty of Vaugirard, which recalls to his mind the events in Bethlehem. In all the storms of passion he found in prayer a precious oil to throw upon the troubled waters of his soul, and calm ensued. When humiliation pursued him, he had a chosen retreat to which he betook himself for strength and resignation; he had a bosom friend to whom he addressed himself with the certainty of being heard. To Him he opened his bleeding heart, and there received the embraces of the Divine Consoler; there he rested, free from the imputations of men who could not understand his acts, nor the intention with which they had been performed. When his soul was in agony, caused by the malicious tongues and the wicked pens of exulting enemies, he had a chosen harbor whither he directed his steps; he prostrated himself in silent, but imploring prayer before the Divine "Prisoner of the Tabernacle."

Each morning, even when excruciating pain was his portion, the Venerable servant of God hastened to the altar to offer the Lamb of propitiation therewith all the actions of the incoming day. In presence of this Spouse he could spend not only one, but many hours, watching with the Sacred Heart that never slumbers. His ardent belief in the real presence made him see the love, the beneficence, the beauty of the mystery of the Blessed Eucharist. There he was inspired with that hope that led him to expect all from Him who strengthens us; and when the day was over, when another bead had been added to his chaplet of life, with what love he prostrated himself anew before the " Silent Watcher," and begged Him to bless the closing hours of a day in which he had endeavored to procure His glory and to extend His kingdom! The holy Founder's only desire was to be dissolved and to live with Christ; and as he knew that we cannot suddenly love that which we have studiously or through carelessness avoided, he ever bore in mind that, to sing the praises of the Lamb in eternity, men must learn the first notes of the heavenly music on earth, by prayer and good deeds.

To maintain this spirit, he recommended and practised devotion to Jesus, to His blessed Mother, Mary, and to His foster-father, St. Joseph. From meditation on the sufferings of the sacred humanity of Jesus, he learned how to bear up with the trials that surrounded him in life; from his affection for Mary, in whose immaculate heart he loved to find refuge in hours of temptation, he imbibed that unsullied chastity that shone so conspicuously as to enable Brother Barthélemy to say of him that he "believed him to be among the virgins;" from his contemplation of St. Joseph—his retired life, his sublime charge, his sanctity—he strengthened in himself that spirit of retreat and flight from the world which he so urgently recommends to his children, and found in him a powerful protector in whose name he consecrated his institute to God; and under his patronage it became so useful to the Church as to lead Pius IX to say that "it seems to have been established rather for our day than for his own time." To preserve his Brothers in this spirit of faith and piety by which he and they were animated, he urged upon them to practise mental prayer. This he regarded as the most powerful means of preserving union with God. "Mental prayer," he used to say to them, "must be your principal support; never, therefore, fail in it, save when ill. It will dissipate the darkness and ignorance of your mind. . . . You are in the presence of God: what a favor! Be not anxious for sensible devotion: rather fear and distrust it."

Such a life, in which the glory of God was procured, not only in the practice of the most heroic virtue, but likewise in the benefits mankind have derived therefrom, could not remain without the public recognition of the Church and her children; and there is every reason to look for the near approach of the day when the "true friend of youth" will have altars erected under his patronage wher-

ever stands a school in his name and that of his
institute.

On the eighth of May, 1840, Gregory XVI permitted the cause of La Salle's canonization to be
introduced into the Roman courts, and then declared him Venerable.   On the twelfth of September, 1840, the decree stating that no public homage
had been rendered the Venerable, was published;
the twenty-second of September, 1842, another
decree, determining the reputation of the Venerable,
because of the sanctity of his life, was issued; on
the sixteenth of April, 1842, the proceedings at
Rome were approved; those of Rheims and Rouen
were also admitted on the sixth of September, 1846.

The Archbishops of Paris, Rheims and Rouen
were next instructed to collect all the writings of the
Venerable, and to submit them to the examination
of theologians.   The research was prolonged and
close; and though many writings had been in part
prepared by La Salle, it was decided, on the tenth
of January, 1852, that, with the exception of thirty-
four autograph letters, it was not certain that the
works submitted had been written by him.   They
were, therefore, thrown out as of no value as
testimony.   Next, the process of beatification was
continued by an examination of the virtues of the
Venerable servant of God.

On the thirtieth of November, 1873, the Sacred
Congregation of Rites, in public session, presided
over by the Sovereign Pontiff, decided that "the
Venerable servant of God, Jean Baptiste de La
Salle, has practised the theological virtues of faith,

hope and charity, toward God and toward his neighbor; as also the cardinal virtues of prudence, justice, temperance and fortitude, and their dependent virtues, in a heroic degree."

The Church, therefore, has for the present given all the honor to the Venerable servant of God that the circumstances, and the rigid character of her proceedings, will allow. But the world, which sees the good that is derived from the work of the Venerable de La Salle, has not waited for the final verdict of our holy Mother before paying its debt of gratitude. This it generously requited on the second of June, 1875. On that day, in the city of Rouen, it erected a monument to the Venerable Jean Baptiste de La Salle.

The monument is worthy of the subject. The arms of Rheims, his native city; those of his noble family; those of the institute that he founded; those of Rouen, the beloved city in which he placed the cradle of the institute, where he died, and where his precious remains are preserved, will be found represented. The bas-reliefs, which perpetuate the memory of two remarkable incidents in the Venerable's life, will also be noticed: the first represents him distributing his patrimony to the poor; in the other, James II is seen visiting the school-room in which the fifty young Irish lads were instructed. At the four corners are figures of the children who represent every part of the world. This is one of the most pleasing features of the monument. "O little children! how eloquent you are! and how much better than the most brilliant discourse you speak the glory of the Venerable de La Salle!"* From the base of the fountain gush forth limpid streams, symbolical of the instruction which has been distributed to the people by this great servant of God.†

France has paid her tribute to the genius of modern education, but the Catholic world still clamors for other honors: she appeals to Rome to crown the saint. Four hundred thousand children and twelve thousand Brothers ask to repeat aloud: "*Blessed Jean-Baptiste de La Salle, pray for us who have recourse to thee.*" The supplication would be reëchoed by millions, from all quarters of the globe. Rome abides her time; but the day cannot be far distant when the pious wish will be fulfilled.

---

* Chantrel, *Monument du Ven. de La Salle*, p. 88.

† Historical justice makes it worthy of mention that the initiative in the erection of this monument was taken by M. Doudiet d'Austrive of Rouen.